I0729804

# Where Monsters Hide

The Moonchildren Trilogy #1

Emily Agnew

# WHERE MONSTERS HIDE

## EMILY AGNEW

Copyright © 2025 Emily Agnew
All rights reserved.
This novel is entirely a work of fiction. All names, locations, characters and events
are fictitious, and all a work of the author's imagination.

No part of this publication may be reproduced, stored or transmitted in any form
or by any means, including but not limited to, electronic, mechanical, photocopying,
recording, scanning or otherwise without permission from the publisher.
It is illegal to copy this book, post it to a website or distribute it by any other
means without permission.

Cover design: Anna Agnew

ISBN: 978-1-7640979-0-1

*To Danica, for taking me on this journey.*

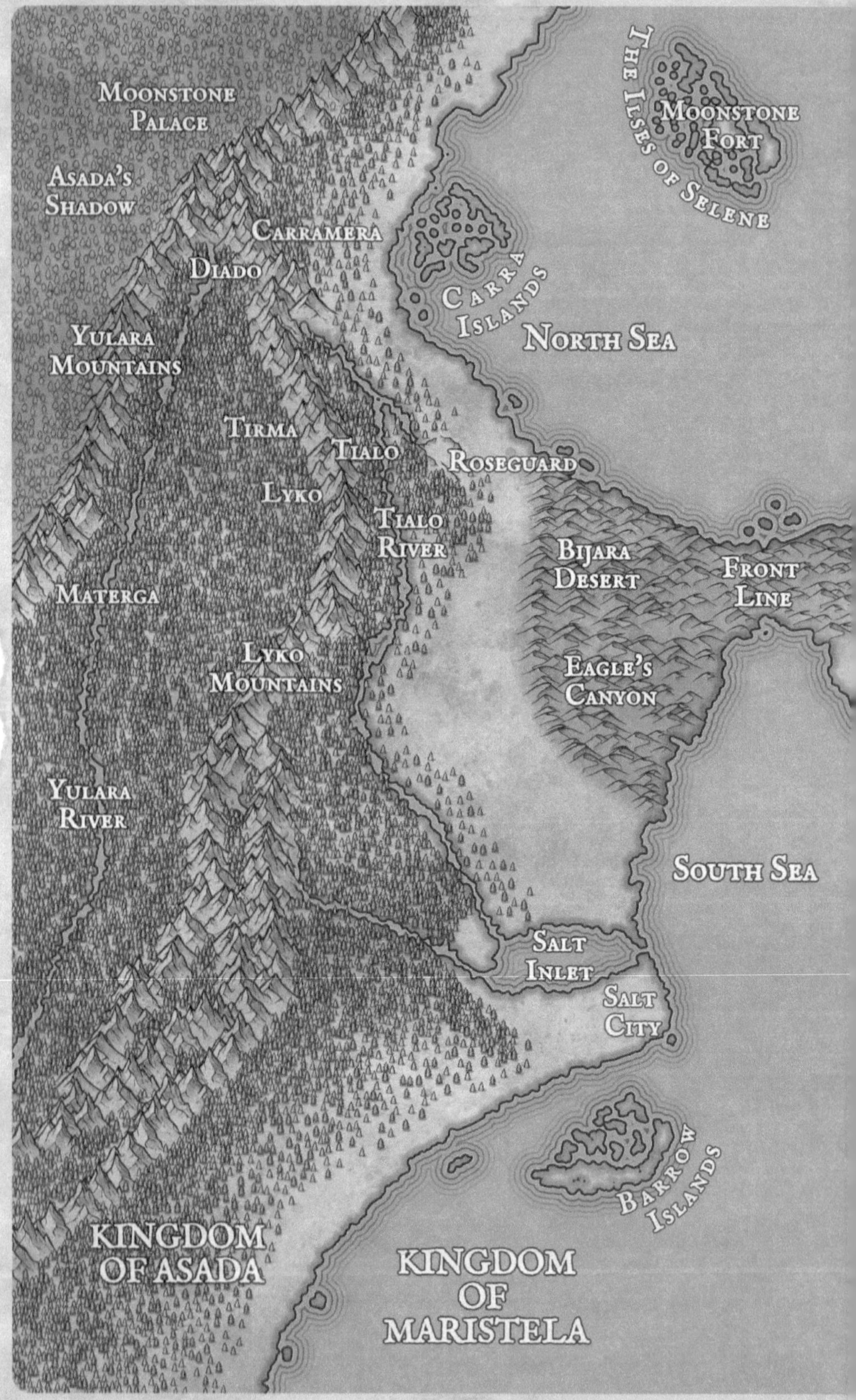

MOONSTONE PALACE
ASADA'S SHADOW
CARRAMERA
DIADO
YULARA MOUNTAINS
TIRMA
TIALO
LYKO
TIALO RIVER
MATERGA
LYKO MOUNTAINS
YULARA RIVER
THE ILSES OF SELENE
MOONSTONE FORT
CARRA ISLANDS
NORTH SEA
ROSEGUARD
BIJARA DESERT
FRONT LINE
EAGLE'S CANYON
SOUTH SEA
SALT INLET
SALT CITY
BARROW ISLANDS
KINGDOM OF ASADA
KINGDOM OF MARISTELA

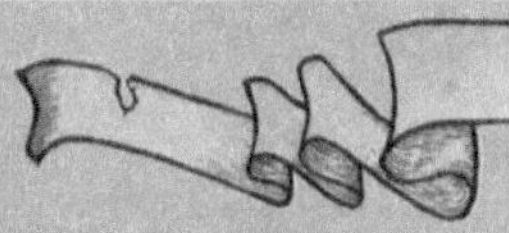

RAGUIA
NORTH
ELATOR
VAHLA MOUNTAINS
MOONSTONE CASTLE
YERMEN
ZAHALA
VAHLA LAKE
KINGDOM OF MARISTELA
KYO
KINGDOM OF RITENVOLD
THE IRON STRONGHOLD
CACIA

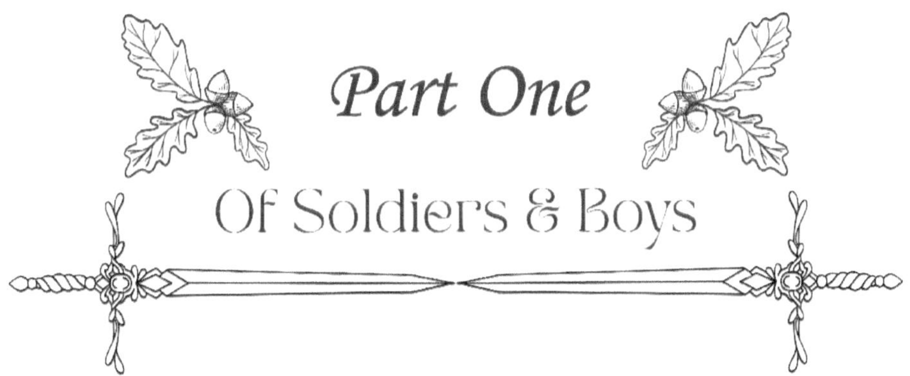

# Part One

## Of Soldiers & Boys

# CHAPTER ONE

## HUNTER

I enjoy moving soldiers around on a map, to where they're likely going to die. I forget that they are real people and pretending that they are toys makes my job easier. I stare long and hard at the map, at the wooden figures spread across the strip of land between Asada and Ritenvold. Ten long years and we haven't made a dent in Ritenvold's lines, not a single dent. Ritenvold seems to be enjoying themselves. They put almost no effort into their own lines, just enough to hold us back, but not enough to win. It's like they're waiting for something, letting us play at war.

I let out a breath of frustration, and my eyes glance at the grey area on the north-west corner of the map, at Asada's Shadow, home to all sorts of beasts and creatures.

Two years ago, Mother promoted me to captain, but other than a few minor successes, I haven't done anything noteworthy in that time. I want to make a story and a name for myself.

I slide the little red wooden figure with the rose engraved on the back, across the map, the wood has been smoothed out after years of use. I then reposition the black figures that represent the Kingdom of Ritenvold.

Fortunately, Ritenvold hasn't sent a fleet of ships to destroy us yet; and we haven't dared send ours, not with the beasts that lurk in the oceans. The Ocean Kingdom, Maristela, hasn't made a move in the last ten years, keeping to themselves and not interfering. I know that their trade had suffered in the beginning but somehow, they've managed to continue importing and exporting supplies out of Asada with Ritenvold. We have yet to figure out how. Our soldiers have patrolled the coastline and found no signs of ships dropping anchor anywhere other than the Carra Islands, yet goods from Ritenvold had been discovered in Carramera, and even in our home city, Roseguard.

We still trade with the islanders, mostly sea food for building supplies as well as red meat, they have enough fish and chickens over there to keep them fed. Only trade ships from Carramera are safe to cross to the Carra Islands. The island group govern themselves until a leader is named. If Maristela found someone to lead their people, they could wipe out the human race in Asada — yet the ocean remains leaderless and wild. And both Ritenvold and my army are smart enough to keep our war away from its shores.

I move another red figure to Ritenvold's border, trying to figure out how they have enough strength to have merrily played with us for ten long years. Have they been sending their younger troops to the front line for training? They have their monsters fighting for them, but we also have the monsters we've captured too. Centaurs and minotaurs have the strength that our human soldiers lack.

A knock on the door interrupts my concentration and never-ending frustration, and I look up as Mother walks in. She looks pristine in her red blazer, the Roseguard crest over the breast pocket, paired with a neat white shirt and black pants — the uniform of Roseguard's commander. Her signature scent of roses wafts into the room.

Mother has painted her lips bright red, as she does every morning. One of her neatly groomed eyebrows rises as she pins her black eyes on me, her gaze shifting from the map spread over the table to me.

'Well?'

I sit back in my chair, running my fingers through my hair and stretching out my stiff legs. 'We need more force in one spot to really punch through the line, and we need more soldiers.'

'Be careful, you don't want Ritenvold to fall through the holes.' Mother says, striding across the room to take a seat across the war table from me. It's a conversation we've had a thousand times over the past six months.

'Trust me — you did when I said we should move the northern trenches back two hundred yards, and it then proved to be a wise move. The death rate dropped once we had the empty trenches between Ritenvold and us.' I sigh, changing the topic. 'How many men are we sending to the front line this week?'

'Forty men, also a banshee that was caught outside of Salt City and two centaurs found roaming the grasslands.' Mother's scars crinkle slightly as her mouth moves and I wonder, as I always do, if she feels the imperfection every time she talks.

'Centaurs?' Although they're highly beneficial once caught, it's the catching them part that proves to be more difficult. They tend to stay hidden within the Shadow.

'Mhmm, they acknowledged they were trespassing into our lands, so went with us without much of a fight.' They often do, they're quite noble when dealing with them. Mother turns to look out the window, her dark hair, now showing signs of grey, falls over one shoulder. 'The banshee was a bit more difficult.'

'Send them to the middle.' I state, and Mother nods in agreement.

The middle of the front line is where the fighting is the heaviest and has been for the past ten years. When the war began, Mother hadn't known that it would last a long time. That was her one mistake, and the mistake I intend to rectify. She had been prepared to fight Ritenvold's fiercest attacks, but she hadn't been prepared to hold a line for a decade. It is obvious that Ritenvold is not too concerned with the war. They don't put much effort in and haven't sent their full forces to the front line yet, which is fortunate for us. For if they do, they will break through our lines in a matter of hours. But why?

'I think you should take a trip to the front line again.' I nod as Mother talks. Everything is easier to understand from there. 'And this time, you should go to the middle.'

'Why?' Whenever I travel to the front line, I go to one of the outer areas, where it's safer for someone like me.

Mother stands, her heels clicking as she walks towards the bookshelf in the corner, running her finger along the spines. 'What I am about to tell you is confidential. Only the generals, myself and now you will be privy to this information.' She turns to look at me from over her shoulder. 'Six months ago, we had two criminal soldiers flee the front line. From the middle. These soldiers are still missing.'

'And I'm just being told this now!' I stand, fisting my hands at my side. We've never had a soldier escape the front line. All who tried had been caught and punished. The fact that I'm only being informed has my jaw clenching.

'We didn't want word to get out.' Mother turns to look me straight in the eye, and I can't help myself from dipping my head slightly. 'Who those soldiers are is highly confidential. Only the generals know who they are. I want you to go to the middle to make sure no-one else will even think of pulling that kind of stunt.' Her voice is angry, but there is also a hint of something else, nervousness? Fear?

'Who escaped?' She knows I'm not asking for their names.

'Two girls; one is thirteen, the other is twenty and dangerous.' She taps a finger on the edge of the shelf, as if considering how much to tell me. 'Despite her age, the thirteen-year-old is a criminal, and an orphan from the Salt City.' We often send orphans to the front line, but usually only to the training grounds. One of Roseguard's rules is no-one under the age of thirteen is allowed to participate in the fighting. 'The twenty-year-old ... her details are classified.' I raise an eyebrow but don't push it, despite my position, there is no one who can get Mother to talk if she doesn't want to.

'We sent soldiers along the western perimeter of the Bijara Desert, but no girls ever appeared, so they are assumed dead.' Mother hesitates, as if she doesn't believe what she has just said. 'I would like to know how they escaped and managed to steal a wagon full of supplies in the process. Since information about the escape is classified, the soldiers were told they were hunting a minotaur that was causing havoc and relocating it to our army. If the information got into the wrong hands, we would have a big problem.'

The Bijara Desert is a massive expanse of sand dunes that stretches between the city of Roseguard and the front line. So even if Ritenvold smashed through our lines, they would have to trek the unforgiving desert to reach us. It is hard travelling with guards, no water, just the wind, and if you're unlucky, desert wolves, for two weeks across the narrowest point. So, for two girls to survive … it would be impossible. Despite having supplies, they wouldn't have enough to out-wait the soldiers riding the perimeter. And that's if they hadn't run into the desert wolves that hunt anything that strays too far into the dunes.

I walk to the open window, gazing out into the yard around the war room. There is a cool breeze that gently kisses my face, and I close my eyes, taking a moment to figure out my plan.

'When are the next group of criminals heading out?' I ask, not bothering to look at Mother.

Criminals are offered a deal when they're captured, fight for the Red Army with the possibility of freedom afterwards, or execution. Most criminals choose to join the Red Army. Mother and I have discussed the outcomes when we win the war, and what will happen to the criminals. I am of the belief that once one has become a criminal, they are always a criminal, and we should rid our kingdom of the filth. Mother is a bit more sceptical of my belief, but once she steps down from her position as commander after we win the war, I will step into that role and I will not hesitate to rid the kingdom of any criminals that will threaten our peace.

'The wagons roll out tomorrow. Sorry it's late notice.'

'Right, I'll see what I can learn. I'll ride out with the criminals.' I turn to face Mother. 'There are only two ways we can win this war. We either continue like we have been for the last ten years and hope our limited soldiers will make a difference in the next ten years, or we attack with full force to put a hole in their lines. To do this, I think we should start clearing out the outer villages of Tirma, Lyko and Materga.'

Mother is silent. So, I elaborate my reasoning for those particular villages. I was promoted to captain for a reason.

'Salt City has rumours of a rebel group uprising fighting for any halfbreeds that aren't hiding in the Shadow. It would be wise to stop any possible expansion of these rebels before word spreads even further. Stop any hope from growing there.'

Although no halfbreed would willingly admit they have diluted blood, they are often easy enough to find through traits or mutations of their non-human parent. And those villages were all mining villages for the old dwarven city of Diada. There had been rumours that those dwarves never truly left their great city, but to confirm whether those rumours were true or not, we'd need to cross the Lyko Mountains and we'd risk our own soldiers. Therefore, we only send patrol parties to the base of the mountains. Although Tirma and Materga are on the west side of the mountain range, the villages are small enough that we wouldn't be risking our resources by sending a small team of soldiers there.

'I agree.'

'Good, I have a few things to get in order before this mission.' I stride back to the wooden desk and begin rolling the maps up.

'Like?' She questions.

Although Mother can't see my face from where she stands next to the bookshelf, I scowl. I am not a child that needs to be monitored.

'Well, I'm meeting with Tyke in the Underground after your dinner party.' Despite the huge differences between our lives, me being a captain and Tyke being a club owner, we've been friends since we were little and he's like a brother to me. He's always managed to get information quicker than the Red Guards — gossip flies faster than messages travel.

*****

The sun is starting to dip below the city walls, the last of the rays warming everything before the cool night sets in. The smell of smoke, sweat and spices saturates everything. Another summer is coming to an end, and with it, the end of the scorching hot days and bitterly cold desert like nights.

My footsteps bounce off the cobble stone street, I'm taking a short cut through the back alleys to get to the Underground. My suit jacket will look slightly out of place, but I've just come straight from Mother's monthly dinner party. It's called the Roseguard Dinner Party, but really it's just Mother's party to make sure that her social standing doesn't move.

Everyone with any sort of status is invited, and of course with Mother being the commander of Roseguard, and being the best captain Roseguard will ever have, I have to be in attendance at these events. The dinner party is always hosted at Mother's home, the mansion overlooking Thorn Gap, the massive canyon to the north of Roseguard. Roses adorn every surface, tables covered in deep red cloths. Women wear elegant gowns, and we dance in the small ballroom. The champagne and red wine flows and the food is rich. And Mother attempts to find me a woman of high enough status for me to marry.

I turn down another street. There is nothing special about the heavy door that sits under the small bridge. Plain, boring and uninviting, just how Tyke liked it. The Underground had been built long before my time, and even Mothers. Roseguard sits atop of many underground caves, and I have to admit, I'm shocked we haven't had a cave in yet.

I glance over my shoulder once before pulling the door open. The Underground is exclusive, only those who have been approved by Tyke can access the club. And of course, anyone approved by myself as well.

The staircase on the other side of the door leads down, the stone walls and single torches makes it look quite intimidating. But that's not the worst part, many times I've had to tackle climbing back up the steps drunk as a cricket. There's been even more times that I've just stayed the night in Tyke's private office.

The sound of music slowly creeps in, getting louder as I make my way down.

Reaching the bottom of the steps, I knock on the door. The small rectangle slider opens, and I stare at the plain brown eyes that are crinkled in the corners as the bouncer squints through the slider.

'Captain Hunter Cole.' I say clearly.

The slider closes and I hear the door unlock over the music. It pulls open away from me and I step into the Underground.

It's a little bit too early for people to be dancing. Most are standing by the bar, drinking and gossiping. I notice the two boys that have been trying to get into my inner circle for the last two weeks and I groan. I just want to find Tyke and maybe a girl to keep me entertained. I move my way across the dance floor, keeping out of sight of the boys.

Klara isn't here yet; the type of girl Mother would never approve of. Normally I don't touch whores, but she's made it far too easy for me to get her into bed. It doesn't hurt that she's exactly my type as well. Small, skinny, dark hair and blue eyes.

I make my way across the dancefloor and lean up against the bar. The bar maid notices me immediately and stops what she's doing to tend me. The last time a bar server treated me as less than a VIP, I had them fired.

'What can I get you Captain?' There is a nervousness in her voice. I look her over, blonde hair, blue eyes.

'Two reds, and nothing cheaper than fifty gold marks.' She nods and jumps into action.

Moments later, I have two chalices filled with red wine. I take both by the stems and stalk over to the last booth against the wall. The thick red curtains are closed, Tyke must be entertaining a client.

It doesn't take long before the curtains are pushed back, and a young boy leaves. One of Tyke's spies. He sees me and dips his chin. 'Captain.'

I ignore him and slide into the booth, passing one of the wines to Tyke. Smoke and cedar fill the booth, the scent that always follows Tyke around.

He sits there grinning like a fool as he eyes me up. 'What?' I instantly return the grin as I get comfortable in the padded booth seat.

Tyke picks up his chalice, swirls the glass and takes a sip of the wine before leaning back in the seat. His blond hair is loose around his shoulders this evening.

'Did you manage to fend off Tamika?'

I throw my head back and let out a long groan.

'How'd you know?' I let out a laugh. 'Actually, why didn't you warn me you bastard?'

Tyke laughs. Tamika, General Edward Valor's daughter, had been hanging off my arm the entirety of the dinner party. She was pretty, but far from my type with light blonde hair and light brown eyes.

'Yeah, rumour has it, Melissa spoke to Edward about potentially setting you up with Tamika.' Tyke laughs. 'I figured you could suffer for a dinner party.'

I take a sip of my wine. 'She wouldn't leave me alone. At all.'

'I know.'

'You could have warned me.'

'Yep, but I thought it would be funnier not too.'

I roll my eyes at this. 'I'm going to need a few more drinks to help recover from her advances.'

'Aren't you heading out on that mission tomorrow?' He leans forward.

Tyke and I had been friends since childhood, always running amuck together. Then I started working in the war rooms and he found a way to be the city's unofficial source of information. Nothing happens in Roseguard without Tyke's knowledge, and I often use that to my advantage.

'Aye,' I don't say anything about the two escapees. 'Doing my duty.'

'I heard there is quite a few rolling out?'

'More banished beasts as well as some human criminals from Salt City and Carramera.' Apparently Carramera was ruled by the fae before the banishing, but humans outnumber beasts one hundred to one, and humans have taken over the cities.

Tyke stares at his wine for a moment and I know he is contemplating telling me something.

'Spit it out.' I grin at him.

He looks up at me, his dark eyes watching me for a moment.

'Rumour has it patrols have increased along the Bijara Desert. Correct me if I'm wrong, but it appears that Melissa is looking for something, and not just the minotaur they say it is.' I stiffen, that's the other frustrating thing about Tyke, he's incredibly smart. I clench my fist under the table. 'Rush has been sighted multiple times outside the city walls. I think Melissa is trying to catch Rush.'

I breathe a sigh of relief. Dimitri Rush is infamous. Mother once said that she'd met him, that he'd been quite close to her and my aunt when they were growing up. He'd been sent by Roseguard to kill a Nightwalker but had refused to injure the beast. There was supposed to be repercussions, from what Mother had told me, but you'd have to catch him first. From then on, Dimitri had been roaming Asada, and when all the beasts were banished, he'd grown restless. It's been said that Dimitri is the one human alive that has travelled into Asada's Shadow and made it out alive again.

A while ago, Tyke and I created a list. We'd called it *The Rush List* with the hope that if we ever met the sharpshooter, we'd give him the list of seventeen names to kill. It had originally been Tyke's idea; Dimitri was the one true God in Tyke's life. He had listened to every story about him and had tried to track him down whenever he caught the hint of a trail, to no avail.

'Aye, Rush would be very beneficial to the army.' I lie easily.

I had no idea that he been sighted outside of the city. Mother said she had tried enlisting him many times, with promises for of dropping the repercussions of denying orders almost twenty-five years ago, but the problem was, according to Mother, he had loyalties elsewhere.

Tyke doesn't second guess my lie, he just nods, watches me for a moment and then takes another sip of his wine before bringing up a topic about the wine trade.

We chat long into the night, and eventually Klara shows up. I let her know of my mission and tell her to save herself for when I get back, whispering promises I know I don't care to keep in her ear. We drink, we chat, we laugh and eventually I end up staying the night in Klara's small house atop of her parents' bakery. She helps take away the pressure of being a captain and I can forget my worries for the rest of the night.

# CHAPTER TWO

## DANICA

I check all my blades are in their sheaths—two on my hips, two strapped to my thighs, two on my calves, one in each boot, plus a few hidden in my long, black leather jacket. My hood is up, my hair is in a loose plait, with small braids that Vixy plaited amongst my dark brown hair.

I smile as I stare along my wooden arrow into the small farmhouse on the southern side of the famous Roseguard city. Vixy is hidden behind the barn with the horses, waiting for my signal.

I have watched this farm for the last two days, learning its secrets. We rode our horses here and plan to take the two farm-horses, along with as many supplies as we can carry home with us. Vixy made camp a few hours away, on the edge of the desert, while I spied on the farm.

The farm is owned by a man, his wife and their two sons, who are off playing at being soldiers.

The sun dips below the horizon and I double-check all my blades are still strapped down before moving from my hiding spot. As I stalk towards the house, I ready my bow with an arrow. I learned long ago how to move silently. All that can be heard as I move through the wheat field is the gentle breeze and an owl in the distance.

I figured out the layout of the farmhouse by watching the people and what they carried in and out of rooms that didn't have windows. I sight the kitchen window, where the wife, a small woman with blonde hair, hunches over a chopping board, carefully slicing up some food. The feathers of the arrow tickle my cheek; the feeling almost second nature as I line up the woman, taking into account the glass window smashing and the husband who will come to investigate.

I let my breath out and release my fingers. The arrow finds its home right between the woman's eyes, and I watch across the wheat field as the glass flies inwards and the woman collapses.

I am already pulling out a second arrow as the husband sprints into the room. Shock sprays onto his face as he sees his wife and I release the second arrow. He drops to the ground like a sack of sand.

I swing my bow back over my shoulder; it sits snugly next to my small quiver of arrows.

Nine and a half years in the muddy, rat-infested trenches of the front line have hardened me enough that I don't think twice about killing someone.

Cupping my hands, I make a bird sound almost identical to an owl, signalling Vix. The breeze is gentle on my face as I carefully walk towards the house, keeping an ear out for any suspicious noises. The wheat parts easily and occasionally, there is a slight rustle as a rodent takes off. There is a small wooden fence around the house, and I push the gate open. I grit my teeth as it creaks.

Entering the old wooden farmhouse, the coppery tang of blood fills my nose. I retrieve my arrows, wipe them clean on the dead couple's clothes before carefully placing them back into my quiver.

Other than the scent of blood, the smell of fresh bread is heavy. I lift the lid off a pot and take a deep breath, smiling, breathing in the scent that reminds me of home. Pulling out a hessian cloth from my pocket, I wrap the loaf and place it on the wooden bench, smoothed from years of use. I look around the kitchen, we'll have a big job of packing all the supplies. I crack my fingers, stretch my neck then crouch as I begin opening cupboards and drawers, pulling out food and anything useful.

Vixy soon appears, red braids spilling out behind her hood. She grimaces at the bodies, and I give her a stern look. She was only on the front line for two months, so she hasn't witnessed the horrors I have and still flinches at death. When she was assigned to my *team*, I had made an effort to protect her from the truth of war.

'If you show mercy, they'll remember you wanted to kill them.' Vixy mutters the sentence I've drilled into her.

'Good girl,' I say, and add, 'There can only be one survivor.'

Although I've tried to protect her, I've corrupted her in a way. She might not have seen the brutality of war, but I cannot let her think that the world is full of rainbows and butterflies. The only way she will survive in this world with the word *Wanted* above her head, is if she knows that she must show no mercy and take what she needs without hesitation.

Vixy hurries into one of the bedrooms.

Over the next couple of hours, we clear out the house, barn and meat room. We pile our new supplies onto the four horses before finally climbing into the saddles. It will be a long trek back through the desert with the extra weight on the horses, but we have the supplies we need: water, food, clothing, weapons, and other bits and pieces to add to our temporary home hidden in Eagles Canyon.

I had planned to head to Salt City to retrieve Vixy's sister before heading west after six months of hiding in the desert, but Red Soldiers patrolled the desert perimeter heavily. I wanted the commander of Roseguard to believe we perished in the desert. However, this summer has been a short one, and winter will come early this year. I don't think Vixy will cope well travelling into the mountains with a snowstorm beating down on us. Winter isn't so bad on the forests and grasslands, but there is too much activity by locals, and we would be discovered if we remained. If I was alone, I would have aimed for the mountains and not looked back. So, I had tried to turn the dusty and hot canyon into a home, a safe and loving place for Vixy. It might not be my real home, but I would do my best to make it a home for her.

I take a deep breath and breathe in the twilight air, already planning the next raid. These supplies will last us a month if we're smart, three weeks if we aren't.

*****

The desert during the day can kill one if not prepared. During the day, Vixy and I sleep, the horses hobbled. We try not to exert ourselves whilst the heat burns us. If we ride throughout the day, it will take us twice as long to reach Eagle's Canyon.

Standing at the top of the dune, I watch the sun dip below the horizon, soaking up the last of the warmth before the light disappears. The sunsets in the desert are beautiful.

Once the sun has disappeared, I make my way back down to Vix and the horses. The temperature will drop quickly now.

Vixy is grooming her horse, rubbing the brush in circular movements across the horse's rump to ease the sweat from her coat. The mare is curling her upper lip in pleasure.

I pull down the scarf that covers my nose and mouth so I can talk clearly, then crouch next to my dark bay stallion, unstrapping the hobbles.

'Only two more nights until we're back home.'

Vixy glances over at me, 'including tonight?'

'Yep,' I shake the sand out of my saddle pad before placing it on the stallions back. 'Did you think of some names for the two new horses?'

I let Vixy name all the animals we manage to steal. She'd named my stallion Eagle, after the canyon, and her mare, Sparrow. The calves we'd herded home a month ago are called Dusty, Demi and Deliah. And then there were the desert wolves we'd tamed.

'I think so,' I glance over at her as she pulls down the cotton scarf covering her mouth. 'The bay is Cherry, and the chestnut I want to call Autumn.'

I stop what I'm doing and turn to look at her.

'You will see your sister again, I promise.' Grabbing the stallions lead, I stride over to her and gently squeeze her shoulders. 'Once winter is over, we're heading south to find her and then we'll all go hide in the mountains.' We'll go home. Nervousness and excitement always fills my stomach when I think of starting the journey home.

Vixy doesn't meet my eyes. 'I know but it seems so far away.'

I pull her in for a gentle hug, her small body is so lean. I try my best to make sure she has enough food and protein but she's still so small.

'I know, I know.' I crouch down so I am at her eye level and look her in her hazel-coloured eyes. 'I promise you; you will see Autumn again.'

She gives me a small smile and I feel myself frown, my tummy clenching. I am keeping her safe but also keeping her from seeing her sister again, keeping her hidden in the desert is safer than marching into Salt City where every Red Soldier will be looking for us.

A breeze drifts across the dunes, carrying grains of sand with it. We both pull up our scarves, back to covering our noses and mouths. The material irritates my skin, especially with the dry sweat and sand that has got caught in it.

Through the scarf, I nod at the horse. I can't smell anything other than the salty tang of sweat.

'Do you need help putting the saddle on?'

Vixy picks up the saddle and hands it to me. 'Yes please.'

She's still too short to reach Sparrow's back, and Eagle is even taller. I place the saddle gently on the mare's back, the leather is smooth in my hand, and I carefully adjust the saddle pad, so it's not pulled tight across the horse's back. Reaching beneath the mare, I grab the girth and pull it tight, latching it into the buckle tight enough to stop the saddle from slipping.

'How about I'll help you finish tacking up, then you can hold Cherry and the chestnut that still needs a name while I finish saddling up?'

'Deal.' Vixy grins, and I hand her Eagle's lead.

I unhitch Sparrow's bridle from her saddle and gently place my finger in the gap between her teeth, encouraging her to open her mouth before sliding the metal bit in and the bridle over her head. I notice the leather is beginning to crack.

'Do you want a leg up?' I ask Vix.

Vixy passes me Eagle's lead. 'Yes!'

I grin and stand behind her, one hand on her knee that she's holding up and my other hand next to her behind.

'On three.' I say. 'One, two, three.' I spring her upwards. She throws her right leg over Sparrow as she grabs onto the front of the saddle.

I take a step back, then pass her Eagle's lead once she's adjusted herself in the saddle.

'Alrighty, give me a moment to get the pack ponies sorted.'

'Yes ma'am!' Vixy laughs and I let a small grin slip onto my lips.

Turning my back to her, I unhitch the two new leads from the new bay and latch it onto the horses' halters before undoing the hobbles. I brush off their legs where the hobbles sit, to checking that there is no chafing. I go over the packs and make sure everything is secured before leading them to Vixy. I take them to her right side, as Eagle can get a bit painful to deal with around new horses. I pass Vix the leads, duck under Sparrow's neck and take Eagle's lead, leading him away from the three mares while I finish saddling him up.

I swing myself into the saddle before walking around to take one of the pack ponies' leads.

Eagle starts to prance as we approach the mares, despite having one of the mares led from him last night as well.

'Settle,' I growl at him, feeling his movements becoming quicker. I squeeze the reins and that gets his attention.

I reach and take the horses' lead, Vix letting go of the remaining lead. I manoeuvre Eagle and the chestnut away from Vix, letting her get her lead and reins adjusted.

'Ready?' I ask after a moment.

Vixy gives me a nod. 'Yep.'

'Let's go home then.' I say and ease Eagle and the pack pony into a trot.

Using the stars and moon as a compass, we ride through the night. I like to think the moon is aiding us, with the light it provides. The moon has always been there for me, from the darkest moments in the trenches, to the night we escaped. It was a full moon that night, we could see the dunes for miles ahead. But fortunately, the moon wasn't bright enough for Vixy to see all the blood that was spilt that night.

In the early hours of the morning, we have to pull out blankets to keep the cold away. As sunrays appear in front of us, we ease our horses to a halt. We'll continue our journey home tonight.

# Chapter Three

## Hunter

I don't regret staying up late last night, and I don't regret going home with Klara and using her to make myself feel good, but I do regret drinking so much. My head thuds as I pack the final folder of paperwork.

The red rose on the shield is stamped on every document. My bag is packed and ready to hand over to my personal guards. Mother has already said her goodbyes earlier this morning, before she had to leave to meet with one of the other generals.

There is a knock at the door. Rubbing my forehead, I stand up and make my way over.

The door is thick wood, painted red, and I open it, pushing it out.

My father stands there. 'I heard your mother is sending you out to the front line.'

'Hi Pa,' I don't make a move towards him.

'You don't have to go if you don't wish to.' His once blond hair is now grey, and he runs his hand through it. His skin is faring better than his hair.

I scowl. 'Mother is the commander, and I do as she orders.'

Pa tilts his head, and I notice that his red suit jacket is faded. 'She needs to discuss these sorts of things with all the generals.'

'No, she doesn't.' I fold my arms across my chest. 'I have an important mission she has entrusted me with.'

'She will get you killed if you're not careful.' Pa takes a step forward.

'If you want your opinion heard, you never should have left Mother and I.' I snap. 'I need to leave now, or I will be late.'

'Hunter.' Pa doesn't move.

I close the door in his face. He left Mother when I was eleven, just after the banishing. He left Mother when she was struggling with keeping the city running and keeping the beasts to the Shadow.

And yet my father never once gave up his position as a General of Roseguard, not when his last name was still the same as Mothers.

I pick up an hourglass sitting on the table and throw it with all my strength towards the wall. Rage burns through me, how dare he have the audacity to tell me what to do after he walked out on us. Glass shatters as the hourglass hits the wall, sand spraying everywhere. Some cleaner will sort out the mess.

I want to punch something.

I take a deep breath, the smell of roses always thick in the Roseguard war rooms. I grab my folder from the desk, pick up my bag and make my way out of my office.

The gates of the city is where I'll join up with the soldiers that are heading to the front line. Outside the war rooms, a groom has my blood bay stallion tacked up for me, I think the horse's name is Atlas. My broadsword is strapped down to the saddle bag, not that I know how to use it … well, I know the basics. I may be able to command armies and plan battles, but being in a battle is not my thing. I prefer controlling the armies. It is truly something to control a number of people, to position them in places, to move them around like stones on my map.

Most boys my age are trained to be soldiers for our kingdom, Asada. But I fear what lay beyond the front line. For years, Pa tried to train me in swordplay and teach me how to fight, despite having walked out on us. I wasn't interested and never put in any effort, much to his disappointment. When I was fourteen, I went with Mother to drop something off at the war rooms in Roseguard's Red Towers, the headquarters of the city. I had caught one look at the maps and knew that was how I would prove myself as a Cole, without having to shed blood.

Pa had been trained as a soldier from an early age and worked his way up until he became a general. He had once fought with the Nightwalkers. The God-like beasts that Mother had banished to the Shadow. Therefore, he wasn't impressed that I didn't want to become a soldier and work my way up the ranks like he had, but I can't stand the thought of cutting flesh open, of fighting on the front line and living in army camps while we battle a seemingly endless war. I do not have a death wish! So, here I am, planning where I should position our army, deciding where others will die. I had only just started to impress Mother; it was difficult, not having the experience of a seasoned soldier, but I did it. And I enjoy it.

Mother had also been trained as a soldier, but instead of working her way up, she earned her reputation by banishing the beasts. She had spent her childhood learning warcraft. She is undefeated, cunning and loved by everyone in the city.

Arriving at the barracks, I scan the criminals as I ride past them, towards my personal guards. The stench of sweat, mud and shit wafts towards me and I scowl. Filthy. All shackled to the floor of their wagons, a few are my age. One of them I know. The banshee is gagged, drugged and shackled to a cart with her own personal guards. I take in her humanlike body, all old and crinkled with long grey hair. Despite her deceiving appearance, she could throw a full-grown man through a brick wall. If these precautions weren't taken and she were to scream, none of us would hear anything for the next week.

The centaurs, one a dark brown female and the other a light grey male, are handcuffed and collared, chains connect them to the back of the heavier carts. I avoid the cart with those beasts, keeping my eyes low as I urge my stallion to hurry past trying to remain out of their line of sight. The banshee and centaurs could kill a trained warrior in seconds and are always helpful on the front line — when they cooperate.

The prisoners are fed twice a day — breakfast and dinner. They get water three times — with meals and also at noon when the Red Soldiers stop for their lunch. They are only allowed to relieve themselves twice a day, before breakfast and dinner. They aren't allowed to talk.

I find my personal guard closest to the city gates, and I trot towards the group that are all mounted on horses. They are all in silver armour with red clothing peeking out from beneath.

One of the soldiers sees me and raises an arm 'Captain!'

'Boys,' I say despite being their junior. I need to make sure they're well aware I out rank them.

I notice a glance between two of the soldiers but don't comment on it.

'We're riding out in half an hour.'

I nod. 'Good.'

*****

Trekking across the desert is the most dangerous part of the trip to the front line. Occasionally there are bandits, or beasts that haven't been captured yet, desert wolves, poisonous snakes, spiders. All are waiting for me to get a little too far from the group to attack.

The first day of riding isn't too bad, my horse keeps its pace at the front of the convoy of soldiers and criminals, with my guards. It takes us three days to reach the desert with our large convoy. The routine is simple, and we stick to it. I look forward to retiring to my tent each night, a soldier having set it up for me. I read my book by candlelight as the soldiers' drink and play card games. I tried joining them once, but found they were hesitant to play with their captain, so I left them to it.

Last night we had arrived at the perimeter of the desert, the grasslands thinning out and becoming bare, the dunes appearing in the distance. I hate the desert.

The heat is worse among the dunes, the scent of sweat and body odours thick. My stallion's neck is coated in sweat by lunch time. Midafternoon, the wind begins to get strong, blowing sand into everything and we pull out our scarves to protect our faces. By nightfall, the wind drops off again and we can enjoy our dinner, venison stew, without sand through it.

That night, with nothing to do but flinch at each sound, worrying what the sounds could be, and watch the moon, I think of the task ahead. No one has ever escaped the front line, let alone two girls. There would have been a reason that Mother withheld this information from me for six months, she's smart. Perhaps it's has something to do with making sure Ritenvold didn't know that our soldiers weren't willing to fight under our crest. From the way Mother described the girls, I doubt they were sisters. However, the age difference suggests that the older girl broke out to protect the younger one. Perhaps … but there would have to be some reason for a twenty-year-old girl to help a thirteen-year-old escape, so maybe they are sisters or blood relatives.

The breeze rustles my tent, sand always managing to creep in. I don't get much sleep, as I worry about what I might see at the front line, as well as what could be lurking in the desert. And when I do sleep, disturbing dreams haunt me. The nightmare that always follows me when I'm travelling to the front line, a reminder to dread what I might see. The nightmare I had witnessed on my first visit to the front line. A man, maybe a couple of years older than me, swinging his sword. His red uniform is brown with mud, and not nearly as visible as that of the man he fights, a warrior in black and gold, smudged black paint over his face. The man in red is nothing compared to the warrior. The warrior slashes his sword and the soldier's intestines spill into the mud. Another swing and the soldier's head goes flying, landing yards away from the rest of his body. Even from two hundred yards away, I could see his pale blue eyes that make him a monster, a Nightwalker. I fear one day I will cross that Nightwalker again and not have an army ready to protect me. The first time watching my soldiers fight had been horrific and truly traumatic, for Ritenvold had never banished their monsters. I hadn't been able to sleep for months.

Morning arrives, bringing a red dawn with it. As the train of soldiers and prisoners roll forward, I linger with a group of guards, having a slightly larger breakfast that had been prepared for us—sausages, bacon, eggs, beans. Criminals only eat bread and dried beef.

I join in on the big breakfast and I listen as they tell horror stories from their times on the front line.

The next four days are uneventful and incredibly boring. We stick to the routine and don't stray from it. Breakfast, I ride ahead with the lieutenants and deputies, while the soldiers pack up my tent. There is minimal talking, as sand will get into our mouths. Most of the day is spent shielding our face from the blowing sand. We pause for our lunch and then march on through to dusk. The dreams haunt me every night, but I know my personal guards would put themselves in front of a blade for me. The Red Guards hold a higher position than the Red Soldiers, usually they have to earn that title and are often enlisted to protect the captions, generals and of course, Mother.

I don't know where I fit in with the guards because I'm the young boy playing at being captain, whereas the men around me are trained soldiers. If I was in Roseguard, I would act as my authoritative self, as a captain. But out here? I don't have my father's ranking of general to fall back on. In Roseguard, I am General Cormac Cole's son, *and* I am Commander Melissa Cole's son. Out here, I am just a young, inexperienced captain surrounded by seasoned soldiers.

I try to keep quiet and out of the way.

The sun rises over another day and again we all sit down to breakfast. We have, roughly, a week before we make it to the front line. A week left of roughing it out and then I can stay in the front line headquarters, in a proper bed.

We drag breakfast out a little longer and enjoy the morning coffee as clouds cover the sun. The sun hasn't been able to begin heating up the sand yet.

I watch as the soldiers and prisoners disappear over the dunes. We're at the back of the convoy now, my personal guards finishing their coffees. We'll be able to catch up quickly and canter back to the front. I rub warmth into my hands as I stand next to my horse. The group of guards take their time getting ready, two are laughing while saddling their horses.

Finally, the camp is cleared, and we are ready to go. I'm about to swing my leg over my horse when he collapses and I topple backwards, using my hands to catch myself behind me, a horrible noise coming from my stallion. A dark, wooden arrow with black feathers has pierced his chest. There is a band of blue painted just below the feathers. I freeze, watching the other soldiers leap onto their horses. More arrows are fired and more horses collapse.

Then I see them. The bandits … or rebels. Traitors to Roseguard, to Asada.

In sand-coloured shirts and pants, they come charging at us with bows and swords. The leader, with a slimmer but curvy build, obviously a woman, stands out with her white cloth wrapped around her head, covering her mouth, nose and forehead from the sun, only her eyes are visible. The others all have similar clothing wrapped over their heads.

I watch as the leader reaches the closest guard. Now that they're in close combat, the traitors won't stand a chance. Especially with a woman of her size and up against my trained guards.

Getting to my feet and backing away slowly, I keep my gaze on the traitors. I watch as a Red Guard raises his sword, and then it falls suddenly, his arm following, flying into the sand; then his head rolls, spraying ruby blood over the traitor's white clothing.

Sapphire eyes meet mine. The leader prowls closer as her companions murder my guards. I turn and sprint, I don't even know where I'm running to. Behind me, I hear laughter, I dare a glance over my shoulder as I sprint across the dune. She's watching me, giving me a small wave before turning back to the blood bath behind me. I don't know why she doesn't pursue me, and I don't want to find out.

I don't run far, just over a dune or two before I dive down and bury myself in the sand. While the traitors steal what we had left, I stay hidden.

My mind races. I'm alone in the Bijara Desert with rebels patrolling the hills. I am a captain and what a bloody useless title that is when I don't even know how to fight off a small band of traitors.

My heart doesn't slow down all day, and I flinch at every sound as I hide at the base of the dune all day, finally making my move as twilight falls. The guards are either dead or long gone. As I slowly make my way to the top of the dune, my stomach grumbles with hunger, but as I reach the peak, it turns to dread as I gaze out over the endless desert.

# Chapter Four

## Danica

Eagles Canyon had been a myth my entire childhood, just old stories to exaggerate and add to. The bones of the stories centred around the rocky canyon with a sacred stream that runs far below the desert. Hidden between the rocks, it rises briefly to the surface before diving back down. My father had told me that all stories had an element of truth to them, that there would always have to be something the myth could be built on.

When Vix and I had made our desperate dash from the front line, then after a week of travelling through the unforgiving desert with nothing around us except sand dunes and the two horses hitched up to our stolen wagon, I began praying that I had picked the right truth to believe about Eagle's Canyon.

I was exhausted, dehydrated and tired, Vixy even more so, when I'd spied the nymph beckoning me towards her. At first, I thought I was hallucinating, but I followed anyway, clinging to the hope that Eagle's Canyon was more than a myth.

I think the nymph knew at the time that I was a criminal in the eyes of Roseguard, and I think she knew that I wouldn't bring any harm to her, so she had led us to where the stream touched the surface and left us to recover.

After almost a day of sleeping in the shade and a constant water source, I had explored the canyon, realising that the nymph had built a well around the water source. I'd found caves hollowed into the canyon walls, twisting mazes, natural barriers and paths, even an old human-like skeleton hidden in a cave. Occasionally the nymph would beckon me down a path, and I'd follow. The nymph always disappeared when Vixy was near, but I understood why, and I think the nymph knew that.

We're exhausted after the hard ride home, the uncomfortable days and bitterly cold nights, but riding through the canyon, following the track, I hear a growl and smile.

'It's just us!' Vixy calls out and the growls instantly stop.

Moments later, our eight desert wolves come bounding along the track. The horses spook, but we hold them steady. The dark yellow pelts of the wolves' flash along the track. They reach us and bound around us joyfully, a few of them barking and yapping as we greet them. A couple of months ago, I found a dead wolf bitch with full teats, so I tracked down the pups and brought them home, training them as guards for our small rocky home. It had been a wise decision, for they kept the wild wolves from entering their territory, our home.

We continue the rest of the way along the track with our wolves, Vixy chatting to the loyal animals.

I take a deep breath, early morning air crisp on my skin.

Vix and I put the horses back into their makeshift stables, untacking them and grooming them after the big ride. I'll have to find some more rope to fence off another bigger cave for the horses now that we've gained another two. We've got five now in total, one from our original escape, the other had died after arriving at the canyon. We carry the packs to our home cave and organise all of our new supplies. We store the food, fill up water buckets, put new clothes away and find homes for new tools, utensils and weapons.

As Vixy prepares meals for the evening, I cut up the last of the older meat to give to the wolves. We have to dry a lot of the meat, otherwise it wouldn't last us.

Once all the jobs are done, we retire to our little bedrooms, just a hole in the cave wall that we've fitted some old sheets across. My bedroll lays there, the blanket folded neatly over it.

It feels good to be home, I can let my guard down for a bit.

I unbuckle my belts and sheaths and place them neatly at the end of the bedroll. I then pull off my dirty clothes and place them next to the door.

'Hey Vix?' I call out.

I get a muffled reply, 'yeah?'

'I'm going to go clean up outside.'

'Okay.'

I smile, then walk over to a small chest. On top sits a soft grey sheet, which I use as a towel, and inside are a fresh change of clothes.

Wrapping my towel around me, and slipping my feet back into my boots, I take the clean clothes and wander outside to the well.

I place the towel and clean clothes on the wall of the well and slip my boots back off. I cringe at the feel of sand between my toes. I pull the bucket up; splashes and droplets of water is all I can hear. Reaching the surface of the well, I pull it up over the edge and begin scooping water with my hands and cleaning myself. There had been a lovely little freshwater creek Vix and I had used while we were still in the grasslands, we'd even managed to wash our hair properly, but since then, we hadn't been able to clean ourselves.

Once I've climbed back into clean clothes, I aim straight for my bedroll, collapsing on the thin mattress. Sleep hits fast and hard. I don't wake until the evening.

*****

After an easy dinner of boiled potatoes and some small beef steaks, I head outside to feed the wolves. Throwing the chunks of dried meat to the wolves, I watch as they devour their feeds. They do hunt within the canyon, their territory, but I like to give them extra. Watching them finish the meat, I untie my braided hair and run my fingers through it. In the distance, a howl cuts across the desert and I hold my breath as I listen to the sound of the wild desert wolves. I glance at the cave; Vixy is inside and will most likely be climbing into her bed.

Taking a breath and letting a small smile slide onto my lips, I climb up the cliff face, my hands and boots finding the worn but strong footholds and cracks. The rock is rough against my fingers but it's a quick, easy climb for someone like me.

I pull myself over the top of the cliff and gaze out across the canyon. From here, I can see the three calves huddled against the cliff of their small yard. Those calves are our emergency food. Below me is our home cave and across from it is the barn cave. The well is in between.

I watch as our wolves sit up and listen to the wild wolves.

I take a deep breath, staring out over the rocky cliffs all the way to the dunes. I let my gaze drift north-west, as if I can see all the way to the Shadow.

The nymph appears beside me quietly, her almost invisible form moving as she stares out at the desert with me. I've always had a lot of respect for her kind and always trust in their wisdom.

'What is the wind saying?' I ask quietly.

The nymph doesn't say anything for a few moments, long enough that I begin to doubt I'll get an answer.

'The wind tells me that somewhere, someone is waiting for you, Danica.'

I turn to look at the nymph. 'I know what it is to be hunted.'

'You have many people who hunt you,' she tilts her head slightly as if considering what to say. 'Many will continue to hunt you, but trust in your blood, and no-one else, for only your blood will help you.'

I grunt at this. So much help my blood has been.

# CHAPTER FIVE

## HUNTER

As the sun makes its way across the sky, I decide it would be wiser to travel south for a day or so before turning west towards home. The rebels would assume I'd make a beeline home, especially since I have no food or water. But if I stay smart, keep my wits about me, I can survive. As I lay covered in sand, I decide to only travel at night, once the heat of the day has disappeared with the sun.

As dusk settles over the desert, I climb out of the sand. My limbs are stiff. I stand and stretch and realise just how alone I am. No-one travels through the middle because it's nearly impossible to cross. The beasts or rebels will kill you if you don't die of dehydration or insanity first. The endless rolling sand dunes are a quick pathway to madness.

I turn to face the stars; I really should have paid more attention in astrology classes. Although, I never should have needed to pay attention, I should have had better guards, ones that don't get killed by pathetic rebels. If the sun is setting west, then I turn my body to face the south.

I take a step forward, then another and another. Forcing myself to keep walking, I travel through the night, often hearing the howls of desert wolves. They are my real concern. Their hides are a yellow-brown and they are smaller than the average wolf, but they roam the dunes, preying on anything stupid enough to walk alone in the desert—like me—and they are known to be vicious.

The wolves and the traitors that viciously killed my guards.

Fortunately, all the beasts were banished to the Shadow ten years ago, so I don't need to worry about werewolves, Nightwalkers, dragons or wraiths in Asada. Only the few that decide to risk being captured and to then serve in the Red Army. Mother had told me the story of the banishing and although I had been there, all I remember was a meeting, Mother telling me to keep quiet and being incredibly bored. She told me the monsters had come to kill the humans, but she had banished them to Asada's Shadow, threatening them with death if they trespass. Sometimes I get a feeling that Mother hasn't told me the full truth yet, because surely the beasts would lash out, but there wasn't ever any record of a battle playing out, so I always end up deciding to trust in Mother's words.

I keep to the tops of the dunes, seeing for miles in the moonlight. There is nothing.

How did everything go this wrong? If I had just ordered the guards to leave with the carts, then I wouldn't be trekking alone across the Bijara Desert in the middle of the night. I am a captain. I have more authority, but I was intimidated because they had more experience than me.

I flinch as another howl echoes over the desert. There is no way to tell how far away the desert wolves are.

By dawn, I am hungry and thirsty. I've never gone this long without food, and I feel a low nauseous feeling at the bottom of my stomach. I force myself to keep walking.

By mid-morning, the heat sets in, and I sit in the shade at the base of a dune. If I don't find food or water by tomorrow morning, I'll be in big trouble. I try not to dwell on what will happen, but it haunts my thoughts all day.

I tear a strip from my shirt attempting to use it as a makeshift scarf across my face. I roll my jacket up – a sorry excuse for a pillow – and lie down, listening to the soft sound of sand being carried by the wind between the dunes.

The sun seems to take longer to travel across the sky than it did yesterday, beating down on me, heating the sand around me. The wind then carries the sand, stinging any skin showing. I am grateful that I still have my scarf. My lips are cracked; my neck, face and hands are sunburned and my whole body is sore, forcing myself to give up.

That night, as the sun sets on the desert, I find it harder to get up and walk. I think of home, the smell of bread in the oven, and Mother sitting down at the dinner table, notes and food in front of him. I think of the paintings, how Mother had decorated the house to look as if it belonged in Carramera, on the tropical beaches near the North Sea. I think of my bedroom, with its view of Thorn Gap, and I think of the late nights spent in the Underground with Tyke, dancing with gorgeous women, drinking ourselves stupid, bantering and plotting grand schemes that will probably never happen.

My throat is so sore.

As the moon begins its descent, I notice a glint of something, as if it's winking at me. It looks like water on the horizon. I hesitate, I might be hallucinating. So, what if I am? It might be real, and if it isn't then I'm already a dead man walking.

I aim for the glint, but after a few steps, it vanishes, my glimmer of hope along with it. Hopelessly, I continue to walk towards my now non-existent chance at survival.

After an hour, I feel no closer, but I notice the landscape has changed slightly. The sand dunes have turned into rockier terrain. And as I walk on, rocks start to pile up, bigger boulders and rock walls appear.

Relief washes through me, I'm out of the desert. I must be somewhere at the edge of the desert… unless… there was an old childhood story of a canyon in the middle of the desert. I can't remember any details from the story.

The darkness fades and I keep pushing myself forward. If I'm going to die, I may as well make it as far as I can, that way, someone might find my body.

I stop. Something in the distance doesn't match the rocky terrain. A small collection of rocks has been piled up. I walk closer and notice the wood frame above it. My hope renews as I realise it's a well. I rush forward, climb over a rock wall and limp towards the structure. The bucket is already at the bottom, and I pull it up with all the strength I can muster. When the bucket reaches the lip of the well, I pull it towards me, dunking my head into the water and drinking as much as I can without making myself sick. I pull my head out and take a deep breath.

That's when I hear the low growl.

My heart pounds in my chest as I freeze; my hands let go of the bucket. I turn around, shaking. There are eight desert wolves in front of me, a few crouched ready to pounce and a few standing, all growling at me. I notice a low stone wall behind the beasts. If I can get over that I might stand a chance.

I back up a step.

Another wolf walks forward a few paces and stops.

A sharp whistle slices the air, and I flinch. The sound is certainly from a person, and the wolves all turn towards where it came from before slinking back towards the wall, glancing back at me, knowing that I'm fair game. I don't take my eyes from the creatures, even as another whistle sounds and they sit at the base of the wall, their pelts the same colour as the stone.

I don't want to take my eyes of the animals, but I figure that I'll hear them if they move. I turn around and discover a young girl with freckles over her nose and hair the colour of a fox's pelt loose around her shoulders. She watches me from beside a rocky cliff wall. She doesn't look any older than thirteen and is wearing a dirty skirt and pale green shirt. I am definitely hallucinating!

She stares at me, and I stare back, noticing her bare feet.

'You're lucky I found you before they ripped you to shreds.' The girl says in a low but excited tone. 'Sandy and Shadow will literally rip you into tiny pieces, they won't eat you though. Rosie will do that.'

I keep quiet.

'How did you find this place?' The girl walks forward a few feet, and I scan the area behind her.

I realise I've walked into a canyon similar to Thorn Gap, but much smaller, as I take in the rock walls dotted with cave entrances. One of the caves has a wooden door and a smaller cave has an old and dusty bed sheet hanging down, a couple of tears in it.

'I …' My throat is dry and sore, but I force myself to speak. 'I got lost.'

'You escaped the front line too, didn't you?' The girl's eyes widen slightly.

I nod, letting her believe the lie.

She grins and that's when her words truly sink in. She had said *too*. My blood starts to race through my veins, having only just calmed after the wolves. I look her over now with more interest. She would be the younger of the two girls that escaped.

'I'm impressed you found this place.' She skips forward. 'I'm Vixy.'

'Hunter.' I take another look around. 'How have you survived out here?'

'Luck.' Vixy grins.

She doesn't strike me as someone who's been on the front line. Even though I never fought there, in a crowd of people I can pick out exactly who has fought. It leaves a mark on them, like a memory that chases them from bed in the early hours of the morning, a nightmare that haunts them when the sun sets. Like the nightmare that always comes when I travel to the front line.

Vixy looks over to the smaller of the two caves before turning back to me. 'What is your plan?'

'I …' What is my plan? Figure out exactly who she is and bring her back to the custody of the Red Soldiers. 'I don't know.'

'You can have breakfast here.' Vixy smiles and turns around, as if she doesn't have a care in the world.

I warily follow her to the smaller of the two caves, making a wide circle around two of the wolves that is now laying between us. Vixy pulls the sheet back and walks into a massive open room, the cave hollowed out by years of erosion. In the middle is a table with four stools around it. Pushed up against a wall is another table with cooking utensils scattered over it. Three wooden boxes are tucked underneath it, and a bucket next to it. Charcoal drawings cover the walls. Drawings of trees and flowers, mountains and rivers, deer and wolves, with the night sky shining down over the landscape.

Vixy's hazel eyes land on the table with the stools around it, potatoes half peeled on it. 'Danica is not going to be impressed when she gets back.'

Danica …

'I'll talk to Danica. You'll only be here for …' Vixy turns to me. 'How long do you want to stay here for?' Vixy sounds like an excited kid with a shiny new toy.

I shrug. 'Just 'til I know it's safe to go home, if that's alright?' Or until I can work out a plan to get this girl back to where she belongs.

'Yes.' Vixy is grinning at me. 'I'll talk to her, and we'll put you to work. Danica has been so busy, especially now that we've got to fix up the barn.' She heads for the table, sits down and picks up a potato. 'We hadn't planned to stay this long, but she doesn't want to travel through winter.'

Vixy tosses me an apple from out of nowhere and I catch it, greedily shoving it into my mouth. I sit across from her. She asks me questions about my life and I tell her most of it. That I am from Roseguard and have lived my whole life there. I tell her what the school was like, how the city was built around the Red Towers, what my house was like, the streets and the stores. I leave out my parents' occupations and how I ended up out here. Who and what I am. I answer her questions, despite my own questions buzzing around my mind. How did Vixy control the wolves? How did she find this place? Where did she get all this food?

A sharp voice sounds behind me, a voice so cold and hard as if it's never felt warmth. A voice that gives me goosebumps, especially when Vixy falls silent. I turn to face the doorway. Standing there is the most beautiful girl I've ever seen. Her small, slim but fit body stands still and tense, like a coiled spring. Her dark chocolate hair is plaited back but strands have fallen loose, framing her around her face, her skin fair with a dusting of sand from wherever she's come from. She watches me, with pale eyes as if she is about to kill me.

# Chapter Six

## Danica

Last night I heard the wild wolves howling. It was the type of howl that would let other wolves know that something else was out there among the dunes, so with the rise of the sun, I had gone scouting.

I arrive home after dawn; everything seems to be in order. My pack of wolves were content and relaxed, yet I can sense something is off. The footprints in the sand told me someone else had been through our little yard, the quiet chatter coming from the cave makes my skin crawl. The nymph doesn't chat with Vixy and is nowhere in sight. I put my horse with the others in the massive open cave that acts as our makeshift barn, before opening the door to find Vixy sitting at the table with a stranger.

Neither of them noticed my arrival, not with Vixy's never-ending chatter. This gives me some time to take in the stranger. He's obviously been trekking through the desert, as he is still covered in sand. He has dark blond hair, cut short in a military style. He looks like he's wearing a faded army jacket. It's similar to those that the captains would wear.

'What is going on?' I say sharply.

Vixy looks up. The stranger jumps, stands up and stares at me. He gulps once, twice.

'You better have a bloody good explanation, Vixen.' I set my eyes on the young girl.

Vixy ducks her head. 'Danica, I can explain.'

'Oh, you will.' I snap, not moving from in front of the door.

The stranger speaks up. 'I'm Hunter.'

My glare doesn't move from Vixy. 'I didn't ask.'

Vixy's eyes dart between us. 'He's a front liner. He's one of us.'

'Vixen Kyler, you know our rules.'

She stops in front of me. 'Danica, please!'

'Please what?' I finally move my gaze to Hunter. He looks about my age, maybe a year older, with light brown eyes and a sharp face, all burnt and cracked from the sun. Although he is muscled, he looks soft. His clothes are filthy, almost unrecognisable. 'He's not a front liner.'

Vixy frowns at me and turns to look at Hunter, who is sizing me up nervously.

'The carts I was travelling with were ambushed by rebels before we made it to the front line.' He says carefully, not stating whether he is a soldier or prisoner as he takes a step forward. I raise an eyebrow at his confidence for taking that step and he freezes, like a rabbit.

For a moment, I stand in silence, watching Hunter. My gut instinct is telling me that he is bad news disguised.

'Where do you want to dig a nice big hole, Vixen?' Vixy's eyes go wide, she knows exactly what I mean.

'Danica, no!' Vixy grabs my arm, and I'm tempted to slap her off. I can feel my heart rate increase, my muscles tense with fury burning through them. She brought a stranger into our home, putting her life at risk. 'Please, no!'

'What's going on?' Hunter asks, bravely taking another step forward.

I pull out a dagger and point it at him. 'Don't move!'

Hunter freezes again, eyes darting between me and the dagger.

'Please, Danica! You were saying about how much work needs to be done. He can do it!' Vixy argues. 'He can work for us and we can give him food and water for it.'

I look back at Vixy. If I could control how he behaves, and what he says around Vixy, then it would be good for her to be around other people, and it would also be good for her to have a break from the constant workload. It would be good for her to be a kid.

'Why were you sent to the front line?' I direct my question at Hunter, dagger still pointed at him.

He's either smart enough to not lie, or brave enough to tell me the truth. 'I am a Red Captain, and I was supposed to inspect the front line.'

I look him up and down. The dirty clothes, the messy blond coloured hair, the light dusting of freckles and dirt. Just a soft boy who has too much money.

'How did you manage to become a captain so young?' I laugh mockingly.

'I'm smart.'

I look at him again. Not just at him, but at all the small tells. He stands there fidgeting, eyes darting—no good in a stressful situation, especially since he freezes every time he gets a scare. But his tone and punctuation are educated, confident, it doesn't have the slight slur that the soldiers have. The voice of someone spoilt, someone used to living in luxury and getting what they want.

'You look like you've never even been on the front line.'

'I have been a couple of times, but I handle more of the strategic planning.'

My heart rate increases again as I realise where his *strategic planning* is based. Roseguard's war rooms.

I laugh again. 'Well, that just makes you a lousy captain.'

He clenches his jaw for a moment, as if my words had hit home. 'I'm the best strategist since Melissa Cole.'

I clench my jaw and force myself to take a deep breath at the mention of *her*. 'Melissa Cole?'

He frowns and nods.

I stand there for a moment, considering my options. I could either kill him now and be done with him or risk having him around, get some work done and deal with him later. I look down at Vixy, and she's staring at me hopefully. Maybe having another person around will be good for her. And if he grows comfortable around me, he'll be more willing to talk. If I play my cards right, I can find out what's happening in Roseguard.

I yank my arm out of Vixy's grip and stride forward. I place my dagger at Hunter's throat and watch him panic, his eyes darting around the room looking for an escape.

'You do exactly what I tell you.' I pause, to let the weight of my words sink in. 'If you don't do as I say, if you harm Vixy, if you steal, lie or reveal us, I'll kill you and feed you to my wolves. Clear?'

'Crystal,' Hunter says.

I watch him for a moment, the dirty skin, the clenched jaw. He's tense, but I put it down to fear. I sheath my dagger but then pat him down. He flinches when I touch him but holds still.

'If you flee, I've trained those wolves to hunt strays down and kill them.' I finish patting him down, finding only a pocketknife in his pants pocket. 'I'll be keeping this.'

'Did you like feeling me up?' He replies and I tilt my head at the tone.

'Aye, even more so when parts become disconnected from the body.'

His face pales. He doesn't have a smartass response to that one.

'Good.' I step away. 'Go clean out the wolves' cave. It's the small cave at the end of the rock wall. There's a small shovel in there against the wall. Tell them to *sit* if they start misbehaving.'

Hunter nods his head and almost runs out the makeshift door.

Vixy quietly sits back at the table putting all the sliced vegetables into a pot. I sit across the table from her, resting my head in my hands. Today had certainly not gone as planned.

'What do you think of him?'

Vixy considers the question. 'I think Hunter is nice. Even though you say he isn't one of us, I think he could become one of us. He may be a captain, but he obviously doesn't like the title. And I also don't think he knows how to fight. He was like when one of the wolves find a bunny, frozen. Let's just help each other out.' Wise words from a thirteen-year-old girl, but she does also see the best in everyone and fails to see the worst. 'That's what Autumn would have done.'

He had also flinched when I called him lousy and had seemed proud to be following in Melissa Cole's footsteps.

'I, however, think Hunter is loyal to his family and home, I don't know what he does in Roseguard, and being a captain, he's in a position of power.' I say quietly to Vixy, quiet enough that Hunter has no chance of overhearing. 'But … I also think he'll put his survival first.'

Vixy tilts her head slightly as she considers my words. I give her a small smile and begin helping with tonight's dinner.

*****

Hunter finishes his work and pulls the sheet back. I don't look up as I give him a list of jobs to do before dinner. All jobs that needed to get done anyway, but I give him a few to test out, see if he'll challenge me on anything, especially with how exhausted he is. The day passes slowly, my focus is always on Hunter no matter where he is or what he is doing. If he is cleaning out the horse yards, I'll be nearby watching while I complete another task. Or if he is fixing the gate in the calves' paddock, I'll be checking the calves. Not only is he exhausted, but starving and I can tell that he is not use to the work I am making him do. I don't think Hunter knows who I am, for if he did … he'd be dead.

As Vixy finishes preparing dinner, I stand up. She watches me before skipping to her bedroom, another small cave with a curtain as a door, and I wander into the sunlight. Hunter is busy filling up buckets, and looks like he is struggling to stand up straight. I tell him to go and prepare for dinner, and he nods his head slightly before hurrying into the main cave.

As soon as he is out of sight, the nymph appears. She shyly floats out of the well, her semi-transparent body rising and gliding over the sandy ground until she is in front of me.

'Please,' I say quietly to the nymph's grey but beautiful face. 'Any advice on the Roseguard Captain?'

'Humans are greedy creatures … only trust him when you've got something he wants enough to be loyal.'

'I don't know what I would have that would keep him loyal to me.'

The nymph gives me a small tight-lipped grin, 'Humans are greedy. The answer to your question is obvious. To survive.'

I'm about to push for more answers when the nymph looks over towards the well. She floats over to the well wall, its rocks worn from years of erosion and sun. Her body becomes solid as she touches the ground, pale skin and long hair. 'There is something in there that should you retrieve, keep it close to your blood.'

'And what is that something?' I tilt my head slightly as I consider the nymph's words.

'Your world is about to change, and I think this item needs to go with you. Hold your breath and dive.'

'I can't leave Vixy with Hunter while I go for a swim.'

'I will watch over the girl.'

'And what can you do if Hunter attacks her?'

'You know better than anyone else to trust me.'

'I do, please reassure me though.'

'I'll command the wolves.' The nymph's eyes travel to the well, then she fades with the sunset.

I sigh in frustration, shrug my jacket off and sit on the edge of the well. The nymph is one of the few creatures, beings, that I trust, so if there is something down there she wants me to have, I'll get it. And if she says she'll watch over Vixy, I trust her. Even though she fears the wolves, I know that her magic will allow her to call them to protect Vix.

Looking down into the water, I wonder what could be so important that the nymph wants me to retrieve. I guess I'll have to find out. I take a big breath, the scent of wet earth thick, and let my body fall forward; moments after falling through air, a huge splash and then every nerve in my body tenses as the freezing water engulfs me. I push myself down as I dive. Although the water is freezing cold, it's soothing in a way. I pump my arms and kick my legs as I make my way to the bottom of the well. It seems to go on forever, my lungs begin to burn and I fear I may have to turn back to the surface. A glint catches my eye in the wall of the well. It's hard to see in the murky darkness so I reach out blindly.

As I grab onto the object, a rush of electricity travels up my arm, the feeling like raw unfiltered power. The power feels too big for this world, but it doesn't feel like its bursting to escape, like it's sleeping. It calls to my blood, like a summer storm calls to every wild creature that is alive with youth, like the darkness calls the predators and the beginning of spring calls on the birth of animals.

It gets harder to hold my breath, so I kick off the well floor, my body spearing upwards, parting the fresh water.

As I break the surface, I take a deep breath and tread water, before pulling myself over the lip of the wall. I sit there as I unfurl my hand. The object is a small chunk of Moonstone-looking metal, twisted like silver vines. I hold it up in front of me; looking at the metal and the powerful feeling that follows is like an old memory, it nears the surface of my mind but falls just short each time. I can't place where I may have seen it before.

# Chapter Seven

## Hunter

By nightfall, I'm exhausted and starving. My hands sting, blisters having appeared on the skin, and my muscles ache. At least I am nice and cool from all the sweat that drips down my body. All day I did general jobs; more labour than I've ever had to do. I keep my mouth shut and when I finish one job, I move onto the next. Vixy came around with bread, a bit of cheese and an apple at lunch time, but after no food or water for the past few days, I have very little energy left.

All day, I think of the dinners and balls in Roseguard's grand hall. The platters of food along the tables covered in red silk with gold trim, roses in vases. The women dancing between my arms, with dresses that cover just enough to remain elegant. Sneaking Tyke in right under Mother's nose.

I have absolutely no doubt that if I step out of line, Danica will kill me. Mother certainly described her correctly. *Dangerous.* The women in Roseguard are nothing like Danica, they are elegant, soft and easy to read. Danica is cold and aloof and would be stunning if she ever wiped the look of hatred from her face. She moves like a wild cat—every step, every movement calculated. Every breath considered.

The profile I was given from Mother of the girls was correct, Danica with her brown hair and pale eyes, small and lean stature. Although she only reaches my chest height, I feel so much smaller than her. Vixy of course with her red hair, young age and freckled complexion… it would have been hard to miss her.

I've noticed Danica watching me as if I am prey or something she can't quite figure out. She made a point of feeding the wolves while I cleaned out their small cave, throwing them chunks of meat as they growled and devoured it within seconds, teeth snapping at one another, the stench of raw meat and wet-dog strong enough to make me gag. Where she got the meat from … I've no idea.

And then she walked out as the sun set, running her fingers over the rocks of the well before sending me inside as if I were a child.

Vixy is in her bedroom, so I watch Danica from the cave entrance. I watch as the air around the well shimmers, like mist or fog. Then the mist thickens and transforms into a naked young woman. Danica then speaks to the … thing, and it says a few words, too quiet for me to hear, before dissolving back into thin air.

I take a few steps back, blinking.

'That's the nymph,' Vixy says from behind me.

'They're banished.' I glance back at her.

Vixy rolls her eyes, walks up and collects a handful of cutlery to set the table. 'No, Danica says they aren't part of the Treaty.' The Treaty of Asada that kept all beasts and monsters controlled until the banishing. 'But that nymph is really shy, she won't talk to anyone other than Danica. She'll flee if I walk outside, but sometimes she leaves gifts by the door. Usually a flower she's found.'

Vixy walks over to the table, and I follow as she begins setting it. I hate my ignorance, but I have to ask. 'What is a nymph?' I've only heard the name muttered around taverns and inns late at night.

Vixy looks me up and down. 'They are guardians of nature. Usually, the spirits of women killed by ill intent but who have not committed a crime. That's what Danica told me anyway.'

'How does Danica know that?'

Vixy bites her lip, and I watch as she considers my question, her brow furrowed. 'I don't know, maybe her mother told her.'

I lean against the rough wooden table. They've placed a rock under one of the legs to keep the surface even. Now is probably the best opportunity to get information out of Vixy. 'What else has Danica told you?'

'What do you mean?' Vixy finishes setting the cutlery and picks up three mismatched plates from their so-called kitchen bench.

I probably should have narrowed that question down a bit, she is a child after all. 'What else does Danica know about the beasts?'

Vixy places the plates on the table. 'A lot, she said most of her friends while in the Red Army weren't humans. She said that she learned a lot about them.'

'Right, and what did this include?'

I flinch when I hear Danica's cold voice. 'Like how each beast would be willing to kill a little red captain.'

Danica walks in and leans against the doorway, watching me, raising an eyebrow. She's soaking wet, and her wet clothing does very little to hide her fit and toned body. I can't help but take in the sight of her, she's certainly a dangerous woman if she knows how to use her body… She doesn't say anything, and I don't know what to do. I've never come across a woman that hasn't been scrambling for my attention—a captain of Roseguard's Red Army.

Luckily Vixy saves me from doing anything as she points a sour look at Danica. 'Danica! You tell me off for getting my clothes wet.'

Danica's eyes flick over to Vixy. 'That's because it's just you and me. There were no boys before.'

'Well, I finished making dinner.'

I watch Danica as a soft smile appears on her face, cracking that hard cold exterior. 'Thanks, Vix. Give me two moments.'

Danica strides past us, aiming for a small room with an old sheet as a door. I can hear her getting changed, and she emerges moments later in new clothes that look similar to the ones she was wearing before, a dark brown long sleeve shirt and brown leather pants, worn and a size too large.

I follow Vixy to the table and sit next to her to avoid sitting next to Danica. Finally, Danica walks over and sits directly across from me. She starts eating her stew and I wait until Vixy is eating before touching my meal. I keep my gaze down as I try to ignore the fact that I am a captain dining with two criminals. The people I normally dine with have titles.

'So, Stray,' Danica finally says. 'Where abouts in Roseguard do you live?'

I consider her question. Do I want to provide criminals information on where I live? No… but a small grin plays on my lips. This will impress her, and it'll be worth her reaction. Plus, she'll be in chains before she can do anything with the information.

'Highhill.'

Danica's face is completely blank, uninterested. Not the usual reaction I get when I say I'm from Highhill. Usually, it's absolute jealously or admiration. Only people with money and status can afford to live on that street.

'What's Highhill like?' Vixy grins, her grey eyes watching us.

'It's different from here,' I begin. Danica snorts and I clench my jaw, tighten my fists under the table. Disrespect is not tolerated in Roseguard, and Danica will pay for that reaction once I have her back in custody. 'Highhill has a view of Thorn Gap, closest to the Red Towers and has the best clubs, taverns and parties in the city. My Mother's house is at the end of the street with the best view of the Gap.'

'What's Thorn Gap?' Vixy keeps watching me and I frown.

'Where are you from?' I ask. Everyone knows what Thorn Gap is.

'I was from Salt City. Never been to Roseguard before, except when I was a prisoner. I wasn't able to see much.' Vixy rolls her eyes, as if it were completely normal.

I bite my tongue for a moment, she wasn't a prisoner, she's a criminal.

'Thorn Gap is a massive canyon north of Roseguard. No man can make the climb down, but the view is spectacular, and my bedroom balcony looks out over the Gap.' I hesitate, about to ask Danica where she is from, try to get some information out of her.

'What are the Red Towers like?' Danica asks, as if sensing the question on my lips.

I tense. 'Tall, boring, all four in the middle of the city, with all the important rooms guarded behind the towers.' I add with a smirk, because if she ever gets the idea into her head to break in, I'll shut that idea down before it grows.

'What is the Red Army's next moves?'

'Wouldn't you love to know?' I grin.

Danica just stares at me, putting her cutlery down. Vixy nudges me under the table, and I realise that although this information should definitely not be shared with criminals, it might be my only way to survive.

'We're going to begin the next phase in recruiting soldiers. We'll be taking anyone who can hold a sword or bow from Lyko, Tirma and Materga.' I wait to see if her reaction indicates whether she may be from one of those villages. Her face remains perfectly still, except for a slight clench in her jaw. There is some anger tucked away behind her stunning face.

'When will that phase start?'

'Soon. I'm not in charge of that mission so I don't know when.' I take another bite from my meal. 'How did you two get here?'

'Wouldn't you love to know, Captain?' I tense as she throws my words back at me. Vixy might be oblivious, but she and I both know we're enemies.

I notice Danica shoot a sharp look at Vixy who quietly begins clearing plates. Danica soon leaves to another room, when she moves, it's like watching a cat, every step smooth and calculated. I sit and rub my face as Vixy clears the dishes and she asks me more about life in Roseguard. I give her everything she wants to hear, whilst leaving out important information as I know Danica will be listening from the other room. I ask Vixy about the wolves and she tells me how Danica found the litter after the mother had died, so she took them and raised them as guard dogs.

Eventually she finishes the dishes and leaves to her small bedroom, and I realise I have no place to sleep. I walk to the room Danica had gone into and pull the sheet back.

She's sitting on a bedroll, with a map in front of her. She is in a cotton shirt and matching pants, her shirt is quite thin, old, worn and a little bit transparent. I wonder if maybe she wore it on purpose, to try and distract me. Her long dark brown hair is loose around her shoulders. She doesn't even look up as she tracks a finger across the map.

'What do you want, Stray?'

'Some place to sleep.' I look around the room and notice black figures painted on the walls. Three female figures that look like humans with daggers and swords painted in their hands, a moon above them. Nightwalkers.

Danica looks up at me and narrows her eyes as she notices where my gaze is. 'They're supposed to be the Three Sisters: Zodia, Selenia and Celestial.' Danica's voice hesitates ever so slightly before she mentions the final sister.

Mother had told me bedtime stories of the monsters with those names. The stories were used to keep children from roaming the streets after dark. They were the goddesses worshipped by the Nightwalkers and had once ruled over Raguia during an age of darkness. One had ruled Asada, one for Ritenvold and the last sister ruled Maristela. During this reign, humans had been forced to remain hidden in small villages scattered across the countries while those very monsters who said they saved us, hunted us down.

'Those Three Sisters are a bad omen,' I say warily.

'Do they scare you? They were here when we found the place.'

I look at Danica, the girl sitting on the bedroll. 'Yes.' I do not lie. 'They are monsters.'

Danica doesn't say anything for a moment, her pale eyes watching me. 'In the trunk in the kitchen, there are spare rugs and blankets. Take one and sleep in the kitchen.'

I nod my head and turn to go. 'Goodnight Danica.'

I'm out the door when her reply floats through.

'Goodnight.'

The blankets are rough and scratchy against my skin, and smell of must and moths. I lay on the hard cold rock and close my eyes. I need to figure out a plan. I am the best strategist since Mother. I will come up with something, I just need all the information and then I can put these criminals into chains and punish them.

*****

The next day is more of the same. At least there is a bit more cloud coverage so it's not quite as hot. My clothes are disgusting, I know I stink. I have never been this filthy my entire life. I can feel the dust coating my skin. All I want is a nice long hot bath.

Vixy had given me some strips of cloth this morning to use as bandages to protect the raw blisters on my hands. Breakfast had been simple, some eggs I don't know where they found and a bit of dried meat. I ate everything they gave me anyway, I can feel my body losing its energy.

Danica watches me all day, as if sizing me up for a fight. And I watch her as we complete the jobs. She's in brown pants and wears a white singlet. I'm surprised her pale skin doesn't burn in the sun. I admire her body from a distance, and I wonder what it would feel like against mine. I watch as she gives Vixy a lesson in fighting. I can see them, but I can't hear whatever they are saying. Despite that, I can see that Danica is a very talented soldier. The Red Army taught her well.

Vixy follows me around all afternoon as I carry water buckets to and from the well, add more rocks to the wall around the little clearing and slowly complete the list of jobs Danica has ordered me to do. Vixy asks about Roseguard, about life in the city. I lose track of where Danica is in the late afternoon, and I get a nauseous feeling when I can't find her, worried that she'll be setting an ambush for me.

Towards the evening, Danica reappears, and I feel instantly relieved being able to keep an eye on her.

I keep shovelling dirt out of the trench she ordered me to dig. She watches me, leaning against the rock for a while before speaking.

'I don't trust you, Stray.' I look up at her. 'And I don't trust you around Vixen.'

'I gathered that much.' I frown and stop what I'm doing it. 'What is your plan for me?'

Danica watches me for a moment. 'Dinner is ready.' Is all she says.

She turns her back and I roll my eyes before checking out her ass. I bite my lip. She's a criminal. Then again, that would be a good story for Tyke, to bed a criminal…

I lean the shovel up against the hard rock wall of the canyon and stretch out my aching arms before following Danica back to the home cave.

The scent of stew wafts up my nose as I inhale deeply and close my eyes for a moment. My stomach gurgles and I open my eyes again, Vixy has served some cooked venison and potatoes for the three of us. To a hungry man, it looks delicious. Everything seems to be the same as last night. Vixy is her usual chatty self, asking me questions while Danica stays quiet, watching us, sizing me up still. I clear off my plate again but don't dare ask for seconds. Finally, as Vixy cleans up, Danica pulls out two bags and dumps them on the table.

'What's going on?' Vixy asks, glancing between Danica and the bags.

What is going on?

'You are going to stay here by yourself for a couple of weeks, Vix.' Danica says, checking the two packs. 'Take it as punishment for inviting a stranger into *our* home.'

'What do you mean?' Vixy stops drying the dishes.

'I mean, the Stray is going to prove he is worthy of staying with us.' I almost believe her lie, but there is no chance she would ever trust me, a captain of the Red Army.

Vixy looks up at me and back at Danica. 'You and Hunter are going on a raid by yourselves?'

Danica does the buttons up on one of the packs. 'Correct.'

'But you need me.' Vixy whines.

'I don't need you this time, Vix.' Danica taps her finger twice against the table. 'And if you keep complaining, you won't be coming on a raid any time soon.'

Vixy throws her towel on the bench and looks ready to have a temper tantrum. I'm almost tempted to sit down and watch the argument erupt between the little fox and the wild cat.

But Danica only runs an eye over Vixy, as if knowing exactly how the argument will play out and turns to grab a pack. 'Come Stray, we're leaving now.'

'Now?'

'Yes, now.' Danica turns towards her bag.

'But we're not rested.' I argue.

'You can sleep when you're dead.' Danica snaps, then a small smirk appears on her lips, and she looks up at me. 'I can have that arranged if you wish?'

I swallow.

Vixy grimaces and rushes forward to hug her. Danica hugs her back then presses a kiss to her forehead.

'This will keep you safe.' Danica whispers as she places something into Vixy's hand. 'Be a good girl, show no mercy and make sure you do all your chores.'

A strange group of words I think as I shrug the pack from the table onto my shoulders, always keeping an eye on where Danica is standing.

'Bye Danica. Bye Hunter,' Vixy says quietly.

I hesitate for a moment before saying, 'Bye, kid,' and follow Danica out of the door, to the barn cave.

I look over my shoulder once to see Vixy standing by the doorway, watching us leave. I grimace as I imagine her on the front line, a thirteen-year-old girl fighting the monsters on the other side of that precious line, trying to protect our kingdom from the evil in the east. But she was there for a reason. She's a criminal and became even more so when she betrayed the Red Soldiers and Roseguard by escaping and running away. And as soon as I can, I will have soldiers sent to this canyon to capture her again.

Inside the makeshift barn, two horses are tacked up both with saddle packs full of supplies. Danica hands me the reins of a small chestnut mare. I watch as Danica climbs into the saddle of a big dark brown stallion, her long leather jacket flowing around her, the split up the back perfect for riding. I can tell instantly that she is a natural rider.

I climb onto the mare and once Danica has arranged her weapons, she urges her horse forward and I follow her out of the maze that is this canyon and into the desert. Hoofbeats echo against the hard rock. The only other sounds are of the horses breathing, and one neighing from the stables. Danica remains silent. I watch her as she rides, her body moving as one with the stallion. Her long dark hair is braided and tied close to her head; the braid finishes two thirds of the way down her back. She has a sword on one hip, a dagger on the other, blades in sheaths on her long slender legs and a bow across her back, the quiver of arrows strapped to her saddle. I have yet to see her make a kill, but I have no doubt she won't show any mercy.

I ride up alongside of her. 'So, what exactly do we do on a raid?' I ask, testing out how far she'll go with this lie.

Danica turns to face me, moonlight and shadows playing on her face, she doesn't look entirely human, but like something that would haunt your dreams. 'We're not going on a raid.'

I clench my jaw; I had expected some more dancing around the truth. That is something I can do, after bantering and making deals and finding out information in the Underground.

'Oh.' I frown. 'Where are we going?'

'Roseguard.'

'Roseguard?'

'Roseguard.' Danica lets a small but wicked grin fall onto her lips and a shiver goes down my spine.

'Why?'

'You're going to get me into the Red Towers.' Danica finally turns to look at me. 'I want to find out when the soldiers are leaving for the mountain villages.'

'We won't need to go into the towers to find that out.' I frown. There is no way I will let Danica into the Red Towers.

'So, you know when they're leaving?'

'No, but I can find out through the Underground.' I clench my jaws. I need to figure out a way to get her back into shackles whilst preventing her from wreaking havoc in my city.

'The Underground?' She tilts her head slightly.

'Aye, an underground club. I have a friend there who will have the information.'

'Good.' She looks back out to the desert.

# Chapter Eight

## Danica

As the rays of sunlight spill over the horizon behind us, I sit deep in the saddle, easing my stallion to a halt before dismounting. Normally I would take a different horse out each trip as I like to alternate them, but Eagle is my most reliable. The chestnut mare I gave to Hunter, who Vixy had later renamed to Sweetie, had been a little bit lazy. Not wanting to leave her companion, the two of them neighing out to each other for the first hour – Sweetie had been trying to turn back to the canyon any opportunity she had. Hunter was a better rider than I thought he would be and follows my lead through the desert. He'd asked once how I knew where I was going, and I told him I was following the stars. He asked me to show him how to read the stars, and I smirked at him, nice try Hunter, nice try.

I offer my horse some water from my small bottle as I contemplate the journey ahead, we'll reach the grasslands in just under four days without the extra weight of the pack ponies.

'Hobbles are in your saddle bag, and then make yourself comfortable,' I say through my scarf to Hunter as I pull the leather straps from my saddle bag. 'It's going to be a long hot day.'

I hobble and untack Eagle, rubbing the saddle marks from his back. I quite enjoying grooming the horses, it's therapeutic. Once I've finished tending to Eagle, I pull a small blanket from my pack and sit down. I take off my bow and my sword and leave them by my side, before laying down on the blanket.

Hunter goes about tending to Sweetie before he sits down near me, but puts enough distance between us that I can't reach him with a sword. I keep my gaze on the sky above me.

Hunter is silent for only a few minutes before speaking.

'Vixy said you killed a chimera a few weeks ago. I thought those only roamed Asada's Shadow,' he says carefully.

I don't know whether Hunter is genuinely curious or just trying to make conversation.

'Vixy isn't a liar.' But she is a chatterbox. The creature with the huge cat like face and a thick mane, eagle like front legs and a scaled tail had started coming too close to our little desert home. It had started harassing the wolves and I knew it wouldn't be long until it began preying on our loyal pets.

'Why was one of those beasts all the way down here?' A note of worry laces Hunter's voice, and I look over at him.

'A chimera is a desert creature. I'd be surprised to find them anywhere else.'

'All creatures were banished. Chimeras were included in that banishment,' Hunter states, with a tone of certainty and belittlement.

I sigh and roll over so I'm looking out into the dunes. 'I don't understand how you could be a captain when you know so little of the truth of the world.'

'And what is that truth supposed to be?'

'Your people have been spreading false lies through Roseguard and beyond, making the people of Asada believe what benefits the commander of Roseguard.'

'And you know this how?' Hunter pushes, and I can tell I'm stirring him up.

I grin to myself. 'Over nine and a half years being forced to fight for your Red Army ... lies don't last long in trenches.'

'So, what is it that you know, that I, a captain, don't know?' Hunter pushes.

'Chimeras were never part of the Treaty. Roseguard can't control creatures such as chimeras, dragons, griffins and goblins, although you normally only find those in the swamplands in Ritenvold.' I turn to Hunter. 'No-one can control those creatures. Not even the Nightwalkers as you call them.'

'How do you know all that?' Hunter's eyes narrow.

'My mother spent a lot of time teaching me about Raguia before the front line. I picked up the rest between trenches.' Not a lie, but not the entire truth.

*****

By evening, I'm itching to be back in the saddle heading for Roseguard. The night passes by slowly, with the moon covered by clouds. Despite this, I know my compass bearings well enough to not get lost among the changing sand dunes, and the few stars that peek through aid me. Hunter is quiet and I don't encourage any conversation. Eagle trots steadily through the desert, never tiring. One of Vixy's jobs is to keep the horses fit, so they can survive days of hard riding until we reach the grasslands.

The moon gives off just enough light that I can see Hunter's dirty blonde coloured hair in my peripheral vision. During the night, Hunter stays quiet, keeping his gaze on Sweetie's neck in front of him. Over the next few days, I will have to make sure that Hunter believes he can't escape from me, for if he did, Vixy's life will be at risk. He needs to fear me enough, or realise that I am smarter, more cunning than him. It will be difficult getting the information about the Red Soldiers departure plans. Especially without alerting the city that their missing captain is asking for information he should already know.

*****

The nights of travelling through the desert allows me to have plenty of time to contemplate what I'm going to do once I have my information. I might need help taking down the Red Soldiers. I know how to survive and how to kill, but that's about it.

I realise while I ride through the desert that my only purpose in life is to survive and look after Vixy. At least now I am taking small steps forward. Determined to stop any other young girls from suffering the same fate as Vix. Sent to the frontline scared, afraid and completely unprepared.

*****

The next few days take us into the grasslands without anyone taking much notice. As soon as we had reached the grasslands, I began changing our travel time. In the desert, it's safer and quicker to ride through the night, when no-one will see us. However, in the grasslands, we start riding at noon and finish at midnight. That way, if anyone questions why we're riding so late into the night, an excuse such as *a cow calving* or *we spied a broken fence at dusk and we're on our way home* will be believable. Once, when raiding with Vix, a farmer had come across us in the early hours of the morning. We had told him that we had to help a friend move some cattle, but the farmer believed us to be stealing. He wasn't wrong and I had learnt to avoid being sighted that early.

Hunter remains relatively quiet, and I don't bother making small conversation as we ride between the large farms. The farms are used for both crop and livestock, supplying Asada's cities with most of its foods.

Before the Treaty, the grasslands were home to a lot of halfbreed creatures, mostly human crosses. However, those with mixed blood were some of the first to be sent to the front line, if they hadn't fled to the Shadow. I had met quite a few of them while fighting. Now, humans have taken control, and most report to Roseguard. I'm not sure about what happened in Salt City and Carramera, but from what I had heard, after discovering that humans could gain more power, they all rallied to Roseguard's banners.

It's easy enough to stay hidden in the grasslands, even when we travel along the small roads. No-one questions or considers two riders on horses, especially as we often spy others on horses going about their daily life.

We had run out of food supplies on our second day into the grasslands, so I had hunted down a few rabbits. I told Hunter to start a fire, but after watching his pathetic attempts at getting a flame to ignite, I had done it myself. A city boy through and through.

A few days later, I spy Roseguard in the distance above the trees. We had entered the forest south of the city yesterday, the scent of pine a welcome change. The uneven ground made it impossible to clear the trees and turn it all into farmlands, making the forest an ideal place to hide in.

I find a small clearing with a few old pine trees to keep us hidden and decide that will be where we spend the remainder of the night. I don't think Hunter had noticed the city, for he had not raised his head the entire ride. He just kept his head bowed as his horse followed all day.

'Your city is close now,' I say, watching as Hunter's eyes fly to meet mine. Turning my voice cold and brutal, the voice I had used on the front line, I add, 'This is your only warning to not do something stupid while we're in there.'

I watch Hunter flinch, and know that my words and tone convey just how serious I am.

'I hope you've got your plan, Captain,' I say, staring between the trees while I pick at the rabbit carcass.

'I do, but I don't think you'll like it,' Hunter says quietly.

I look over at him. 'I don't have to like it, as long as it gets me the information I want… and you're not going to try anything that will get you beheaded.'

'As I said before, I've got a friend who will know what's happening.'

Hunter looks up at me and I say carefully. 'He betrays me and he's a dead man.'

Hunter only nods. 'I understand. He holds a position of power, unofficially of course, within the city, and he'll receive news, gossip and rumours first, normally before the Red Soldiers.'

'Sounds like my type of person.'

'You and him …' Hunter trails off and shakes his head. 'Promise me that if he gets you the information, you won't harm him.'

'If he threatens me or Vixen, then I can't hold that promise.' I say, before tossing the rest of the rabbit carcass into the small campfire and turning on my side, ending the conversation. 'I also don't owe you anything Stray, and you owe me nine and a half years of my life.'

82

# Chapter Nine

## Hunter

I do not owe Danica *anything*.

The reason she is, was on the front line, is because of her actions. Only criminals are sent to the front line.

Fury burns through me. She doesn't know me and assumes so much. I fist my hands, wanting to hit something. I roll over and stare at Danica.

She lays there, her body so still that I can't tell if she's breathing or not. Her eyes are closed, but I can tell that she is still awake.

I can't wait to get her in chains and make her beg, threaten her as she has done to me. Force her to work as she has forced me.

I will see Danica on her knees one day.

The shadows from the pine trees play patterns on her and I stare, taking in the shape of her body. The breeze carries her scent with it, a woody scent I can't place and something almost smoky. It's a soothing scent and I close my eyes.

At the moment, she needs me alive, so I don't have to worry about her trying to kill me in my sleep.

I'm going to have to hint at Tyke, somehow, that Danica is holding me hostage. I imagine that this is the only thing she knows how to do. Act like a criminal. Tyke would love besting her, challenging and outwitting her. It'd be such an exciting challenge for him. Although on one hand, I'm dreading the interaction, on the other, I'm excited for it. I'm excited to see how Danica handles the Underground, how I'll end up capturing her.

I decide there and then that *I* want to be the one to put her in chains.

# DANICA

I wake before noon but find myself not moving. I enjoy the silence while Hunter sleeps, the smell of the trees and soil, the quiet rustle of wind through the leaves, birds fluttering between branches and small animals moving across the forest floor. When it reaches midday, I pack up the few items and tack up the horses before waking Hunter, it's easier and quicker to do it myself.

I nudge my boot against Hunter's leg to wake him. 'Wakey-wakey Stray.' I mutter at him.

He groans and sits up rubbing his face.

'You can use the remainder of your drinking water to wash yourself if you want.' I mount Eagle and adjust my jacket. 'We'll be passing a creek in an hour and can refill then.'

'Thanks,' Hunter mutters and walks behind a tree.

I can still see him as he pulls his shirt off over his head. His back toned but not muscled. Not a single blemish marks his skin, and I watch as he uses a bit of rag to wipe off the grime.

I turn my gaze to the sky, the canopy above us. The wind has picked up and I watch the leaves whip back and forth. The forest floor is much more still.

Hunter returns, his shirt back on and I sit comfortably on Eagle as he puts his bedroll and blanket away.

'Thanks for tacking up Sweetie.' Hunter mutters as he takes the reins and mounts up.

I take the lead, picking the trails through the forest that will take us to Roseguard's front gates.

For the next couple of hours, I focus on the city, coming up with escape plans should things not go my way. I know that the moment I get an uneasy feeling, Hunter will try to take advantage of that. The moment I think he is plotting against me, he will have my knife to his throat and Melissa Cole will learn exactly who is in her city.

Riding towards Roseguard, we follow the trails, and then onto a dirt road that becomes paved the closer we get to the huge city ahead. When we reach the end of the tree line, I halt my horse and watch the city for a time. Between the tree line and the city is a massive green field, the sweet scent of the wildflowers growing over the field reminds me of the mountains in summer, and temporary market stalls are scattered across the grass. I assume most of the market stalls will trade with hunters and farmers. A few soldiers roam between the stalls, all in pairs. I watch as one soldier taunts a trader while the other laughs.

Finally, after deciding there are no nasty surprises between the tree line and the city walls, I turn back into the forest to find a place for the horses to hide and wait.

Hunter grows more impatient the longer we wait – fidgeting, fisting his hands and chewing his lip. I try my best to look completely at ease, unbothered about what is going on. I can't afford to show any form of weakness.

As the sun sets, we begin the walk towards the city that ruined my life, and I feel strangely confident. I had been in Roseguard once before, but I can't remember most of that *visit*. I had been terrified when I was conscious, and delirious the rest of the time, with a knife stuck in my gut.

I remember waking in a cell to find my stomach covered in dried blood, but the knife gone and the skin healed but scarred. I had screamed and threatened and hit my fists against the cell bars and walls for hours. The soldiers had refused to feed me until I was too weak to fight, then *she* had appeared in front of my cell …

I take a deep breath, pushing the memories back as I walk through the city gates. I'm back for revenge, and I am no child with a knife stuck in my stomach this time.

'Why do you even want the information?' Hunter turns to look at me, snapping me out of my thoughts.

'You'll find out later,' I say, looking forward.

I notice him swallow and a guilty look passes over his face. I don't care, not after what the Red Soldiers have done to me, to Vixy, to Asada.

'Okay, here's my plan.' Hunter hesitates for a moment, as if he can't quite believe that he is about to tell me his plan. I keep my gaze on him as he leads me between a row of houses, out of sight of the main streets. 'My friend, who will have the information, is king of the Underground. He owns it, runs it and rules it. When you're in the Underground, you play by Tyke's rules. But to get in … you're going to need to look and act as if you're there to party.' Hunter grabs my wrist, and I instantly snatch it back.

'You may be quite capable of looking after yourself out there, but I know how to live inside the city. This is where I thrive. So, if you want to get your information, you'll do as I say.' Hunter raises an eyebrow.

I fold my arms and stare back at him for a few moments. I don't appreciate the tone, the challenge in his voice as he tests how far he can order me, push me. But I do realise I'm in his playground, his home, and I want him to cooperate without any hassle. 'Okay. What do you want me to do?'

Hunter shakes his head. 'I need to find you some clothes.'

'Better find me some clothes then,' and I raise my eyebrow at him in expectation.

*****

Travelling around the city is easy enough. I keep my head low, gaze to the floor and avoid locking eyes with anyone as I follow Hunter towards the centre of the city. Red Soldiers patrolling the streets don't give us a second look as we trail behind others as they finish up for the day and head home to their families.

I memorise the route we take, the soldiers, the weapons they hold and their stances. I notice who is paying attention and who isn't too worried about the people walking through their city. The exterior wall is guarded by twelve lookouts, except on the north side where the city overlooks the canyon, and Thorn Gap protects the border. Slightly north of the heart of the city are four tall towers with a thick wall running between them— the Red Towers.

I don't fail to notice that Hunter weaves back and forth through the city, trying to confuse and disorientate me. He'd have to try much harder to do that.

As we walk through the crisp evening air, I ask Hunter questions about Roseguard as he leads me through the back streets of the city, disguised questions that will get me the city's layout, slowly with gathering curiosity.

'You said you were from Highhill, where's that?'

'Do traders use different gates to the city?'

'Where are your favourite and least favourite areas?'

Eventually, Hunter finds me some clothes from a quiet store in a back street. I stand just inside the entrance of the building as Hunter pays for the clothes with his eyes averted. Listening to make sure he doesn't expose me. I had cut a coin sack from a man's belt while in a busier street and no-one had noticed, fortunately there was enough money to pay for the clothes.

After leaving the store, I follow Hunter to a dirty but quiet alleyway and take my jacket off, laying it flat on the filthy ground before taking the clothes from Hunter.

'Turn around.'

'If you want me to get you the information, you better stop ordering me around.'

I look up at Hunter and he's got a small smirk on his lips, testing me now that I'm out of my comfort zone – and in his.

'Careful, Stray,' I mutter and turn around, then add over my shoulder. 'If you want to stay alive, you better do as I say.'

But I do like *playing* with this new confident and cocky Hunter. I know I should be shutting it down, but it's exciting. I haven't had anyone challenge me in this way before. I decide to let him keep playing until I get what I want.

I pull my shirt up over my head and drop it on my jacket by my feet. I can feel Hunter's eyes on my bare back as I pull the new shirt over my head. It's low-cut, dark red and leaves my shoulders bare. I let out a huff of amusement at the red. Of course, Hunter would put me in Roseguard colours.

The night air is cool and kisses my bare skin. I turn around to Hunter as I unplait my hair and run my fingers through it, the dark strands falling around my face and shoulders.

'Do I look like a Roseguard girl now?' I smirk as Hunter's eyes drop towards my exposed skin.

His eyes shoot up to meet mine. 'Never. But close enough for now.'

Smart answer Hunter. I glance down at my dark leather pants and combat boots.

'Your pants and boots won't be too noticeable.' Hunter says quietly.

I pick up my jacket and glance around the alleyway for a spot to hide it. Finding an uneven row of bricks along one wall, I make my way over and reach up to hide my jacket, my shirt riding up.

Convinced that no-one will steal it, I turn to Hunter. His gaze on my stomach, I realise that he'd caught sight of my scar.

I say loosely, 'Well?'

He stares at me as he pulls his shirt off over his head. I refuse to break his stare as toned but lean stomach comes into view. He grins and tosses the old shirt onto the ground, the new one still in his hand.

'Cat got your tongue?' He grins.

'There would need to be something far more interesting and better looking to catch my tongue.' I look down at my nails, inspecting them and letting boredom mask my features.

Hunter laughs and pulls the clean white linen shirt over himself, adjusting it before stepping towards me.

'Shall we?' He asks and offers an arm, a small smirk pushing at his lips again, and I narrow my eyes at it.

I size up the challenge and take his arm, my enemy's arm. He is comfortable in this city, I realize as I watch him stride out of the alleyway beside me. This city is a hunting ground, and he's a hound within it. Fortunately, I'm holding his leash very tightly.

We wander through the quieter streets, red brick homes that belong to the wealthier residents of Roseguard. The gardens are neat, and most are full of rose bushes the scent thick. The street is clean, and a few empty carriages are left in the open. When we pass under the shadow of a bridge, Hunter stops and pulls me to the side of the bridge wall. His hand is soft against my skin, other than where the blisters were. The night air is cool, I gulp it down.

He looks down at me, his mouth inches from mine. 'Just let me do the talking. The women here are not like you,' he adds, his breath warm against my cheek, 'and we don't want Tyke to know what type of woman you are.'

'What type of woman am I?'

'The type men don't survive. And if he finds out you're not the usual sort, he'll follow you through the desert to get you, to claim you as his.' Hunter grins. 'Tyke likes a challenge and loves to conquer it.'

'I'd like to see him try,' I say with only one side of my mouth pushing up into a small grin.

Hunter sighs and turns to the wall, pushing a brick back. The whole wall begins to move inwards, and I realise it's a door. I peer inside to a staircase winding further down than I can see. Torches line the wall.

Hunter goes to walk forward, and I yank his shoulder back, turning him to face me as I step closer, pushing a dagger against his groin.

'You betray me, and you'll lose your manhood.' I raise the dagger to his throat. 'Try anything, and I am more than capable of getting this information myself, in a much more brutal manner.'

I let Hunter go and he stumbles back before turning and making his way down the stairs. I follow warily, a hand casually resting within quick reach to my dagger. I wish I had the daggers I'd left hidden in my jacket in the alley. The descent is long, dark and cold, and I can't help but feel like the walls and roof are pressing down on me.

The further down we go, the worse I feel, especially when a dull thud starts echoing through the walls, making them feel like they'll start to creep towards me, trapping me. I don't mention it but the lower we go, the louder it gets. I then realise the thudding sound is music, not the few songs I know but heavier, louder music.

Eventually the stairs finish at a door. Hunter knocks on it and a small metal slit in the door opens, revealing a pair of dark eyes. 'Open the door, it's Captain Hunter Cole.'

Cole. My eyes flash to Hunter, to what he just said. Hunter Cole! As in Melissa Cole!?

My heart rate increases, my blood beginning to burn. My mind starts racing. He obviously has no idea who I truly am, by what he's said and done so far, I think he only knows me as an escaped criminal.

*Think, Danica. Think.*

I take a deep breath as I realise how close I am to the woman that destroyed my life. While the door opens, I give myself those few moments to plot a new plan. Hunter had told me where he—where Melissa Cole—lives.

The door opens, revealing a massive stone chamber shaped like a cave with paint, tapestries and curtains covering most of the walls. Men and women dance to loud, pulsing music. The men wear loose plain clothing, and the women wear even less. My heart is still racing as I watch a couple walk past and look up at Hunter with awe, who looks completely at home. I step closer to him, putting a hand around his waist. I am stronger and faster than he is, I am not letting him slip out of reach otherwise my bargaining chip disappears. He looks down at me sharply, obviously surprised at the touch, he puts his arm around my shoulders casually and says over the beat of the music, 'Careful, Danica, you might decide you like the social life.'

'Don't get your hopes up, Captain,' I say, forcing a wicked grin to keep him from thinking twice, and to keep myself from spitting on him, a Cole. Hunter's eyes narrow at me slightly before looking back up.

He walks us through the middle of the floor, everyone looking up at him and getting out of the way. People glance over at Hunter, do a double take then go back to dancing. They must be used to seeing their captain in the Underground.

The scent of perfumes is thick, and I feel like I can't get a fresh breath of air.

I can't see where the music is being played from, but I notice booths along the far wall. Some with curtains drawn but all with people filling them. I realise Hunter is aiming for the one in the farthest corner, where two men and a woman sit.

We make it halfway across the floor when a woman appears in front of us. I realise I don't like being in here because I can't hear the footsteps of someone approaching, the breathing of prey or predator. The woman has dark brown hair, cut to chin length, with dark paint over her eyes making them look bigger. Her lips are painted red and she's wearing a tight red dress, which is more like a piece of fabric wrapped around her torso. Her heels match her dress, and I eye the stilettos quickly. If things become nasty, I'll have to keep an eye on those heels.

The woman steps a bit too close than I am comfortable with, and she doesn't even look at me.

'Oh Hunter, we all heard tales of how you went to protect us and disappeared in the desert.' She pauses, as if waiting for a response as she runs her tongue along her lip. 'I've been lonely.'

'I left something behind and had to return,' he sighs.

The woman angles her body slightly, cutting me off and I'm tempted to laugh at her behaviour. 'I'm assuming you'll be staying now, because I missed you.'

Hunter just eyes the table at the back of the room, so I make my presence known. 'There really isn't that much to miss.' He looks down at me, raising an eyebrow and the woman's dark eyes slide to me, and to where Hunter's hand rests on my waist, a bit too low to be causal.

'See you later, Klara.' Hunter gives her the cold shoulder, and I wink at her as he leads me towards the furthest booth.

We reach the table and one of the men catches my eye. It's not his appearance that strikes me, but rather the look of being a predator in a house full of prey. Not like Hunter who has the look of someone who knows he's the boss and is completely at home, but this man … he will be the one to watch, the one who moves like a wolf through a flock of sheep.

I let myself smile at the familiar look—well not a smile, but a wicked grin of acknowledgement that I'm sure he'll understand if he notices it. I take in the dark blonde hair tied in a small bun at the base of his head, the dark eyes half paying attention to the person across the table from him. The girl on his side, plain as paper, kisses his cheekbone and I almost shake my head in pity.

The wolf looks up at us. 'Ah Hunter, I thought you'd be long dead.'

Hunter laughs. 'Good to see you too, Tyke.' He addresses the second man across the table. 'Excuse yourself.'

The man scrambles to get out of the way of the captain, and Hunter slides into the seat. I follow him, resting a hand on the table as his hand sits on my hip.

Tyke's eyes travel over me before turning to Hunter. 'I heard you were attacked on the way out.'

'Unfortunately,' Hunter leans forward. 'I need to ask a favour of you, brother.'

Tyke smiles at Hunter, the type of smile that would have prey running. 'Let me guess, you want me to get you into Ritenvold?'

Hunter hesitates. 'Worse.' He then looks at the woman beside Tyke and nods his head to the door.

Tyke removes his hands from the woman and says to her, 'Close the curtains on your way out.'

She quickly gets out. I don't take any notice of her.

'What about your pretty little lady?' Tyke motions at me.

'Call me that again, and you'll quickly learn that I am no lady,' I let that wicked grin reappear, and Tyke laughs, a deep sound that sends shivers down my spine.

'My pretty little lady stays.' Hunter bites his lip for a moment, another excuse to procrastinate before betraying his people. 'I need information. And I can't get it by playing captain this time, not with her.' He nods at me.

# Chapter Ten

## Hunter

'She wants information.'

Tyke's eyes slide to Danica, looking at her properly for the first time since we slid into his booth. His gaze narrows for a moment as he takes her in, the tense and alert body and the too wary eyes. He's smart enough to know that someone like Danica isn't from Roseguard.

Tyke bites his lips, his gaze meeting Danicas. 'Pretty eyes.'

'So I've been told.' Danica eyes don't leave his, and something in Tyke's posture changes, he becomes slightly more tense. I frown, I've never seen him like this before.

He would probably have made a better captain than myself, as he is excellent at reading people, crowds and atmospheres. He can read between the lines and notice the slightest of reactions.

It's what makes Tyke so good at getting news, rumours and gossip, and because he is my *brother*, whatever he hears, goes straight to me. Anything useful, I take to Mother.

'Why?' Tyke turns to me.

'I think her ulterior motive is to destroy the entire Red Army, but that's only a guess.' I look down at Danica, her hand tapping on the table, as she slowly turns her gaze to me and gives me a glare. Under the table, her hand squeezes my thigh hard enough to leave a bruise and it takes every bit of willpower not to react.

'Among other things,' she says as she turns her gaze back to Tyke. 'Hunter told me you're my best chance of getting information regarding the movement of Red Soldiers. Is that true or did Hunter give me incorrect information about the so-called owner of this particular underground club?'

Tyke's face remains blank as he takes in the challenge. I realise he's carefully turning over her words, trying to pick out any clues or hints. He runs his tongue over his teeth and doesn't say anything for a couple of long moments, as if considering how to react to the not so little lady beside me. 'What will you give me in return?'

As much as I'd love to hear Danica's response, I know Tyke will not take it well, so I respond quickly. 'I ask you for a favour Tyke, get her the information.'

'I want something in return, Hunter. You know what the deal is.'

'Information for information,' I snap, growing agitated the longer I sit here.

'Why do you want the information?' Tyke asks Danica.

Danica doesn't miss a beat. 'My lover is in that army.'

'About one hundred Red Soldiers were seen.'

'Heading in which direction?' Danica asks him.

Tyke shakes his head. 'Tsk tsk tsk. I need more information.'

Danica narrows her eyes for a moment. 'I need him to return home with me.'

'West.'

'I need him to return because I'm pregnant and have no way to look after myself.' Danica lies smoothly but by the look on Tyke's face, he does not believe a word she says. 'Weapons?'

I snap. 'Enough.'

Tyke tilts his head slightly as he looks Danica over yet again. 'Now I have given you more than enough information. I want some information that is true.'

Danica glares at him before huffing and leaning back in her seat.

'I do not have any information to offer,' she says. 'If you want information about me, you can ask any of the Red Generals. As I am sure you will the moment I leave this city with Hunter with me.'

'Why is my brother here with you, requesting this information from me instead of visiting the commander?' Tyke tilts his head in a challenge.

'Because once I have my lover back, I will expose a hidden community of rebels to him. The one that caused him to go missing…' Her lies keep building. 'But we can't let word get out, as they have spies.'

'Any other news?' I ask, changing the subject.

'Some. But first, what's your plan, brother? You're a missing man. Your mother went absolutely nuts when she heard rebels had attacked and you were missing. She's been sending search parties out for you.' Tyke leans back.

I can feel Danica's stare on Tyke, but I know her attention is on me. 'I promised Danica that I would help her find her lover, in return for the location of the rebel community.' I say carefully. 'If you could let Mother know that I have decided to assist the Red Soldiers that are heading West, I would appreciate it.'

So, she knows where I'll be to rescue me. I feel Danica's blade replace her hand against my thigh.

'Of course.'

'Thank you.'

'And what's her story?' Tyke nods to Danica. 'She isn't your usual sort.'

I don't say anything.

'She isn't from around here.' Tyke says sternly and turns to me. 'You're not telling me everything.'

Danica speaks up. 'That's because you don't need to know everything.'

'Careful sweetheart, I know that you aren't from around here and I know you've got a price on your head.' Tyke leans forward and glances over at me when he notices the subtle shake of my head in warning. Of course, I can stop Tyke, I can pull rank. Yet, I respect that this is his club, his business, his territory.

'Careful making false threats.' Danica looks as if she wants a fight to happen.

Tyke laughs. 'And what are you going to do, Princess?'

Danica tilts her head slightly at the nickname, as if she hadn't ever expected to be called that. 'Are you sure you want to find out?'

'I know I don't want to find out,' I interrupt. 'What is your news, Tyke?'

Tyke rolls his shoulders and his gaze sets on me. 'Dimitri Rush was spotted trailing the Red Soldiers that left the city.'

I feel Danica tense at Dimitri's name. A lot of people would, he's a legendary sharpshooter who has hunted and killed as many beasts as the Nightwalkers.

'Well, that is interesting news,' I say, 'But utterly useless to me.'

'We better get going,' Danica says, standing up.

'When are you leaving the city?' Tyke asks.

'You're welcome to come wave us out.' Danica grins and I stand up.

'I think I will come say goodbye,' Tyke says a bit sharply and I grimace, knowing he is only going to follow as he wants to challenge Danica and win.

Danica steps out of the booth and into my side, her arm around my waist. Tyke steps up to my other side and as we stride through the room, everyone gets out of our way. As usual, eyes follow us.

I let Tyke lead the way up the stairs, making sure to stay between him and Danica, I move her hand from my waist to my own hand. I can feel her eyes on my back the entire way up and as I step onto the deserted street, I finally feel Danica's eyes move from me to Tyke.

We make our way back to the alley where Danica had hidden her jacket, and I keep Tyke's attention on me as Danica puts her jacket over the shirt that had almost distracted me all night.

Quietly we make our way through the streets until we're standing in the wall's shadow.

'Wait.'

I turn to look at Danica.

'There is one more thing I need to do.'

'And what's that?' Tyke pushes.

Danica glances between Tyke and me. 'I need some ink, paper and wax.'

I close my eyes for a moment.

Tyke is the one that answers. 'This way.'

We follow him to a partially empty store, and he produces a key from his pocket. It must be one of his newer meeting rooms. He ducks inside and returns moments later with what Danica has requested.

He holds the items in front of Danica and just as she goes to take them, he brings his arm back, out of her reach.

A scowl appears on her face.

'Tsk tsk tsk,' he grins, stirring her up on purpose. 'Give me one truth tonight please.'

The scowl doesn't leave her face. 'My horse's name is Eagle.' Tyke's brows furrow. 'That's one truth.' She adds, grinning now.

She takes the items from him and walks across to the other side of the street for privacy, but not out of earshot.

Tyke leans against the wall beside me.

'That's quite a lady you've got there.' He laughs suddenly.

'You shouldn't have provoked her,' I say, watching Danica from across the street hurriedly writing on the paper.

'What's she going to do? Bite me?' Tyke sits down, leaning against the wall.

'She probably would,' I say, keeping my voice low and following Tyke to the wall.

'You've never been one to let a woman boss you around. What did she do? Bite you too hard?' Tyke laughs, looking over at me.

'She does exactly what she needs, to get what she wants, but I think she's overconfident in her ability and she'll slip up pretty soon.' I watch Tyke frown.

'You're the one chasing your tail.' Tyke shrugs, but I can feel him watching me. 'And that girl, she is more dangerous than you and I.'

'After the rebels attacked us, she was the one that found me and offered me shelter, so I kind of owe her one,' I add, just to stop Tyke from pushing, even though it's not entirely true.

# DANICA

In the half hour I sat at the table in the club, a new plan formed. One to really make Melissa Cole suffer.

I took the pen and paper to the other side of the street, away from Tyke's prying eyes, and paused for a moment to collect myself and plan out my letter. Fortunately, I'd learned enough of my alphabet before the front line, and then it had been just a case of practicing when I could. I'd read letters that weren't addressed to me, from people I'd never met.

I grin at the thought of Melissa's face when she finds my little letter as I bring the ink to the paper.

*MC,*

*I am free, and I have your son hostage. Maybe I should show him what I learned while I was your slave? All the wonderful and wicked things I learned on the front line. Should I show him what your soldiers showed me? Shall we see if he survives like I did?*

*Here's what's going to happen.*

*You're going to surrender to Ritenvold and pull all your soldiers back to Roseguard.*

*Once every human who willingly wears the Rose is within Roseguard's walls, then I'll be in touch.*

*Yours truly,*

*D.A.R.*

*(Just know that Hunter will die should you fail to do as I order.)*

I fold the letter over and poor some wax over it, sealing it.

# ḦUNTER

'You underestimate her,' I say quietly, watching as she keeps her back to us.

Tyke rolls his eyes. 'I don't like her.'

'Neither do I.'

I sit back down and wait for Danica to turn around.

'What's her deal though?' He pushes.

'I don't know.'

'And the scar?'

I turn and face him, 'You saw that?'

'When she was getting out of seat, her shirt came up a bit.' Tyke rolls his head, as if to release some tension. 'To me, it looks like an old knife wound that never had a healer see to it.' Of course, he would be able to guess at what caused it.

Tyke had grown up not knowing his father, and his mother had worked in the Underground. When he got old enough to fend for himself, he'd started building his reputation bit by bit, until he got to where he is now; boss of the best and biggest social and dance club in Roseguard. And he has control of almost the entire city's social system—eyes and ears everywhere.

I had met Tyke when we were forced to go to early childhood school. He was the only boy that didn't whisper about me—General Cole's son. He'd even picked fights with me, but I liked him because he treated me like any other person. Despite our fights, we'd become good friends and looked out for one another.

'If you're heading out of the city, I would be careful.' Tyke looks out over the street, watching as Danica seals the letter with the hot wax Tyke had provided. 'I had four men come to the Underground a day or so before Rush was sighted. Not the usual lot.' Tyke turns to look at me again. 'They had that same look as your little lady.'

'What look?'

He shakes his head. 'Just be careful.'

It's then that Danica turns around. 'What look?'

Tyke and I stand as Danica walks across the street.

'What look did these men have that is the same as me?' Danica pushes.

Tyke raises an eyebrow as he stares Danica down for a moment. 'Well, for starters, they had the same attitude as you. Rude, pushy, thinking they were better than everyone else.'

I grit my teeth, preparing myself for whatever Danica is about to spit back.

She stares Tyke down, then one corner of her lip pokes up. 'Sounds like my type of people.'

I blink, confused.

'Come, Captain,' Danica turns towards me, 'we're leaving now.'

I nod at Tyke, hoping he'll let Mother know that I need help.

# Chapter Eleven

## Danica

I slip my letter into one of the small post boxes that are scattered across the city on our way out.

'Why did you want to know when the Red Soldiers left the city?' Hunter asks.

I look at him carefully. We're still in his city, but I doubt he'll cause trouble, especially since I'm the one holding his leash. 'The soldiers Tyke said were heading west, you said they are going to Tirma, Lyko and Materga to take every resident and send them to the front line.'

Hunter remains quiet for a few moments. 'You never answered my question.'

'Because I'm not going to let them force any more people to fight on the front line.'

'That's ridiculous!' Hunter hesitates and his eyes skim over the buildings around us. 'We need more soldiers on the front line, it is the only way to put a dent in Ritenvold's line. Do you want this war to continue for another ten years? Sure, we have bloody great defences, and most people haven't been affected but neither has Ritenvold. But you would know that, wouldn't you Danica?'

I roll my eyes at his little monologue. 'You sound just like the little captain you've been trained to be.'

'You're a criminal, you deserve to be on the front line,' Hunter snaps and I let my gaze settle on him as he has his temper tantrum. He hasn't noticed that I've pulled him into a side alley. 'Escaping from the front line is enough of a crime to be sent back there.'

'So, send me back.' I snap. 'Go on, call the city guards!' He hesitates for a moment. 'But if you do, you will die and so will every guard that comes running because there is no way I am going to go back and fight a war that me and mine did not start. And I will not let you send any more children to pick up a sword and to be killed by warriors twice their age. So go on, call them.'

Fire burns through my veins. The reason I had to get Vix out. The reason that's made me change my plans and try to stop the horror from happening to more people.

Hunter clenches his jaw. I know he is smart enough not to call them, especially when his gaze lands on the hand I've got resting on my dagger.

'And for the record, I was never a criminal. I never deserved to be forced to fight on the front line. I was a child when they took me.' I turn on my heel and march back into the city with Hunter following. 'Oh, and the reason you haven't made any progress or had any major losses on the front line the last decade, is because Ritenvold is deciding what happens, not Roseguard. Roseguard has hundreds of thousands of humans, and more in the other cities scattered throughout Asada, but if Ritenvold decided to smash through your lines tomorrow, it would be a massacre.'

It's not until we reach the city gates that Hunter opens his mouth again, curiosity getting the better of him. 'Why were you sent to the front line, Danica?'

'I ask myself that question nearly every day.' It's a lie; I do know the reason. But I don't know why everything happened as it did, that's the question I ask myself daily.

He falls silent and we walk back to the horses in that silence. I catch him opening his mouth to ask a question a few times, but he never says a word.

When we reach the horses, we ride hard west, towards Tialo, one of the cities in Asada. Hopefully when we reach Tialo, we will have caught up to the soldiers … and hopefully I'll have a plan figured out.

When we pass over the first creek west of Roseguard, I turn Eagle sharply down stream, the horses' legs splashing through the water, before finding a clearing on the creek bank to make camp for the remainder of the night. We don't bother making a fire, simply tie the horses up. I roll out my bed roll, and take the saddle off my horse, leaning it up against a tree. Hunter follows my lead hesitantly. I imagine that he wouldn't be too sure what to do now that he knows my plan, after he was so close to home.

I walk to the river and Hunter follows a few steps behind. I ignore him as I tie my hair up on top of my head and shake my jacket off, hanging it over a branch. As I wash my face, I can feel Hunter standing behind me, fidgeting, a foot tapping on the grass.

'What does the tattoo on your neck mean?' Hunter asks.

I debate whether to tell him anything about the circle with a moon on one side and an oak tree on the other. Vixy had asked once and I'd told her.

'I got it as a child, it's my mother's family symbol,' I say, drying my face on my shirt.

'You realise I can't allow you to stop the soldiers.' Hunter chews his bottom lip. 'Roseguard needs soldiers, and we do not have enough volunteers or criminals. Ritenvold will break our lines soon.'

'Ritenvold will break the lines, and unfortunately for you, I hate Roseguard more than I hate Ritenvold.'

Hunter frowns, his steps making so much noise as he cracks twigs and crinkles leaves as he follows me back to the camp. I sit down on my bed roll and allow myself to shut my eyes.

The wind sings softly through the trees, the branches gently swaying. In the distance, small animals tread lightly, grazing in the moonlight. An owl flies overhead, its wings almost silent.

I don't sleep until Hunter's breathing has steadied, until the wind picks up slightly, bringing the scents of the forest with it. The wind lulls me into sleep.

*A woman sitting on a thrown, a crown of Moonstone on her head, midnight hair flowing around her. Young children playing barefoot in the forest, climbing trees and wandering through streams, all with smiles. Soft grass between my toes, dirt under my fingernails.*

*A small cabin in the mountains, snow floating through the air and a fire crackling in a pit. A man with light brown hair and the woman with midnight hair sitting by the fire.*

*A dagger glinting in the moonlight. A woman with a kind face making bread and the same woman with her throat ripped out, blood pooling on the floor. I can feel blood dripping down my chin, my shirt soaked.*

*Small cabins filled with beds and children of all ages, a dagger lying in the sand forgotten behind a target. An arrow flying, multiple arrows flying. The crack of a bull whip, the crack against my bare back.*

*Trenches and shackles keeping me from running. Dry, hot sand, and rats. Endless trenches and smoke. Screaming. Blood everywhere. Ice eyes looking at me from across a trench, those eyes widening and a bow lowering before blackness. The skin around my neck, my wrists and ankles rubbed raw from having to fight in shackles. So much screaming.*

My eyes fly open, hand on my dagger. My breathing has become faster, my pulse quicker. My senses are alert.

I can feel myself shifting into my killing calm. I prick myself with my dagger on the palm of my hand, bringing my attention to the present as I try to pull as much air into my lungs as possible.

I scan the small glade, the two horses are still tied to the trees, one asleep and the other nibbling at the grass. Hunter lays against a tree across from me, his head fallen forward. I stay quiet as a small fox trots around the edge of the glade, watching Hunter, and I relax slightly.

I look up at the sky, the sun should be rising shortly. I take a deep breath as the breeze kisses my skin.

Hunter stirs and I watch as he slowly wakes up, rubbing at his face. He groans and finally looks up to me staring at him from under my brow.

He holds my gaze, not breaking it, and I don't know if I begin to feel more challenged by it or if it begins to feel more awkward.

Instead, I stand up and move to one of the saddle packs that I'd taken off my saddle last night, pull out some dried meat and throw a piece towards him. He catches it and nods his head.

Soon we're on the horses heading west again. All day we ride as hard as we can without causing the horses to become sore. We walk them up streams to keep their legs cool and reduce any swelling.

Hunter doesn't say anything for the next two days, and I only speak to him when I must. Otherwise, we ride in silence.

While we ride, I keep an eye out for rabbits, always having my bow prepared. Hunter watches me warily whenever I nock an arrow. I don't shy away from his judgement, I let him see me, see who I am with a weapon in my hand. I let him see the skilled precision—never missing, always hitting my target.

Three days since leaving Roseguard, we're setting up our camp within the pine trees when Hunter finally breaks the silence.

'Your scar, how did you get it?' Hunter asks quietly, poking at the small fire.

'Which scar?' Usually I don't scar, but I have a few.

'The one on your stomach.'

I roll my shoulders before pulling out my arrows and inspecting all the arrowheads, checking that they are all still in good condition and I try to think back on when he may have seen it. 'From a knife.'

 'How?'

'This is not the night for my story,' I say in a dismissive voice.

'Why not?' Hunter pushes.

'Because I don't want to tell it.' Because it was your mother that ordered that knife to stay in my gut until I was too weak to defend myself.

Hunter frowns at me, then shrugs as if deciding he doesn't care to know that much about the scar. 'Can you at least tell me why and how you escaped from the front line?'

'Why? I lost all hope, all motivation when I was sent to the front line. All I did was kill who I was told to. They sent Vixy to the front line for pick pocketing. You and your generals sent a homeless thirteen-year-old girl to the front line for *pick pocketing*.' I take a deep breath and continue. 'I couldn't let Vix witness the horror I had seen. She and I are different. Those horrors would have haunted her for the rest of her life, they don't bother me.' I meet Hunter's gaze, there is disgust in his eyes. 'We did what we do best. I figured the way out, Vix stole a knife for me, and we vanished without a trace into the desert.'

It had been a bloody mess.

Vixy had managed to steal me a knife, then, while we were unpacking a wagon, Vix had slid underneath it, hanging onto the framework. I then went and killed all those soldiers that stood between Vix and I, and freedom, the soldiers that had been too eager to whip me, starve me, beat me, chain me, cut me. If Vixy had peeked out from under the wagon…

she would have had nightmares for the rest of her life – it was a blood bath. I wonder what Hunter would have thought if he saw me then…

I used the knife, my hands, my teeth, anything as I killed every Roseguard soldier within sight before taking off into the desert with the wagon. The Red Soldiers stood no chance against me, especially after I had found a reason to escape.

Vixy had then spent an hour unlocking the shackles around my wrists as the horses had walked through the desert. Our only chance of surviving without being caught again was if the rumours about Eagle's Canyon were true.

Although it had been tempting and would have made the escape easier, I hadn't slipped into my *killing calm* that day. I hadn't wanted to horrify Vixy if she had peeked.

'I don't understand how you could abandon the army that was protecting you. Yes, you're a criminal but that army is protecting this kingdom from the beasts on either side of it, it's protecting *you*,' Hunter says, watching me warily. 'I don't doubt that you know what the punishment is for escaping.'

'They wouldn't kill me, Stray.'

'Why?'

'Because I was the best soldier your Red Army has ever had and ever will have.' Not a lie, but not the full truth. 'We do what we must to survive. When I was on the front line, I witnessed many horrors that gave grown men nightmares, but the worst would have been how your Red Soldiers treated me, despite being their best.'

I don't know why I just told Hunter that, but he holds my stare. 'I'm surprised they didn't send Dimitri Rush to hunt you down after you escaped.'

I laugh, the sound almost a cackle as I imagine Dimitri Rush hunting me down. 'Tell me, when did you learn that two girls had escaped the front line? One of them a thirteen-year-old.'

'My mother told me a few days before I left Roseguard. She said the information was confidential, I was only told your ages and gender.'

'There is a reason why that information is confidential.' Hunter raises an eyebrow. 'What would the other front liners do if they knew they could escape and never have to fight again? Or was it confidential because your mother didn't want word out about who had escaped.'

'It was confidential for both those reasons, I assume.' Hunter looks forward, gritting his teeth.

'I'm surprised your own mother kept you in the dark.'

I put the arrows down and then turn to the cooked rabbits, prying them off the small spit I made. I hand one to Hunter, then cut pieces of meat off with my dagger, eating until my stomach can't take any more. After living on the front line, my body has adapted to smaller food portions. Often, I would go a week with almost no food so the soldiers could keep me weak and easy to control.

I don't say anything else that night; just let myself fall asleep. My sleep is not heavy enough to let me dream.

*****

I watch the last of the stars disappear through the canopy of pine trees above, and as the sunlight touches the world again, waking up the creatures of the forest. I lie on my bed roll, watching the leaves move in the wind and birds flitter between branches.

A breeze drifts through camp and the birds stop whistling. I cautiously sit up, my muscles tensing, senses alert. I relax, though, when an imp creeps into our camp and I remain silent, a small grin forming on my lips, as I watch it approach Hunter, preparing to play some nasty trick on him.

Hunter stirs and wakes. His eyes go wide as he sees the imp's small, knobby form approaching him and scrambles back.

Quietly I stand up, easing a knife from its sheath on my belt.

'Hello, human,' the imp laughs.

They're usually harmless, however can be nasty to anything weaker or more vulnerable than themselves. I'd once seen an imp torture a litter of kittens, yet it had fled when it saw me ready to put up a fight.

Hunter is now pushed up against the tree and I can see his hands shaking.

'What do you want?' he says in a single short breath.

I almost laugh at Hunter's panicked voice. All you need to do to scare an imp off is show that you're not afraid of them.

The imp does laugh. The brown crinkled skin moving over its body as it throws its bare wrinkled head up to the air before saying, 'I only want to play a game.'

I don't think Hunter has noticed me as I stand behind the creature, he's fixated on the imp.

'I'm going to ask you a question.' The imp brings a long, crooked finger to its mouth. 'Every time you give a wrong answer, I get one of your fingers.'

Hunter's face pales, his mouth going slack.

'When the moon rises, what children rise with it?'

I know the answer to the riddle, it's based off the Treaty.

'Nightwalkers.' The imp spins around, seeing me. Its brown eyes and small but crinkled face take me in.

The imp turns and flees the clearing. I tilt my head as I watch it go.

Once I can no longer hear twigs snapping and leaves crunching under its feet, the imp far enough away that I can't hear it, I turn back to the horses, knowing that Hunter will be right behind me. As soon as it took off, I heard him scramble to his feet.

'What was that?' Hunter demands.

I look back over my shoulder at him, his hair still mussed from sleep. 'An imp. Practically harmless, but if you show fear, they can have a nasty bite. They never allied with the Treaty, therefore it is allowed into Asada, but it also means you or I have free rein to kill it should it become a nuisance.'

Hunter blinks once and nods. 'Why did it run off when you spoke to it.'

I turn back to readying Eagle, and I realise that Hunter doesn't know that I answered the question correctly.

'Because I'm scarier than you, Captain.'

Hunter hurriedly begins tacking up his mare. 'How do you know so much about the Treaty? I mean it was practically abandoned when all the beasts were banished.'

I turn to Hunter. 'My mother taught me about it at a young age. You, as a captain, should know it thoroughly. It's really quite shameful that you don't; that you aren't aware of what previously happened and what is actually going on in the world.'

'And what is going on?' Hunter turns to watch me.

'You should ask your mother that question.'

Hunter lets out a groan and mutters something I choose to ignore.

*****

It's another two days of riding through the forest until we catch up to the Red Soldiers just outside of Tialo.

The smoke was heavy where the soldiers had been, grass trampled into mud. I made the decision to dismount the horses and leave them hidden a distance away from the small army. Hunter didn't know why I decided to leave the horses, but it was because if he got the idea of running for the army, I would have more of a chance at catching him on foot than if he were on a horse.

We're at the edge of the forest, where the trees give way to the grassland just outside of the city. Hunter is sitting up against a pine tree, refusing to answer any question about the Red Soldiers. It doesn't matter that much though as I am able to work out the answers from watching the small army go about its evening routine. I watch the soldiers for over an hour, until there isn't enough light to gain any new information. I have a couple of different plans, but I'm not completely committed to any of them yet. I want to get a feel for the small army, what the morale is like among the soldiers, how quickly they will turn around if faced with an obstacle. I need to make this army turn back to Roseguard, as it'll send more of a message to Melissa and the residents of Roseguard than a full-scale slaughter.

'Come on,' I turn to Hunter and he looks up at me, a scowl on his face. 'Let's head back to the horses and get some sleep.'

'You know I could scream right now, and those soldiers would capture you again.' Hunter snaps.

'The problem with that, is I would still be able to kill you before they reach you,' I stalk towards Hunter, my gaze set on him and he swallows. 'And yes, they would come, but I'd be gone. All they would find is their little captain missing his head.' I reach up and run a finger along his jawbone, his eyes widening. 'So go on, I dare you.' I smile wickedly at him.

He steps back, muttering, 'whatever.'

'After you,' I say and point towards the trail we had followed earlier.

*****

As the sun rises on another day, so do we. We trail the army all day, heading west of Tialo towards the Lyko mountains. Hunter refuses to talk to me. I don't mind as I would rather the peace and quiet. It lets me think clearly.

My thoughts drift to Vixy and how she's going. How much food she has. With Hunter and I gone, the food stocks would last much longer. I will need to bring some fresh food with me when I go back. Maybe I'll get a treat and find some biscuits or a cake to bring back with me. Or the ingredients to make a cake. I would also like to bring her some more clothes, she manages to ruin hers pretty quickly.

As we follow the soldiers, I learn their routines. How many scouts they send ahead, how many soldiers guard the supply wagons… I make mental notes on all and any details that could help me commit to one of my many plans to stop the Red Soldiers.

I use the day to learn their routine, and the next day to confirm their routine. Each day they are packed and ready to march by dawn, but they set up camp an hour or so before dusk. They stop their march for an hour over midday for lunch, most of the soldiers are still in training. All still learning the rules of the Red Army.

As the sun is setting, an hour after the Red Soldiers have made camp in a paddock, I pick up a hidden set of tracks. The tracks of a single shod horse are hidden well enough that my suspicions go on high alert. I check my surroundings subtly, and I don't tell Hunter. Last thing I need right now, is Hunter aware that there is someone else out and about in the forest. I simply follow the tracks until I can hear the quiet grazing of a horse and the hiss and crackle of a fire. I turn to Hunter and bring a finger to my lips, dismounting slowly and quietly before tying Eagle up. I slip my bow over my head, pull the quiver out of its hook on my saddle, and attach it to my belt, on the opposite side to my sword. I nock an arrow, keeping it pointed at the ground in front of me and nod at Hunter to follow. If my suspicious are right, the rider may attack first and ask questions later. And despite who it may be, I would rather not have to tend to an injury tonight.

Carefully, I tread through the forest, grimacing at the noise Hunter is making. I make sure we stay downwind.

Up ahead, a small fire is visible. A black horse is tied to a tree; its saddle slumped against the trunk. On the other side of the clearing sits a man fiddling with his bow.

I step closer and my heart skips a beat; my suspicions are correct.

I walk into the clearing, my arrow still pointed at the ground, but relief washes over me. The weight that's been sitting on my shoulder ever since I could remember, disappears.

A genuine smile appears on my lips. 'Hello Dimitri.'

# Chapter Twelve

## Hunter

Danica's words make my blood freeze.

Dimitri. Dimitri Rush.

Of course, Danica wouldn't have forgotten the little titbit of information Tyke had let loose. Of course, she would have been on the lookout for the legendary sharpshooter and Nightwalker hunter trailing the army. I've underestimated her while trying to guess her plan, despite telling Tyke not to underestimate her.

Dimitri moves faster than I can track. One moment he's sitting, the next moment, he's crouched with a dagger ready to throw. His pale blue eyes fly to Danica's face and disbelief covers his face; he lowers his throwing arm.

'Danica?'

I frown, biting my lip and look at Danica who has a huge smile on her face, her cold exterior broken. Then back down to the legendary sharpshooter as he slowly puts his dagger away, carefully, like he knows Danica is slightly insane.

Danica relaxes her bow and puts the arrow back into the leather quiver before slinging the bow across her back.

Dimitri stands and runs a hand through the light brown hair cut close to his head. He's a bit taller than me and a lot older than I thought he would be, maybe late forties. His pale blue eyes run over Danica quickly.

'How?' Dimitri doesn't even acknowledge me.

'I escaped six months ago.' Danica says hesitantly, as if unsure how to proceed.

'I have been within range of Roseguard the past decade and nothing hinted at you escaping.' Dimitri lets a long breath out. 'I've been waiting for an opportunity to rescue you. I have tried so many different ways to get you out. I never once stopped trying to find a way.'

Mother's words shoot through my mind. She had warned about the information getting into the wrong hands … Dimitri Rush is definitely the wrong hands!

'If you knew I was out, Roseguard would lose any advantage they had.' I notice Danica start to tremble slightly.

Why would *the* Dimitri Rush know or look out for Danica? Danica! Bloodthirsty, criminal Danica! My mind is spinning so fast I can barely keep up, I feel like I need to sit down.

'That's why we couldn't act.' Dimitri takes a cautious step forward. 'If we made a move, you would die.'

Danica breathes out and starts nodding her head. 'I know. I know.'

Dimitri takes another cautious step towards her, and then Danica springs forward, throwing her arms around the sharpshooter. He wraps his arms around her, holding his face to her neck. He squeezes her tight, lifting her from the ground.

I take a step back as I watch the biggest criminal I've ever met, embrace the legendary sharpshooter. This is not how I had planned on meeting Dimitri.

After a moment, I avert my gaze. How do Danica and Dimitri know one another? I need to find out this information before I escape, it would be invaluable for Mother.

Finally, they break apart and I notice tears on both of their faces. Not many but one or two. Just enough to make me glance around the clearing, avoiding looking at them.

Dimitri finally glances at me before returning his gaze to Danica, and frowns. 'Melissa Cole and her soldiers took you that night.'

Mothers name catches my attention and my gaze snaps to Danica. How she had acted towards me, the comments about my mother. She deserved to be sent to the front line, however, if Mother had been present when she was arrested … that explains the reason for her hatred.

'I beat your mother to Roseguard and told them you were a Rush. Cole knew who you were though.' My heart completely stops for a few moments. The meaning behind Dimitri's words sinks into me like a stone in a pond … he is Danica's father! I look between them again spotting the similarities — the eyes, Dimitri's are pale blue and hers more of a white-blue ice colour, the similar nose, the full lips.

'She tried enlisting me when the war came, with promises to release you but I knew it was to make sure she kept us separated. Your mother had to return home, as expected with the rest of our people, and I hung around Roseguard, waiting for a moment or a hint that I could get you out. That you had escaped.

'But your mother bargained with Roseguard, threatened to go to war with them, with Asada, if you weren't returned.'

Danica bites her lip at Dimitri's words.

'Cole threatened that if your mother went to war with Asada over you, she would slit your throat and hang you from the gates of Roseguard. Our hands were tied.'

I don't believe what Dimitri says, about the threat Mother made. She's not violent like that, she does what she has to but she's never vicious.

'Mother had told me that I would soon have to be very brave. I think she thought I would be at her side then.' She squeezes her hands together. 'I don't think she ever expected Melissa to come for me as she did.'

'No, she didn't know you were going to be taken.'

Danica nods her head slightly.

Who would her mother be? There's no way Danica could have a Ritenvold mother, Dimitri has been an Asadian his entire life, maybe it's one of the noblewomen of Salt City…

Dimitri's eyes widen. 'You said you escaped half a year ago, why did you not come home?'

'I had someone with me when I escaped, and so we had to keep hidden, then I didn't want to travel through winter. She's still hidden safely away,' Danica says softly. 'I… I am very lost. I don't know what to do, other than survive. But I am trying to stop more people from being recruited.'

Dimitri nods his head, listening and I take in her confession about how she truly feels.

'They know who you are Danica. You'll never be safe until you're back home with us.' Dimitri takes a step closer.

'I know.'

My mind is still reeling.

Dimitri Rush. Danica Rush.

Dimitri looks over her again. 'You look like your mother.'

Danica turns to look at me. 'Go fetch the horses.'

Fine. Fair enough. Although Danica is a criminal, she has just been reunited with her father after ten years, I can allow her this privacy, even if her father is Dimitri Rush. I nod and head back the way we'd come. The horses are still standing tied to the pine trees. Danica's horse stands silent; however, the lazy mare Danica gave me is grazing at the end of her lead. I stand for a few moments trying to comprehend my thoughts. No wonder Danica's information is confidential, if she's Dimitri Rush's daughter.

Danica being Dimitri's daughter changes so much and explains even more.

She had said she was the best soldier the front line had ever had … she would have been invaluable if she had the sharpshooter's line of sight, if she has Dimitri's skill.

I untie the horses and lead them through the forest, arriving back at the camp to find Danica and Dimitri sitting by the small fire. I listen to Danica tell Dimitri our plans while I pull the saddles off the horses, having tied them up next to Dimitri's black stallion.

As I sit down next to Danica, I realise that I just missed an opportunity to escape. I keep my mouth shut as I silently scold myself for letting this distract me.

Dimitri looks at me properly for the first time. I try to be as inconspicuous as possible now that I know why they don't particularly like the Cole family.

'So, who's this?' Dimitri asks Danica, and I avert my eyes. If I had another Red Soldier with me, I would have said who I was with confidence.

'A stray.' Danica sighs.

Relief floods through me when Danica doesn't say my name. She must have known how Dimitri would act, should he know my bloodline. However, Dimitri is looking at me like he might recognise me. I turn and unbuckle my bedroll from the saddle and lay it on the grass.

'Feel free to catch up,' I say, trying to appear completely oblivious to who I am sharing camp with. 'I'm going to get some sleep.'

I lay down, the bed roll uncomfortable, with my back to Danica and Dimitri.

Danica is breathing softly and I can't hear anything from Dimitri for the moment. The crackle of the campfire is loud. What would Mother think if she knew I was sharing camp with the legendary sharpshooter?

I should have figured it out, the whole situation about her information being confidential to even myself, then when Danica aimed at those rabbits as if it was second nature, I should have realised despite no other clues about her blood. There is a reason I am captain, because I can figure out this stuff. Dimitri is quietly telling Danica how he'd heard rumours and had been tracking the soldiers to see if he could help the people in the cities I had sent soldiers to.

'There are people there like you.'

'I know. Why do you think I came?'

'You should go back home instead. See your mother.'

It's silent for a while. 'I want to.'

'But?'

'I want to finish this war. And I've got a thirteen-year-old girl whose survival depends on me. I didn't want her travelling through the winter months,' Danica says softly, then adds, 'and now there is this one too.'

They fall silent and I hear Danica and Dimitri moving around, getting ready to sleep. I don't know what Danica implied when she added me to the reasons she can't go home. I don't dare move, especially when Dimitri next speaks.

'The day after Melissa betrayed the Treaty and the *banishing* happened, I arrived back at the cabin, it was a bloodbath.' He is silent for a moment and the only sounds are the fire and the horses shuffling about quietly. 'There were six dead soldiers and the maid with her throat ripped out.'

My stomach churns as I visualise the scene, imagining the blood makes me feel nauseous.

'The maid sold us out. She knew mother would be visiting Roseguard, and you would be watching her back.' Danica goes silent. 'The maid thought I was asleep, she tried tying my hands up, so I ripped out her throat with my teeth.'

My eyes go wide in the dark, as I realise just how much of a monster Danica is. I need to stop her.

'And you *became* your mother in those moments?' Quiet, careful words from Dimitri, as if he knows I'm listening.

'It was the best feeling when I fell into my *killing calm*. I had no thoughts other than what I was seeing before me, and I just flowed. I forgot that the maid had read me bedtime stories, and that she had sold me out to Roseguard. I didn't think, I just did. I killed six guards and I can't remember their faces … but Melissa Cole, her face I'll never forget.' Danica's words are quiet and cold. 'She sent enough guards to restrain me, but the only way she could stop me from killing everyone was to have one of her soldiers put a dagger in my stomach and leave it there. Because of how long that dagger was left in my gut, I have a scar I'll carry to the grave.'

I don't believe Danica's words. Mother is not cruel. Everything she has done is to look after the people that live in Roseguard. To protect them from the monsters that prowl through the night.

'She sent me to the training grounds for a year. Usually, soldiers train until they are thirteen, but you know me!' Danica laughs, a cold sharp laugh. 'They sent an eleven-year-old girl to the front line because they knew I would kill without hesitation. I didn't know what happened to you or mother and Melissa fed me lies and more lies those first few years.

But I worked it out. I was a hostage, and the only way she could control her hostage was to put her in the thickest patch of fighting.'

Dimitri says quietly. 'Does he know?'

Silence. I assume Danica shakes her head because I knew none of that, but her anger and hatred makes so much more sense. And yet I am left feeling even more confused… who is Danica's mother?

'And the one you have relying on you, the young one?'

More silence. I assume another shake of her head.

'For nearly a decade, I fought Ritenvold soldiers. But they weren't the bad part.' Danica falls silent for a moment then says sadly, 'The Red Soldiers never allowed me to touch a bow, and I always had three armed guards that were allowed to kill me if I so much as blinked the wrong way. When I got older, they would keep me in shackles, force me to fight in shackles. I wasn't allowed to go anywhere armed unless I was about to engage Ritenvold soldiers, or in the yard with all the other criminals. I was fourteen and sharing a tent with murderers and rapists, and I wasn't allowed to kill them.' Danica had said the Red Soldiers were the bad part of the front line …

'Everything is in motion once again. You'll be home soon. And I'll never let Roseguard take you again. I promise.'

'I'm never going to get caught again.'

'Your mother would be … is very proud of you.'

There is silence for a while. Then I hear Danica yawn. I've never heard her yawn before. She must be feeling comfortable within Dimitri's company.

A quiet whisper comes, 'Goodnight, Dimitri.'

For a moment, I wonder why she call's Dimitri by his first name, and not with a fatherly name. Then again, he'd be almost like a stranger to her.

I can hear Danica move, and I assume she's rolling out her bed roll. Danica Rush.

Dimitri Rush has permission to kill freely in Asada. He was originally granted that permission by the Treaty of Asada, and after that … it's difficult to hunt down and kill someone who is the best out there. So, it has mostly been forgotten by Mother. Danica, however, doesn't have that permission. Even though she's threatened to kill me and could surely beat the living daylights out of me, I never realised what a cold-blooded killer she is. She killed seven people when she was only ten years old and who knows how many since! She is a criminal, a murderer.

Most criminals are sent to the front line. But the really bad ones? They have a trial and are usually executed, decapitated by the four Red Generals on a small rock jutting out over Thorn Gap. I doubt they would even need to trial Danica. I chew on my lip for a moment, I think I'll let Danica think she's the boss. Let her believe she has scared me enough that I would never cross her. I'll get her onto that rock one day.

# CHAPTER THIRTEEN

## DANICA

Ten long years without a parent to remind me what truly matters. Ten long years of pushing down who I am, what I have to do and where I am from. Ten years of putting my own survival first.

When I stepped into the clearing, when I saw him… it was like a weight came off my shoulders, one I hadn't realised was there. The memories of my childhood had come forward, flashing through my mind as I had seen him, heard his voice, smelt the burnt wood and citrus that was so uniquely him. Every lesson and value learned came rushing forward. The motivation to fight for my survival was replaced with motivation to fight for my people, my home.

When I was on the front line, it had done no good to think of the years before, it would have made my survival harder to fight for. If I wasn't focused on the present, I would have been suffering from the past. It was easier to block out everything that had happened before Melissa Cole ruined my life.

Now, I let all those memories pour through me like a waterfall.

Winters spent in Dimitri's small hunting cabin in the mountains, hidden away from the rest of the world where we could just be a family and do our own thing surrounded by the endless forests and mountains. We wouldn't see another soul for months on end, especially since the mountains were almost impossible to travel through during winter if you didn't know the small tracks, the secret hidden passes through.

A fire was always crackling in the small hearth and mother, when she was home, would make dinner or teach me to swing a sword or learn to ride one of the five rare Natari horses we had owned.

Dimitri taught me how to shoot, first with a small bow then a bigger one and another one, then onto the long bows and hunting bows until I could hit a bullseye with any bow and arrow. We had to replace the small target frequently, Dimitri showing me how to chop down a tree to make the target. He also taught me how to survive in the forest, the mountains and the desert; how to find water when it didn't want to be found, same for food. He taught me how track and gut a rabbit, how to stalk and skin a deer, to catch and fillet the small fish in the streams.

I would spend the evenings listening to stories, some myths and some legends.

I rise early the next morning, hoping to get a look at the movements of the Red Soldiers. Dimitri is already awake, quietly pulling some bread out of the small fire. Rubbing my face with my hands, I realise that I had slept better than I have in a long time, the knowledge of having someone I trust be able to keep me safe had let the much-needed deep sleep find me.

'Good morning,' I say quietly as I sit up, stretching.

Dimitri glances over before turning back to carving up some bread. 'Good morning, my little warrior.'

I smile at him, a genuine smile before glancing across at Hunter, who is still completely oblivious to the start of the day.

'What's your plan now?' Dimitri asks.

I take a moment to consider his question whilst I begin rolling up my bedroll. 'I don't know… I will continue on my way to see if I can stop this small army, I'm thinking I can probably do that at one of the mountains passes, but after that I am not sure.'

He passes me a slice of bread with some jam spread over it. 'Is there a chance Cole knows you're alive and west of the desert?'

'Aye, she knows now.'

'She's going to pull all her soldiers back to Roseguard,' he says thoughtfully. 'Which means Ritenvold will make their way across the desert. It will take them possibly three weeks to reach Roseguard, they have healthy and fit warriors and plenty of supplies, but the army is large and that will slow them a down a bit. How long ago did Melissa learn of your reappearance?'

'About a week ago, when Hunter and I visited Roseguard to gather some information.'

Dimitri stares down at the ground in thought for a moment. 'It'd take a week and a half for a message to get out to the front line to withdraw the army. They might only be a day or two ahead of Ritenvold, but they'll also have fewer numbers, which means quicker travel.'

'Why didn't Ritenvold ever wipe out the Red Army while I was there?'

'They were waiting for the word of our queen before doing that.'

'Right.' I take a bit from the bread, consider Dimitri's words. 'If Ritenvold is coming for Roseguard, that'll mean that the Asadian Army will come down from the Shadow?'

He gives me a dark look before glancing at Hunter, checking that he is still asleep. 'Melissa Cole is a dead woman walking.'

'Good.' I finish my bread and then walk over to the small fire, crouching in front of it and warming my hands. 'Once I've stopped this small army in the mountains, I want to race back to Eagle's Canyon and retrieve Vixy.'

'Aye, I'll head towards Roseguard to meet with you there, I'll accompany you to Eagle's Canyon.'

'And the Asadian Army? How will they get word that the Red Army has retreated?' I ask, standing back up.

Dimitri cracks a grin, 'they have eyes and ears everywhere, little warrior.'

I return his grin, and he offers me another piece of bread.

It's about time Hunter wakes up, I walk over to where he lays, the blanket pulled up over his face and I nudge him in the side with my boot, waking him up. He pulls the blanket from his face and blinks.

'Time to wakey-wakey Stray,' I say before turning back to Dimitri.

He's watching me with narrow eyes and I think he might be close to working out Hunter's identity.

Instead of saying anything, I head over to my horse.

'Danica …' I look over my shoulder at Dimitri. 'Take my horse. It's a Natari.'

I smile, a genuine smile. 'Thank you.'

'That's a Natari?' Hunter suddenly asks, glancing at the stallion from where he sits on his bedroll, on the other side of the small campfire.

Dimitri nods.

'How have you got a Natari? I thought they had almost vanished completely during the banishing.' Hunter stares at the stallion. 'They say they were originally bred for the Nightwalkers.'

Dimitri and I share a quick glance at one another, hiding our grins of amusement.

'Very few exist, and most have been diluted with other breeds. There's more in the Shadow,' Dimitri explains, putting the small fire out before looking over towards me again. 'He was one of the last foals we bred at the cabin.'

I look back at the horse. 'Hello, old friend.'

'You named that one.' Dimitri walks over and runs a hand along the stallion's spine; the horse rests a hind leg, relaxing.

I throw my saddle over the horse then place a hand on his neck, whispering to him, 'That must make you Oak.'

'Aye.' Dimitri returns to his bedroll.

'The mare was called Maple and the sire was Auburn?' I ask as I tighten the girth.

'I'm astonished you remember.'

I finish clipping on the breastplate, then begin piling my things into the saddlebags. 'I always did have a better memory than you,' I tease.

Hunter watches me. 'What's the plan for today?'

'I am going by myself today,' I say as I carefully arrange my bow and quiver of arrows on Oak. 'I'll check on the Red Soldiers' progress then I'm going to ride into the village outside of Tialo, see if I can pick up any news. I'll be back by noon.'

'Be careful.' Dimitri says to me quietly. 'I don't want to lose you again.'

He knows better than to try to stop me, I'm too much like my mother. 'They'd have to catch me first!'

Dimitri comes to stand in front of me, resting a hand on my shoulder and raises an eyebrow in Hunter's direction.

I bite my lip as I look over at Hunter before whispering. 'That's Hunter Cole. Melissa Cole knows I'm holding him hostage … it's a long story.'

Dimitri's eyes go wide, and he discreetly glances at Hunter. 'Well, you've certainly been busy. I'll leave once you get back. I'll meet you outside of Roseguard.'

I nod, then wrap my father into a hug, breathing in that familiar scent of burnt wood and citrus.

*****

Sitting on Oak is like sitting on pure raw power. The stallion's powerful black body moves through the forest like flowing water, never missing a step or miscalculating a stride. Staying light on Oak's back, the wind in my hair, the adrenaline of working with an animal as large, as powerful and dangerous as a stallion in his prime, it humbles me to be able to ride him and reminds me of my own humanity, that I am just another creature from the darkness.

I sigh when I have to bring Oak back to a steady trot, rising and falling with his footfalls. The ride through the forest doesn't take as long as I thought it would, and all too soon I am on a road heading towards the village. I close my eyes for a moment, gathering the mental strength to get back to work before I walk past the first few small log houses.

The village is small and consists of a temple, a tavern and inn as well as the few small houses and stores.

Most of the road is mud, puddles of murky water splash up Oak's legs as he steps into them. I can see clearly where the soldiers marched through the village, the leftover carnage. As I ride, I can feel the villagers watching me, assessing me.

I tie Oak up outside the tavern before quietly slinking in and occupying a table in the darkest corner of the room. I know no-one would be foolish enough to try to take Oak; Natari horses are bred not only for their strength, speed and bravery but for their loyalty as well and rarely let anyone but a few chosen riders touch them. This trait has always been a mystery, but I believe it's because they're not often sold, and usually having one rider their entire life, therefore they never gained a lot of exposure to different riders. I guess it became a part of their instinct and bred into the bloodline.

The tavern is nearly empty, and the few who are there only talk about the mess the Red Soldiers left behind and their crop and livestock, so my mind drifts to the captain sharing my camp.

He is the perfect hostage. Too scared of me to try to escape or challenge me. And even if he did escape, he and I both know he would be lucky to last a few days without soldiers to protect or look after him.

And it was because of Hunter's dear friend, Tyke, that I knew to keep an eye out for the nearly invisible track of a horse. I'd picked up the tracks the day before last. The set of hoofprints would have been invisible had I not known what to look out for, where to look out for the tracks.

Dimitri had taught me how to stay hidden one year when we were travelling back from the cabin. How to travel along riverbeds to avoid leaving prints, to follow the deer tracks through the meadows so the grass won't be brushed to the side. To follow well-travelled roads if I need to lose someone tracking me, as the prints on a road would be impossible to tell apart. It'd been Dimitri that taught me how to veer away from the road and back into the forest like a ghost in the wind.

I sigh as I study the small man behind the bar, carefully cleaning glasses and trying to keep an eye on me as he quietly chats with a customer. I can hear him talking about the soldiers that went through the village, the front line and the war.

The customer takes a mouthful of stew. 'They say Ritenvold doesn't care about what happens 'ere. Sloan was saying they barely fight anymore, they just sit in the trenches drinking and playing cards.'

'Yee, well Roseguard needs to figure out what they want to do.' The bartender glances around the room before continuing. 'I heard if Ritenvold sent their whole army, we'd be beat in moments.'

They would be. If Ritenvold sent their entire army, anyone with a rose on their armour would be slaughtered. They would break through the lines in a matter of moments. I was forced to kill those warriors in Ritenvold. If I didn't kill, I was lashed, beaten and tortured by Red Soldiers. I change my thought as memories of those beatings come to mind.

Ritenvold hadn't broken through the lines due to their alliance with the Queen.

When Melissa had gone to war with Ritenvold, she had expected the country to be battling civil wars after the death of Prince Luca. Instead, Ritenvold sent enough warriors to the front line to keep the Red Soldiers occupied, and life within their country carried on as normal.

It had taken me a few years to learn why Melissa had attempted to go to war with the powerful Ritenvold, why creatures that call Asada home were now named criminals. Eventually, I realised the truth, Melissa Cole simply craves power. She schemed a way into blackmailing the Queen and the creatures of Asada into staying west of the Yulara Mountains. She realised Ritenvold was a threat to her power, so had their heir assassinated and went to war with the kingdom to the east.

What she didn't realise, though, was that the Queen was playing the long game, waiting whilst the creatures thrived in the Shadow.

'Yes, well, the crops aren't harvesting themselves without the boys.' The customer continues, and I grimace as I realise I'd completely zoned out of the conversation.

'Half the fields weren't even seeded.' The bar tender turns to place the glass on a shelf. 'And we'll have no-one to look after the livestock with winter coming. I reckon the wolves will come down from the mountains this year.'

'I reckon more than wolves will come down.' The customer talks through his mouthful. 'I reckon some of the beasts will come east again. They've been hiding too long.'

'Nah, the Nightwalkers will keep them in check.'

I grin at the turn in conversation.

'I bet you five gold marks the beasts will come before the end of winter.' The customer leans forward.

Their conversation is becoming less and less useful, so I stand up to leave. As I pass the bar, I pause and lean in to speak to the customer.

'The beasts are already here.'

Neither the customer not the bartender says anything as I walk out the front door.

What small amount of news I had gathered is that the people left in Asada are few in numbers and beginning to lose faith in Roseguard. They believe that it is only a matter of time before Ritenvold breaks through the lines. I throw my leg over Oak and canter out of the small village.

As we move through the forest, I breathe in the smell of the pine trees, so different from the smell of oak wood back home - forever my true home.

I feel more awake than I ever did on the front line. I'm doing something, not just surviving but going to help others.

I canter Oak through the forest, detouring to spy on the army for an hour before making my way back to Dimitri's camp.

Oak's strides are large, and cover the ground quickly, his hoofbeats echoing through the forest. He never missteps, never hesitates as I guide him through the pine trees. I let myself smile and enjoy the ride.

I ease Oak back to a trot and then a walk as I arrive back at the small camp. Dimitri is sitting on Eagle, the stallion chomping at the bit with the weight of a new rider on him. Hunter is standing, holding his mare by the reins, talking quietly with Dimitri, what they're talking about, I don't know. I bring Oak up next to Eagle, and Dimitri growls at the stallion for pinning his ears back at Oak. I squeeze the reins slightly, before Oak charges the other stallion as they compete to be the more dominant stallion.

I keep my voice low as I tell Dimitri what I had heard and he listens before telling me that the people have been losing faith for a while now. He also tells me that more and more fae have been moving back into Carramera, and that Melissa hasn't done anything about it. It is one of the many reasons the people have been losing faith.

I take a deep breath, inhaling the damp scent of the forest air, and run my hand along Oak's strong neck.

'Who started Oak?' I ask, changing the topic. I had never had the chance to teach Oak how to be ridden, he'd been a foal before I was taken. He'd have turned three when I turned thirteen. Had life played out how I had planned, I would have started him then, teaching him how to be ridden and learning how to teach those lessons.

Dimitri doesn't speak for a moment. 'A girl from Carra Islands. She was a couple of years older than you.'

'Well, she did an excellent job,' I say, as I shift my weight in the saddle.

'She loved him as much as you did—do.' Dimitri picks up his reins. 'I'm sure you'll meet her one day.'

'Thank you for letting me continue on Oak.' I nod.

'Well, I guess I'll see you in what, a week? Two?' He asks.

'If you haven't heard from me in two and a half weeks, then come find me.' I say.

'I'll see you soon then, little warrior.' He gives me a wink and a nod as he trots the horse off into the forest. Dimitri has never been one for long goodbyes.

Hunter is watching me from where he remained standing the entire time, leaning against a tree with his arms folded.

'Come on, let's get moving. The Red Soldiers have half a day head start on us.'

Hunter mounts his mare quickly, as if he has been waiting for the order all morning.

It is silent for two whole minutes before Hunter breaks the peace. 'When were you going to tell me that *the* Dimitri Rush is your father?'

'If I hadn't picked up Oak's track, you would never have known,' I say, looking forward.

'Why?'

Something in Hunter's voice makes me look over at him and I say truthfully. 'For that first year at the front line I let myself hope that Dimitri would come for me. And then I realised there was more at stake than me being uncomfortable and lonely in a trench.'

Hunter remains silent for a few moments. 'Who is your mother?'

I had been preparing for this question all morning. 'Ask your own.'

'Why do you call him by his first name if he's your father?'

'We've been strangers for the last decade, it feels weird to call him *pa*.' I say, not adding the bit about how it's not really a custom I was raised with.

He falls silent again, and then, 'I heard what you and Dimitri spoke about last night.'

'I know.' I let my eyes slide over to Hunter. 'You have much to learn before you can start playing war on our level. One day, when you're not so blinded by your mother, you'll understand. Or perhaps not.' His face changes slightly.

He falls back behind me, and I keep my body still as I listen to his quiet breathing.

Hunter truly has no idea about the real world, but I don't think he would intentionally ever hurt someone. Threaten them – definitely – but that is a product of his job and his upbringing.

148

# CHAPTER FOURTEEN

## HUNTER

Danica thought I was sleeping this morning when she discussed what was going to happen with Ritenvold. Why would Mother care if Danica had reappeared? Why would she retreat her army to Roseguard because of Danica? She thinks she's so damn special if she thinks Mother would do that because of her. And the Asadian Army? The Red Army is the Asadian Army.

Danica is wrong about me.

She doesn't know what I did to create a reputation within Roseguard's walls, to live up to the expectations of being a Cole. I've planned where to put armies to battle Ritenvold, and people have died because I put them there. She believes that I'm weak because I'm not a solider like her.

I hate how Danica thinks I rely on her; that I need her to survive outside of Roseguard. And I hate how I can't control her, I have nothing to control her with. She's cold and cruel and won't show me, a Captain of Roseguard, any respect. She treats me like I'm a stray mongrel dog that has been nipping at her horse's hooves.

I want to control her, I want her to bow before me, then I want to have her executed over Thorns Gap, just to prove that I can.

I watch her as she rides in front of me. Danica Rush. A girl who fought for nine and a half years on the front line of the biggest war in history. A girl who at aged ten ripped out the throat of her maid with her teeth like a monster. She has blood trailing her wherever she goes. Her shoulders are pushed back like a queen and she sits still, her hips swaying with the stallion's steady walk. Her stillness irks me. She seems to know exactly what is going on around her and watches the world as we walk past, taking everything in.

It's not natural, that stillness.

Yet, her father wasn't nearly as vicious or as cruel as she is. Dimitri Rush hadn't seemed at all like the tales made him out to be. I had imagined him to be a big, scary man covered in tattoos, scars and weapons, the legendary Nightwalker hunter. But, in reality, he was a fit middle-aged man, a father. Yet he had said to Danica that he'd be waiting outside of Roseguard for her, if I can escape and get word to mother, we could arrest him as a criminal and put him on the front line.

This morning he had packed quickly, barely glancing at me. I had been bursting with questions, but I only asked a few. Mother had told me stories about how for years Dimitri had worked for her - with her - before they had a falling out. She had told me he had been involved with the banishing, but never told me what he had done, how many monsters he'd slain.

Finally, I had gained the confidence to ask around mid-morning. 'How did you banish all the monsters and beasts to the Shadow?'

Dimitri had grinned wickedly, and it had looked too much like one of Danica's grins. 'I never banished a monster or beast to the Shadow.'

I remember how Danica had told me about the chimera. 'What do you mean?'

'As you call them, the Nightwalkers,' he says the word like he's never said it before, 'are the only ones capable of hunting down the beasts and monsters that haunt everyone's thoughts on a dark night.' He had hesitated, as if considering what to tell me. 'I'm just a sharpshooter, I was taught how to kill the beasts, but the Nightwalkers are the true protectors of Asada.'

He had then mounted Danica's stallion, I think its name is Eagle and had waited until Danica appeared. After a decade of being apart, I thought they would have spent more time catching up but obviously not. I had managed to get one more conversation out of him, asking him how he survived in the forest, and he'd told me about the kind of animals he would track and kill for food.

Danica pulls her horse to a halt, and I realise I haven't been paying attention. We are overlooking a small valley, the road travels through the centre of it. Up ahead in the distance, we can see the Red Soldiers. Their flags fly in the wind, the red rose just a speck. The hundred or so soldiers march at a steady pace; wagons and horses in the centre as they make their way west. To the north-west, dark green smoke from a fire darkens the sky. It makes me nervous, the unnatural smoke.

I turn to watch Danica. She is surveying the small army below; her mouth moves silently. She watches the smoke for a moment, chews her lip, tilts her head slightly then shakes it as if deciding on something in her cold mind. Finally, she looks back down at the army.

'That doesn't make sense.' Danica says quietly, almost to herself.

'What doesn't?'

She glances over at me, as if she's only just realised she's spoken out loud before she turns to look back out over the army. 'There are only ninety-three soldiers.' She hesitates for a moment as if considering her next words. 'There were one hundred and five before Tialo, and one hundred and five just after the village. I counted that night.'

'So that means twelve soldiers have gone missing?' I look out over the valley again, kicking myself for letting Danica distract me enough to not count my soldiers.

'Not necessarily missing. Watch the army; see how their supplies are in the middle. Soldiers have weapons at the ready. And they have sent a scout out.' Danica points a few hundred meters in front of the army, where I spy a chestnut horse and armed rider. 'I think they were attacked.'

I look at Danica again, as she watches the army. Her hand resting on the sword at her side. I grimace at the thought of being watched, especially if it's someone who is willing to attack Red Soldiers. She surveys the rest of the valley before turning her horse away from the cliff face and encouraging the stallion through the forest.

She urges her horse into a trot, and I follow, regularly looking back over my shoulder. I haven't seen Danica with her alarms going, and although she looks relaxed, I can tell she isn't impressed that there is someone else out there, someone who is capable of taking out twelve trained Red Soldiers.

We hurry through the trees all day, and I notice Danica is more cautious about choosing a camp. She doesn't light a fire and hands me dried meat instead. She sits against the tree that her Natari horse is tied to, the saddle propped against the tree next to her. I stay across the small clearing from her. I can barely see her in the dark, but I can see she's fiddling with something.

Every so often, I scan the clearing, trying to pick up what Danica notices. It is eerily quiet. No wind, no animals calling in the night.

I almost flinch when she suddenly appears by my side. Her hand is outstretched, offering me something. I take it from her and turn it over. It's a dagger, plain and simple. I look up at her, and one side of her mouth lifts slightly before she turns to go back to her tree. I stand up quickly and grab her wrist without thinking.

Danica spins around, eyes going to the hand on her wrist before flying to meet mine.

'Let go of me,' she says quietly.

I let go of her wrist but grab her hand, pulling her in closer. I'm genuinely surprised when she takes a step forward, watching me.

I lean forward and whisper in her ear. 'Thank you.' I'm not sure if I whisper because I want to see her reaction or if I'm nervous that whoever is out there might hear me.

Danica is watching me, not with her usual wariness but with something like uncertainty. I release her and sit back down.

'Your friend Tyke said he had some people come through the Underground that he didn't particularly like?' she asks quietly. 'Said they had the same look as me?'

I look up at her. 'Do you think those could be the people that attacked my army?'

I make sure I say *my* army, to remind her that she is plotting against *my* people.

She chews her lip for a moment, thinking. 'Possibly.'

She doesn't say anything else and walks back to her side of the clearing.

My charm must be working if Danica is beginning to trust me enough to give me a dagger and I decide then that I want her to trust me. Completely trust me so I don't have to deal with her questioning. I have noticed how her snapping has softened over the past few days, and she has been giving me a proper answer more often than not. Whatever her motive is, I don't care. I want her in my chains to do as I want with her, to command her as she has me, to force her to respect me as she should, and I want to make her second guess all her thoughts of me. By getting her to begin trusting me, telling me more pieces of information … she'll slip up and give me something that I can use to control her with.

I smile as I look down at the dagger. She would never have given it to me unless she had begun to trust me enough to believe I am hers to command.

I roll over and close my eyes. I know Danica won't sleep with even the slightest thought that there might be someone else prowling through the forest, and if she's given me a weapon, then she isn't going to kill me any time soon, so I let myself sleep.

*****

When I wake, she appears to be sleeping lightly, huddled beneath a blanket. I don't believe for a moment that she is actually asleep. As quietly as I can, I tack up my mare, and then I go to tack up Danica's stallion. Running a hand over the Natari's neck, the horse steps away from my touch, his ears pinned back, and I frown.

'Nataris are loyal to their riders. I hand fed that horse when he was a foal.' Danica's voice echoes through the clearing and I turn around to find her watching me, still huddled under the tree.

'He's beautiful.'

She doesn't say anything, only gets up, rolls her blanket and straps it to her saddle. She then begins tacking up the Natari. I watch as she effortlessly mounts the massive horse before I climb onto my mare and follow them through the forest. We ride through the forest in silence, and I let her take the lead, trying to show her that I trust her enough to follow her.

We haven't been riding for long when she stops, dismounts her horse and nods for me to follow. I tie my mare's reins to a tree before carefully following her. She crouches down beside a large fallen tree, and I follow suit. Peering over the large tree, I realise that about a hundred feet ahead, through the trees, is the clearing that we slept in last night. I start to open my mouth when she looks at me, finger over her lips and I wisely shut it.

We stay crouched behind the tree for a few hours. The forest makes its usual sounds, and Danica sits patiently watching the clearing, never once moving. My body starts to ache and go numb, but I resist the urge to stretch my limbs. I am tougher than her.

My blood goes cold when a rider enters the clearing, then another three enter behind the first. All are on massive black horses similar to Danica's stallion. They wear capes and hoods that hide their faces but the swords at their hips are easily visible. Despite their coverings, I can make out that the first and last riders to enter the clearing are definitely male with their bigger, broader builds. The hilts of the swords are like nothing I've seen before. All Red Soldier swords have a gold rose on the hilt; these swords have slender silver handles. The four riders move around the clearing, one getting off where I had been sleeping last night, toeing the base of the tree and then prowling over to where Danica had slept. The rider crouches by the base of the tree and lets a gloved finger trail over the base of the trunk then raises the finger to their hidden face.

I look at Danica and she's watching carefully, curious to see what the riders will do next.

The riders talk amongst themselves for a few moments, too low for me to hear, then the rider on the ground swings back onto his horse and they leave the clearing the same way we had.

Danica doesn't move for over another hour; I assume it's in case a rider has stayed to spy. She doesn't make a single sound until, when the sun is at its highest, she quietly stands up and I follow her back to the horses. I keep behind her, checking over my shoulder.

'I bet the reason the twelve Red Soldiers are missing is because of those riders,' she says quietly. 'And I bet they were the four that Tyke was talking about.'

'Any idea who they were?'

She doesn't answer my question. 'They know they're not the only ones tracking the Red Soldiers, so be on your guard. Those riders will want to know who we are and what we're doing.'

I wonder if Roseguard knows there are traitors roaming the forests, tracking and killing Red Soldiers that are trying to defend this country. At least when I get out of this mess, I'll be able to report all this to Mother.

'Were the horses they had Nataris'?' I keep my gaze on the back of her hooded head.

Silence, then; 'They probably had Natari bloodlines.'

'So basically, they're going to be hunting us now?'

She turns to look at me; a grin on her lips and my heart skips a beat at her words. 'Scared, Hunter?'

I match her grin. 'Danica darling, do I look afraid?'

I'm not afraid, I am terrified.

She runs an eye over me, her grin turning to a smirk, as if she was impressed by my comeback. 'I don't like being the prey; I much prefer being the predator.'

I raise an eyebrow. 'You intend to hunt down our hunters?'

Danica's grin deepens. 'Yes, and you're the bait.'

'What?'

'You heard me, Hunter.'

I want her to trust me. 'What do you want me to do?'

'Tonight, you'll set up camp. And we'll see if that draws any attention.'

She is looking like she's just been given a shiny new toy.

'And you?'

She looks forward. 'I'll be watching and making sure you're safe.'

My grin falls from my lips. She doesn't think I'll be able to look after myself. Even after surviving this long, after escaping the traitors in the dunes, after trekking for nights through the desert and then proving myself useful. She still doesn't think I can look after myself.

# Chapter Fifteen

## Danica

For the rest of the day, we follow the Red Soldiers. I haven't seen any signs of the riders but I'm not overly surprised because I made sure to keep Hunter and myself hidden, only riding along the smallest of deer tracks.

By the time the soldiers settle down for the night, I have already found the perfect spot to set my small trap. I doubt the riders will fall for it but if my suspicions are true, their cockiness might be their downfall.

Hunter had been growing more and more silent as the day passed, and late in the afternoon I hand him another dagger, telling him to only use it as a last resort. I need to make the trap look convincing to these riders, if there is an unarmed boy, they'll get suspicious.

The camp site I chose is a cave cut into the side of one of the cliffs, with only one entrance. The cave was easy to find in the forest, cliffs occasionally shooting up from the trees and then falling back to meet the forest floor. I dismount outside the cave and let Hunter walk the horses in, making camp, leaving only one set of footprints in the soil.

I climb a tree outside the cave and watch the entrance as I pull my daggers out and inspect them before putting them away. Tonight won't be the night for a noisy fight, as I'd rather not draw the attention of every Red Soldier in the country. I left my bow and arrows with Oak, but my two swords are ready, and the daggers are within easy access.

I watch as Hunter moves around the cave nervously. He makes a small fire within view of the entrance and sets out his bedroll. I told him to leave the horses tacked up in case we have to make a quick exit.

As the moon travels across the sky, my legs get stiff, and the breeze keeps me from being comfortable, raising goosebumps along my arms. I watch as Hunter drifts in and out of sleep, his restlessness obvious. When he's awake, he paces around the cave, wearing a track between the fire and the entrance, occasionally he peers out, gazing into the darkness.

It's not until after midnight that the forest falls silent. Not completely silent, but the silence that those who live under moonlight would understand; a silence that means a predator is prowling through the forest.

Fortunately, Hunter is awake when the four cloaked riders step up to the cave entrance on foot. I quietly climb down my tree as one draws a long sword. I let my own slide free as the rider in the centre steps into the light.

'Well, well, well!' the man with the sword says. He's tall, taller than Hunter or Dimitri, a lot taller than me.

Hunter's attention snaps up. 'Who are you?' he asks hesitantly.

His hand hovers by his side, where the dagger is hidden beneath his shirt.

One of the others moves towards the side of the cave, as if to circle around to get behind Hunter, to surround him. 'Hmm, this is interesting. Look at him all by himself! What will he do?' The rider teases in a wicked way.

Hunter puts his back to the wall. 'What do you want?' I watch as he sizes up his opponents.

Unfortunately, he is a city boy and will fight like his parents taught any Red Soldier to fight, but the people circling him are warriors and they will fight like warriors. Hunter is used to planning battles in the war rooms of Roseguard. Like myself, these warriors have been trained from birth. Hunter won't stand a chance.

Another man steps forward and I see the familiar strategy of herding Hunter away from the wall. 'What is a little human boy doing tracking Red Soldiers?'

My blood chills slightly, hoping that Hunter doesn't catch his words.

'Where's the woman gone?' The fourth says, glancing at the two horses.

'I'm here on business. For Roseguard.' Hunter says clearly, but his eyes nervously dart behind the men into the darkness outside the cave, to where I am hidden.

Wrong answer Hunter, I grimace.

I notice the leader tilt his head slightly, using the movement to keep Hunter's eyes on him. 'Business … You know we really, really don't like Red pricks.'

'I can't imagine why,' I say sarcastically, before they let anything else slip out. 'They're really quite wonderful people.'

All four spin around. And I raise my sword to the figure closest to me, the one with his sword already out.

*Despite who or what he is, I show no mercy. My survival comes first.* I tell myself the same words I repeated every day on the front line as I size up the male before me.

'How did you manage to sneak up on us, girl?' The man laughs. I don't like how I can't see his face under the hood.

'Leave him alone,' I say clearly, my voice even. 'He's mine.' I add with a hiss.

The man laughs. 'I don't think so.'

I keep my gaze on the leader, as one of the others begins circling behind me. 'First of all, why were you snooping around our camp this morning? Secondly, call your little dog off.' I nod my chin to the male trying to herd me.

The leader stills, a type of stillness I've grown up with. I notice the glances between the other three as they try to figure out how I knew they were in my camp.

Then the male swings his sword, a perfect arc to knock mine out of my hand. I raise my own smaller sword and effortlessly block the blow. He hesitates, no doubt thrown off by my speed, my strength. He didn't expect me to match him. He didn't expect me to stop his sword, and he steps back slightly to re-assess the situation.

Instead of letting him figure out what just happened, I swing my blade at him. Each movement perfectly executed and each one matched by speed and strength similar to my own. I am faintly aware of Hunter watching, his eyes wide and mouth slightly open with awe, he has never seen me fight before.

I jump forward, aiming my weapon at the man's torso, and I'm met with a blade before a sword comes flying towards my shoulder. I block it easily and let my second sword slide free. Gripping a sword in both hands, I hammer at him. If I let myself fall into my *killing calm*, I could have the male dead in one blow. But the rider is still holding back, he's not fighting with everything he has just yet. I want to see how far I can push him before he starts getting more aggressive in his attacks.

I jump back slightly, to allow myself a moment for a quick breather and to assess the situation again.

'I said leave the man alone,' I repeat, eyeing the other three who have now drawn swords. 'He's mine.'

The swordsman grins a nasty wicked grin. 'Why let the boy live?'

'Because he is mine,' I snap and throw a bit more strength and aggression into my next attack.

The swordsman matches me before jumping out of reach. He's silent for a moment.

'You…' He laughs suddenly. 'You're one of us!'

I hope Hunter doesn't understand what he means.

'Let's show the human what we do to their kind, eh?' The rider says to me, to his riders, finally pulling his hood back to reveal a face vaguely familiar to me. He runs a hand through his midnight hair as he turns to Hunter, and my heart skips a beat.

'Falcon?'

The swordsman turns to me. 'How do you know my name?'

I sheath both my swords and pull my hood back from my face. He frowns.

'It's me, Danica!' I grin.

Realisation crashes onto his sharp face. 'Danica?' He whispers with disbelief, pale eyes widen.

'Long time, no see.'

Falcon is still staring at me with disbelief. 'You're … Roseguard took you!'

I nod.

I look at the other three who have all removed their hoods; their pale blue eyes watch me.

Hunter slowly takes a step forward but doesn't say anything.

'Falcon was my childhood friend,' I explain to Hunter.

'We all thought you were still in Roseguard's torture chamber. How are you here?' one of the others asks.

'Cole thought I would be of better use on the front line,' I say and turn to Falcon who's still staring at me like I'm a ghost.

'How?' He asks quietly, taking a small step forward and sheathing his sword.

I nod my head towards the camp. 'Join us for the night.'

'Danica … we're not leaving you now.' A male with an ugly scar across his right cheek says.

I only smile.

Over the next half hour, Falcon introduces me to the three other riders. Crynn with the scar, and Ryker and Caden who are twins, the only difference between them is that Ryker keeps his black hair in a long braid. The twins leave to retrieve their Natari horses and take longer than I would have thought necessary. I half-heartedly introduce Hunter, who wisely remains silent, watching me as I make room for them. I do take the daggers back from Hunter, however.

Falcon doesn't leave my side, as if he's scared that if he looks away, I might vanish into the night. Seeing Falcon again … he had lived in my mother's home, and we had played in the oak forests together, playing at being warriors. Seeing Falcon now … he is no longer a little boy with a stick sword, he's a full-grown male. A warrior, with a sleek sword made from Moonstone strapped to his hip. When we finish our training, we are gifted a custom Moonstone sword. Being on the front line, I had never finished my training. I study him as we wait for Ryker and Caden; his face is sharp, his build lean but muscled like mine, Crynn's and the twins. He's also so much taller than me.

Fortunately, no-one says anything vital in front of Hunter, but then, they know he is human, and they would know there is a reason he is here with me. I do, however, mention to Falcon to be careful what he says around Hunter just in case, while we wait for Ryker and Caden to return.

Once Ryker and Caden have returned and settled the horses, they join us by the campfire, rolling out their own bedrolls. I keep an eye on Hunter, who is sitting on his bed roll further away.

Crynn asks in a low voice. 'How did you know we were tracking you?'

'I was, still am, tracking the Red Soldiers. I noticed some of them start to go missing.' A satisfied smirk appears on Crynn's lips, confirming that they were behind the disappearances. 'I also had a gut instinct to make sure whoever was tracking the soldiers wasn't also tracking me. I stayed behind when you four decided to check out our campsite earlier.'

Crynn nods, the shadows hiding his scar.

'Those Red Soldiers got a bit of a shock when they found some of their own missing their heads in the middle of the camp,' Ryker says quietly, then adds, 'We hid the heads through the camp. They spent the rest of the day finding them.'

I cough, half in amusement, half in horror. I couldn't imagine opening my saddle bag to find a head.

Caden groans. 'That last bit was Ryker's idea. He wanted to send them a reminder that not everyone likes them.'

Falcon sits beside me, watching Hunter who has his head against the cave wall behind him. 'How much does that one know?'

Hunter answers before I open my mouth. I hadn't realised he could hear from where he is sitting. 'I know that Danica is the daughter of Dimitri Rush and that was why the Red Soldiers took her.' Falcon turns to look at me while Hunter speaks. 'But what I don't know is what she is, if she isn't human.' Hunter finally looks at me. So, he had kept up with our little exchange of words.

'I used to make fun of Danica because she is Dimitri's daughter,' Falcon lies smoothly. 'I tease her about not being human because Dimitri … well, Dimitri is the legendary sharpshooter.'

Hunter's gaze doesn't leave Falcon, and I almost sigh with relief when he nods.

I decide that now is a good time to change the topic. 'I saw Dimitri.'

Falcon raises an eyebrow. 'You did? We saw him not long ago. He's the one who told us to track the Red Soldiers.' He chews his lip for a moment before continuing. 'I think he was still hanging around, though… Is he heading home? If your mother knows you're safe and out …' He trails off.

'I know. Once I'm done with the soldiers, I have one more place to go,' I say quietly. 'I'll be meeting Dimitri outside of Roseguard as soon as I'm done here.'

'We'll come,' he says.

I dip my head in appreciation and smile at him.

Crynn interrupts. 'Why were you tracking the Red Soldiers? And why is that one with you?' He nods towards Hunter.

'This one is a Cole.' I almost laugh as the others all tense. 'He's the one that told me about the Red Soldiers' plans. And he's the one that got me the information, via the Underground in Roseguard.'

Crynn hesitates. 'We visited the Underground.' He says the word as if it's hard to pronounce.

'And?' I push. Hunter's attention is fixed on Crynn.

'We had a run in with a man named Tyke. He figured out where our alliances lay, as we were asking questions that we shouldn't have been asking,' Crynn says casually.

Caden adds, 'And you got into a fist fight with a couple of guards in there.' I stiffen, I had sat across from Tyke. Hopefully my pale eyes hadn't given my identity away, especially if Tyke had worked out that Falcon, Crynn, Caden and Ryker were Narakuya. All Narakuya have pale blue eyes and usually so do the halfbreeds. I'd been born with ice eyes, paler than most, a trait of my mother's bloodline.

Falcon leans forward, cutting off whatever Crynn was about to say. 'We managed to leave without a wanted poster, but I doubt we'll be welcome back anytime soon.'

Hunter's eyes dart to me and then back at Crynn. 'Why did you get into a fight with the guards?'

Crynn raises an eyebrow but doesn't snap at Hunter.

'Not everyone likes us,' Falcon says smoothly.

'Now what?' Crynn asks.

'We take down the Red Soldiers,' I grin.

# CHAPTER SIXTEEN

## HUNTER

My heart races, adrenaline had been sitting low in my stomach since Danica's *friends* had appeared.

The dread had been my companion all night, especially when Danica had walked out into the darkness, her footsteps fading, I had felt entirely by myself until she reappeared like a ghost behind those riders.

I knew Danica would have known her way around a sword, but I had never thought that she would have been that good.

Soldiers had spent years practicing in the training rings in Roseguard, they were some of the best swordsmen I had ever seen, yet Danica made them look like toddlers with stick swords. She had moved like a wraith through the shadows, and Falcon had met her every swing. The nauseous feeling in my stomach had only grown worse as I had watched the criminal's fight. The speed, the strength… I would need my best soldiers to best them and to put them into chains.

But, while their swordsmanship had been impressive, Danica had forgotten that she had Roseguard's best strategist in her company. While they fought, I'd been paying attention to their words. They had repeatedly called me human, as if they were something other. They had called Danica the same as them.

Then Danica had recognised the leader, introduced them as childhood friends and invited them into the camp. Fear had pumped through my veins as the criminals sized me up, considered how much of a threat I am. If I can get them to believe that I am not a threat to them, they will underestimate me and that will be their downfall, I had decided.

The remainder of the night, I shudder every time I move, talk, breathe. I feel like I am walking on thin ice around them. Especially as the criminal who calls himself Crynn watches me as if I am his next meal, and the twins can't look at me without disgust on their faces. Falcon is the only one to keep a carefully blank face whenever he glances in my direction.

Having kept their voices low, they had talked into the early hours of the morning, Falcon looking at Danica as if she isn't a crazed killer and cold-hearted bitch, but as if she were a goddess, even as she tells them stories of the horrors on the front line.

And then there was the whole thing about Danica being not human because of Dimitri? Well, that's certainly bullshit. I saw the quick looks between Danica and Falcon, smelt the lie like it was pig manure.

Danica and I will need to have some words, there's a reason I have my title and it's because I can make anyone talk.

The criminals had seemed to make a point of ignoring me, and I made a point to look as uninterested as possible. I waited for them to let something slip out that wasn't supposed to be said, but they're too well guarded with their words, other than their exchange whilst they were fighting.

None of us slept that night, and in the morning I'm quiet as I put the bridle back on my mare, well aware all the others are on Natari horses. When I am back in Roseguard, I will send out a team of soldiers to hunt down a Natari for myself, considering they don't seem to be as rare as I thought.

Danica is about to swing a leg over Oak when I come up beside her. She pauses and I take the opportunity. 'How have they all got Nataris?'

Danica says smoothly, 'They're family friends and Dimitri always has a few extras.'

I don't believe a word she says. 'Sure, they are.' I snicker.

Crynn calls over his shoulder, 'Don't talk to Danica like that or she might cut out your tongue. If she doesn't, I will.'

I almost let a reply snap out, one I would have confidently said if we were in Roseguard. But we're not; we're in the middle of a forest and I am outnumbered. And I don't want to lose my tongue because I don't doubt one of them would actually attempt to cut my tongue straight out of my mouth.

Danica only sends Crynn a small, wicked grin before lowering her voice slightly as she looks back to me, her ice eyes running over my body. 'Believe what you want.'

'Does Vixy know about any of this? About Dimitri, these friends of yours?'

She shakes her head.

So, I decide to do what I am best at, use words to get what I want.

The others have finished mounting their horses and are waiting outside the cave. So I take step closer to Danica, the scent of her, of oak wood and smoke, makes me want to kiss her. I blink at the thought, then think for a moment how she would look sprawled across my bed, tied up so I can do what I want.

I take a deep breath, I have a mission that I can't get distracted from. 'I want to work with you; I want to be a part of your team. I want to be one of you.' And I know Danica knows I'm not talking about the riders at the cave entrance, but the small family she has in the desert. 'I've proven where my loyalties lie, I've let you use me. For bait, for information; I've betrayed my position and family for you. Why won't you let me in? Why do you keep secrets from me?'

I know my words hit home when Danica's gaze darts down to her boots. She doesn't say anything but bites her lip guiltily.

So, I say the words that I hope will hurt her enough. 'It's ok … I understand. I'm a Cole and I'm not what you want in your group of warriors.' I turn to my mare. I hope she doesn't smell the lie as easily as I smell hers.

'Hunter,' she says, grabbing my arm. I look over my shoulder at her. 'I've said it before, and I'll say it again; you have much to learn before you can start playing war on our level. Before making that offer, wait until you understand what is truly at play.'

She releases my arm and turns to her horse.

I frown. I hadn't expected that, I'd been expecting her to feel guilty for the lies I had just spat at her.

I climb onto my own horse and follow her out of the cave.

*****

All day, I make a point to ride next to Danica, with Falcon on her other side. I can hear Crynn's horse chomping at the bit as he rides directly behind. Ryker disappeared somewhere in front of us, scouting ahead and Caden keeps a distance behind, as if Danica is a goddess they have to protect.

Danica and Falcon spend the entire day discussing how to take down the Red Soldiers, what each of their little criminal team's strengths and weaknesses are. They discuss different locations and how to take down the army. The audacity they have to think that they can take down an entire small army and save the villages from recruitment is incredible.

Roseguard has been struggling to recruit soldiers for the last five years and now is the time to enforce stronger rules in order to defeat Ritenvold … but I can't understand why Danica wants to save the villages. She has witnessed the front line firsthand, she should encourage the enforcing, because the only way to truly protect the people of Asada is to destroy Ritenvold.

I know my words have changed Danica's view of me, because instead of being all secretive, she's letting me listen to her conversations with her little criminal team.

As the day progresses, I keep my ears open.

There is one question that caught me off guard, I thought Falcon would already have known the answer. We've been riding in silence for a while when Falcon asks Danica what the front line is like.

I look at Danica too, waiting for her response. She stares straight ahead, not meeting any of our gazes.

She replies quietly, 'I trained for a year before they sent me out. You aren't supposed to go into conflict until you turn thirteen, but I was just eleven when they decided I didn't need any more training and sent me to where the fighting was the thickest. Roseguard is losing because they don't have enough strength. They only have humans and unwilling warriors fighting for them whereas Ritenvold never banished their *beasts* …' Danica glances at me, suddenly aware that I am listening. 'Ritenvold have *Nightwalkers* fighting with them, against the Red Soldiers. I was forced to fight them.'

'Once, I saw one who looked as if he understood that I wasn't there willingly.' Danica glances at me again, like she's been really careful with how she tells this story in my presence. 'Then a Red Soldier knocked me out and I was put in the thickest part of where the humans were fighting.'

'Why did they knock you out?' I ask quickly.

Danica hesitates for a moment. 'Because I didn't try to kill him.'

'Why not?'

Falcon interrupts. 'The past is in the past. Now, do we want to take on this entire Red Army or simply pick them off one by one as they enter the mountain pass to Lyko?'

'Both,' Danica says, and my stomach twists.

*****

With the sun at its peak, we stop for a quick lunch break, and when Danica slips into the forest alone, I decide to follow. Falcon watches me leave, raising an eyebrow at me but I ignore him. As I follow the small trail Danica took, I can hear the gentle trickle of water, the forest branches blowing in the breeze. I can smell the scent of damp soil and as I round a corner, a little stream comes into view, the water clear as it runs over the bare earth. Danica is up ahead, crouched over the stream. She cups her hands, dipping them into the water before raising them to her lips.

'I know you're there,' she says quietly, her voice soft and sending shivers down my spine.

Even though she's not watching, I shrug and wander to the stream, standing beside her.

'What do you want?' She stands up and looks at me, her eyes running over my body quickly.

'A lot of things.' To see you back on the front line where you belong. To see you bowing before me.

'You're looking at me like that again.' Danica's words snap me out of my haze, and I have a moment as I blink to let any expression fall from my face.

'Like what?'

Danica hesitates before answering. 'Like there's something about me that you do not necessarily agree with.' She looks back to the trail that we'd followed to the stream. 'I would like to know what that particular thing is.'

So, I decide to give her a sliver of truth. 'I have to say it occasionally shocks me how young you were to have killed so many people.'

Danica's eyes narrow. 'I didn't have much of a choice, and yet one day I will still have to pay for those deaths.'

'We all have a choice.' I lower my voice. 'I am a Captain of Roseguard's Red Army, and I have never killed another person.'

Danica blinks and then bursts out laughing. I watch as she laughs for a few moments, her head thrown back.

'No, but you decide who is going where to die. I like you Hunter, because you are so oblivious to the real threat in Asada. You play games in your expensive war rooms, get bruised and call it a day. You have a choice.'

'And you?' I say coldly.

The amusement vanishes from Danica's face. 'I wake up and fight for my life every day. The first time I killed someone, it was because I knew the maid had sold me out and I would be going wherever your mother thought would be a suitable place for me. I did it to protect myself and I do not regret it.'

'You know I'm not as oblivious as you think.'

Danica raises an eyebrow.

'You deserved to be on the front line because you are a murderer. You are a cruel and a cold bitch, and the only thing you know how to do is kill.' The rant comes out of me, sudden and quick. I swallow, instantly regretting saying anything. There goes the trust I was trying to earn.

Danica doesn't say anything for a long moment. 'I was tortured by *your* soldiers if I *chose* not to kill. That is not by choice. I never *ever* wanted to kill anyone on the front line. I dare you to tell me that I had a choice again.'

I swallow, not saying anything. If she made the choice not to kill the maid, then none of this would have happened. But I don't say that right now, and I decide I will pick up this battle again once her temper has cooled.

Danica pushes past me, shoving me as she goes and I turn, never putting my back to her, only to find Falcon standing there, his sword drawn and a death promise in his eyes.

Danica stops beside Falcon and says something I can't hear before striding back to the horses, her temper evident in her step. I keep staring at Falcon.

Falcon is watching me. 'If Crynn heard you say that, you wouldn't be alive right now.'

'And you?' I say cautiously, preparing to run if I have to.

Falcon puts his sword away. 'Danica think's it'll be wiser to let you live. For now.' With that, he turns on his heel and follows Danica back to the horses.

I close my eyes and take a deep breath.

What am I going to do? I just want to go back to my city; I want to put Danica and her little entourage of murderers back on the front line. Being in charge means getting to make threats, getting to kill someone without being the person to put a hole in the target.

The next two days are the same, wake up, breakfast, saddle up, ride behind Danica as she refuses to talk to me, untack, dinner, sleep, repeat. When Danica needs to tell me something, she lets Falcon do the talking. When I ask a question, there is always that silent conversation between Danica and Falcon before he says anything to me. I'm not sure when, but Crynn had learnt of the nasty name Danica had called me by and whenever he spoke to me, he would address me as *Stray*. Ryker and Caden didn't say much to me at all, and they kept their duties of scouting in front and following a distance behind. Although, one of the nights, Ryker had *accidently* tripped on my legs as I had been laying on my bedroll and had kicked me hard enough to leave a nasty bruise.

There was movement in the camp well before dawn on the third morning. It was cold when I woke to find Caden putting the fire out. I watched, sitting on my bedroll as the criminal team all very quietly saddled their horses, armed themselves with weapons. They moved through the clearing quickly, quietly and efficiently.

'What's happening?' I ask, standing up.

Falcon glances at Danica, that silent conversation playing out before he walks over to me.

'You're to watch the camp today.'

'Why?'

'Because I said so.' Falcon then spins on his heel and strides over to my mare. He takes the lead before mounting his Natari. Danica is the next to swing a leg over her horse. Ryker finishes checking his tack and Caden counts the arrows in his quiver before mounting up.

'We'll be back shortly.' Falcon says and they all turn towards the forest.

The criminal team disappear from sight, and not long after, the echo of hoofbeats vanish into the forest.

It dawns on me as I stare at the empty camp, that today is the day that Danica is going to attack my soldiers. They had taken my mare to stop me from running and left me in the forest by myself, with nothing to defend myself with.

And I realise that this might be my only chance to escape. I had made sure to take notice of the direction we'd travel, so, I run. I run back to my home, to my city, to my position and family. The one place that I have any control.

# CHAPTER SEVENTEEN

## DANICA

Hunter watched us leave the camp, taking his mare with us. Just in case he gets any ideas about running.

I felt a little guilty about leaving him there... if anything stumbles across the clearing, he will be fair game with how defenceless he is. Yet, I am still furious with what he said by the stream. His mother sent me to the front line and he has the audacity to call me a bitch and a murderer. His mother made me, and he's decided he doesn't like the end result of her creation.

We told Hunter we'll be back shortly, when we'd actually be back in the late afternoon if everything went as planned. It would take a couple of hours of hard riding to make it to the mountain pass. The hours go past slowly, with anticipation fuelling me. As the forest gives way to the mountain range, the anticipation only heightens. Falcon knows the land here like the back of his hand and I follow him along the deer tracks up the mountain, passing the marching Red Army on our way.

We arrive at the mountain pass with half an hour to spare. Ryker takes the horses and hides them in a small cave where the soldiers will never find them. I tread lightly through the mountain pass; the aim was to arrive just before the soldiers. The pass is just wide enough for two horses to walk through side by side, and it is the quickest way through the small mountains on the east of the villages, the range finishing just north of Diada. The small mountain range, known as the Lyko Mountains, is nothing compared to the Yulara Mountains. My jacket keeps the cool wind from biting. I haven't had a moment to braid my hair, so it's swinging loose around my shoulders, much to my annoyance, and I try tucking it into the back of my jacket.

Falcon looks over at me, his gaze lingering and I grin as I nudge him with my elbow. I have told him more in the past few days then I have to anyone in years. Falcon's mother had been friends with my mother, and he had grown up in my mother's home. I would spend spring, summer and autumn with him and we would often spend hours playing and causing trouble in the oak forests. In winter, I would travel with Dimitri to his cabin in the mountains, where we could be a family. The winter before my first on the front line, Falcon had stayed with Dimitri and me.

Crynn had never met his mother, she died giving birth to him. So his father raised him. Ryker and Caden had spent their childhood in Lyko, where both their parents lived, but would often travel to and from the Shadow.

Caden strides a few feet ahead and raises his hand, stopping us. We have reached our destination.

We all get into position, preparing for the battle ahead and Ryker arrives back shortly, going straight to his position.

The mountain pass is covered in a fog, which helps us. We wait patiently for Hunter's Red Army. I stand relaxed in the pass, both swords out, daggers on my hips and up my sleeves. Falcon is hidden on the pass wall just beneath the layer of fog, where he has a perfect view of the soldiers, and perfect aim with his bow.

I hear the soldiers before I see them, and I rest one of my arms behind my back, with both my swords hidden from view. My other arm leans against the wall, my hand resting on my belt.

The first two that appear are on horses, one bay and one chestnut. The rest are on foot. The man on the bay is leading, and I can make out grey hair and a clean-shaven face. The man on the chestnut… I recognise him. I clench my jaw, my heart beginning to pick up speed as I remember how he took pleasure in leaving the scar on my stomach. I take a deep breath, I need to have my wits about me. I had seen him multiple times over the last decade, and I had made sure he was well aware that I would kill him one day. Last time I had seen him, I was sixteen. I had been cursing him, acting like a madwoman, my head was shaved, my face gaunt, and you could count my ribs. I'll be impressed if he recognises me now. I let the wicked grin appear on my lips.

The leading soldier pulls his horse to a halt as he notices me leaning against the mountain wall. His hand rests on his iron sword, a sword good for hunting faeries that live in the Shadow.

'Move out of the way, girl.' The soldier raises an arm, the tiny army halting behind him.

I don't look up at the soldiers as I say clearly, 'Your mission, unfortunately, has been cancelled.'

The soldier laughs, unaware of the weapons hidden out of their sight. I turn and raise the swords; the laughter dies instantly.

'How have you got those swords?' the soldier asks without thinking the question through. Although the swords look silver, the Moonstone is unbreakable. Falcon had a few spare, so I was able to swap my steel swords for Moonstone.

I only smile. 'We can do this the easy way, or the hard way. The easy way being you turn around and march all the way back to Roseguard.'

'You're a bit outnumbered girl,' the guard says smoothly, despite the two swords aimed at him.

I let a nasty smile appear on my face. 'Who said I am outnumbered?'

The soldier on the chestnut steps forward and looks me up and down. 'Little girl, it is a criminal offense to harm a Red Soldier, so move out of the way and we'll be nice.'

I'm kind of insulted now that he doesn't remember me, so I decide to jog his memory. 'It is also a criminal offense to put a dagger in the stomach of an innocent ten-year-old girl, take her from her home and force her to fight on the front line,' I say sweetly, poison dripping from my words.

The man's eyes go wide. 'Danica Arlet Rush.' His eyes go to my stomach.

I don't think as I throw my sword like a spear with all my strength. I watch the sword fly through the air, through the mountains and land home, straight through the man's right eye. I never learned his name, but it is one less person on my death list.

The man with a sword through his head slides out of the saddle, flopping onto the ground. I turn to look at the soldier on the bay; he has his sword drawn now.

'Leave,' I say with perfect timing as screaming and chaos breaks out at the back of the army.

The soldier looks back over his shoulder and a moment later a foot soldier runs forward, his red clothing flashing under the silver armour worn for protection from werewolves. I smile as I think of how useless the amour would actually be against a werewolf. I start swinging my second sword with expert precision. I leave the soldier alive as he backs his horse out of the way; more soldiers running forward. They'll need the leader to take the army back to Roseguard and explain all of this.

I keep swinging until I lose my sword in the chaos. A soldier laughs at me, but I only smile and take my daggers out. Another runs forward, jumping the bodies of his fallen brothers and an arrow hits him mid leap. An arrow from Falcon's bow.

The soldier that laughed at me hesitates, sword still in his hand, an arrow protruding from his right shoulder.

'Take your soldiers and leave. Do not take the innocents from Lyko, Tirma and Materga. Tell the Red Generals that Danica Arlet Rush is coming for revenge,' I say clearly, and their eyes widen, jaws clenching as fear flutters across the soldier's face as he orders his army to turn back.

'Tell them Queen Rayven is coming for Melissa Cole.'

They all begin to back away.

'Don't think about trying to sneak past us, we'll be following you back to Roseguard,' I lie, letting a cruel smile onto my face. I hadn't expected the soldiers to run so quickly, but Crynn, Ryker and Caden would have helped scare the soldiers in the fog.

The soldier watches me as he leaves. 'You'll regret this!'

I raise my eyebrows. 'We'll see.'

The soldier backs out of sight, and I wait there. It's half an hour before Falcon appears at my side.

'You can certainly be persuasive.' Falcon grins, his eyes shining.

'I could always get you to do what I wanted, so a few soldiers are nothing,' I reply with a smirk.

'I only got to let one arrow fly.'

'You'll get to release a lot more by the time everything has been dealt with,' I say quietly.

As we wait for the others, I tie my hair back, which has been blowing around my face all morning. Falcon catches my hands.

'Don't.' I look up at him. 'You look more terrifying with it out.'

I laugh, a proper laugh for the first time in what feels like forever. 'Thanks, Falc.'

Falcon only grins before releasing my hands, his pale blue eyes watch me carefully. 'Why do you let Hunter talk to you like that?'

I sigh and look away. 'He is so oblivious to what is truly going on. I don't want to be the one to break the news that his mother is the real monster,' I reply truthfully.

I can feel Falcon still watching me.

So, I add, 'He annoys me.'

'You let him get away with it.'

Fortunately, Crynn and Ryker return, saving me from Falcon's interrogation.

'Caden is tracking the soldiers and will regroup with us later,' Ryker says before I can ask.

'All went smoothly then?' I ask.

'Only a few dead soldiers.' Crynn grins.

'Good. Let's head back to the horses.'

Once we reach the horses in the cave, we have lunch to celebrate our small victory before continuing on back to the campsite, back to Hunter.

*****

A clammy, nauseous feeling builds in my stomach as we make our way back to the campsite. I can almost smell it in the air, something is wrong. The feeling prepares me for the worst, something had stumbled into the camp and found defenceless Hunter, leaving a corpse behind.

It's worse than that.

He's gone.

I stand there staring at the clearing. Hunter is gone.

His saddle bags are still there, his bedroll still out.

'The bastard pissed off at a hundred miles an hour,' I hear Crynn say as he inspects the clearing.

Falcon is watching me. 'Do you want me to go after him?'

I don't answer as I stare at the clearing. I had underestimated him. I never thought he'd attempt to run without a horse, without anything to protect himself with. He is well aware that he knows nothing about surviving outside of the city walls.

'I'll kill the prick,' Crynn growls.

His words snap me out of my daze.

'He's my kill,' I snarl, my words echoing through the clearing. 'Don't bother going after him. I know where he's heading.'

'And where's that?' Falcon asks gently.

'Back to his beloved mummy,' I say quietly. 'So, we'll be going to Roseguard.'

# Part Two

# Of Monsters & Men

# CHAPTER EIGHTEEN

## HUNTER

After nearly a full day of running through the forests, hoping that I was running in the right direction, I came across the soldiers Danica had turned around. They recognised me instantly, gave me a horse and organised eight men to be my personal guards as we rode the rest of the way back to Roseguard. It took a week of hard riding to reach home. A week of looking over my shoulder, hoping and praying not to see a black stallion come galloping behind me, the murderer on the stallion's back with her sword raised ready to cut me down.

After two days of riding with the Red Army, a team of twenty Red Soldiers found us. They told me that my mother sent them out to rescue me after receiving a tip off.

The soldiers asked how I escaped my captor, and I'd told them that although my captor thought they'd had the upper hand, I had allowed them to underestimate me and waited until I had all the knowledge I needed before disappearing into the forest. I informed the soldiers that I had Mother send them as part of the ruse. When they asked who my target was, I told them they would be better off not knowing, and I told the soldiers nothing about Danica and Dimitri, best to discuss with Mother first.

Once I was surrounded by Red Soldiers and during that hard week of riding, harder than anything Danica had made me do, I felt safe again, and I breathe a sigh of relief when we reach Roseguard without seeing any big black horses and their cruel riders.

Mother and Pa are waiting for me at the walls of Roseguard with hundreds of soldiers through the streets. As I dismount from my tired horse, they sweep me into a hug before ushering me back to our home with a convoy of Red Soldiers guarding our backs.

As soon as I walk beneath the gates of Roseguard, I feel like my old self again. Nothing can hurt me here, as I am Captain Hunter Cole. Pa urges me to wash up, and then we shall sit to discuss what had happened. I linger in the water, making a list of things to tell Mother so I don't forget anything important. I then change into crisp, clean clothes, the red Roseguard crest on a new jacket.

I make my way downstairs towards the kitchen, the smell of warm bread and roast floats down the hall. A servant has prepared a meal for me, but when I sit down to eat there is no sign of her. Mother and Pa sit across from me, watching me eat, watching every mouthful. Waiting expectantly for me to finish. They don't acknowledge one another as they watch me, but I would imagine that having me back safe and sound would be enough to make them put their differences aside.

Despite the last few weeks of living like a commoner, Danica had been able to provide filling meals.

When I am done, I explain what happened in detail. How I had lagged behind the carts heading to the front line and been attacked by rebels. How I had wandered through the desert and found Vixy, and Danica Rush.

I watch Mother's face when I mention Danica's name, expecting to see shock or surprise or anything other than her expectant nod.

I don't say anything for a moment, then I realise.

'You knew I was with Danica Rush?' I raise an eyebrow and sit up a bit straighter at this news.

Pa shakes his head in disappointment, scoffing at Mother.

Mother doesn't say anything but puts her hand in her pocket and pulls out a piece of paper.

I take it and unfold it, not recognising the handwriting.

*MC,*

*I am free, and I have your son hostage. Maybe I should show him what I learned while I was your slave? All the wonderful and wicked things I learned on the front line. Should I show him what your soldiers showed me? Shall we see if he survives like me?*

*Here's what's going to happen.*

*You're going to surrender to Ritenvold and pull all your soldiers back to Roseguard.*

*Once every human who willingly wears the Rose is within Roseguard's walls, then I'll be in touch.*

*Yours truly,*

*D.A.R.*

*(Just know that Hunter will die should you fail to do as I order.)*

As I read the letter, my heart races faster and faster, a nauseous feeling building in my stomach.

That was the letter she had written that night. While I stood across the street, she was threatening me, my mother and my city. She'd had Tyke find wax so her letter couldn't be read until it reached Mother. I read the letter again, my hands shaking as I read further down. I'd been a pawn in her game. My fear and dread turns to white hot anger. How dare she! How dare she drag me along and threaten my city!

I slam my fist down on the table.

'Easy Hunt,' Pa says, placing a hand over mine.

'The bitch!' I hiss at him.

Pa rubs his thumb over mine, 'you're back safe and sound, that's all that matters.'

I am going to make her pay for this.

Taking a deep breath, I look up at Mother. I am a captain, and I need to re-strategize, I need to get my revenge on that bitch.

I take another deep breath, trying to put myself into the mindset I use as a captain. First thing first, I need all the details, and I won't let Mother keep anything confidential from me again, not now.

'I met Dimitri Rush, and he said some things that got me thinking, but there is one thing I can't work out.' I look at mother, her red uniform matching the red and gold kitchen of our home. 'Who is Danica's mother?'

Mother glances at Pa, his dark eyes narrowing, deciding how much to tell me.

Pa lowers his voice. 'Hunter has a right to know, especially after everything he has been through. You should have told him years ago.'

'I do,' I interrupt their silent conversation. 'I was her *hostage* for the last couple of weeks. I am not going to accept anything but the full truth.'

Mother lowers he eyes slightly, but I don't miss the glare she gives Pa. 'Everything I have done, is to protect you, to keep you safe in a world built to kill humans.'

'Tell me.' I snap at her, impatience making me want to hit something.

'Danica is dangerous. She's a born killer and was training to be a warrior before she could walk. She is perhaps the deadliest creature in all of Asada and its Shadow.' Mother stands suddenly and walks to the window overlooking Thorn Gap. 'Danica's father is Dimitri Rush. And her mother is Rayven Arlet.'

I frown, not recognising the name. 'Who?'

It's Pa who answers. 'Rayven is the Queen of the Narakuya—or as you call them — Nightwalkers. Danica is her only child and possibly the sole heir to the Moonstone Palace hidden in the Shadow.'

My blood goes cold, I forget to breath, my jaw goes slack. Danica is princess of the Nightwalkers…

'Rayven is the law; she is Queen of Asada. She is the one who enforces the Treaty of Asada,' Pa continues, his eyes becoming darker as he talks. 'And she was doing a perfectly fine job until your mother got greedy.' Pa adds with a pointed look in her direction. 'Danica is their princess. She's the best weapon Melissa has ever had, not only against Ritenvold but against the Narakuya themselves because as long as we controlled Danica, we controlled the Queen of Asada. And that's how we were able to force the beasts to remain in the Shadow.'

The only thought that goes through my mind is, *I was held hostage by Narakuya royalty.*

Mother turns around, leaning against the wall and glares at Pa. 'Sooner or later, Rayven would start wiping out the human race. We were weak, vulnerable, and I was the only one who did something to try and balance the scales of power.'

'Rayven never gave you any inkling that she would do that.' Pa growls at Mother, I've never seen them argue like this before. He turns to me, 'the reason I left this family was because I didn't want to put our people through unnecessary suffering.'

Pa leans back in his chair and raises an eyebrow at Mother before rubbing his chin. 'Dimitri Rush's father was Narakuya, his mother human. He knew about his father's blood, but as his father had barely been present for most of his childhood, he did not care for that blood, until he was sent to assassinate Rayven.'

I stay silent for a couple of moments, gathering my thoughts.

'Who sent Dimitri to kill Rayven?'

'I did,' Mother says quietly.

'What?'

'I did,' mother repeats. 'Dimitri lived with my family as a child, it was always the three of us, him, me and your aunt. Dimitri was always stronger and faster because of his blood, and he was only half Narakuya. I knew the queen was deadly, a threat to humankind, so I took the risk and asked Dimitri to assassinate her. I offered him more than anything he could want. Yet he ended up becoming that queen's bedwarmer,' Mother adds with a scowl.

'So let me get this straight,' I say, looking mother in the eye. 'Dimitri chose Rayven over you, so you kidnapped their child?'

Mother folds her arms, unimpressed with my wording. 'Correct. But the reason behind taking Rayven's child is incorrect. I took that child because with every generation born, the Narakuya become stronger. They are only mere steps away from calling themselves Gods. I intend to stop that from happening and keep humans as the ultimate species.'

I turn mother's words over in my mind. 'That makes sense,' I agree. If someone like Danica was to call herself a God, we'd be ants beneath her boot.

I rub the back of my neck, considering everything said. 'We have something against Danica though…' I say slowly, my thoughts collecting. 'Danica was looking after a human girl. At Eagles Canyon. If we control the girl, we control Danica.'

Pa shakes his head. 'We're all going to die.'

Mother suddenly snaps, shocking me. 'Shut up you useless bastard.'

I raise my eyebrows at her outburst.

She turns to me. 'Aye, I was able to take a calculated guess that that's where the girl was. We have soldiers retrieving her as we speak.'

'Vixen Kyler might be the only weapon we have against Danica,' I say carefully.

'The girl should arrive at Roseguard any time now.'

'Danica's poisoned the girl, but she didn't deserve to go to the front line in the first place. Despite her crime,' I say quietly.

Mother walks over and places a hand on my shoulder. 'The law is the law.'

I nod. 'We can use Vixen to control Danica the way you used Danica to control Rayven. Once we have control of Danica, it's a chain reaction. We'll have control of Rayven again.'

*****

Later, in my bedroom, I laze on my bed with my sketchbook. Pa had insisted that I have a sleep to recover but sleep never finds me so as I lay across my bed, I sketch out images from the last few weeks. Of the pine forests I rode through and the canyon that hid criminals for six months, of Danica and Vixy, of the sand-coloured desert wolves and the rebel woman with the sapphire eyes. Of the nymph and of the black Nataris.

I flinch when a loud thumping knock sounds against the front door. There are soldiers guarding the house, so I know it's not anyone dangerous. I make my way downstairs, checking my appearance in the mirror in the hallway before pulling the door open, revealing Tyke in his usual black attire.

'Hello, brother,' I grin, opening the door for him. 'Come in.'

'Good to see you're still in one piece, brother.' Tyke grins, 'I heard you were back in the smoke again.'

I lead him to the living room, keeping silent until we're seated comfortably.

'The last few weeks have certainly been interesting,' I say, crossing one leg over another as I watch Tyke sitting across from me.

'Danica Arlet Rush, hey? As if.' Tyke shakes his head.

I set my gaze on him. 'How do you know that?'

Tyke shrugs, looking away for a moment. 'I was able to put two and two together.'

I stare at him. 'What was two and two?'

Tyke watches me for a moment. Normally I would have let that sort of information slide by without pushing further. 'She looks like Dimitri. Yes, I do know what Dimitri looks like, I've seen him in Roseguard before.'

I take in a sharp breath. 'And you never cared to tell me?'

He shrugs again, looking away. 'I did tell you, and you took the piss out of me for day drinking.'

Rubbing the back of my neck, I lean back in my chair. 'Okay, that's fair. How else did you figure it out?'

'I know of the rumours from returned soldiers that there was a child on the front line that could take Ritenvold beasts down in the blink of an eye. They called her Danica. Put two and two together, a skilled warrior that looks like Dimitri Rush…? Obviously, his child.'

'And you waited this long to tell me?'

'I didn't figure it out until I saw her.' When she dragged me to my city and paraded around sending death threats to my mother.

'And the Arlet name?'

'You're getting good at listening now.' Tyke laughs and I know that he means that he'd led me down the Dimitri path to avoid talking about the Arlet name. And I had caught onto it. 'Now what was the big scandal with Dimitri? He didn't kill the Nightwalker. Danica has the same eyes as a Nightwalker, and from the rumours, the same heightened senses, strength and speed. So, it is obvious that Dimitri didn't kill the Nightwalker because she was his lover and they had Danica.'

'And the Arlet name?' I repeat and Tyke grins suddenly, and I realise this is now a game to him, to see if I can get the answer out of him.

'Now, why was Danica so important? Why didn't your mother just kill her instead of keeping a deadly pet?' He leans back in his chair. 'Why had we heard nothing from the Queen in the Shadows, and why, every so often, do Nightwalker warriors come snooping around Roseguard?'

'What?' Nightwalkers came snooping around Roseguard?!

'Let me finish.' Tyke is grinning, he's enjoying this. 'Why else would the beasts in the Shadow stay in the Shadow? They could best us any moment, yet there was something important enough for them to stay where they were. It led me to believe that Rayven Arlet must be the mother. So, you see, I worked out that she was Danica Arlet Rush the moment she sat in my booth holding onto your leash.'

I shake my head. 'Why didn't you go to mother?'

'And tell her that I, a commoner, was able to work out that she had somehow been able to capture Rayven Arlet's daughter? No-one knows, Hunter, except for who she chooses.'

I clench my jaw and change the subject. 'Last time we spoke, you mentioned four riders?'

Tyke's eyes narrow on me. 'What about them?'

'When were you planning on reporting to the Red Soldiers that four Narakuya had been to the Underground?' Pa had explained exactly what Falcon and the others are.

Tyke clenches his jaw. 'They've been snooping around for years, always a different bunch.'

'And why didn't you tell Mother or the Red Soldiers.'

'They knew I knew and threatened to slit my throat. And I'm more scared of them than I am of the Red Soldiers.'

It's the first time I have heard Tyke admit to being afraid of anything.

'Turns out they found Danica, so they made camp with me.'

Tyke's eyes go wide.

'Danica Arlet Rush is coming to Roseguard. Prepare yourself, Tyke.'

'Nah, she may come,' Tyke says slowly, 'but it's not like she's got an army to back her up. She's a lone wolf, Hunter. It'd take months for her queen to rally an army and march it here. And besides, she's used to only looking out for herself. On the front line, she only had herself. Why would she turn to people to help her now? She hasn't been to the Shadow or seen her people for at least ten years, and she would have been a child then. Her people will be strangers to her. It'd be easier for her to rely on herself.'

# CHAPTER NINETEEN

## DANICA

We take over a week as we follow the messy trail the Red Soldiers had made in their hurry back to Roseguard. We had managed to track Hunter and discovered that he had found the small army. Caden had tracked the soldiers back to the outskirts of Tialo, the city hidden among the forests, before we regrouped with him. Falcon explained that before the war, Tialo had been home to the Cyclopean, the one-eyed people that were forced to seek refuge in the Shadow. Now, it's inhabited by humans. So many humans everywhere, they had always outnumbered all other species, thanks to how easy it was for them to breed.

We take our time as we ride back to Roseguard. I enjoy the ride, hearing stories from the last ten years and learning about my people and home, realising how much more there is to learn.

Hunter's betrayal angered me, but I realised that I was to blame. I underestimated him and gave him the perfect opportunity to escape, assuming that he relied on me enough to think escaping then surviving the journey back would be impossible.

The days had passed quickly, filled with banter and stories. The journey back to Roseguard didn't present any obstacles and it was easy riding. A day out from Roseguard, we start keeping any eye out for Dimitri, for his near invisible signs. Caden and Ryker would ride ahead each day, looking for those little signs of my father, but as we're drawing closer to Roseguard, I've asked if they can go and investigate what's happening within the city.

The pine trees sway in the breeze as we ride through the forest to the south of Roseguard, the wind carrying the scent of pine and earth.

'The supply routes through Carramera have been unaffected the last decade,' Falcon explains as he rides beside me. 'There were a few issues at the beginning, with the fae folk taking refuge in the Shadow. But some of the half fae were able to remain undiscovered due to their appearances.'

'I heard rumours on the front line that more and more fae were making their way back into Carramera?' I ask as I guide Oak along the trail.

'Aye, the fae glamoured themselves to appear human. Hence why we were able to then continue trading with Ritenvold.' Falcon pauses for a moment, glancing across at me. 'The fae remained glamoured so no harm would come to you.'

I nod. 'And news of Maristela in the last decade?'

'Still unclaimed,' he says.

Crynn speaks up from behind us and I turn to look at him from the saddle. 'I've heard that pirates are to blame for the attacks on Roseguard's soldiers during their trek through the desert.'

Falcon scowls, his face scrunching up in disgust. 'Makes sense, what happens in Asada and Ritenvold doesn't affect them as long as they don't get caught.'

'What was that look for?' I laugh.

'Wait until you meet one of the pirates, then you'll have the same opinion.'

'Right.' I laugh, then take a deep breath in.

The scent of pine and damp soil fills me, along with something else, something almost smoky.

I sit up straight in the saddle, pulling Oak to a halt.

'What is it?' Falcon asks.

I glance between him and Crynn. 'Dimitri is here somewhere.'

Taking another deep breath, I follow the scent, carefully guiding Oak off the trail.

Falcon falls behind me and Crynn takes the rear. We slowly ride through the forest undergrowth following the barely there smoky smell.

Slowly, the scent becomes stronger. I let out a sharp quick whistle. Moments later, a whistle is returned, and I turn Oak towards the sound.

Urging Oak to trot, we create a new path as we follow the sound to a small clearing. The clearing is against a small cliff, with a cave entrance at the base. A small creek trickles out of the cave and into the grassy clearing, to where a horse line has been set up, the brown stallion I had swapped him with grazing but looks up as we walk into the clearing. There is a fire going with a rabbit on a spit roasting. A log is laying near the fire, with Dimitri sitting on it, wearing a loose black cotton shirt, the sleeves rolled up, and dark brown riding pants. His hair is tied back and a sword in its sheath leans against the log beside him.

I jump off Oak and rush forward to hug my father. The scent of burnt wood and citrus is strong as I breath into his shoulder.

'I am so very glad to see you again little warrior.' Dimitri breathes into my neck.

I take another moment, embraced in his arms before stepping back. Dimitri looks me over before smiling.

'I take it your mission was a success, judging from the army that had to do the walk of shame back through the gates three days ago?'

I grin. 'It was successful.'

'Can you go and find the twins?' I glance over my shoulder to Crynn. He nods and vanishes into the forest.

'Good to see you Falc,' Dimitri says. 'I was just about to carve up the rabbit, are you guys hungry?'

'Aye, let me just untack Oak,' I say going to turn back to the stallion.

'It's alright, you sit and have something to eat.' Falcon dismounts and takes Oak's reins. 'I'll take care of Oak.'

I smile at him. 'Thank you.' I say before joining Dimitri on the log and telling him about how the mission went.

*****

It's just as the sun is setting that Crynn and the twins reappear.

I stand as they canter into the clearing and instantly frown at the looks on their faces. Their jaws are clenched, muscles tense, and brows furrowed as they halt their horses.

'What's wrong?'

Dimitri stands up beside me.

They all dismount quickly, Ryker taking the horses to the stream.

Caden looks directly at me. 'Vixy was a red-haired young child, correct?'

My blood goes cold, thoughts emptying out of my head.

Dimitri speaks for me. 'Yes, she is, what is it?'

This time Crynn speaks. 'We watched about two dozen soldiers, half of them severely injured, all mounted on horses return through the gates with a young girl matching Vixy's description tied to a horse. Unfortunately, we only arrived on the eastern side of the city to see them walking through the gates. We weren't able to reach her in time.'

All thoughts empty from my head. The others are still talking but none of it makes sense. I sit back down on the log, my hands holding my head with my elbows on my knees. My heart feels like it has stopped.

Melissa has Vixy. And it was my fault.

I made a mistake provoking Melissa. And it's cost me Vixy's safety.

Dimitri crouches down next to me. 'Listen to me Danica,' he begins. 'We're going to come up with a plan, and we will rescue Vixy.'

Nausea fills my stomach as he rubs my shoulder.

Falcon crouches on my other side. 'We're here to serve you, and I promise you we will rescue Vixy and get her back to safety.

I nod, stand up, shaking off Dimitri and Falcon's hands as I walk into the forest. They follow me and as soon as I am far enough away from the clearing, I crouch over and vomit.

Dimitri rushes over, pulling my hair back and rubbing my back. 'Breathe Danica, breathe through your nose.'

Once I am finished, I take a deep breath, the smell of vomit thick enough that I almost gag.

Dimitri offers me his arm and I lean on him as we walk back to the clearing. My mind is blank as Dimitri sits me gently on the log.

'Falcon, roll out her bedroll.' Dimitri barks commands, 'Crynn, in my saddle bag is a small tin with some tea in it. Please go get it.'

I don't know how much time has passed when Dimitri places a mug of tea in my hands.

'Drink this little warrior,' he says gently, crouching in front of me. 'You're in shock and the best thing you can do is get some sleep.'

I nod and raise the tea to my lips. It tastes a little bit different to what I normally have, and I feel my eyes start to droop as I sit there. It's not long until Dimitri takes my hands and guides me to my bedroll, helping me get under the blankets. Sleep sets in quickly, and the darkness is heavy.

*****

After Roseguard had captured the few that had not returned to Asada's Shadow at the start of the war, they had realised that they would need many more soldiers if they hoped to stand a chance against Ritenvold. So, they had begun recruiting other humans. Many humans spread out across the cities of Asada had joined the Red Army willingly, believing that if *Melissa Cole can banish all the beasts from Asada, we can win against Ritenvold.* They believed that until they realised all they were doing was holding a line against a country that was holding them there with minimal resources.

One of the human representatives in the Salt City had the idea of sending criminals to the front line, impressing and aiding Melissa Cole. Criminals that would be there for a set amount of time were fighting daily, however criminals with a life sentence would get one day each week behind the trenches. A day to rest and recover so the Red Army didn't lose their soldiers to insanity as well as Ritenvold blades.

It was one of my days off, and I had got into a fight with a lowlife criminal twice my age. I'd let myself get a bit beaten up that day, I hadn't wanted to draw the attention of the soldiers. My personal guards had watched with amusement. I didn't care if I got hurt, I just wanted to blow off some steam and forget where I was. Let myself focus on the target before me. It was easier to keep fighting than remembering where I was, who I was.

I had received a fist to the stomach and gone flying into the mud, a punch I had seen coming from a mile away, and I relished in the pain.

When I made myself look up, I saw the older man advancing on me, laughing despite his broken nose. I spat the blood and mud onto him before launching myself at his face, nails tearing skin.

It was when he screamed, like a rabbit in a wolf's mouth, that the soldiers stepped in, and my guards pushed me back. I had let them drag me away, throw me towards the water trough. I had spat at their feet then turned to wash my face. Standing beside it was a young girl with vibrant red hair, watching me like a fox. Like she knew exactly who I was. She looked so out of place, her scared and wary yet curious face watching me carefully.

I asked her what her name was and told her if she wanted to survive, she'd be safest by my side. Hours later when I was huddled against the trench wall hoping for sleep to find me, Vixy had sat down almost silently beside me and given me a small smile. That night I had dreamed of barefoot children dancing between oak trees, moonlight shimmering down on them. I had dreamed of waterfalls and hidden caves, big black war horses grazing in fields, foals at foot. There had been music and laughter. I had woken up crying silently and had looked across at that little girl and realised that I couldn't let her childhood be ruined by war. I wanted her to grow up under oak leaves, laughing and dancing with that smile on her face.

I woke up and knew it was time to fight. Time to fight the Red Soldiers and Melissa Cole. It was time to escape.


*****

I swing my sword towards Dimitri's head, and he ducks just in time, his own sword aimed towards my upper thigh. I leap back and duck to the side, aiming to catch him by surprise. He blocks my long sword with a dagger from his belt. I spin back, my footsteps light as he launches towards me. I take my sword in both hands and swing it towards his neck, and he blocks again, the clang echoing through the forest. I pause, panting, watching Dimitri take a step back.

My head snaps up, hoofbeats echo through the forest, heavy against the ground. Pain lashes through my arm and my attention snaps back to Dimitri as he draws his sword away. He had hit me with the blunt surface of the sword.

'And you're dead.' Dimitri raises an eyebrow. 'I thought I taught you to always focus on what's in front of you.'

'Can you not hear the horses galloping towards us?'

'Aye, I can.' He sheathes his sword. 'It sounds like your mother's scouting party has found us.'

Excitement and nervousness fill me as I sheath my sword and follow Dimitri into the clearing.

My gaze scans the pine trees around us, the ferns, the rocks and the bushes, but nothing meets my trained eye. I turn to look at Falcon, who is now sheathing his own sword but leaves a hand resting on his dagger.

I let my hand rest on my sword. I catch Crynn's gaze, he has a grin on his lips.

The wind whispers through the trees, I frown as I fail to smell anything on the wind. The scouts must be downwind, but near enough to hear the hoofbeats cantering. I become more and more anxious.

I completely freeze when a bird flies from a tree. The horse's footfalls echo through the forest, against the trees, the wind carrying the sound further.

There.

I focus on a flash of black, identifying it as a horse. I try but fail to identify the rider; the trees are too thick to see clearly. I do make out another horse behind the first, and another. A total of seven horses and riders.

The horse at the front, a big black Natari, with an elegantly carved saddle, bridle and breastplate is the first to canter into the clearing. I can feel the weight of the horse's power and strength as his hoofbeats vibrate through the ground. He snorts; his eyes wide as he slows to a trot as he approaches me. I let my gaze travel up, to the woman atop in fighting leathers, oak leaves carved into the leather. There are twin duelling blades at her hips, Moonstone peeking out from between the leather wrapped handle and sheath. A dark cape falling from her shoulders and flows onto the stallion's rump.

Her midnight hair flows behind her with small braids and plaits throughout, her eyes the colour of ice and her skin fair. A crown sits atop of her head, a crown made of Moonstone.

A queen. A queen I would recognise anywhere.

Her eyes meet mine.

My own go wide as I take in the face I haven't seen in almost a decade. The face that I have dreamed of, a face that stopped me from giving up all hope, even in the darkest hours in the trenches, those hours I'd considered that maybe the best option would be to turn the blade on myself. The face that reminded me to keep fighting, whispering words of wisdom from years before. A face that warriors bow to and serve with unquestionable loyalty. A face that has songs sung about it, the face that is my mother's.

'Danica…' she breathes softly.

I open my mouth to say something, anything, but I can't seem to form any words.

I close my eyes and pinch myself. This is real.

'Your Majesty,' Falcon says behind me, bowing his head.

'Mother…' I let out a shaky breath. And despite the day, despite what is at stake, I don't stop the smile from lighting up my face as I race forward to be with my family once again after ten years.

*****

Slowly, we make our way back to where Rayven's army is camped. We ride spaced apart, with Falcon and a rider I don't recognise far ahead, scouts on either side and more riders trailing at a distance. Rayven and Dimitri on either side of me, and as we walk through the forest my mother quietly explains what had happened all those years ago.

Rayven had never guessed that Melissa would retaliate when Asada's army refused to offer her aid. Asada's Queen had never considered that her enemy would have been bold enough to take on Ritenvold with only an army of humans to aid her. Sure, the human population was much greater than all other species combined, but it was still a fool's move. Yet,

Melissa was cunning and knew Rayven's weakness, knew what to do to keep Rayven from making a move against Melissa. That was me.

The maid that had put me to bed ten years ago while my mother was negotiating terms after the assassination of Luca Vold, had been a spy for Melissa Cole. And Melissa knew that Rayven would get in contact with Ritenvold and plead with them not to attack Asada for my safety. To simply hold the line. What Melissa hadn't anticipated was that Ritenvold would be able to hold the line for a decade. She had believed that with my safety a concern, her soldiers would have easily been able to best Ritenvold.

When she had kidnapped me, Melissa knew that, despite my age and training, I would have bested that defenceless maid easily. And I did, especially when I shifted into my *killing calm*. With Celestial's blood coursing through the veins of the royal family, my forefathers, Rayven and I were stronger than other Narakuya.

Before Rayven had left for Roseguard, she had warned me that the way I lived was going to change greatly and I would have to be brave, especially as the heir to the Moonstone crown. I realise now that her warning had come from a very different belief, and because of what had happened I thought it had meant to keep my head bowed and behave for my mother's sake on the front line.

And for the past ten years, while Rayven waited for me to break out of the front line when I was ready to challenge Melissa, to prove to the leader of Roseguard where my loyalties lay, Rayven prepared her hidden army just inside the Shadow.

Before the war, Ritenvold had been a strong and powerful kingdom. The people were always patriotic towards their royal family, with few issues between species, but they always kept themselves within their borders, so Rayven was able to provide intel to the Ritenvold army. The plan was to keep Roseguard busy enough until I could escape, and when I was no longer in the firing line, we'd smash Roseguard together.

When I ask how she knew I had escaped the front line, she explains about the dark green smoke Hunter and I had seen when chasing down the Red Soldiers. Unknown to many, including myself, the Narakuya have a bonfire in each kingdom. Alchemists had created a powder, that when fed to the flames, would turn the smoke a particular colour. It would alert other Narakuya that an event of great significance had occurred. The other kingdoms had different coloured powders to add to their bonfires.

When Rayven saw the green smoke rising above the mountains, she began marching the army straight to Roseguard's front doors. Rayven knew that the only reason the fire would have been lit, would be to announce that I was free.

As Rayven's army isn't as big as Roseguard's, it can easily hide in the forests south-west of the city, with scouts watching Roseguard and the many species making up Rayven's loyal forces not complaining about the rough living.

A tent had already been set up for me, including a bath brimming with warm water. I spend longer than necessary in my tent, bathing and recovering before striding through the camp. All the Narakuya, cyclopean, centaurs, minotaurs, satyrs, shapeshifters and werewolves do a double take before acknowledging me as I make my way past. When I arrive at the main tent, Rayven, Dimitri, Falcon and a few others are inside. I sit down and tell them my story and my plan to get Vixy back.

# CHAPTER TWENTY

## HUNTER

I stare out of my bedroom window, the window that overlooks part of the city. I've been standing here for a while, and I don't move when the door opens quietly, the clicking of heels making their way through the door.

'It's quite impressive, those caves that Danica made for herself,' I say, and for a moment I try to imagine if I would have been able to do what she and Vixy did.

'Those creatures will turn anything into something they can use to their advantage,' Mother says from behind me. 'Like you. She turned you into a hostage.'

I shake my head at the fact before turning to face mother. 'And the nymph that was living with them?'

'No sign of it.'

I don't say anything for a moment, then blurt out everything on my mind. 'Danica is going to come for Vixen, and she's going to do it the only way she knows how, with all swords out. She's currently with four Nightwalkers who are completely loyal and would step in front of an arrow for her.'

Mother watches me carefully. 'Why are you so anxious about this Hunter?'

'I'm anxious? How are you not?' Mother doesn't say anything, so I give her my reason, her reason to be anxious. 'Because Dimitri Rush has gone to find Danica's mother. We no longer have a leash on Rayven Arlet.'

'I am aware of that, Hunter,' Mother says, 'And I have prepared for it.'

'What?'

'Walk with me.' Mother turns on her heel and strides out of the room, shoulders back like a queen.

She doesn't say anything as we climb into a carriage that takes us to the Red Guard Towers. The doors are opened for us and Mother aims for one of the small barracks that I have never visited before. I raise an eyebrow as she produces a key. She pulls the doors back to reveal a staircase heading down, torches lit on the wall.

Mother pulls a torch off the wall and begins the descent. I follow warily.

'Did you really think I would not be prepared should Rayven decide to march on Roseguard?' Mother glances over her shoulder at me before turning to look back to where she is taking us. 'Rayven would not have sat in her Moonstone Palace for ten years twiddling her thumbs, hoping Danica wasn't killed on the front line. The Narakuya are faster, stronger, more powerful than us humans. And the ordinary Narakuya are feeble in comparison to those of the royal bloodline, with each royal child more powerful than the last. No, Rayven knew that Danica would survive, the only one able to kill Danica would be her equal, as an heir to the crown is always more powerful than their parents.'

'And is there anyone of equal power to Danica?' I ask, glancing down at my feet as the stairs change from stone tiles to plain rock.

'None in Asada,' Mother pauses for a moment, considering her next words carefully. 'Ritenvold has always had a strong and peaceful relationship between their humans and Narakuya, as the Ritenvold throne has always been powered by one with Narakuya blood that flows back to the original queen, Zodia. To keep the humans of Ritenvold from rebelling, Zodia married a human man named Tanix Vold. The Narakuya blood is always more dominant, and therefore, the heirs would usually marry a human. Occasionally they would marry another Narakuya to strengthen the bloodline again, but usually human. The only one possibly capable of defeating Danica would be King Darius and Queen Ada's child, Prince Luca Vold.'

'But you had Luca Vold assassinated.'

'Correct.'

'Why?'

'When Ada died during childbirth, so did the Narakuya's queen. I thought it would cause a war between the humans and Narakuya, but I was wrong.' I notice Mother duck her head as she finishes her statement, and I refrain from making a comment as I know how ashamed she is of her overconfidence in her belief.

We continue down the stairs in silence for a while.

'Would the Ritenvold army ally with Danica?' I ask cautiously as we reach a door.

'I made the wrong choice once before and was not prepared.' Mother unlocks the door then says, 'I will not be unprepared again. I have requested an alliance with another species that could pose a considerable threat to the Narakuya, should they have an army large enough, but they have yet to confirm or arrive.'

'What species?'

Mother looks at me out of the corner of her eye. 'Think, Hunter. The only magic wielders in Asada, who are greedy and would wish to have their own city. A species who does not wish to bow their heads to anyone stronger. The Fae. Unfortunately, the Narakuya have a natural defence against the small magic that the Fae are able to conduct, but they are stronger, faster and stand a better chance than humans. I have offered them Carramera in return for their alliance.'

I'm about to push for more details, but my breath catches as I take in the sight behind Mother as she pulls the door open.

Inside is a cavern, cliffs reaching high, and I realise as my gaze trails up, that this is the bottom of Thorn Gap, the river winding through the cavern, flowing fast from the waterfall at the far end. The sound of the waterfall is deafening, almost disguising the sound of the clanging steel and yelling from the camp. On either side of the river are thousands of

Red Soldiers camped, training, practicing. The scent of smoke and sweat is thick down here.

'How?' I gaze at the army, the rose and shield banners blowing in the wind. Any previous thought about this new alliance is gone from my mind when I behold this massive army.

'Rayven Arlet spent ten years preparing her army. So did I.'

'But … the front line?'

'The front line is where we send our criminals, our undesirable and disloyal soldiers. Clearing out the villages kept the front line from wondering why they only had enough soldiers to hold the line. The last six months, since Danica escaped the front line, we've been recruiting soldiers from every city and sending them here to prepare for war.'

'But how have you been able to keep this quiet? Feeding hundreds of thousands of people?'

'There's another entrance to the cavern, on the north side of Thorn Gap. But that entrance is guarded at all times and is going to be destroyed shortly.'

'Why didn't you tell me about any of this?' I frown at mother.

'Because I love you and I wanted to keep you safe. And you were still learning. I was going to explain everything once you got back from investigating how Danica escaped.' Mother looks at me. 'Come, we have the girl down here.'

'Vixen Kyler?'

A nod before mother marches through the soldiers, heading towards the wall. I notice all the glances towards us, the small dips of chins, of acknowledgement as Mother walks past. I want that. I want that respect.

'I'm impressed Mother, I really am.'

She sends me a sly smile, and I grin back.

The wall has small cell-like caves dug into it with bars across the front. The first cell is empty and I can't help but reach out and touch the metal bars, smooth and cool against my skin and a shiver runs down my spine. I run my hand over the stone wall beside it with bones cemented into it, rough beneath my fingers.

'Basilisk bones.'

I snatch my hand back as if those bones were still alive, as I spin to look at Mother. 'What?'

'Rayven slaughtered this one herself, when she was Danica's age.' Mother walks along the row of cells.

I had only seen drawings of basilisks, huge snakelike creatures. If you stared into one's eyes, it would hypnotise you, making you easy prey.

'So, Rayven knows about this place?'

'Yes but, she doesn't know that I have access to it, though.'

Mother is silent as she comes to a stop in front of a cell. I bite my lip, guilt in the bottom of my stomach as I look down at a small red head huddled in the corner. Mother quietly unlatches one of the doors, and I push my shoulders back as I walk between the cage bars before crouching down a distance away.

'Hey Vix.'

Vixy looks up at me and my blood goes cold as I spy the bruising over her face. She turns to look at Mother over my shoulder before turning to stare at the wall. My eyes go to the piece of metal in the shape of a small wave that hangs on a leather strap around Vixy's neck. Danica had given that to her before she left, promising her that it would keep her safe. I need that more than her.

'Vixy …' I hesitate, not sure what to say.

'The girl hasn't really said much since the desert.' Mother leans against the bar behind me.

'Vixy, I can help you,' I try quietly, inching a step closer.

'I should have listened to Danica,' Vixy mumbles, and I cringe, understanding what she means by that. She should have dug a grave that day.

'Hey, I haven't forgotten that you called those wolves off to save me, so I'll help you in return, if you help me.' I hesitate, unsure how much she'd know about Danica. 'It's about Danica, she is more dangerous than you realise Vix.'

'Danica says there are two types of monsters in this world. Killers and liars. I think there is only one, the liars. Danica may be a killer, but she'll never lie. You, however, you are the biggest liar I have ever met.' Vixy turns to look at me. 'The nymph spoke to me only once, when we first arrived at the cliffs. She said I can always trust a Moon Child. I didn't know what she meant then, but she was talking about Danica. I've always known Danica was something more than human. But she is not a monster.'

'Vixy …'

'Leave me alone.'

She turns back to the wall and I sigh, getting up. I hesitate for a moment, then as quick as anything, I snatch the leather strap with the metal fragment from her neck. Vixy tries to grab the piece back, but I hold it out of reach, not failing to notice the chains keeping her attached to the wall.

'You should have cooperated with me, Vixen,' I say and leave the cell, my head spinning and my guts churning. Danica is the monster, not me!

I put her necklace in my pocket.

Mother is standing outside. 'She said more then, than she has since we caught her.' She turns to look out over the army, her black hair swinging around her neck. 'You know Danica Arlet Rush best, what do you think she'll do?'

I bite my bottom lip slightly before answering, fear now in the bottom of my stomach. 'She's going to come for Vixen Kyler, and she's going to try to kill us.'

*****

After hours spent in the war rooms, discussing every possible way Danica will retaliate, we finally decide that the best strategy is to set her up and herd her towards the Red Towers. She will come barging into the city, swords out, demanding what she thinks she is owed. And so, we wait for her to make her move.

# Chapter Twenty-One

## Danica

If Hunter thinks he can play a game of power with me … then I'll show him how it's played. And I'll show him and his mother exactly who I am. Melissa would believe that my reaction would be to attack with everything I have, like I had been trained to on the front line. She would expect me to make a rash, hasty decision to go straight to Vixy without thinking it through, as I had jumped into armies without thinking it through. She would be ready for me to come marching straight through Roseguard's city doors, killing anyone that stands in my way. She will forget that I am not just a mindless soldier.

Hours later, after discussion with my parents, Falcon, Crynn and some of Asada's best warriors on the countless ways we could retrieve Vixy and eliminate Melissa Cole, I decide on a plan. It's quite simple, a plan that Melissa and Hunter would never see coming, and one that will make them question their own values as well as how well they think they know me. My plan will also offer me the opportunity to learn how much sway Hunter holds over his mother.

As the sun dips below the tree line, I get dressed for revenge and envision every possible outcome should my plan go wrong. Should I get caught before even arriving, what I will do if I am ambushed, what I can do if there are unknown traps…

Sitting on my small bed, I braid my hair, five single braids finishing just above my hips. My hair has grown dramatically since leaving the front line; we had been required to keep our hair short, and mine had been pushing the boundaries when I had escaped, just below my shoulders. It moves through my fingers like water, smooth and silky against my skin. My health had also improved after escaping as well. My hair had been thin and brittle, the ends snapping easily and I could count my ribs from a distance. They had only fed the bare minimum to keep me fighting and I remember nights feeling so hungry that I felt nauseous.

Finishing the last braid and tying it off, I stand, stretching my arms out. The soft floor mat tickles my bare feet as I walk across to the small table next to the bath and reach for the little wooden box resting there. The wood is smooth under my fingers, and I open the lid to expose the small sticks of kohl. I stare at it for a moment, debating whether I should change my appearance.

The women in the Underground had worn thick black eye makeup. It would make my ice eyes pop, however if I avoided eye contact I would look like all the other humans there, dancing and moving their bodies to the music. I pick up a small handheld mirror and a piece of kohl, grimacing at the feel of the rough flaky stick. It's awkward drawing the lines on my eyelids, trying to make sure both sides are even, and I don't like the feel of the rough stick so close to my eyes. The black lines beneath my eyes and on my lids are thin, the contrast of my ice eyes and the dark kohl makes me worry I have gone too heavy with my attempt at makeup. I try to blend the dark substance with my finger. It takes me longer than I would have liked before I am happy with the look I have created.

Next, I lift the red paint to my lips, coating them to match the ruby banners of Roseguard. I also find some jewellery in another little box. I silently thank whoever set up my tent as they really did make sure to pack anything I could need! I stare at a pair of earrings, beautiful little diamonds. I don't have my ears pierced like the women in Roseguard, like some of the females in my own camp. I lift one small earring to my lobe, then, holding my ear with my other hand, I grit my teeth and punch the metal through the skin and out the other side. It stings for a moment before fading, and a drop of red blood spills onto my shoulder. I do the same on the other side before wiping away the blood.

A bird calls, reminding me that I want to be ready to go just after dusk. I browse through the small drawers in the tent, finding something suitable to wear. Something I can fight in, yet something that suits the Underground. I pull out a plain singlet and pull it over my head, the fabric soft against my skin. It's a deep black material, no sleeves, with thin straps, yet it sits perfectly, exposing a little bit of my cleavage without feeling like it will slide down. Finding a skirt in the drawers, I hold it up in front of me, it's long, black and with a slit up one leg. I wiggle out of my pants and pull the skirt on, the material is light and silky. The skirt finishes by my ankles, with the slit running all the way up my leg to just below my hip. At least it won't restrict my movement.

I take a deep breath, pull my leather jacket on over the top before buckling my boots up. I count each blade as I strap them on to myself, hidden under my clothes and in my boots.

Stepping outside my tent, I take in a deep breath, the cool breeze of sunset kissing my face and making me shiver. The clanging of metal, the crackling of fires, the voices talking quietly and birds whistling in the trees fills the camp.

Walking over to the meeting tent, I notice the stares of my people, the Narakuya watch me carefully, as if they're not sure who I am, if I am sane. The centaurs all dip their heads towards me in respect, and I offer them a smile. The satyrs all grin at me, and the werewolves watch me as I walk past. I probably look ridiculous in these clothes.

I spy Crynn standing by a small cart pulled by two Nataris. He's wearing a black buttoned-down shirt and black pants, and despite looking quite plain, I know he will have daggers strapped to him beneath the clothes. As I approach, he turns around, holding a quiver of arrows.

He whistles, 'Damn, Danica!' and I let out a laugh, tension relieving from my shoulders.

'What Crynn meant to say was you look lovely, Danica,' Ryker laughs from behind me and I turn to see him carrying coiled up rope. He places it into the cart before climbing in.

'You look lovely,' Crynn grins and gives me a dramatic bow.

I elbow him in the ribs. 'Well, you scrub up alright yourself.'

He places a hand over his heart, 'thank you, Princess.' He says sarcastically.

'Is everything ready?'

'Aye, just waiting on Caden with the hessian sheet and Falc, wherever he is.' Crynn rolls his eyes as he mentions Falcon's name.

'He's probably talking to the Queen.' Ryker adds as he continues sorting out gear in the back of the cart. I narrow my eyes at his comment. We had already discussed all necessary details.

'Ah, here he comes,' Crynn nods towards someone approaching from behind me.

I turn to see Falcon walking towards us.

'Hey.'

Falcon pauses as he looks at me, his eyes travelling over my body, slowly, pausing at the exposed skin on my leg. I can feel warmth spreading across my cheeks. He doesn't say anything, just watches me and I force myself to swallow, I don't know what to do.

'Is everyone ready?' Caden's voice breaks the tension, and I tear my gaze away from Falcon.

'Sure am.' I turn and climb into the cart.

'Danica!'

I look up and see my parents striding towards us.

Rayven looks like a goddess, in tight fitting black clothing and leather armour, she walks with purpose, never hesitating and never doubting herself. Dimitri is wearing his usual attire, however with a cape strapped to his shoulders and is a step behind Rayven, always respecting her position and her power, but always there to guard her back.

Rayven reaches us and I crouch down at the edge of the cart, eye level with her.

'Ritenvold scouts arrived an hour ago, the army will not be far behind. If they have spare riders, we shall send them to assist with your return from Roseguard.'

'Good. I don't think we should need them, but it'll be comforting to know that if the plan goes array, we will have back up.'

'Full moon tonight, be careful my child.' Rayven nods her head, her gaze piercing as she watches me carefully. I don't know what she is looking for, but I hope that I can prove that I am worthy of being her daughter.

She takes my hand, squeezing it tight. She knows better than to try to get me to stay behind. I am a warrior; I fought for my enemy and came out the other side.

'It's no fun without a bit of danger,' I add, letting one corner of my mouth grin.

Rayven matches my small grin, wickedness in her eyes.

Dimitri shakes his head. 'You're too much like your mother. Don't do anything reckless and prioritise your safety above all else.'

Rayven and Dimitri step back, so I nod my head once before the rest of my team take up their positions. Caden at the reins, the rest of us in the tray of the cart. We lay down strategically, and Caden throws hessian rags over us, hiding us. The hessian is itchy against my skin and I crinkle my nose as I realise that there will be no reprieve from the material until we reach Roseguard.

We make our way towards Roseguard at a slow, steady pace, and we pass through the forest and fields with no trouble. We aim to arrive just as the night life of Roseguard starts up. Hunter doesn't know I can sneak through a city. All I can hear is the rattle of the cart, the footfalls of the horses and Caden's quiet commands. As we get closer to Roseguard, the sound of city life gets louder and louder, my heart rate increasing as the cart slows to a stop. We've made it to Roseguard's walls.

'What you got there, boy?' I hear a soldier say.

'Venison.' Caden leans back, smacking Ryker a couple of times, and I smirk under the hessian as he glares at me. 'Got to get it to Artie's restaurant so he can prepare it for tomorrow. You know how Artie gets about late deliveries.'

Silence for a moment.

'Clear.'

I let out a breath as the cart rolls forward.

I can hear the quiet chatter of the city, horses' hooves on stone, pans clanging. The air is thick with smoke, sweat, spices and animals, vastly different to the camp hidden in the forest. The smoke here is foul and smothering, the animals wail with irritation. A stark change from the forest where the smoke is soothing, and the animals' sighs are content.

The noises fade as Caden pulls into a quiet alley, and I stay laying down between Falcon and Ryker until Caden pulls the hessian from us.

We don't say anything as we quickly climb out, Caden waits by the cart as our getaway, the plan now in motion. Ryker heads to the wall of a red brick building, looking up as he prepares to climb to the rooftops. He will keep an eye on the surrounding streets to make sure we won't be ambushed.

I bite my lip and pull my hood over my head as Falcon, Crynn and I make our way along the streets of Roseguard, keeping to the shadows and taking our time as we aim for the Underground. I keep my senses aware, ready for a trap of any sort. Hunter knows I'm coming, and Melissa will be prepared. We pass a few others, yet none give us a second look.

We arrive at the bridge and slip through the door. I cringe as our footsteps echo down the stairs until we finally reach the second door at the bottom. I push my hood back, and pull my jacket off, carefully folding it and placing it in the corner by the door. Quietly, Crynn steps in front, pushes the door open and vanishes inside. Moments later, four knocks sound on the door and Falcon and I step through. Crynn has the security guard knocked out and hidden in a black sheet, the same colour as the walls. Inside, despite being just the start of another long night in the Underground, there are enough people that the guard in the corner won't be noticed. My plan relies on Hunter not being here; on him being safely by his mother's side.

We split up as we move through the crowd. Not one person looks twice as we stalk across the dance floor, like wolves stalking their prey, heading for the farthest booth. Halfway across the dance floor, a hand grabs my wrist. Instinct kicks in and I twist my wrist out of the grasp of the other and reach for a blade.

'Can I buy you a drink?' a man says before my blade makes an appearance. I can tell he's already drunk and hasn't comprehended that he has lost his grip on me.

I take a good look at the man. Attractive, but quite a bit older than me.

'I can buy you every single bottle of wine in this fine establishment, my lady.' The man leans in.

I lean in and whisper in his ear. 'Touch me again, and I will gut you like a rabbit.'

He pulls away, concentrating hard I let myself start to fall into my *killing calm* – only pulling back into my humanlike body when my canines have lengthened and my pupils disappeared, my eyes becoming wholly white.

The man stumbles backwards, glances around and by the time he's looking at me again, my eyes are back to normal, and my teeth are human like once more.

He blinks, staring at me.

'Have a lovely night.' I smile and turn on my heel.

By the time I reach the booth, Falcon is already waiting. I grin at him as we pause to prepare ourselves for what might be on the other side of the curtain. The music is loud, almost deafening, but I can still hear two men talking over the music. One of them is distinctly Tyke Carter, with his rough drawl.

I unsheathe my dagger and keep it hidden beside me. I wait on the side I know Tyke will be sitting on, the side where he will have his back to the wall. Falcon stands on the other side, Crynn has returned from doing a lap around the club, checking for any hidden traps and he stands prepared between the two of us, at the head of the table once the curtain is drawn back.

We wait casually at the sides of the booth until a young man finally pushes the curtains back, he looks us over once and aims for the dance floor as Falcon slips in in his place. I push through the curtain, sliding in next to Tyke with the dagger aimed at his throat. I let it rest against the stubbled skin on his neck.

The woman on Tyke's other side opens her mouth.

'Make a noise and you're dead.' Falcon smirks, more intimidating than serious.

She wisely shuts her mouth, shaking.

Tyke's face pales as he looks over at Falcon once before returning his eyes to me.

I watch as he moves a hand under the table in my peripheral vision.

My own hand ducks under the table, grabbing Tyke's dagger, and passing it to Falcon.

'I know who you are, Danica.' Tyke leans back in his booth, his face still pale but he changes his demeanour to look relaxed. 'Have you come to get your revenge?'

'Aye,' I say, 'You're smart enough to know that your best chance of survival is to do exactly as I say.'

'Why?' He runs his eyes up and down my body in the way any man would, and I know he does it to ignite my temper, to make me slip up. With him acting relaxed, it undermines my power, my authority over him and he knows it. 'Who says I want to survive?'

'You're not in a position to be asking questions.' Falcon laughs, matching his behaviour.

'I think you and I, Tyke, have come to realise that we are more or less the same. The Underground is your personal hunting ground. What we hunt is different, but nonetheless, we both hunt, making us both predators. Prey will accept death, a rabbit will freeze if it believes it cannot survive, but a wolf will fight. Now, you're going to stand up and walk with us. Walk as if everything is normal. Your little girl in the corner will come as well.' I nod at the girl, then look at her a second time.

It's Klara.

'You!' I laugh. 'Well, I certainly didn't expect to see you again.' I turn back to Tyke. 'Anyway, Klara comes too. Both of you will die if one of you tries anything silly, because to me it doesn't matter if you're alive or dead, I just need your body.'

I stand up, pushing Tyke in front of me. One arm slides around him, the other rests under his jacket with the dagger, the blade aimed to slide straight under his ribs. Falcon moves into a similar position around Klara before leaving a note on the table. Tyke stretches his neck, tilting his head to both sides and I know he can feel the blade against his ribs as he casually rests his arms around my shoulder. I swallow, this wasn't part of the plan.

'We'll if this is the closest I'll get to a princess, then I may as well make the most of it.' Tyke whispers in my ear. His thumb begins stroking the skin above my breast and I glance up at him to see a grin on his face.

'Mmm, make the most of it while you can.' I hiss back.

I refuse to look at Falcon as we begin making our way across the dance floor, people moving out of our way, but no-one does a double take.

'You know,' Tyke whispers into my ear. 'We could have been really good friends.' His finger brushes the skin between my collarbone and breast, my skin tingling in its wake.

'Oh I am sure we could have been really good *friends*.' I don't give him the satisfaction of looking uncomfortable at the contact. 'You, a manager of a shady club, me, a princess of a kingdom … I couldn't imagine a better *friendship*.'

'It works quite well for Hunter.'

Now I turn to look at him. 'You know the type of person Hunter is, why are you friends with him? You don't strike me as the type of man to be friends with a coward.'

He raises an eyebrow at me. 'And what type of man do I strike you as?'

I give him a little jab with my dagger, not enough to draw blood, but enough to remind him who is in charge.

He rolls his eyes at me, and I almost laugh at the audacity.

But he continues, 'Yes, I don't normally befriend people like Hunter, but I also know it's good to have a friends in a position of power, hence why I think we would make good *friends*.' He says that word again, implying that we'd be anything but just friends.

Crynn opens the door for us, and we walk through. Klara goes first, followed by Falcon who raises an eyebrow at me, glancing at Tyke. I know he would have heard everything. I pull my blade back from Tyke and he gives me a grin.

'Ladies first.'

'In that case, after you.' I grin back.

He only raises an eyebrow before walking through the door. I grab my jacket, and I hear Crynn close the door behind us.

'You know, Dancia darling, I think the Coles have underestimated you.' I grimace as the name he calls me, remembering when Hunter had called me that name the last time we were here.

'They always did.'

He glances over his shoulder. 'I never did.' He gives me a wink and I let my face go completely blank.

'Did you predict getting kidnapped tonight?' I ask, as I follow him up the stone staircase.

'Admitting to your crime, I'm impressed.' He says. 'I did, I was so looking forward to seeing the gorgeous princess again. I cleared out the rest of my schedule for you.'

I snort, 'you're so full of shit.'

'Does he ever shut up?' Crynn asks from behind me.

'Apparently not.' I huff.

'Danica loves the sound of my voice.' Tyke says.

'And I would love to cut out your tongue right now.' Crynn growls.

Tyke pauses and turns back to face me.

'You wouldn't want to disappoint your princess, would you?' A wicked smirk forms on his lips. 'Dancia likes my tongue.'

I choke on air.

Falcon spins around in front of Tyke and grabs him by the back of the neck, lifting and slamming him into the wall. Tykes face is to the wall and Falcon squeezes his hand. Tyke's arms instinctively try to free himself as what I can see of his face starts to turn red.

'Disrespect the princess again, and you'll lose more than your tongue.' Falcon growls, his voice echoing along the stairway.

He then let's go and Tyke drops to the floor, glaring at Falcon, who turns his attention back to Klara.

'No rest breaks,' I say, kicking him with my toe.

He's silent the rest of the way up the stairs.

At the top, the door opens as Klara steps through and his greeted by Caden and Ryker. They quickly bind rope around Klara and Tykes hands before pushing them forward and into the cart. Ryker is quick to hogtie the two humans as Crynn and Falcon climb in. I pull my jacket back on and then climb in so I'm laying with my face to Tyke's, watching him. He winks at me and I roll my eyes.

Caden takes up the driver's seat again after pulling the hessian over us, and we make our way out of the city. Pressed between Falcon and Tyke, I listen to the horse's hooves and the cart wheels echo along the streets as voices get louder, as the city smells drift over us.

At the city walls, we stop.

I hold my breath, my eyes meet Klara's over Tyke's shoulder.

She's shaking slightly. I shake my head at her. Ryker is behind her, and I meet his pale eyes.

'Oi!' We hear a soldier say. 'What you got there?'

'A couple of bags of cattle grain,' Caden lies smoothly.

Klara starts shaking more violently in fear and I glare at her. Caden must have noticed, as he shoves her a few times, allowing Ryker to shift in the cart, moving so his arms encompass her, squeezing her tightly to stop her from shaking. Ryker's shift is impossible to notice with Caden distracting the movement.

'Mind if we check boy?' My blood freezes. 'It's a bit late at night to be out shopping. And that doesn't look like grain.'

'What does it look like then?' Caden asks in a wary tone.

'Why have you got the rug covering your *grain*?'

'Because it'll stop the rain from damaging the grain.'

'It's a clear night.'

'I have a long way to travel.' Caden starts to sound irritated.

'Where are you travelling to boy?'

'Farmland just south of the Salt City.'

Silence for a moment.

'Protocol, still going to have to check your load.'

A whistle from one of the soldiers and our cart suddenly lurches forward, soldiers yelling and Caden encouraging the horse on.

A different pitched whistle fills the air and that's my cue to climb to my knees, the hessian falling away, and I reach for my bow in place behind Caden's seat. The last thing I need is the soldiers' arrows hitting my team.

Falcon passes me a quiver and I pull an arrow out, nocking it before looking down along its length. I sight the first soldier, standing on the bridge above the gate and I release my fingers, the soldier falls over the wall. I pull another arrow out of the quiver, Crynn does the same on the other side of Klara. Instinct and years of practice take over, loading and releasing arrows is second nature. Soldiers aim at us, and I don't hesitate as I down one soldier after another. I keep my hand steady, my breath even and always, in the back of my mind, Dimitri's lessons of archery.

Mounted soldiers give chase, the horses galloping fast. The horses will gain ground quickly, and with our horses having to tow all of us in a wagon; the extra weight will slow them down significantly.

The moving targets are harder, but not difficult. I aim for their mount, an arrow for the chest. The first horse falls, flipping forward over itself and crushing the rider beneath. The other soldiers go around and continue to chase.

The sound of hoofbeats is heavy and shouting loud. The full moon is bright and gives me so much visibility to aid in our escape. Rider after rider fall from their saddles, horses tumbling and crashing to the ground.

After I use the last arrow in my quiver, I reach for Caden's quiver, Falcon having it ready for me. Slowly the distance between us and the city walls increases, the soldiers still gaining.

'Will we make it to the forest before the soldiers?' I shout over the wind to Caden.

'By ten yards,' Caden's reply comes.

The soldiers continue to gain, only fifty or so left. A thump sounds in my ears as a bolt hits the wood of the cart beside me and I sight the soldier who released it. He has a crossbow, and his horse gallops in a steady line as he loads another wooden and steel bolt. He lifts the weapon and aims it towards us. I release mine as he releases his. I watch as my arrow hits home, and pain bursts through my stomach. I glance down; the thick bolt is lodged above my right hip. I gauge how far we have before we make it to the forest, twenty yards as a burning sensation begins to fill my stomach.

I keep going, nocking and releasing, another horse comes crashing down, its rider beneath it. Another arrow releases from my fingertips and a soldier falls back on his horse, his stirrup coming loose and he falls to the ground. An arrow lodges itself in another soldier's throat.

The pain is stinging in my stomach, but I ignore it. I've had worse. I continue protecting my team until there are only about thirty riders left as we enter the forest.

I look down at the bolt in my stomach, its bleeding, the blood dribbling down onto my bare leg. The bolt is too thick to snap the end off.

I glance at our prisoners, both fortunately still alive.

Tyke grins at me, 'that wound will kill you.'

I take a deep breath and lower myself to the cart floor. Falcon rushes to my side, having heard his comment.

Meeting Tyke's stare, I grin at him. 'You forget that I am not human.'

His smirk disappears.

Falcon lifts my hand off the wound, inspecting the protruding end of the bolt.

'You're losing a lot of blood,' Falcon presses a cloth to the wound. 'That one will knock you out if you're not careful. It'll take your body longer to recover from the blood loss than the injury.'

I nod my head, my eyes closed. 'How many more soldiers?'

'Don't you worry about the soldiers, Crynn's got it covered.'

'Where's my bow?' I ask, 'I'm good for another five minutes.'

'No.' Falcon orders, 'Ryker! Help me get her up next to Caden.'

Ryker lifts me, a hand around my back and another under my legs. Falcon helps place me in the front seat as the horses gallop through the forest. The arrows have slowed with the trees, however the soldiers have not given up their chase.

'Crynn, keep picking off the soldiers.' Falcon orders, 'Caden, make sure none follow us back to camp.'

I glance back. Falcon, Crynn and Ryker are all knelt in the cart with bows drawn. Tyke and Klara are still hogtied.

I squeeze my eyes shut and take a deep breath, focusing on not shifting into my *killing calm,* into my true form, where the pain would be more bearable, and the blood flow would slow significantly.

'How are you going Danica?' Caden asks.

'The sooner we get to camp, the better. It won't be long until I black out.' I grit my teeth.

'Danica,' Falcon says, suddenly beside me. 'I need you to look at me.'

I open my eyes and stare at his pale blue ones.

'We've still got a while to go, so I'm going to bandage you up as best I can until we get back to the camp.' He watches me carefully.

I nod and pull my hand and the cloth back, blood soaking into the sleeve of my jacket. He presses some dark material to my wound, to the bolt, and I groan again, fire flooding my body again, and I grip the wooden seat beneath. He goes through the emergency pack Ryker takes with him everywhere and finds a bandage. Falcon pulls my singlet up, bandaging the wound and around the end of the bolt. Every bump sends splinters of pain through my body as the horses canter further into the forest.

'The bolt has to stay in until we can get you to a healer. Otherwise, you'll black out for a week,' Falcon says, and I groan. I know already, first rule of impalement, even though we heal quickly, there is still a chance of infection.

Closing my eyes, I take a deep breath, and gasp as pain shoots through me.

'You good Danica?' He asks, keeping one of his bloodied hands against my wound.

'I'm fine,' I murmur, feeling dizzy and nauseous. 'How much longer have we got?'

'A fair while.'

'How many soldiers left?'

'Twenty or so, they've dropped right back.' He rubs my shoulder. 'They've realised that if they get too close, Crynn will pick them off. They no longer have safety in numbers and will try to be a bit smarter about approaching.'

I open my eyes again and lean back. The sound of horses behind us fades. The soldiers are still following, but the forest is thick here and they don't know if we've set an ambush. I can feel my body wanting to black out.

I take in the forest before me and the hair on the back of my neck pricks; my senses go on high alert. Adrenaline shoots through my body again, pain flaring. I'm not sure which of my senses have picked it up, but I know we're not alone. I nudge Falcon who instantly sits up.

'Slow the horses, Caden.'

The horses come down to a trot and my eyes scan the forest once, twice before I pick up a black horse leg, I pull the reins from Caden, stopping the horses as my eyes run up the horse's black leg to meet pale ice eyes, almost white. The eyes watch me through the trees, hidden from all but me, and I feel as if the world could end and begin anew, and I wouldn't notice as long as I watched those eyes, the person behind them. I stay frozen, not thinking, the pain temporarily forgotten.

An arrow hits the side of the wood cart, jolting me out of my stupor, and I blame it on the injury.

'No-one move.' I struggle to lean over and inspect the arrow, spying three white strips beside the black feathers. 'It's Ritenvold scouts,' I say quietly, not moving as my eyes go back to find the ice eyes. They've disappeared.

All Narakuya in Ritenvold know of the symbol on the arrow. Scout groups will fire an arrow within distance of someone they cannot identify, and if it happens to be another Narakuya, they'll be able to read the arrow as a scout's *identify yourself* message and a warning to do as they ask.

In the back Klara starts panicking and tries to move towards the back of the cart, despite the rope. Fortunately, Ryker overpowers her quickly.

I scan the area for the ice eyes again, but to no luck. So, I say as clearly as I can remember in the Language of the Moon, the True Language, 'I am Danica Arlet Rush, daughter of Queen Rayven Arlet and princess to Asada's Moonstone Palace.'

Silence falls through the woods, the silence so heavy with tension that not even the owls call.

'Who are you with, Danica Arlet Rush?' comes the reply in the common tongue, an accent thick and smooth.

'Falcon Rhodes, Crynn Balathasar, Ryker and Caden Thindrel of the Moonstone Palace. As well as our prisoners, two humans from the city of Roseguard,' I say, having to take a few breaths afterwards.

A few more silent moments before three black Natari horses step through the trees, and I sigh in relief then grimace in pain.

I study the riders. Two with the typical pale blue eyes of the Narakuya and one with pale ice eyes, lighter than the other two and an easy grin, tan skin with dark thick hair. Definitely has Narakuya blood, but it must be very faint if his skin is that tanned, much darker than our usual olive to pale shade. The grin annoys me, but the ice eyes, the ones that were watching me ignite my curiosity, and I don't know why.

The Narakuya on the right, the male with pale blue eyes and brown hair speaks quietly. 'You are Queen Rayven's daughter?' I nod. 'We've been expecting you.'

I nudge Caden and our horse walks forward. 'How many scouts do you have with this group?'

'Five. How did you get injured?' The pale-eyed Narakuya female speaks this time.

Falcon then reaches around and presses a hand to my wound, using his other hand to take the reins and pass them back to Caden.

'What are your names?' I ask.

'I'm Sage and that's Flint,' Sage nods towards the pale-eyed male and then finally nods towards the ice-eyed male, who hasn't said anything yet. 'And that's Kai.'

Kai's eyes are on me, and I watch as he runs them up and down, his gaze hovering over the hand Falcon is pressing against my wound.

Falcon notices Kai's stare and speaks for me. 'A stray bolt on our way out of town.'

I take a deep breath, about to open my mouth when Falcon speaks again. 'There are twenty soldiers behind us, tracking us. We must continue back to camp.'

Our horse moves forward again, and the Ritenvold scouts escort us. Silence hovers through the forest, the only sound is the creaking of the cart. As we travel through the trees, I find myself unable to focus on my surroundings, and blood keeps seeping through the cloth. Despite my inability to focus for longer than a few moments, I notice Kai's eyes on me more than once. Each time I turn to meet his gaze, he only smirks, as if he knows something I don't. During one of these focused moments, a horse bursts through the forest beside us, and I instantly jump up, pain splintering up my side almost forcing me down again. I brace my arm around Falcon's shoulders, trying to support myself.

It's a black Natari horse and female rider with pale blue eyes, she quickly looks us over before turning to Kai. 'Twenty humans are coming for whoever is in that cart. They must have called for reinforcements as there are a hundred soldiers that have just entered the forest.'

I wonder why they would turn to Kai, when Sage seems to be the leader of the scout group.

Tyke begins to laugh from the cart. I glance at him and frown. I'll worry about him later.

Falcon's eyes flash to mine. 'We need to get you back to safety.'

My heart misses a beat. 'I'll fight alongside, don't worry about me.'

It's Caden who speaks up. 'Danica, I would say yes if you didn't have a bolt in your stomach, but this one isn't your fight. Your fight is another day.'

I turn to Caden. 'I am staying with the prisoners.'

Kai speaks up. 'I'll get the princess back to the camp, you lot stick with the prisoners and follow us back.'

I grit my teeth as he brings his horse up beside the cart. 'Not happening.'

'Can you get her back to Rayven?' Caden asks Kai.

'I'll die trying,' Kai says, that easy smirk disappearing for a moment.

'No!' I demand.

'Get on the horse Danica,' Falcon finally says, pushing me forward.

'But Vixy …' I try again, feeling slightly faint.

'You'll be more help to Vixy if you're alive and well.' He helps me stand up.

I close my eyes for a moment, trying to gather my strength to argue and fight, but I realise Falcon is right. I let him help me into the saddle of his horse, Kai having shifted to sit behind the saddle, on the horse's rump. Blood drips down my side as Falcon finally removes his hand. An arrow whistles through the forest. Falcon smacks the horse across the rump as Kai spurs it into a gallop, I hold onto the horse's mane, hunching forward, the only thing stopping me from falling off is Kai's arm around my waist, his hand pressed around the end of the bolt. I grimace as the horse's gallop sends throbbing spears of pain through me.

I take a deep breath, finding my last burst of energy to sit up and look over my shoulder as we ride through the trees, spying the first of the Red Soldiers, the cart hurtling towards us and the Narakuya pulling out swords, and I watch as they unleash themselves on the soldiers.

The horse jumps a log, and I groan as it lands, jarring my wound, my hands struggling to keep a hold of the Natari's mane.

I barely hear Kai's words as we gallop through the forest. 'Hold on, Princess.'

'Don't call me princess,' I snap, despite the pain echoing through me.

'If you say so, Princess.'

We gallop through the forest for what seems like hours, the horse keeping to the shadows until in the distance I see a small black tent, then another and another. Relief floods my body, and my eyes drift shut as I realise that we're in the army camp. My body finally letting unconsciousness take over, knowing it is now safe.

I need sleep. I haven't slept properly for weeks. Sleep sounds good.

'Hey! Hey! Hold on, Danica,' Kai says behind me. 'You lasted ten years on the front line. Don't die on me now.'

'I'm not going to die stupid…' I mumble.

The horse slams to a halt and I jolt forward into its neck, but I can't find the strength to do anything. As I'm pulled from the horse into strong arms, the warmth of hard muscle wrap around me, and I let myself relax as sleep starts to creep closer.

'RAYVEN!' I hear someone shout mother's name.

It seems like a while before I hear some panicking from beside me. 'Danica, Danica. Thank you, Kai, thank you.'

'Where do you want her? She's lost a lot of blood. She'll be fine, she only just blacked out then.'

'Take her to her tent. Thank you, Kai.'

250

# Chapter Twenty-Two

## Hunter

The door of the war room slams open as a soldier rushes through, panting.

'What is it?' Mother demands.

We are all on edge today, waiting for Danica to make her move, especially since a cart with stolen goods managed to escape the wall inspections yesterday. Mother had insisted that we send soldiers after the cart, to prove a point now that Rayven will be watching, she had told me.

I am beginning to worry about why Danica is taking so long to make her move, I was expecting an attack almost as soon as I knew Vixy was captured.

'You should see this, Commander, Captain,' the soldier pants, his eyes wide beneath the helmet as he addresses Mother and I. Outside, there are three horses waiting for us, all blood bay stallions. I mount one of the horses, and once Mother is ready we follow the soldier through the city towards the southern gates. The city is quiet, restless, and faces watch us through windows as we make our way along the streets, hoofbeats echoing off the walls.

When we reach the lookout, my breakfast almost makes a second appearance. Beneath the walls, on the field between the city and the forest, the soldiers we'd sent to deal with the thieves lay spread out in the shape of a mountain and crescent moon. All the soldiers are dead, limbs hacked off.

'Danica,' I say, nausea building in my stomach.

Mother shoots me a look, as if embarrassed I had just said that. 'No. Ritenvold, King Darius is here.'

'I know that that's the Ritenvold crest, but Danica is behind it,' I grumble, now embarrassed myself.

Mother shakes her head. 'Not this one, this is all Ritenvold. Danica is brutal but she's not a savage.'

I raise my eyes at Mother's comment. 'She held me hostage.'

'And yet you escaped in one piece, and she never hurt you in that time.' Mother then adds, 'her threats are empty. The fact that she hasn't attacked Roseguard for that girl yet is the perfect example.'

I shake my head. Danica is a savage; she's no doubt sharpening her sword right now.

'There's more,' the soldier says, and leads us outside of the city walls where he points at a message written in blood across the stone wall.

We remember what you did to our prince.

## Prince Kai Vold is coming for Prince Luca Vold's murderer.

I crouch down, head between my legs and force myself to take deep breaths, the coppery tang of blood heavy in the air. Slowly my stomach settles, and I stand again.

'And no-one saw the Narakuya do this?' Mother shouts suddenly, and I flinch.

No-one answers.

'Who is Kai Vold?' I ask.

Mother turns to look at me. 'Ada died giving birth to Luca, this Kai won't be a legitimate heir to the throne, as it was Ada's bloodline that was royalty. They must have kept this secret. He can't be older than ten.' Mother then tilts her head. 'Again, empty threats. King Darius is trying to scare us, by adding a bastard to the bloodline. I made sure the Zodia's bloodline ended with Ada and Luca.'

I frown. 'Then why would they write that on our walls?'

Worry flashes through Mother's eyes, then she lowers her voice, only loud enough for me to hear, 'I don't know.'

I realise then that Mother is simply guessing everything at the moment, she'd made some mistake in underestimating the power of Ritenvold, and the strength of Danica.

'Tyke will know who saw it,' I say, Mother follows as I head back to my horse and aim for the Underground. If there is any gossip about it, that's where it will travel to first.

We mount the stallions again and turn towards the Underground. The steel of the horseshoes clang against the cobblestone streets. We stay at a walk, trying to look as if we are unconcerned about what we've just seen.

The streets are eerily quiet. I bite my lip as I think about the consequences to this city, to my life, if we don't play our only cards right.

Mother turns in the saddle to look at me. 'You know what this means, right?'

'That Ritenvold is here. And if Ritenvold is here, then Danica and Rayven will most likely be trying to ally with them.'

'Correct. And that girl, Vixen Kyler, is going to be the only thing that might make them hesitate from hitting us directly.' Mother takes a deep breath.

We are playing with fire, I realise, and we have nothing with which to put it out. Our only chance of containing the fire is Vixen.

'How are we going to survive this now?' I ask.

'We play dirty, and we do anything to survive.'

We remain silent as the horses walk through the streets. I haven't spoken much to Tyke since I got back, only to see if he's heard anything through the gossip that passes through the club.

We reach the street to the Underground, and I tie my horse to a rail before starting the descent. It's early in the morning; therefore, it should just be the staff cleaning from the night before, and Tyke meeting with clients. I had once asked Tyke if he ever slept, as he always seemed to be awake no matter what hour. He had just laughed and had told me that he slept in the afternoon, and between meetings.

If Tyke's not here, then he would be in his apartment in the centre of the city. He had managed to buy himself a fairly large apartment above a warehouse. Although he didn't have the best view, he was in the centre of the town and no one suspected him to be living there.

We reach the final door, and I push it open. A few people are picking up rubbish and sweeping the floor, some are at the bar cleaning glasses. The curtains are drawn in the last booth, meaning that it is occupied. At least that's one good thing about this morning, I don't have to go hunting Tyke across the city.

'Come on, he's here,' I say to Mother.

I stride across the room, feeling the eyes of those cleaning. I push back the curtains, not caring if someone else is having a meeting with Tyke. I am higher priority.

The booth is empty.

There is a knife, the tip stabbed into the table pinning a note to the timber. I pull back the knife and unfold the creased and worn paper, revealing elegant handwriting. I instantly recognise the writing, Danica's. I read the letter, once, twice, three times before handing it to Mother as she clears her throat.

*Melissa Cole,*

*Tyke Carter is alive for now.*

After a moment, I sink into the booth chair and stare blankly at Mother. She is standing at the head of the booth.

Danica had outsmarted me, out manoeuvred me yet again. I thought I understood her, understood how she would react and what she would do. I so strongly believed that she would have gone straight for Vixy, killing anything and anyone in her path.

Yet she had gone where I least expected and where I should have known she'd go. She would have known that I expected her to go straight for the kill.

Danica had simply taken an eye for an eye.

Just as mother had taken Vixy hostage, she had taken Tyke hostage. And I knew that she would not treat Tyke the same way we have been treating Vixy. The little girl has food, shelter, water …

Danica had decided on what she had wanted me to believe and played that character so well that I didn't even consider my best friend's safety.

'Hunter.' I look up at Mother. 'We are not empty handed; we have the girl. I doubt Rayven or Danica will harm Tyke until they know for certain that Vixen is safe.'

'And then what, once they get Vixy back and we've got Tyke back... then what?' I ask, any hope I had for my safety disappearing.

Mother closes her eyes for a moment. 'I have one more card up my sleeve that will pose a considerable threat to the Narakuya, they don't know about the Fae.'

# Chapter Twenty-Three

## Danica

The fighting is thick here. Red Soldiers fight beside me, the clanging of swords is loud, the screams are horrific. Its pouring with rain, mud splattered all over me. A Ritenvold warrior comes towards me, I glance over my shoulder at the soldier in the tower, looking down his crossbow, aimed at me. Should I choose to not fight, my only option is torture... I had suffered enough at the hands of Red Soldiers to know that fighting was easier. If I were human, I would have many, many more scars.

The Ritenvold warrior approaches, his sword lowered. I meet his ice white eyes, Narakuya.

'Danica?' he asks, his voice soft like honey, and quiet. Only my ears can pick it up.

I lower my sword, entranced by his eyes, his voice.

*He moves like water through the heavy fighting.*

*A Red Soldier snaps at me, 'Nightwalker, you are to kill them.' The name the Red Soldiers had given me upon arrival. None of the humans would take on a Narakuya.*

*The Narakuya approaches me, only twenty yards away, 'I can help you, Danica.'*

*'Kill him,' the soldier snaps at me.*

*I don't raise my sword.*

*Pain bursts through my leg, and I look down, a bolt protruding from my leg. Then everything goes black.*

*When I awaken, I am strapped to a wooden table, naked. A Red Soldier is leering at me.*

*I snarl at him, and he laughs before pulling an iron branding stick from the roaring pit.*

*'Shall we see if we can make the brands permanent this time?'*

Consciousness floods me, fear and pain ripple through me. Pain on my stomach, my breasts, my thighs from the branding. A headache is thudding against my skull.

The sound of boots marching, soldiers talking, campfires crackling and horses stamping. My heart rate goes up. They won't send me back to the front lines if I am unconscious, the Red Soldiers will wait until I am awake, then give me a day before sending me back out to fight. I try to slow my heart rate, but panic creeps in. *Don't move Danica*, I tell myself over. I don't move, but I peek my eyes open to see if I am chained or not. I try to figure out where I am. I'm definitely in a tent, a black cloth tent.

Black cloth tent… memories come flooding back and I sit up. I'm in Rayven's war camp, not on the front line. Tears flood down my cheek as memories from the last few weeks and from the front line flash through my mind. I am safe. I am almost home. The nightmare wasn't real, the pain in my breasts and thighs fade and I put a hand up my shirt to feel the smooth skin, not raw or burnt.

That nightmare… it wasn't a nightmare, it was a memory. One my mind had made me forget. That male was there, the one in the forest, I had seen him before.

I take a deep breath and pull the loose white shirt up revealing my bandaged stomach, my scar on one side and the new wound on the other. I lift the bandage gently with my finger to have a look. Just an ugly unhealed wound, dried blood sticks to it.

I glance around the tent again and see a jug of water with a glass next to it on a small stool. I stand up and get my balance before making my way over to the water and pour myself a glass, then another. I stand there for a few moments, letting the headache fade as I recall what happened. On another small stool sits a mirror and I pick it up, gazing at my reflection. My ice eyes are dull, with bags beneath them and the makeup smeared, and my face is taut, my cheekbones sharp. My brown hair is still braided. I wash my face and then begin the process of taking out my braids, brushing my hair and pinning it back into a ponytail. I stare into the mirror again and pinch my cheeks, trying to bring some colour into them.

I place the mirror back on the table and turn to find my jacket and blades. There is a trunk behind the small bed. I open it to reveal my few belongings and begin gearing up.

Stepping out of the tent, I take a deep breath and make my way through the camp, keeping my gaze on the ground. I don't quite have the energy to socialise with any warrior that might want to introduce themselves. Rayven's war tent is not too far from mine, I can hear voices coming from inside. I quietly approach the tent and peel back the black canvas flaps. Inside is a massive table covered by a map with warriors standing all around it.

I easily spot Rayven, her midnight hair and posture that is so uniquely hers, that of a queen, is hard to miss. Dimitri is by her side, with his ever-present bow strapped across his back. Falcon and Crynn are also standing beside Rayven; Falcon's eyes are on someone across the table. I look to see who's captured his interest and see Kai, in leather armour that leaves his muscled arms free and dark pants, a sword strapped down his back. His attention is on Rayven, and I let my gaze wander over his features, dark silky hair that is shoulder length and tied back with a band, stubble covers the lower half of his face and thick full lips. My eyes trace his sharp jawline, and then up to his thick brows and ice eyes. I tilt my head as I take him in, trying to figure out why he would be here, why he had been on the front line and how he'd known who I was.

I scan the tent to see who else is present and spy a human in black and gold robes with a crown perched on his head, that would make him King Darius Vold. His hair is grey and skin loose, his light brown eyes are almost golden.

Also in the room is a buckskin centaur with dark hair and a tattoo of a mountain that signifies he's not from Asada; as well as two cyclops men, both from Asada. A few dwarves, minotaurs and satyrs are standing among the Ritenvold humans and Narakuya. I take note of who is here and who isn't; we're missing a few representatives of different species, but I had seen many of them outside. I stand back and listen to the conversation.

'There was no army on the front line,' King Darius is saying.

Kai interrupts, which I frown at. 'Well, there was, but only a handful of Asadian criminals and Red Soldiers left there. Roseguard mustn't have cared enough about them.'

Rayven tilts her head ever so slightly, as if putting pieces of a puzzle together. 'We know that Melissa Cole will have something up her sleeve, she's had ten years to prepare for an attack.'

'So, let's figure out what it is before we attack,' Kai says.

Falcon snaps at him. 'We've been into the city a handful of times now and seen no sign. Danica held their captain hostage, and he shared nothing.'

I watch as Kai looks Falcon up and down once, and a corner of my lip tilts up as I know how much that would annoy Falcon. 'Well, you didn't look hard enough.'

I see Falcon rest his hand on his sword.

Kai must have noticed it too. 'We don't want to see your ass handed to you this morning.'

I frown. Falcon's the best fighter I have ever met, after Rayven and myself of course. The royal bloodline always runs stronger, whether or not the Moonstone Crown has touched our brow.

King Darius puts a hand on Kai's shoulder, and he takes a moment to look at the ing.

'Anyway, the one person who would know the most about the Red Army would be the Ppincess.' Kai looks back towards Rayven.

'Yes,' Rayven agrees. 'But my daughter is still recovering, and I don't want anyone bothering her until she's healed.' I notice as Rayven looks pointedly at both Falcon and Kai.

Kai grins. 'Of course, your majesty. I would never bother the princess if she wasn't up to it.' His grin disappears. 'But despite being recently wounded, she would be up to it the moment she woke.'

I frown, both at him defending me and the sheer boldness at challenging my mother.

Rayven's eyes narrow at him. 'Don't push her.'

'Not unless she's up to it.'

Rayven shakes her head, dismissing the line of conversation and turning her attention to the king. 'You left half your army in Ritenvold to defend the kingdom?'

'Yes, I have brought those who are willing to fight and left enough warriors to defend my people. General Reid is with the army back home.'

I look around the tent again. A thought clicks through my mind as I try to recall all the species I had seen in the camp before. 'Where is the fae representative?'

All eyes go straight to me.

Rayven strides to my side in moments. 'How are you feeling?' Her hands go to my face.

'I am fine. Just a bit of blood loss.'

Dimitri is watching me carefully. 'We didn't want to lose you again.'

'I've had worse. You weren't going to lose me.'

Rayven wraps me into a hug, gripping me tightly enough that I can't move, before stepping back, nodding her head once and turning back to the crowd. 'My daughter, Danica Arlet Rush.'

I let my gaze run over everyone gathered, but it stops at Kai. He is watching me, his body so still that it reminds me that he is not human, his gaze on me, his eyes locked on mine.

'Danica, this is King Darius Vold of Ritenvold,' Rayven nods her head to the King, and I dip my head ever so slightly in respect. 'And you've already met Prince Kai Vold.'

I frown and turn to look at Rayven, as far as I could recall, the only prince I was aware of was Luca Vold.

King Darius answers for Rayven. 'I had two sons. Kai was to become a warrior, receive our family heirloom and become a General for our people. Kai is now our heir. Fortunately, no-one outside of the Ritenvold knew Kai existed. At the time of Luca's death, he had been training with one of the Narakuya tribes and wished not to be seen as a prince, and we respected that. And I have realised that any smart king or queen should keep a backup heir hidden.' Darius gives a quick breathy laugh.

'Right… when did my mother learn about Kai's legitimacy?'

'Rayven has always known. You would have found out eventually.' Darius gives me a small sad smile.

It prompts me to ask; 'I am aware that I am responsible for the deaths of many of your people. I know nothing can make up for that, but if there is anything I can do, that yourself and your people would appreciate, please tell me.'

'My people understand the position you were in and forgive you, a child, for doing what you did to survive.' Darius shakes his head slowly. 'One day, I'm sure my people will ask something of you… but we know why you did what you did, Danica. It's forgiven, and the families of the dead will one day ask you to remember those you have killed.'

I nod my head then turn to look at Kai again. His ice eyes are easy as I size him up. Just to annoy him, I disregard him and turn to Rayven.

'Where is the fae representative?' I ask again as Kai raises an eyebrow in my peripheral vision.

'We had word that they are marching their army.' Rayven's eyes narrow at that, as if I had brought up something she did not wish to discuss at this time and place.

'No news from Roseguard?' I ask.

Dimitri hesitates. 'They have not publicly done anything to the young girl.'

'And where are my prisoners?'

Rayven frowns. 'In the holding cage. Under supervision. No-one's been allowed to talk to them; I thought I'd give you the honour.'

'Thank you.' I nod my head before turning on my heel.

Everyone inside the tent hesitates before following me out. I stride through the camp, everyone following, and the eyes of those in the camp watching us go by. The holding cage is large enough to hold many prisoners, however, today there are only two humans in it.

Inside the cage are two oak posts standing upright a couple of yards apart from the other. A hole has been chiselled through the top of each post and a thick chain runs through. Where the chain protrudes out of each post, it follows the post down a few feet, to where Tyke and Klara are. The warriors guarding the cage nod and open the door for me.

Tyke's head is bowed, his shirt has a few tears in it and his hair is loose. I ignore Klara, who is red eyed and puffy faced from crying; dirt streaks her arms and legs.

I stop in front of Tyke, and he looks up.

I don't say anything as I stare at him, waiting for him to talk first. Waiting for him to decide how this conversation will go.

Tyke looks over at the audience we have before continuing. 'You know, if you wanted me tied up – all you had to do was ask. You'd be surprised how obliging I can be when manners are used.'

A growl sounds over my shoulder, and I glance at Falcon, his jaw is clenched and his hands fisted. I'm not the only one who has given Falcon a second look, Kai is leaning against the open doorway with his eyebrows raised, Dimitri has his head tilted, Rayven's jaw is clenched, and I turn back to Tyke to see him watching Falcon.

'That obviously hit a soft spot.' He grins, his dark eyes turning back to me.

'You have a lot of audacity for someone tied to a post.' I say quietly.

'Only to impress you, Princess.'

'You're a smart man–'

'I knew deep down you liked me.'

I ignore his comment. 'Which means you would know that Roseguard is going to be defeated. If you want to protect your club and still have something once Melissa has been removed from power, you will answer my question.'

'Oh, you want to know whether you can celebrate your victory? Unfortunately, you'll be banned from my club after this whole situation.'

'Vixen Kyler, where is she?'

'No idea who you're talking about.' Tyke laughs, annoying me by keeping that casual, unafraid persona instead of giving me answers.

Everyone is watching.

'Red hair, thirteen years old, human, sent to the front line for pickpocketing.'

'I know that this is something I shouldn't be telling you, even if I did know.'

'Nothing happens in the city that you don't know about,' I say, then fist my hand and punch Tyke in the gut. Hard. Hard enough to wind him for a few moments.

He just stares at me with that cocky stubborn defiance in his gaze. I don't have time to deal with stubbornness. Instead of pushing, I walk around to Klara, her dark hair is messy, and her dress sits high on her legs.

She starts shaking as she realises my attention is on her. 'Please don't hurt me.'

I watch her for a moment. She was with Tyke when we arrived, she would have overheard a lot. And she is vain, she isn't loyal like Tyke and will be more willing to talk.

'Klara, I know you're close with Hunter Cole and Tyke, and I know you hold a position that grants you access to secrets.' The second statement is just a guess. 'So, I am going to need you to tell me anything you know about the girl I just described. Because, unlike Tyke, you don't matter, so your survival depends greatly on what you tell me – and if you don't speak… I'll show you some things that Melissa Cole did to try to make me talk.'

'I don't know.' Klara doesn't meet my eyes.

'But you do know something, don't you Klara?' I step close, getting into her personal space to scare her.

'They took someone to the Red Towers.' Klara starts crying again.

'Klara, I need you to take a deep breath for me.' She does. 'How many people live in the city?'

'A hundred thousand.'

'And how many know how to fight?'

'At least half.'

I nod and walk back to Tyke.

'Anything else to add?'

'I still think we would make good *friends*, Danica darling.'

I lean into whisper in Tyke's ear. 'Oh, I don't doubt that, had our circumstances been different.'

I turn on my heel, meet Rayven's gaze and nod to her. Vixy is somewhere in the Red Towers. Falcon grabs my arm on the way out, but

I shake him off. Quietly, I walk out of the camp and into the forest. Shuddering as I take a deep breath, I need some time alone to process my thoughts.

I walk through the camp and deeper into the forest, listening to the sounds of the small animals and birds, the wind through the trees. I just need silence and to think. I need to not have to keep my guard up and just be able to process everything without judgement.

Melissa has Vixy in the Red Towers, and they have a decent sized human army, bigger than Rayven's. However, where we lack in numbers, we gain in strength, and Narakuya warriors; it'd take a hundred humans to take down one of us. And we also have some of Ritenvold's army.

I reach a small, deep pool, and gaze into the shadowed depths, perfectly clear. I can't see anything lurking down there.

I feel eyes watching me, but I don't care as I let my hair out, shrug my jacket off, then my shirt and pants. I had many men leer at my naked body on the front line. Fortunately, none were brave enough to take it any further than that. Slowly, I unwrap the bandage around my stomach. I run my fingers over the raw wound, the flesh now pink and sensitive.

I sigh, take a deep breath and dive into the pool.

The water hits me, cool and cleansing. I continue to swim down, as far down as I can get. The pool is never ending. My lungs complain too soon for my liking, and I look up towards the sunlight, pumping my arms and kicking my legs until I surface.

I close my eyes as my head breaks the surface, inhaling as much air as I can.

'Tyke got you a bit hot and flustered, did he?'

I grimace. 'Leave me be, Prince.'

I don't open my eyes before sinking beneath the surface again, running my fingers through my hair. I stay under for as long as I can.

I surface and open my eyes to find Kai still there, leaning against a tree.

'I thought I told you to leave me be.'

'I don't take orders from you, Princess.'

I glare at him for a moment.

 Kai chuckles quietly. 'Those prisoners are more friendly than you.'

'Then go irritate them.'

'So, I am irritating you?'

'No, you're annoying me.' I add a sarcastic smile.

'Even better.'

'What do you want?'

'Who's the girl the Reds have?'

'None of your business.'

'If we're now allies, it is my business.'

Instead of answering, I dive deep into the pool. Ignoring him for as long as I can. When I surface, he is still there but has moved to the edge of the pool.

I swim to the edge, and rest my arms on the grass, my body underwater. I make sure the water stays above my breasts as I look up at him.

'You've got a good swing with the sword.'

'I do.' I don't look at him, not even considering or caring where he would have learned that.

'But I have yet to see you fight like we do.'

'Well today's not your lucky day, is it?'

He tilts his head, 'I would say otherwise.' His eyes drop down to the water line, where the curve of my skin is just visible.

I whip my arm through the water, soaking him and he jumps back, out of reach of the water.

'I won't be mad at you for that,' he laughs.

'Turn around,' I order him, and he does.

I climb out of the pool into my clothes, pulling each piece on over my wet skin. My shirt has only just settled over my skin when he turns back around, his eyes burning into me while I pull my pants back on.

'Sorry,' he shrugs, completely unapologetic.

'Creep,' I say and walk into the forest, aiming for the camps. Something about him has me on the defensive, I feel like I can't focus when his attention is on me.

'Princess.' He is hot on my heels. He grabs my upper arm, not harshly but enough to make me stop and turn around.

I stop and turn on my heels, facing him. He's staring down at me, and I hesitate for a moment, caught off guard by him, his height, his eyes and even his smell of summer rains and oak.

That smirk grows slightly as he realises his effect on me. It's enough to make me hiss at him, 'What do you want? I have stuff to organise. So, either go find someone else to annoy or be useful and leave me be.'

He takes a step closer, his body only inches from mine.

'Princess, we're in this together now,' he says, leaning in, raising a hand to my cheek and gently pushing a strand of wet hair behind my ear.

I don't back away from the touch, just the softest of touches and I only feel him there for a moment before he pushes past, aiming for the camps and leaving me behind, my heart rate racing, warmth across my cheeks, fists clenched and a funny feeling in my stomach. He glances over his shoulder once, winking at me.

I don't know what to think of him, the cockiness, the confidence. Why he followed me over to the pool for no other reason than to be painful…

# Chapter Twenty-Four

## Hunter

Thorn Gap is a menacing labyrinth of precipitous rock walls and deep shadows that hide its true dangers. Only at midday can you see what's below, even then it's still difficult. There are so many people down there, and yet no sign of them, the roar of the waterfall overpowers the sound of anything else. The perfect hiding place for an army.

And far behind me, hidden somewhere in the forest, are Danica, Rayven's army and the Ritenvold army. There is no sign of them either, no smoke, no tracks leading through the forest to where they lie hidden. And no scouts sighted either. But then again, I'm not surprised. Danica's kind are predators, they know how to remain hidden among the trees, waiting to strike. I could walk through every inch of that forest, and I wouldn't find any of them if they didn't want to be found.

A door opens and closes behind me.

'Good morning, Mother,' I say, not taking my eyes off the cliffs below me.

The gentle morning breeze runs cool fingers over my face as I turn to face my mother, who looks immaculate in her red suit.

'Good to see you're up.'

'We have a war to win, don't we?' I lean back against the balcony rail.

Mother gives me a small smile. 'Yes. Now, have you done any research on the prisoner?'

I frown. 'Why would I need to?'

She frowns and shakes her head at me. 'She was sent to the front line for pickpocketing a man in Salt City, where she grew up.' Mother comes to stand beside me, looking out over the Gap. 'Her father disappeared when the prisoner was a toddler, and her mother died from illness not much later. That left her older sister to look after her. Vixen Kyler ran feral through the back streets of the city until she was caught by city guards.'

'Wow, how did you find that out?'

Mother's eyes narrow. 'Records, Hunter. You should have already had this research completed for yourself. Especially if you want to end up in my position one day. Anyway, we have someone who might make Vixen Kyler talk.'

'What?'

'When I sent the party out for Vixen Kyler, I also sent a party out to the Salt City to retrieve Autumn Kyler.' Mother grins, triumphant. 'Vixen's sister.'

'And Autumn has arrived in Roseguard?'

'Better yet, she's in the cells in Thorn Gap.'

'Well, what are we waiting for?' I push off the rail and begin the long walk to our hidden army with Mother close behind.

*****

The cavern is a cacophony of sound. The hidden army is busy training, swords smash against each other, soldiers shout and cry and over it all is the roar of the waterfall at the northern end of the Gap.

A soldier appears at Mother's side, and I watch as she subtly nods at the man. He quickly vanishes into the crowd of red.

I let mother lead the way to a cleared area that I assume is used for practice. Shortly, six guards appear with two prisoners between them. Both prisoners have shackles on and hessian bags over their heads.

'Hunter, you can do the talking.' Mother squeezes my arm. 'You can use the practice.'

One of the guards removes the bag from the smaller girl's head. Vixy.

Her eyes instantly scan the area, as if second nature. She hesitates on Autumn for a moment before continuing until her gaze lands on me, fire behind her eyes.

'Hello little one,' I say carefully. 'We need you to cooperate with us.'

Vixy clenches her jaw as she glares at me, every bit of hatred in her gaze. I stay quiet for a moment, giving her an opportunity to respond.

'We can do this the easy way or the hard way,' I try again. 'How will Danica go about trying to rescue you?'

I decide to test the waters and see if Vixy could have anticipated her moves.

She turns her gaze to my mother, turning that hatred to her.

Vixy taps her foot on the ground in nervousness. I nod at the soldier standing by the other prisoner. I watch as the soldier places a long dagger at the prisoner's throat before removing the hessian bag, revealing long orange curls and a freckled face a few years older than Vixy's. The girl's dress is torn and muddy, and she has bruising around one of her eyes. Vixy's eyes widen.

'Autumn!' Vixy shouts and attempts to run across to her, but the soldier keeps a firm hold on Vixy's chain.

'Vixen… the front line…' Autumn says quietly before turning to me. 'What is going on? Why is my sister here?'

'Autumn, you shall remain quiet, or you may get hurt,' I say as evenly as I can. 'Vixen. Answer my question if you want your sister to stay alive.'

Vixy chews her lip for a moment before turning to face me.

'Danica is a Moonchild; she will likely retaliate in the same way you've done. She will find someone to hold prisoner as you are doing to me.' I frown at Vixy's wording, at what she calls Danica. 'Once Danica has saved Autumn and me, she'll destroy you for this.' Vixy stands still for a moment before looking at Autumn. 'Once Danica has her plan, she'll stop at nothing. She'll rescue us.'

'And once she has found a prisoner to hold hostage?'

Vixy chews her lip again, a nervous habit. 'Why are you being so mean to me? I helped you when you found us.'

Her words hit home, and I retaliate. 'I found you because I was hunting both of you. Answer my question.'

Tears fall down Vixy's cheeks. 'Danica was right. I should never have fed a stray dog.'

I snap, 'if you don't give me a useful answer, I will have Autumn tortured.'

'She will probably just trade her hostage for Autumn and me.'

'Thank you, Vixen,' I say, having drawn my conclusion. Vixy has no idea what she'll will do next, but she's confirmed my belief that Danica is unpredictable.

I nod at the soldiers, and they return Vixen and Autumn to the same cell, allowing them to be reunited.

Mother steps up to my side. 'Follow them and listen. Now is when Vixen Kyler will talk, when she thinks no-one is listening.'

I nod my head and quietly follow the guards to the girls' cell, keeping out of sight as I listen as Vixen and Autumn meet again. I listen for a half hour as they explain the last few years to one another. How Vixy ended up on the front line and how Autumn waited by the door of their home for Vixy to return.

Finally, Autumn asks the question I've been waiting to hear. 'Who is this Danica?'

Vixy sighs. 'She is the best person I've ever met, after you of course.'

'Come on, Vix, why do these assholes want to know about her?'

'She helped me escape the front line and saved my life. We made a home in the desert but then I found that guy who was questioning me about her, and Danica told me we'd be better off if we killed him, but I didn't want to kill him and now he's probably going to kill both of us. I should have listened to her …' Vixy begins crying, and I grimace at her words.

Danica is the killer, not me. Threats are useful, but I never follow through with them. I won't kill Vixy as she believes I will.

After a while, Vixy calms down enough to talk again. 'I don't know what's happened, but I know that Danica is one of the Moonchildren you used to tell me about. And I think for that reason they want to kill her.'

'And she saved your life?' Autumn asks quietly.

'When I grow up, I want to be like her. She is my hero.'

I grimace; Danica is nothing more than a cold-blooded killer. No morals, no mercy. I get up to leave and find Mother waiting by the door to the stairs that lead to the city.

'Anything?' She raises an eyebrow.

I shake my head.

'Rayven's army will make their move tonight.' Mother begins the climb up the stairs.

'How do you know?'

'It's going to be a clear night; it hasn't been long since Tyke Carter went missing, the Narakuya won't sit around waiting, and a scout was spotted. The scout was only spotted because of a glint of metal in sunlight, but they're watching the city.' Mother glances back at me.

'Tonight, we're going to kill Danica Arlet Rush, and then we'll win this war.'

'She won't be alone. She'll have those four other Nightwalkers with her. Danica won't let the army attack until Vixen is safe.'

Mother doesn't glance back at me this time. 'I know.'

'Only Danica has to die, the rest will back off if you kill her. Her death will take them by surprise, as she's survived the front line.' I take a few more steps. 'No more deaths than necessary.'

# Chapter Twenty-Five

## Danica

Quietly, I step outside of my tent and into the brisk morning air, the sun streaming through the trees. Tonight, I will get Vixy back.

I walk through the camp until I reach the training grounds. Falcon has agreed to do some practice with me, and I would like to brush up on my skills before tonight. The camp is busy, as I make my way through, the many warriors going about their jobs in a way that feels like they want to, compared to being on the front line. The Red Soldiers treat jobs like chores, putting them off for as long as possible, then once done, they complain about it. Whereas here, the warriors are laughing, happy, and offering to help where they can.

At the training grounds, hundreds of warriors practice, and of course Kai is there, and I'm half tempted to turn around and leave. He's practicing against an older Narakuya woman, one who I'm sure has seen more battlefields than I could imagine. I watch for a moment as he completes a fast movement, where he dodges to the right but manages to attack from the left. His dark hair is damp, and his bare chest is glistening with sweat, his light brown fitted pants are covered in grass stains and dirt.

Falcon appears at my side.

'Want to practice?' he asks.

I nod my head and pick up a sword. I lead the way to a small clearing between a few trees, catching glimpses of Kai patiently destroying the woman's effort and training.

Falcon and I begin circling and for a few moments nothing happens. He attacks quickly. I dodge and counterattack, focusing on the end of my sword. For a couple of minutes, Falcon and I spar before I manage to get him to his knees. He doesn't complain, only nods and smiles. He, and every Narakuya, knows that I will always have an advantage with the Moonstone Crown blessing my royal bloodline. The same goes for Kai.

I help Falcon to his feet and we go for another two rounds, its therapeutic, only thinking about what's at the opposite end of my sword.

After the third round, Falcon pauses to give us a breather for a minute and I turn to find Kai leaning against a tree, sword in one hand. I hadn't noticed him approach.

'What do you want?'

That smirk forms on his lips. 'A round with the princess.'

I frown in annoyance. Falcon sizes Kai up.

He glances at Falcon, recognising that he is being sized up as a threat. 'Careful, you don't want to challenge someone you'll never win against.'

Falcon turns to me. 'Ignore him Danica, he'll only waste your time.'

Frowning, I glance at Falcon, at the comment he made. I don't appreciate being told what to do.

'Isn't that the only thing princes are good for? Wasting time?' I ask Falcon. And I can see that he can't work out if I'm agreeing with him, or to practice with Kai.

Kai grins. 'There's your fire.'

'One round, Prince,' I say, already looking him up and down, trying to spy any weaknesses.

I watch as he straightens to the challenge, raising an eyebrow at Falcon, a subtle middle finger as he gets what he wants. Falcon mumbles something I don't hear before moving out of the way. Kai walks into the area, and I realise I am going to have to work for this win.

He is definitely a trained warrior, but he hasn't spent ten years fighting for his life. He grins at me, realising I'm sizing him up, and he lets his gaze travel down then back up my body again, slowly. I have never felt so laid bare. I hesitate as he begins circling around me, unsure what to do for the first time in my life. His sword is loose in his right hand.

'What are you waiting for, Princess?' He teases, and I tilt my head at his taunt, letting the movement catch his attention.

His attention, however, goes to his surroundings before I spring forward with full force. He doesn't seem surprised by the sudden attack and flicks me off with ease. I step back as I calculate how it went wrong—he had moved his attention to provoke me into attacking.

'How old are you, Princess?' He grins, still circling me.

'I'm surprised you don't already know. Twenty.'

'Your attack would be something I'd expect from someone half your age.' He mocks and I clench my jaw. 'And I did already know.'

I lunge with all my effort, focused on disarming him. Within three movements, my sword is gone, and I freeze as a sword appears in front of my throat. I don't even dare to breathe too heavily.

Kai is standing behind me, almost touching me. 'You fight like our enemy, like a human.' He whispers into my ear and my vision turns red. 'Every move is made like your survival depends on it.'

'I spent the last ten years fighting with my enemy, I haven't had the luxury to train like you,' I hiss back, my eyes focused on the sword.

'Princess,' he lowers the sword and steps back. I spin around. 'Stop being the victim.'

'Excuse me?' I snarl, taking a step closer.

He folds his arms across his chest, his sword in one hand. 'You act like a victim. All temper and no idea. You attack like a cornered dog, snapping at whatever moves. Just because you had to fight *for* the enemy doesn't give you an excuse to fight *like* one of them. If you're one of *us*, then you need to pull yourself together and lose the temper.'

I don't know if he sees it coming or not, but I smack him hard across the face.

'Don't you ever speak to me like that again,' I snarl.

'Make me.' He says, before turning on his heel to start walking out of the clearing.

Falcon stands wide-eyed on the sideline. I launch forward, planning to tackle Kai. Moments before I connect, he spins around, grabs my arm and flings me into the dirt, pressing his knee to the back of my neck. My arm burns as he pulls it back, the fresh wound in my stomach aches.

'A human reaction! You've let your emotions cloud your vision, Danica. Pull yourself together and start acting like the princess of Asada,' Kai says clearly, and I grimace, fire burning through me. 'When you're ready to be one of us, come find me and I'll train you.'

The pressure to my neck and arm vanishes, and I let myself sink into the dirt and grass, squeezing my eyes shut. I listen as his steps fade away and more footsteps come rushing towards me.

'That asshole!' Falcon says, his hand appearing in front of me as I open my eyes.

I don't take the hand that he offers and push myself up.

'Are you alright?' Falcon asks, offering me a rag to clean off the dirt.

I push past him, anger burning through me. 'I want you, Crynn, Ryker and Caden ready to head into the city tonight, ready with my prisoners.'

# Part Three

## Of Moonlight & Darkness

# Chapter Twenty-Six

## Danica

Silence echoes through the night, our army is quieter than the small animals that stay hidden in the shadows. Pulling my bridle over Oak's ears, I prepare for tonight. We had spent hours discussing all the different ways we could go about this hostage exchange, and all the ways it could go horribly wrong. Rayven wants me to take a small army, to show our strength, but I am concerned that if I do that, we would appear too threatening. So, we compromised, Rayven will have her warriors waiting in the tree line, whilst my small team will venture up to the city walls.

I give Oak a scratch behind the ear and lead him out into the grassed area in front of Rayven's war tent, where everyone else is preparing.

Falcon and Crynn are mounted on two Natari horses talking between themselves, Caden, sitting in the driver's seat of the wagon with a Natari hitched up to it, is counting how many arrows he has in his quiver while Ryker is crouched in the back of the cart adjusting the ropes tying Tyke and Klara down. I lead Oak up to the team, and I frown when I notice that Tyke is gagged.

'That was me.' Crynn says and I turn to face him, he nods at the gag. 'He wouldn't shut up.'

I grin at that. 'Fair enough.'

'Ready to get Vixy back?' Crynn asks, nudging his horse to come stand next to Oak.

'More than ready, as soon as she is safe, then we go for Melissa.'

'Melissa's smart. She knows that you will go for her as soon as she gives Vixy back. I'm still not convinced that she doesn't have something planned.'

'Aye, but we're more than capable of tackling anything she throws at us. Plus, Hunter will want Tyke safe first.'

'I know. The plan is as solid as it can be.'

Footsteps sound on the grass and I turn to see Rayven and Dimitri walking towards us. The latter leading two Natari stallions behind them.

'I'll be perfectly fine,' I say before Rayven can open her mouth.

Dimitri pauses halfway across the clearing, his attention caught on something to his left. I follow his gaze, one of our scouts are approaching. Rayven lets him speak with the scout and walks up to me.

'Change of plans,' I go to open my mouth, but Rayven continues. 'Dimitri will join your team. I know this is between you and Cole at the moment, so I will stay in the trees, but I want one of us to stay with you, to keep you safe.'

'Okay, that can work.' I chew my lips for a moment. 'I think if we have him set up in the cart with his bow, that'd be for the best.'

'Yes, he'll be able to cover your backs.'

From between two tents, King Darius appears, with Kai at his side. A grimace forms as I notice the Natari horse he leads.

'Your majesty,' I say to the King as he reaches us.

'I wish you all the best on your rescue mission tonight.' King Daruis replies, before turning to Rayven. 'You are sure you don't need Ritenvold to assist tonight?'

Rayven gives me a pointed look before answering. 'No. Danica is more than capable, and twice as stubborn as myself.'

'Thank you for the offer, your majesty.' I glance at Kai, with his leather armour and his sword strapped to his waist. 'This is something that is personal and your kingdom has already suffered enough at my hands. I will rectify this situation tonight.'

'I understand, Princess.' The king tilts his head, taking me in. 'My son insists, however, on joining you on this mission. If only to better understand our enemy.'

I give King Darius a forced smile. 'Of course.'

Kai raises an eyebrow at my expression. 'Someone's got to save you if you get a bolt to the stomach again.'

I clench my jaw, and Rayven laughs softly. 'Relax Danica, you could learn a lot from the young prince.'

I almost let out a huff at Rayven's words and I don't look at Kai or the grin I know will be sitting on his stupidly perfect face.

Instead, I turn to Oak and vault into the saddle. I look up at the moon, taking a moment to clear my mind, before turning my eyes to the tree line, to where Roseguard is waiting for us on the other side.

A horse comes up next to me, and I turn to see Falcon.

'Ready?' He keeps his voice low, eyes on Kai who is adjusting his saddle.

'I was ready to march through the front doors the moment Melissa took Vixy,' I reply just as quietly.

Dimitri walks up to my side. 'Roseguard is waiting for you, Danica.'

'They have been waiting for me ever since I escaped the front line.'

Dimitri grimaces. 'They have archers ready, foot soldiers on the inside of the wall, and scouts patrolling the bare land in front of the wall. The army that was holding the front line is there. The front line is Roseguard now.' Dimitri runs a hand down my horse's neck. 'I am assuming Rayven informed you of the change to the plans.'

'Aye, and we think it'd be best if you set up with your bow and arrows in the back of the cart, that way you can watch our backs.'

Dimitri nods, 'sounds good little warrior.'

He unstraps his quiver from his Natari and makes his way to the cart.

Kai rides up beside me, giving me a crooked grin. 'Ready, Princess?'

I don't say anything as I give him a side eye.

Rayven strokes Oak's neck, 'we best leave you to it so I can go ride with the warriors.'

'See you in a few hours then,' I grin.

She places a hand on my lower leg, squeezing once. 'Be safe, and I'll see you soon.'

She gives me one more smile before turning back to her Natari, vaulting on easily, and then trotting off between the tents to her warriors.

I glance over to Dimitri, and he gives me a nod.

My heart rate starts increasing. It's happening, we're going to get Vix back.

'Let's go!' I say to my team before urging Oak into a walk.

Caden flicks the rein and the Natari walks forward, the wagon rolling behind. I lighten my seat, Oak easing into a trot. I take a deep breath, breathing in the forest, the cool night air, the smell of horses and leather. Finally, finally I am on the move again. I am able to do something to help Vixy.

For a while we walk in silence. Falcon keeps quiet as he rides on my right, just taking in the forest for any threats.

I grimace as Kai appears on my left. He doesn't say anything, and I certainly don't encourage him. I can hear Ryker and Caden quietly talking in the wagon, Tyke and Klara are silent. The horses tread steadily through the forest, following old tracks wide enough for the wagon.

I look up at the moon several times, tracking the time.

Soon.

*****

When we reach the tree line before Roseguard, we all stop and stare out over the plains between us and the city. Outside the walls of

Roseguard, massive bonfires have been lit. They are scattered across the plain, lighting everything between the forest and the trees.

'They've had these lit every night since we took those humans. They're waiting for us,' Falcon says, gazing at the city.

'I would never have guessed,' Kai mutters sarcastically, and I look over at him. He rolls his head side to side, stretching, before looking over at me. I instantly turn away.

Falcon frowns at him but doesn't say anything.

'We've got the prisoners ready,' Crynn says from behind us.

I dismount, being careful to remain quiet even though I am certain that no humans would be brave enough to leave their city. The others follow suit. Crynn takes the horses and ties them to trees. Ryker pulls Tyke out of the wagon and Caden does the same for Klara. They draw their swords, standing prepared behind my prisoners. Tyke gives me a disgusted look.

I look each of my team in the eye. 'No matter what happens tonight, Vixy's safety is our biggest priority.'

Falcon nods his head. 'I swear it, Princess.'

'You have my word,' Ryker dips his head.

'Vixy's safety first.' Caden glances at Falcon.

Crynn calls out from the horses, 'Promise you, Princess.'

I turn to Kai, who is strapping a small round shield to his back.

'I'm not swearing that, Danica.'

I grind my teeth and grit out, 'Why not?'

'I prioritise your safety over anyone else's.'

My breath catches.

Then he adds, 'Don't let your temper screw this up.'

I clench my jaw and turn away from him.

'Let's go save Vixy,' I say and step out of the tree line. Roseguard is close enough that we'll be spotted and Melissa alerted, but far enough that should we need to retreat we'll be under the cover of the trees in no time. We've barely covered any ground when a horn blows within the city, alerting Melissa of our arrival.

I don't take my eyes off the gates of Roseguard. Kai keeps pace on my left, Falcon on my right. Crynn vanishes into the night to spy and keep watch from the shadows. We pass the first two bonfires. The gates of Roseguard open; I can make out a fairly large group of people.

We slow our pace as we get closer.

When we're twenty yards away from the other party, we stop. My eyes widen when I see Melissa Cole in a suit the colour of blood. Fire burns through my veins as I look her in the eye. I let a hand rest on my sword and hear a slight clink of metal. I frown and turn to look at Kai. His eyes are focused on Melissa, a hand on his sword, and the veins in his neck are starting to show.

Confused at Kai's reaction, I mutter his words back to him.

'Don't let your temper screw this up.'

His gaze snaps to me, his eyes blank for a moment then something like approval shines in them.

I look away, at Hunter. He's standing with his arms folded, a suit to match his mother's, his gaze on me, on my party. Behind Hunter are two hooded figures, one of them, I hope, is Vixy.

I take a deep breath. 'Well Hunter, I certainly didn't give you enough credit,' I pause for a moment to make sure he heard my words, 'but I'm really not surprised, you're just like your mother.'

I watch as Hunter taps a foot on the ground, his nerves showing. It's not Hunter who replies.

'Danica Arlet Rush. The best soldier I ever had. It's a pity your talent is wasted fighting for the Narakuya.' Melissa turns to look at Vixy. 'Well, it seems I have what you want, and you have what my loyal son wants.'

'I want more than Vixen Kyler, but those wants are secondary to Vixen's freedom.'

'The moment you release your prisoners; I will release mine.' Melissa's eyes shoot to my party. 'Hunter made a good guess at who you would bring.'

Hunter finally speaks up. 'You…' He points at Kai, who has a wicked smile forming. 'Who are you? I haven't seen you in Danica's little entourage of vicious soldiers.'

'That's because I am no soldier, boy.' Kai taps a finger against his sword.

Hunter tilts his head as his gaze narrows.

Then Melissa laughs and I know what is coming next. 'So that must make you the little princess's bed warmer.'

Instinct has me grabbing Kai's arm as he launches forward. I've spent enough time listening to Melissa's taunts and I've learned how to deal with her, how to tolerate her snarky comments, but Kai hasn't. Melissa likes to play games and tease and make fun of anyone she knows she has power over. She'd never be brave enough to say something like that to

Rayven, not when she knew Rayven's response would be to cut out her tongue.

And Kai is not the type of male to let disrespect slide.

I look over at Kai and finally I realise the reason behind his reaction when he saw Melissa. Why he, who seems to always be in perfect control, is suddenly struggling to keep control. He has spent ten years knowing who killed his brother but unable to retaliate. Now he is standing in front of the woman who ordered his brother's death, ordered an eleven-year-old boy to be murdered in his sleep.

'Kai,' I say gently, realising that maybe he isn't as controlled as he wants to be.

His ice gaze lands on me for a moment before flying back to Melissa. Hunter is watching us carefully, assessing who Kai might be.

He takes a deep breath.

'Tell me who you are, then we'll begin the exchange,' Hunter demands.

Of course, it's Hunter who will want the information about who Kai is. Not Melissa, she won't care until she finds out who he is. But Hunter … he craves control and power, and knowledge is power.

'Wouldn't you love to know?' Kai hisses, and I pinch his arm. 'Shall I give you a hint?'

'Games are for children,' Hunter snaps.

A thought slips through my head, I could sit and watch Kai and Hunter interact for a while.

'So, I shall entertain you then.' A nasty grin slips onto Kai's lips. 'Hint one, I'm from Ritenvold.'

Melissa's gaze sets on Kai. 'Who are you?'

'A representative for King Darius Vold.'

Melissa tilts her head. 'You're Kai Vold.'

Kai doesn't say anything, not confirming or denying her statement.

'Queen Ada died over two decades ago, you are a bastard to the crown,' Melissa snaps, and I realise that she's getting increasingly anxious.

'Queen Ada died giving birth to myself and my twin, Luca Vold.' Kai tilts his head, 'if you're going to kill one of us, make sure you kill all of us.' I get goosebumps, the authority and power in his voice as he speaks.

I let a smirk slip onto my lips as Melissa's face pops into an *O* shape. She takes a small step back, her hands going to her stomach, looking as if she's going to be sick. Hunter's face is one of pure shock and he glances us, his mother and the gates to Roseguard, ready to bolt.

I realise that this exchange could continue and end in blows, so instead of letting either Melissa, Hunter or Kai continue baiting one another, I interrupt.

'We told you who Prince Kai was, now release Vixen Kyler,' I state.

Melissa raises a finger and drops it.

I nod to Ryker and Caden, who release Tyke and Klara, giving them a push forward.

The guards behind Vixy remove her and the other prisoner's hood. I scan Vixy for injuries as she lurches forward. She's covered in bruises but no visible cuts. I glance at the other person running towards us and do a double take. The girl is identical to Vixy, but a few years older. Her sister, Autumn.

I open my arms and Vixy flies into them, I grip her in a tight hug and her body starts shaking gently.

'I've got you; I've got you.' Relief floods through me. 'You're safe, Vix.'

Vixy pulls away and I smile down at her before she glances across at Autumn. Falcon has wrapped his jacket over her shoulders, and she stands between us, shaking slightly as she watches Vixy and the Red Soldiers across from us.

Kai takes a deep breath. 'We will be back for you Melissa Cole. We will show you what happens when you attempt to tear kingdoms apart.'

I look over at Melissa, at the soldiers undoing the rope on Tyke and Klara.

Melissa takes a single step forward. 'Where's your mother, Danica? Rayven not brave enough to come face me?'

'Mark my words. Queen Rayven is coming for you,' I snap back.

I look over at Hunter, thinking he would have more to say.

'Ready?' Kai asks.

I nod and turn my back on the Red Soldiers, knowing Crynn will be watching them the entire time and Dimitri who has his bow loaded but lowered beneath the side of the cart, out of sight.

'Come on, Vix, let's get you somewhere safe.' Vixy walks beside me, holding her sister's hand.

I take one last look at Hunter and Melissa, they're still in the middle of the open field, only twenty yards from myself. Melissa is watching me. Unease spreads through me. We're out of range of the city walls, and we have the army to our backs.

Melissa nods to her guard, and he raises an arm that's holding a torch.

'Go!' I shout at my team.

A deafening crack splits the near silent night.

'Take cover!' Dimitri shouts from the cart. A weight crashes into me, and I'm thrown to the ground. I am pinned down and can't move.

'Vixy!' I shout, trying to shove the weight off me.

'Don't move, Danica!' Kai shouts into my ear, and I realise he is the weight on top of me. 'Roseguard has attacked, they've used catapults!'

'No, no, no, no!' I scream and shove Kai off. 'I need to get to Vixy!'

Dimitri is at the cart, bow now visible releasing arrow after arrow so quickly that I can't keep up. I don't know how he can see his target from this distance and in the darkness, but I do know that his arrows will be landing, he never misses. For Dimitri, nothing is out of range.

I can hear hoofbeats galloping from both directions. Kai keeps his body between me and the enemy.

'They've got archers approaching on horseback.' I hear Dimitri shout.

They can get close enough to release a few rounds of arrows but they're too close to avoid Dimitri's arrows, and they drop from their horses like flies. Kai unstraps his shield moments before whistling fills the air, arrows raining down on us. Falcon has covered Autumn with his shield while Ryker and Caden shield themselves.

My blood goes cold. There, a huge hole through her stomach from the rocks in the catapult, lies Vixy.

My scream echoes against the walls of Roseguard.

I launch to Vixy's side, this time nothing, no one, stops me.

Frantically, I take in the wounds.

Vixy's chest is still rising.

I put pressure around the hole in her stomach, I can see her intestines. Kai shields us from the arrows.

'Hold on, Vix. I can save you,' I say, tears begin pouring down my face. 'I won't let you die here.'

A hand touches my shoulder. 'She's not going to make it back to a healer.'

'Shut up! She will!'

Blood dribbles out of Vixy's mouth and nose.

'Danica,' Vixy coughs, tears running down her cheeks, terror covering her face. 'Please… please help me.'

'I am.' Both my hands are putting pressure on the wound.

'Danica, we have to get out of here!' Kai shouts over my shoulder.

'Autumn?' Vixy pants, and then she closes her eyes. 'I don't want to…'

Her chest stills.

'No! No! No! No!' I frantically try to restart Vixy's heart.

'The others are back on the cart. We have to go now.' Kai demands, grabbing my arm.

Hoofbeats echo past us, Rayven's warriors forcing the Red Soldiers to retreat.

Tears stream down my face as I ignore Kai and pick up Vixy's little body. I have to get Vixy out of here.

I let Kai guide me back to the wagon; the constant thudding of arrows against the shield is the only thing I can hear.

# Chapter Twenty-Seven

## Danica

I gaze at Vixy's face, her head in my lap. Her orange hair is matted with her blood.

Autumn is on the other side of Vixy's body, tears running down her face as she holds Vixy's hand.

The wagon rattles, the horse's footfalls barely audible. The silence is creeping in.

Vixy's body is not the only one in the wagon; Crynn's body lies still beside me.

Autumn finally looks up at me. At me, who couldn't save a single girl after I had promised to.

'I think you should know that Vixen said that when she grew up, she wanted to be just like you. You are her hero.'

I stare blankly at Autumn. She looks almost identical to the girl whose head is in my lap. 'Melissa is going to die.'

*****

The wagon rolls to a stop, and I see people's faces; their hands touching my face, my hands.

I look down at my hands; they're red. I swallow, my throat dry, and use my shirt to get the blood off, but it won't come off. I spit into my hands to get it off. I run for the nearest water source, a small stream. I dive to my knees and scrub at my hands. I struggle to wash the blood from my skin.

I scratch my hands raw. Someone pulls me back, pulls me into an embrace.

I let my tears fall down my face as I cry into my mother's chest.

# CHAPTER TWENTY-EIGHT

## DANICA

It's eerily quiet through the camp, all in tense and heavy anticipation for the bonfires that await the dead. It doesn't matter now if the Coles know where our camp is, the smoke will drift up above the tree line later today, marking our camp's position. I haven't moved from my tent, haven't moved from the end of the bed since I sat down on it hours ago.

Two people died, two people that should have lived. Ryker had found Crynn, not far from the wagons with a bolt through his throat. He was a warrior, and he died serving Rayven, serving me. Vixy, however… she was a child. A child with a sister and a home in Salt City.

The curtain flaps of the tent move, and I look up to see Dimitri.

He walks over and sits beside me, wrapping an arm around my shoulders and I lean into him, the soft scent of burnt wood and citrus filling my nose.

'I am so sorry, Danica,' he whispers into my ear. 'You didn't deserve to lose her after everything you've gone through. She didn't deserve to die.'

I nod my head. I don't feel attached to my body. We sit there in silence for a while, and I let myself grieve, I let the tears run down my cheeks and into my father's shirt. We sit on the bed, letting the time pass for a while before Dimitri presses a kiss to the top of my head.

'It's time.' Dimitri stands up, holding a hand out for me.

I take his hand, and don't let go of it. The walk to the bonfires is painfully quiet, the air thick and hard to breathe. I keep my gaze on the ground before me, the once green grass now flattened from the army, until I reach those dreaded pyres.

Reaching the clearing, I let go of Dimitri's hand and I stand back as I watch every member of the two armies place a branch on the pyres. Falcon gently places a branch. Kai limps up and places a branch down on each of the pyres, one for Crynn and one for Vix.

There is silence again, only the breathing of the living is heard in the clearing.

Then, from between the two pyres, Rayven finally speaks. Her voice is clear from any emotion, and she recites our ancient words to everyone gathered. Words I haven't heard from another's tongue since I was a child.

'Today, we have gathered to witness the final fight for two warriors.' Rayven's voice is even, and I stare blankly at the pyres. 'Crynn Balathasar was a brother to many and a loyal warrior who will continue his fight in the next life. Vixen Kyler was a sister to many and a born warrior, she will continue her fight in the next life.'

Rayven lets silence hang for a moment longer before the finish.

We all say the final words together. 'You were born from the Shadows and so you shall return. Let the moon guide your path and be a beacon in the dark. May you win your fight and rest during the immortal night.'

I sigh and shudder as the final word leaves my lips. Those words I learned a long, long time ago and had whispered many times. Vixy has now transitioned to the next life under moonlight.

Rayven finds my gaze through the gathered crowd and dips her chin. The air is fresh and cool as I take a deep breath, push my shoulders back and chin up. I need to be strong for Vix now. I stride towards Rayven and upon reaching her, she passes me a torch. I step up to the pyre and let the flicker of flames begin.

I don't move as I watch the flames get bigger and bigger, consuming the bodies within. The sickening smell of burning hair mixed in with the pine wood. I cough once, the scent always a shock to my body. My gaze leaves the pyres once when someone comes to stand beside me. Kai's presence settles around me. He doesn't say anything but offers me his company and support.

*****

The wind stirs through the ashes, and I say my final goodbye to my little fox. The last piece that had me tied to that creature that was fighting for survival, was Vixy. That piece is gone now and only I can decide what sort of creature I become now. I take a deep breath and let go of her, let go of the last six months hidden in the desert. Let go of those years on the front line. I turn my back to the ashes and look out at the camp, at Kai who is still standing at my side.

Kai reaches across and grips my shoulder. His hand is a solid, soothing weight and I want to lean into it.

'You're going to be okay.'

I nod my head. He's the only other person that will understand the pain, the loss, of having family ripped away so suddenly. And yet he hasn't let the grief destroy him. He's a warrior, an heir.

Then I remember Autumn. Poor Autumn, who had been reunited with her sister, only to watch Vixy die days later. She'd be devastated.

'Thank you,' I say quietly, looking him in the eye. 'And thank you for saving my life.'

'Which time?'

I give him a small smile before turning and walking towards my tent, sleep in the back of my mind.

I can feel Kai's gaze piercing my back and I say over my shoulder, 'Every time.'

*****

The smoke from yesterday is still lingering around the camp. I open my eyes and stare at the roof of the dark grey tent, contemplating my options.

What has happened, has happened. I can't change the past, and I shouldn't forget it, but I can't let it ruin my future, my plans. I will avenge Vixen, then let her rest and continue my life. Continue fighting and continue finding my way home. I can let Vixy's death destroy me … or I can learn and become the warrior princess for my people. I can be as human as Hunter, or I can be as strong as my mother. Rayven never stopped fighting, never let any emotion affect her vision. Despite the delay in her war against Roseguard because of me, she used that time to prepare, to be better equipped and to rally her people, lead her people.

I need to become better equipped, better prepared. I need to become a weapon, unyielding and powerful enough to best any obstacle thrown my way.

Yesterday, I had let sleep claim me, only waking for dinner before climbing back into the safety of my bed. Now, sunrays creep in through the canvas flaps of the tent, and I climb out of my bed. Taking my time, I braid my hair, wash my face, prepare myself for the day ahead.

Pulling back the tent flaps to peer outside, I sneak out, keeping my head low so none of the warriors notice me. I don't mind speaking to them, but I would rather not be asked about Vixy, the front line or Roseguard. Not at this moment.

A campfire sits in the middle of a circle of tents, Rayven and Dimitri's tent as well as mine are directly across from King Darius's and Kai's. I make my way across, keeping my steps quiet. I move the tent flaps out of the way and step into Kai's tent. It's almost identical to mine.

Kai sits up instantly, his gaze snapping onto me. He sits on the end of his bed, tying up his bootlaces, shirtless.

I hesitate as I take in the muscles and tan skin, the hair on his chest and the small scars sprinkled over his body.

'You haven't come to murder me in my sleep, have you?' his eyes don't leave me as I swallow and look at him. He raises an eyebrow at me, and I take a deep breath, calming my racing mind.

I shake my head. 'If your offer still stands, I'd like you to train me.'

He bends over to continue his shoelace, 'Of course.'

'Thank you.'

He finishes the lace, straightens up and grabs a shirt that was sitting on the bed beside him. He pulls it over his head, his muscles rippling like water.

'Come sit,' he gestures at the bed, and I cautiously walk over, taking in the small personal belongings around the tent. The daggers lined up neatly on the small table, the swords on a small rack in the corner, the clothes thrown over the chair. A few books stacked neatly on the table beside his bed.

I watch as Kai stretches his leg out in front of him. He had taken an arrow to the back of his calf muscle, fortunately it hadn't gone deep but it was enough to make him sit on the sick bed and limp around camp for the day after. I hadn't even noticed until Rayven had mentioned it sometime between Vixy's death and her pyre. A hazy memory comes to mind, of Kai in the front of the cart that brought the dead bodies back to camp. He doesn't mention the wound, so neither do I.

'Lesson one?' I ask.

He massages his leg almost subconsciously. 'If we're going to make this little arrangement work, you need to trust me, and I need to be able to trust you.'

I glare at him, an almost instinctual response.

'I know you're a very private person, Danica. And I know you're not very forthcoming; you don't trust anyone, and you try to do everything yourself before anyone can beat you to it.' I bite my lip as his words ring true.

'Well, I don't know how to be anything else,' I say, not quite making eye contact. 'I've only ever had myself to trust and rely on.'

'I saw you once before, you know?' Kai begins and I look over at him, tilting my head slightly as I take in the change of topic. 'When Luca died, I trained to be the best warrior I could possibly be, so one day I would be able to avenge him. I spent some time on the front line fighting Red Soldiers.

'We all knew about what had happened. Queen Rayven made sure we all knew how Cole had taken you and how you were stuck fighting for the enemy. We knew that should we see you, we would try to protect you, try to get you to our own trenches where we would wait for Rayven's army. The day I saw you, it was pouring with rain. I was fighting with the archers and had seen someone covered in mud slaughter two Ritenvold soldiers in mere seconds. I took aim and hesitated. I had never seen someone kill that quickly, that efficiently before, not in the mud with those injuries across your skin. And then it dawned on me who you were.

'The princess of the Moonstone Palace forty yards from me, covered in mud. Your hair was loose, matted with blood and mud, and it was caught over your face. The rain soaked your clothes, and you only had one Roseguard training sword, not even a proper sword, and yet you were the most deadly creature out there. You were fighting like a wild cat, taking aim at anything that moved. I saw how you would sight your target and release yourself onto the warrior. I saw the bloodthirst in you as you took in anyone with a rose on their armour. I laid my bow down, and with only my sword, I made my way towards you. You stopped fighting as I approached, and I even called your name, but the Red Soldiers realised what was going on, an arrow hit you and you didn't move, so one soldier knocked you out. One of them came up behind you, and with a hand gloved in metal, struck you in the back of the head. I didn't see you again until you showed up in a wagon trying to hold your guts in.' He looks over at me. 'So, believe me when I say I know what you went through on the front line. What you did there wasn't easy.'

'I thought that that was just a dream…' I look away now, take a deep breath and close my eyes for a moment. 'No, it wasn't easy slaughtering my allies.'

'So, lesson one is turning that to your advantage.'

'How?' I ask. 'I've missed out on ten years of my life, ten years of training to be a warrior. As you said, I fight like a human.'

'Yes, you fight like a human, but you would still defeat anyone other than a royal bloodline.' He taps his finger on the sheets of the bed. 'And how do the humans think you fight? They think you fight like a Narakuya.'

'But they don't know any better.'

'Danica, you've spent ten years learning about the enemy. You know them, you know the way they fight.' I frown, considering what he is saying. 'But you need to learn how to be better than your enemy; how to be greater than them, quicker, smarter, stronger. You need to learn how to be who you are; we all fight differently; you need to learn your way.'

'Which I got my ass kicked for doing,' I say glumly, recalling how he so easily humiliated me and threw me into the dirt only days ago.

'You have a temper. You have anger and hatred in you.' He folds his arms, daring me to snap back. 'You can either fuel it and fight like humans do, throwing everything they have into that anger, or you can block your emotions and turn the anger into energy, into a clear mind where you think and act before your opponent knows what is happening. This is why when we shift into our *killing calm* everything becomes clear and peaceful. Our emotions are locked into a part of our mind where the access door is the size of a pin prick. Only the strongest of emotions can push through that door, and even then, it's faint.'

'And what about your loss of control over your temper that night…?' I don't let myself think about anything else that happened that night, not as Vixy with her bloodied body comes to mind. The night that Falcon, Ryker and Caden broke their promise and failed to save Vixy.

He looks at me guiltily. 'I'll admit that when Melissa didn't recognise me, I let my emotions override my calm.'

'You were about to attack her like a werewolf,' I mutter, and he smiles.

'Aye, I never said I was perfect. Now it's your turn to start talking,' he says, and I tilt my head at him in question. 'I want to know more about you.'

'Like what?'

'The scar on your stomach?'

I try to recall when he saw that, then realise he had followed me to the deep pool. He had watched me strip off and dive into the depths.

'The night the Red Soldiers came for me …' I take a deep breath and decide to tell the story from the beginning. 'Rayven and Dimitri had left me in Dimitri's hunting cabin while they went to discuss the Treaty and Luca's assassination with Melissa. Our maid was looking after me. She had baked me muffins and made me dinner. The food smelt funny, and the maid tried to force me to eat it, so I had thrown a temper tantrum and gone running to my bed.' I hesitate. 'I heard horses approaching and stayed in my room, knowing they weren't Natari. The footfalls were too loud, too heavy, and there was the clanging of heavy armour. I listened as the maid informed the soldiers that I hadn't eaten the drugged food but would be asleep in my bed. The maid told the soldiers that I trusted her, so she would attempt to restrain me.

'I pretended to be asleep, but then the maid tried to tie me up. She was the first to die. I had no weapons, no strength compared to my enemies, so I shifted into my true form for the first time. I remember launching myself at the soldiers and using whatever I could to kill them—claws and fangs. The Red Soldiers had drawn their swords when they saw the blood dripping down my hands, my mouth. Four soldiers attacked, three died before a human put the blade in me. Another three died while

I had the dagger in my stomach. They kept it in there until I passed out and was locked in a cage made for a chimera.'

I look up at Kai. When I told Hunter the story, he'd looked at me with horror, like I was a monster. And maybe I am for what I have done, but I'm not nearly as much of a monster as Melissa Cole. She does not differentiate between warriors and children.

'Well, now you know how I got the scar.'

'I guess I do.'

'And...?' I ask cautiously, looking him in the eye.

'You're brave, Princess.' He bites his lower lip for a moment, instantly drawing my attention to that small movement. 'I would never have been able to do what you did.'

The way Kai says it is completely different in meaning to how Hunter would have said it.

# Chapter Twenty-Nine

## Danica

It has been four days since Vixy died, and I still haven't been able to look Autumn in the eye. Not when I feel like I'm looking at Vixy; not when it feels like I'll be confessing my failures.

But that needs to change now.

I walk through the camp, searching for where Falcon set up a tent for her. Autumn will stay with our camp, safe, until she decides to go her own way.

I find Autumn's tent next to Falcon's. It is the usual warrior's tent, not nearly as large or luxurious as mine, Rayven's or Kai's. But it's big enough that she'll have her own privacy.

I hesitate before pulling open the flaps. This is what a leader does; they push past their pain and move on with life. Part of pushing past my pain is facing Autumn.

Inside the tent, Autumn sits on the bed, Falcon across from her on a stool. They immediately stop talking when they see me, and I don't acknowledge Falcon as I stride into the small tent. He swore to protect Vixy and failed. We all did.

'Autumn, may I talk with you? Alone.'

She nods, her bright orange hair hangs loose around her shoulders. The shade of her hair, the same as a fox's fire coat, reminds me of Vixy's. Although Vixy's had been thicker, the similarity is unsettling.

I wait until Falcon has left the tent before walking over to sit on the stool. I don't say anything as I listen to Falcon hesitate outside, then his footsteps become quieter, muffled by the noise of the war camp as he gets further and further away.

'Vixen spoke very highly of you,' Autumn says quietly, her eyes watching me carefully, eyes that are Vixy's, with the same shades that turn emerald in the sun.

'Likewise,' I reply, my whole body tense, and I can feel butterflies fluttering around inside my stomach. 'I am sorry that it has taken me so long to approach you. Your resemblance to Vix is… you look just like her.'

Autumn sits there for a moment, and I don't know what else to say.

'Roseguard cleared out Salt City.'

'What?'

'When the Red Soldiers came for me, they came for everyone else in the city too.' Autumn looks down at her lap. 'I don't know what happened to them, and I don't know where they are in Roseguard, I was blindfolded the entire time except for when I was in the cell with Vixen. I think they took anyone who could fight. They spun lies about what has truly happened, and when the people have believed those lies for so long, it becomes the truth to them. I think Roseguard sent warnings and insisted on recruiting all who could hold a blade, a bow, a dagger. When they arrived … when Roseguard arrived, all who had decided on chasing glory on the battlefield, joined willingly. Those who chose to stay were believed to be a stain on the city's reputation. In the end, Roseguard took everyone.'

'I promise we'll destroy Roseguard,' I say quietly.

Autumn clenches a fist. 'Do whatever you have to. Vixen didn't deserve to die.'

'No, she didn't.' I stand up, deciding that I would need to speak to Autumn in parts, until my grieving had healed enough that I didn't feel like it was Vixy in front of me. 'Vixy loved you very much. We were going to make our way to Salt City.'

'Vixen knew what you are,' Autumn stands up as well. 'And she loved you.'

I blink a few times and nod my head before turning towards the flaps of the tent. The words… they sting, they fracture the already broken pieces of my heart. But I needed to hear those words, if only to remind me that my broken heart, it is still a heart.

Outside, Falcon is waiting for me across the clearing and he approaches as soon as I spy him. He runs a hand through his dark hair.

'Danica.' He steps up to my side.

'What do you want?' I turn to look at him.

'I'm sorry about the girl.'

'She has a name,' I snap, anger like a viper ready to strike.

He winces.

I take a deep breath. This is not how I want to react.

'Falcon, I think it is best if you stay out of my way for a while,' I say, lowering my voice.

'And who's going to be your right-hand man?' His tone changes slightly, and I don't back down from it.

'I don't need a right-hand man.'

'Who is going to protect you?' He steps closer and I hold my ground.

'I will protect myself,' I say clearly, then add, 'and I will protect my people and kingdom.'

His eyes darken and he goes to take my hand, I pull it back from his reach. 'What about when the time comes that you can't rule by yourself, when you need someone by your side?'

His question catches me off guard.

'I have been free for eight months now. I have a war to win.' My tone drops. 'What are you implying Falcon?'

'I'm just saying that you can't always do everything by yourself.' He raises a hand to my face, and I keep still as he touches my cheek. It reminds me of when Kai had so softly and briefly touched my cheek.

I pull back. 'I haven't even thought that far into my future, and now is not the time to contemplate those decisions…'

He takes another step closer, he's taller than me and I have to look up to match his gaze. 'I won't fail you again Danica. I promise that it'll be you and me one day, just like when we were children.'

'But we are no longer children.'

'I know that, so it's in my best interest to make sure that you are fit and healthy to rule.'

His pale eyes watch me carefully, as if unsure how I'll react.

'Why is it in your best interest for me to be fit and healthy to rule?'

'So you're not the last of your bloodline.'

I choke on nothing, on air, and cough, taking a few steps back from him. Blood rushes to my cheeks and I feel nausea building in my stomach. Falcon goes to take a few steps forward.

'As I said earlier, it'd be best if you kept your distance,' I demand.

He takes another step forward.

'You are disobeying your princess's command,' a voice snarls.

Both of us snap our gaze to where the voice came from, to the edge of the clearing where Kai is leaning against a tree, watching us with his arms folded.

Falcon turns to look back at me, a snarl on his face now. 'You shouldn't be playing around with that arrogant prince, and you know it.'

'I seem to recall it was that arrogant prince who saved my life.' I glare at him, anger burning through my veins at his challenge; at the authority he thinks he has over me; how he thinks he knows best, how he thinks he can have me.

'Princess,' Kai calls from the tree, 'we have practice now.'

Falcon's stare hardens as he spits his words at me, his own anger rising. 'Danica, don't you go with him.'

He does not have the authority to command me, and I remind him of that as I push past, ignoring him.

I keep my back straight as I stride over to Kai, Falcon's gaze like a dagger being pushed into my back. Kai turns to follow me as I aim for a small clearing, far enough from the camp that we'll have some peace.

'You alright, Princess?' Kai asks once we're out of earshot.

'I'm fine, Prince.'

'Do you want to talk about it? About what Falcon said?'

'No, thank you.'

He grins.

I scowl at the prince, but don't say anything as I take him in. The brown leather pants and the loose white shirt. Despite the plain clothing, there is no mistaking him for what he is, a prince. It's in the way he holds his chin high, his muscled shoulders back, and the alert but relaxed walk as he enters the clearing.

He steadily walks around the clearing, taking me in as if I were something other, something more.

He hesitates and turns his shoulders towards me as he says, 'You can't let anyone rattle your emotions.'

'I can't help it.'

'You can.' The circling continues, and I turn on my heel to track him. 'How?'

He stops in front of me. 'Think about why Falcon would be acting in that manner?'

Well, I guess we'll be talking about him anyway.

'Because he is an over-protective bastard who doesn't know where to draw the line?' I tap my foot on the ground, my arms folded, as I start to get impatient.

Kai grins. 'Nice try. It's because he's both threatened by me, and was very comfortable with being in your position as the so-called Rayven's heir while you were on the front line – and I suspect he also has his own motives.'

'What do you mean by that?'

'You heard his comment about continuing your bloodline.'

My heart skips a beat.

'Think it over, Princess.' He passes me a long wooden pole that I hadn't noticed him pick up. 'He is an alpha male in a beta position. He wants to control who and what comes in contact with you. Falcon is aware of the authority you have over him, and I am almost certain that if you did not have that authority, there would be very little to stop him from becoming the one in control of the situation.' Kai falls silent for a moment, letting me process his words before continuing. 'You watch him, how he walks, how he talks and his reaction when a royal orders him. It was oh-so-easy to bait him, as the only thing holding his leash to stop him from striking is his position compared to mine. Watch him among his group of warriors, Ryker and Caden. He is the alpha in that group, Crynn was possibly the only one that could have posed a threat to his leadership but having seen the control and power that Falcon wielded in that group before Crynn's passing … that leadership had always been there and that was routine.

'He has grown comfortable in the role of being a leader. And he has your parent's respect for the warrior he is, which has been earned. However, that respect and that leadership is routine, that makes him think he is more powerful than he is. If Rayven has no more children, and you died on the front line, he would have been next in line for the throne, and he knows that too. He had power. Then you reappeared. He respected you before the front line, but the authority you hold over him, he wants that. I doubt he has admitted that to himself yet. I'm sure he would have schemed a thousand schemes to end up married to you, to be the father of your children, to have access to your power, your authority. Beware of the male with a thirst for power.'

'And what of your statement about him being threatened by you?'

He doesn't grin, and I hadn't realised I'd grown so accustomed to it until it wasn't there. 'I threaten his desires; I have power equal to yourself – as well as being a force he can't control.'

'How do you mean?'

'He has control over you, very little, but he does have some through your childhood relationship with him. Falcon is not your equal, not in strength, title or character. He is your subject.' He takes a step closer, and if I want, all I have to do is lean forward to touch him. 'You and I are equals, Danica.' I nod, knowing it in my mind, my blood and deep in my heart. 'He is threatened by me because of the power we share, the authority we both have. If he has you, my power is still a threat. If he doesn't have you, he has no power.'

I take a deep breath. My previous friendship with Falcon clouds my vision when I see him, and alters his behaviour, but now that Kai has said it, it is so clear. I look down at the wooden pole, then up at Kai.

'Want to play?' He grins, as if he hadn't just laid the truth of my childhood best friend out before me, so raw and bare.

*****

Four hours later I am completely drained, but Kai still hammers me with the pole. I grimace as he hits me on the back of the leg. I am going to be covered in bruises, but the pain is worth it. I have begun to figure out how to be a better fighter, not just quicker and stronger than other warriors but enough to equal Kai's ability.

Kai keeps his emotions hidden, controlled. He attacks through strategy and his movements are precise and brutal, as mine should be. Watching him control his emotions, put them aside and focus on the physical, on what is before him … it helps me know that it is possible. And as I get beaten over and over again, the fury and anger aren't as cloudy as they were a few days ago. I refocus and study Kai, his movements, his reactions to my actions, it's all planned out.

The first hour had been a mess. I went to attack without thinking, just acting. He kept taunting me, my temper came, and I'd throw more into the attack. It never worked.

Then I stopped, focused on Kai, on watching him and started thinking. Like chess, I started plotting my moves ahead. That was when

I started to put some pressure on him. And instead of reacting to his taunts, I started to banter with him.

There is no way I am calling it quits on our first spar and would keep going until Kai calls a finish to the training session, but a ruckus in camp makes me lose focus – and his pole flies straight into my gut.

I grimace and drop my own pole, doubling over as I try to catch my breath.

'The camp is not where your fight is, Princess.' Kai steps back, watching me. 'I think we're done for today.'

I wipe sweat off my brow.

'And we've barely done anything,' He teases, and I glare at him. 'At the start, you were trying to win the fight by force. You attack your opponent with everything you have, you plan one strategy, which would work if I somehow did exactly as the strategy in your mind dictates. You need to plan your attack like a tree, your first move is the trunk. The trunk decides the theme of the attack. Then, based on my reaction, your tree will split into branches, one to counteract the reaction I dealt you. And so on.' Kai walks by my side as I aim for the commotion in the camp. 'Your strategy was beginning to look like a tree towards the end, each branch leading towards the light at the top, where it has won.'

Before the Red Soldiers took me, I had begun basic training on weapons and how to use them, but I was never taught how to fight. I learned by mimicking the Red Soldiers and putting everything I have into the attack knowing I am the most powerful creature.

'It does make sense, what you're saying.' I rub my back for a moment.

He nudges me with his elbow, 'I know, otherwise I wouldn't be saying it.'

Up ahead, the warriors circle around someone. Centaurs and minotaurs stand above everyone else.

I stride up to the back of the gathering and raise my voice. 'What is going on?'

Many turn to look at me, and a female werewolf with long brown hair answers. 'Patrols found a Red spy!'

I push through the crowd as warriors move out of my way. Kai is right behind me, poles still in hand.

Two centaurs are holding a prisoner between them, and my blood goes cold as I meet Hunter's eyes.

Vixy flashes through my mind.

All thoughts of strategy vanish as I launch forward. Arms wrap around my stomach, holding me back. Hunter's eyes widen as he watches me try to free myself from Kai's grip. For one small moment, I am astounded that Kai knew me well enough to have grabbed me.

'Remember who you want to be Danica,' he says evenly. 'Revenge is secondary.'

I squeeze my eyes shut and relax, taking a deep breath.

His grip loosens, hesitating before falling from me.

I open my eyes.

'You have one sentence, Hunter Cole,' I say clearly, looking Hunter straight in the eye. 'And if that sentence isn't good enough, you die.'

Cheering rises from the warriors and Kai steps up beside me, raising a hand, the cheering quietens. The respect and command that he holds, it makes me realise why Falcon would want that.

Hunter's face is pale, his eyes wide and flying over everyone around us, astounded by the brutality and power of the warriors with us compared to the Red Soldiers he commands.

'You were right, Danica,' Hunter's voice wavers.

I certainly hadn't been expecting that. 'You've just earned yourself another sentence.'

'Elaborate,' Kai commands, the authority in his voice catching me off guard compared to his quelling of the crowd. Before he hadn't had to say anything – all had obeyed because of his reputation. There is no denying his commanding presence. Now, he is demanding. A prince aware of the power he has and wishing to wield it.

'My mother is who you thought her to be.' Hunter ignores Kai and focuses his attention on me. 'I told her no-one other than you was supposed to die that night; she agreed.'

'Do you normally start bargaining for your life by telling your captor they were supposed to be killed?' I snap.

'My mother lied and went behind my back and now Vixy is dead because of it.' Hunter is shaking slightly as he takes another quick look around the camp, as if some terrible nightmare were about to erupt from the ground itself. 'I am here to help you, Danica. On one condition.'

I fold my arms. 'You're not really in a position to be demanding conditions. What is it?'

Hunter takes a deep breath. 'I'll help you, give you information, as long as you don't kill my mother.'

I remain quiet for a moment. 'And why is your information so important that I would agree to that condition?'

'Because Mother has two armies. Each almost twice the size of yours.'

'Or I could torture you for the information,' I snarl and he flinches. I know exactly what word flashes through his mind. Monster!

'You could, but then you'd be proving why I shouldn't help you.' Hunter stares me down and I know he's giving me the option of treating him kindly after what he has done or publicly admitting to him and everyone around me that I am a monster.

I walk up to him, like a wolf walking up to a small house cat.

I stop in front of him and don't look at the two centaurs holding him prisoner.

I say softly, 'Release him.'

Relief washes over Hunter's face, knowing his mother is safe from the pain I had intended her to suffer from my bare hands.

It takes a few moments for the shackles to fall off and he rubs his wrists.

When he looks at me, I clench my fist and punch him in the stomach with all my force. He falls back, doubles over, winded and coughing.

'Escort Hunter Cole to the meeting tent. Someone find Queen Rayven and King Darius.' I turn to face Kai. 'I'll be there shortly.'

'Danica!' someone calls from the crowd.

I turn to find the face. It's the female who had first told me what was going on.

'Yes?'

'How do we know he's not lying?' The werewolf stalks forward as if hunting a deer, and I watch as she curls her fist.

'We don't. But it is up to the Queen to decide what to do with him.'

'We want him dead!' the werewolf shouts.

Kai steps in. 'As you all fall under the protection of the Treaty of Asada, it is up to Queen Rayven Arlet to decide what to do with this Red boy.'

None push back on Kai's order. Despite him not being from Asada, they still listen and respect him. I realise that I need to learn how to earn that respect. I want to earn that respect. Kai winks at me and I roll my eyes before nodding at the centaurs. Hunter's eyes don't leave me as he's taken to meet my mother.

I turn and aim for my tent, Kai follows closely behind until I push through the tent flaps. Inside the tent, hidden from the rest of the world, I strip out of my training clothes, still damp. I wipe myself with a towel after dipping it in cool, clean water. I find in the drawers, a neat black shirt and matching pants. I am dressing for a different sort of battle.

Hunter has taken me by surprise yet again. I was so certain that his mother was the one God in his life, but he has potentially proven that she isn't. I chew on my lip as I try to figure out Hunter's intentions, his beliefs and values. He values his life, and trades in gossip and rumours. His battlefield is not like the front line; it's not the one I've grown up on. His battlefield is the mind and words before him, and how to avoid bloodshed. I don't know why he would have risked his life to find our camp when he values his own life so greatly.

Taking a deep breath, I prepare myself for the next couple of hours. I force myself to think of the situation from a leader's perspective and avoid thinking about Hunter's involvement in Vixy's death.

Outside the tent, the wind stirs through the quiet camp. Warriors are busy practicing, preparing and making weapons and supplies. I turn to look at the meeting tent with Hunter inside it.

I don't run into anyone as I make my way over to the tent, and I hesitate before pulling the flap open, giving myself one more final moment before entering the battlefield of words, lies and truths.

I am a leader; a princess, and I do not let my emotions cloud my vision.

I step through the flaps and there sits Hunter.

# Chapter Thirty

## Danica

Ignoring Hunter, I walk directly past him and his guards to pour myself a glass of water, steadily filling the glass and halting at the top without spilling a drop. Letting him see my control over a simple task.

I listen to the centaurs quietly talk between themselves as we wait for everyone else to arrive. A tall, dapple-grey centaur is discussing the best type of armour with a younger buckskin boy. I zone out and make a point of ignoring Hunter. However, I can feel his eyes on me the entire time, especially when I leave the seat across from him empty, taking the seat next to it.

A couple of minutes pass before the flaps are pushed back, revealing King Darius and his small entourage of humans and Narakuya. Kai follows behind.

King Darius looks Hunter over once before turning to me.

'Hello young Princess.' He dips his head ever so slightly. 'I, unfortunately, haven't seen you since the death of the young girl and for your loss, I am terribly sorry.' King Darius dips his head once again, and I realise that part of the reason he said it was to make a jab at Hunter. To let Hunter see how I react.

'Thank you, King Darius. I have grieved for her, but I must be strong in this time of war,' I say evenly. 'Prince Kai informs me you have been well.' I watch as the king takes a seat at the head of the long table.

'Indeed,' Darius says as he watches Kai walk to my side. 'My son has told me he is practicing with you.'

Kai nods, keeping his gaze on his father as he takes the seat next to me, across from Hunter.

'I take it Kai has been teaching you what he learned from both our people.' Darius doesn't acknowledge Hunter, despite everyone in the room understanding that *our people* doesn't refer to Ritenvold and Asada but to humans and Narakuya.

'Yes. I am fortunate to have those hours to practice with an equal,' I say, nodding my head, and a moment of silence follows before Darius turns to look at Hunter.

'You are like me, boy. Human.' Darius leans back in his chair. 'Yet you rage war on your protectors and an innocent kingdom.'

Hunter clenches his jaw.

The tent flaps open again, and Rayven walks in with Dimitri hot on her heels as always. Dimitri looks Hunter up and down before shaking his head. Rayven, however, keeps her stare on Hunter as she takes a seat at the opposite end of the table to Darius.

She taps a hand on the table. 'Hunter Cole. I haven't seen you since you were an eleven-year-old boy tugging on your mother's sleeve.'

Hunter's face pales, looking almost as white as the Ritenvold banners. I look between him and my mother. She has never mentioned that she had met Melissa's son.

'That was the night your mother kidnapped my daughter and forced her to fight for your Red Army against a kingdom we had an alliance with. A kingdom that we *still* have an alliance with, despite your mother's attempt at fracturing our world.' Rayven dips her chin towards Darius in acknowledgement. 'Well, what is it you want to say, boy?'

Hunter's eyes are wide, and he fidgets nervously. A terrible captain, and I realise how little control Hunter has of his emotions.

'I came to offer a deal.' Hunter meets my eyes for a moment before turning his attention back to Rayven. 'My mother is corrupt.'

'Tell us something we don't know,' I snap. Kai squeezes my knee under the table in warning, and I shoot him a look.

*Temper.* I can see the word burning in his eyes, and I take a deep breath.

'My deal is this. In exchange for information about my mother's army, I want to be appointed as Roseguard's leader when you win this war and remove my mother from power. When I am leader, we will re-join the Treaty of Asada.' Hunter pauses. 'It is the easiest path to everlasting peace.'

Rayven tilts her head ever so slightly as she calculates every possible aspect of the offered deal.

I stay quiet. I had my time to get back at Melissa with Vixy, and Melissa won that battle. Now it's time for Rayven to win the war. Rayven's eyes bounce to mine before landing on Dimitri's. A silent conversation ensues between my mother and father. Dimitri moves his head ever so slightly to the right.

Hunter watches Rayven, Dimitri, Darius and I, his eyes occasionally flicking to Kai as if trying to figure him out. We are all players on the board, Kai, however, is a new piece, and that night outside of Roseguard is not a lot of time to figure someone out.

Kai finally speaks up. 'Why have you come to us with this deal? Surely the quickest way to become leader would be to assassinate your mother and take the power from her, stopping this war.'

'I'm not a monster.' He doesn't meet my eye, but I know the words are directed at me.

I decide it's time for payback. 'Hunter is weak and flinches at death, he does not understand that death is a part of life.'

'As I said, unlike you, I don't kill everything that gets in my way,' Hunter finally meets my stare, an eyebrow raising ever so slightly. 'I am not a monster.'

I hesitate, the entire tent is silent, watching, waiting for my response. Maybe I am a monster, I have killed so many. If I hadn't antagonised Melissa, Vixy would be alive. I killed more people than I could count on the front line.

I lower my gaze slightly.

Kai takes my hand. 'If you're a monster, Danica, then so am I.'

I look up at him. And then it clicks into place. Kai clicks into place. When he told me we were equals… I believed him, yet it hadn't sunk in until those words.

Kai has killed many before, but always for the right reasons.

We are all predators in this world, and we are all prey to the more powerful. We are all monsters to someone else, and we all are partly monsters, but as long as our morals are stronger than our actions… then I am not what Hunter believes me to be.

I give Kai a grateful look before turning to look at Hunter, his words not stinging nearly as much now.

'I may be a monster,' I take a deep breath. 'But I am no traitor to my people, to my mother and father. And I am not a coward.'

Hunter doesn't seem to miss a beat, but his eyes go to Kai, sizing him up. 'Apologies, Danica.'

I frown, not understanding what Hunter is apologising for.

'Your mother has never stayed true to her word, so I hope you will prove me wrong, Hunter Cole of Roseguard.' Rayven taps a finger on the table. 'I accept your deal.'

Hunter quietly sighs, barely audibly.

'Well, talk.' Rayven doesn't hesitate to push for answers.

Hunter turns to look around the room at the gathered representatives of each species. 'You're missing one.'

My blood goes cold. I know exactly who Hunter is talking about. 'Yes, the fae.'

'Mother has offered them Salt City as well as Carramera in exchange for wearing Roseguard's colours during the coming war.' Hunter's brown eyes slide to Rayven.

King Jules, the fae king, already had a throne in the tropical city of Carramera, before the war. To expand to another city … to take a seat of power in another city will disturb the balance. Each city is normally dominated by a different species, of course there is a mixture of those species but for the fae to push that line is equivalent to challenging the species for control of the city.

Rayven doesn't let any emotion slip onto her face. 'And where is Melissa's army?'

Hunter hesitates. 'You killed a basilisk beneath our city.'

'There is only one entry into Thorn Gap. Through the top.' I watch as Rayven calculates where she could have missed another entrance.

'There are three entrances into the Gap,' Dimitri finally speaks up. 'The sky, the staircase from Roseguard, and a stone door on the north side of the Gap. Something I learned while staying in Roseguard.' Rayven and Dimitri share a look. I make a note to ask about it later.

'The stairs and the stone door are heavily guarded. The stone door is being destroyed as we speak. And the sky, all Gods watch it.' Hunter folds his arms.

'How did you get in?' I turn to Rayven.

'Through the sky, I fell down with the waterfall. There's a river that runs through the Gap.' Rayven turns to look at me. 'But that was before there were two armies camped there.'

I keep my mouth shut as a plan forms in my mind.

# Chapter Thirty-One

## Danica

The quiet flickering of the flames struggles to quieten the noises of the army as I study the map in front of me, the campfire giving me enough light to see. I trace a finger from where our army is well hidden among the trees, south of a rose imprinted on the map, to Thorn Gap, north of the imprinted rose.

I tap my finger on it once, considering the three entrances, one of them now completely destroyed. That destroyed entrance would have been our best option to gain access to the caverns beneath. It would have been all too easy to take out the soldiers stationed there and bring our own army in.

'Danica.'

I look up to find Kai gazing over my shoulder at the map.

I don't reply and turn my attention back to the map. He sits down on the ground next to me, stretching his legs out in front of him. 'You alright, Princess?'

I nod.

'Tell me about the conflict you have with Hunter Cole,' he asks, and I fold the map up.

'You know I took Hunter hostage.' I fiddle with the folded map, Kai's eyes tracking it. 'What more is there to add?'

He takes the map from me and slips it into his pocket, then takes my hand in his. 'I've seen you furious or unsure, but I haven't seen you this … anxious? Irked? Until the conflict with the Cole boy.'

I gaze into the flames, watching them twist and dance into the night.

'I always manage to underestimate him,' I admit quietly.

'That's not all, is it?' He pushes. 'I saw your reaction when he called you a monster. I see your reaction every time he opens his mouth.' He falls silent and I look at him. 'You think you're a monster because of what you were forced to do on the front line, what you've done to survive.'

I look back at the flames.

Kai's words hit home, they hit the truth I knew but never admitted to myself. I had done terrible things on the front line, right beside those Red Soldiers. I had done those terrible things to Kai's people, my allies. I did it because it was the easy option to give in and fight for them rather than against them, and to avoid the torture that followed disobedience.

'Danica.' Kai pushes, and I don't say anything.

He has just stripped me bare.

'Talk to me.'

I shudder. 'What if I am a monster? What if I am a cold killing creature? What if Hunter is right and the front line is where I belong?'

'Danica. You're not alone.' I turn to look at Kai. 'You and I are the same. And I don't think you're a monster. I heard what Autumn said, Vixy thought you were a hero.'

I lean my head against his shoulder. An arm wraps around my shoulders and for the first time in a very long time I feel like I can relax. The scent of summer rains and oak fills me as I breath in the smell of him. The fire crackles around us and despite the war looming, despite the enemy walking through the camp, I feel like I am in the right place.

Footsteps thud through the camp, one set drawing closer and closer. Kai looks up at the same moment I do to see Hunter approaching from the other side of the campfire, our guards following him, tracking his every move. He stops in his tracks the moment he spies us and bites his lower lip without realising as he takes us in. I have no idea what might be going through his mind, and I doubt I want to know. Not when he takes a seat across the fire from us. I also doubt that he has taken that seat to warm by the flames, not when his eyes don't leave us.

It was peaceful until Hunter arrived. Now my blood is pulsing slightly faster, and the tension sets in as I try to figure out what he is playing at.

'It's interesting that the humans in this kingdom call us Nightwalkers,' Kai states, and I look up at him.

'What do you mean?' I let myself glance over at Hunter, noticing that he is now watching us with a guarded expression. I'm not sure if it is because of what Kai will say or if it is because he is curious to know the answer but doesn't want me to know that.

'It's a name given to create fear.' Kai looks down at me. 'Back home, we're called Moonchildren.'

I had heard the term around the camp but had never spent a second to consider it.

'Rayven said we were originally called Pale Eyes, that and Nightwalker was my name on the front line,' I say, and Kai laughs, a beautiful sound despite the circumstances. All Narakuya have white eyes when we shift into our true form, and always a pale blue in our human body.

'I have yet to see you with white eyes.' Kai squeezes my arm again.

'One day.'

None of us like shifting into our true form, into our *killing calm*, because we lose all our senses, our morals and instantly target anything that moves. However, to shift into that form, despite not liking it, it feels like we are whole, we have no worries or doubts. I had practiced a partial slip many times whilst in the trenches. Just enough to let my eyes and fangs show, before drawing it back whilst I still had enough control.

I lower my voice, low enough that Hunter can't hear me. I don't want his presence to stop me from enjoying this moment. 'When all this is over and done with, what then?'

'Well, I hope you'll visit me in Ritenvold.' He whispers in my ear. 'You'd love the kingdom.'

'Not as much as the Oak forests,' I tease.

He doesn't take the bait. 'I would very much like to show you my kingdom one day,' he says, his voice becoming serious.

'And I would love to explore it with you one day,' I reply quietly, I look over at Hunter, knowing that he can't hear our conversation.

'I look forward to it.' I look back at Kai and swallow when I recognise the longing in his eyes. I've never seen anyone look at me that way before.

It wasn't the way that Falcon had looked at me either. Falcon made me feel uncomfortable. Kai makes me feel like despite what happens, I'll be safe with him. He makes me feel like he would have stepped in front of an arrow for me. For me and not for my crown, my bloodline.

I can feel my cheeks heating up and I swallow.

The motion breaks Kai's gaze, his eyes dipping down to my throat and then up to my lips.

Then, Kai glances over at Hunter, his demeanour changing.

'Let's win this war first.' He suddenly grins, loud enough for Hunter to hear, and it takes me a moment to realise he said that for my sake, for my uncertainty.

'We will.' I grin back.

I look over at Hunter and his expression shocks me; it's full of hatred and anger and I realise it's not directed at just me, but at Kai as well. To avoid the situation, my eyes wander to Rayven's tent, where I see three shadows standing still inside. I narrow my eyes as I consider who the third person might be. Soon the flaps push open, and a man steps out followed by Rayven and then Dimitri.

I tilt my head as I try to work out who the male is, and I watch as he nods his head at Rayven and Dimitri, his lips moving but his words too quiet for me to hear, before turning around. His ice eyes meet mine, and I tense as the man holds my gaze. He looks a couple of years older than

Rayven and Dimitri, but with our extended lifespans, he could be a century older, and his dark hair is chin length, loose around his face.

He walks towards me, and both Kai and I stand.

He stops in front of me.

'Do you know who I am?' he asks quietly.

'No.'

The man looks at Kai for a moment, his gaze narrowing before turning back to me.

'I am glad to see you are in good health, Danica,' he states.

'Who are you?' I ask.

'No-one for now.' The man tilts his head slightly. 'It wasn't only Ritenvold trying to rescue you from the front line. Just know, Danica, you'll always have an ally in the Kingdom of Maristela.' The man glances at Kai again and adds, 'I'll see you around, Kai.'

He nods his head at me before turning and walking into the forest, not once looking over his shoulder.

I look at Rayven and she watches the man leave, then turns and retreats to her tent for the night.

I turn to Kai. 'That was very weird.'

He doesn't say anything.

'Do you know who he was?'

'Aye, I've met him.'

'But who is he?'

'An ally of yours.'

'Kai.'

'He is for your mother to explain.'

I huff, if he won't give me straight answers, I'll ask Rayven another time.

*****

From the back of my horse, I watch as sun rays spill through the forest with the dawn and breathe in the crisp morning air. Rayven's horse is chomping on the bit next to me.

I turn to look at my mother and she smiles at me.

'You did well, little warrior. I am proud of you and how you survived.' She tilts her head slightly, a habit she's always had. 'You're the strongest of the Arlet line yet. You always have been, but now it's visible with every breath you take.'

'I know,' I say quietly. I've known since I killed the maid.

'When the Moonstone Crown is placed on your head, it will enhance all your abilities and senses.' Rayven pushes her horse into a forward walk.

'I don't need a lesson.'

'You let Kai teach you.'

This time I don't say anything, but I do roll my eyes at the comment.

'I have seen how Kai looks at you, and how you look at Kai without realising it…' She turns to look at me.

'Yes, well, I just want to win this war and go home. I am grateful to the help Kai and King Darius are offering us.'

'Of course,' she tilts her head as she looks at me.

'Who was that man last night that spoke to you and Dimitri?'

'His name is Tate.' Rayven is quiet for a moment. 'One day, I'll introduce you to him properly. He is another whole story. There are a lot of stories I need to tell you, about Melissa and how she became the way she is, Dimitri and myself.'

'Okay. He said he was from Maristela? I wouldn't have thought that I'd have allies there. As far as I've heard, they still have no ruler.'

'Yes.' Rayven strokes her horse's neck. 'Maristela hasn't had a ruler in over fifty centuries, since Selenia's three hundred years on the throne. She made her promise, but I think the ocean can never truly have a ruler. It is too wild, and the king or queen to rule it would need to understand that they can never control their kingdom. The ruler would have to be someone as wild and wicked as the ocean, but never greedy.'

'What would happen if someone was able to claim Selenia's crown?'

Rayven tilts her head again, considering the question. 'They would be deserving of the crown, but I think it would change our history. It would be the first time that all three kingdoms would have a king or queen, since the Three Sisters. Our world would change drastically, I believe.'

I consider her words; I have never even seen the ocean before. I take my feet out of my stirrups and stretch my legs, relieving the stiffness that has built.

'Anyway, I am glad to have finally been reunited with you and father.'

Narakuya culture had never encouraged their children to call their parents by their position, but Dimitri, being half human, had always insisted when I was a child that I call them by father and mother.

Rayven smiles at me, winks and then pushes her horse into a canter. I slip my feet back into the stirrups and encourage Oak to match

Rayven's Natari's speed. With that, we're galloping through the forest, south of the army as we race between the trees.

*****

I watch Kai as he pulls his sword out of its sheath, the metal glinting in the sunlight.

Hunter has been irking me this last day, he's been following me around, always appearing where I am busy doing something, watching me, never saying a word but judging my every word and action. I don't acknowledge him from where he leans against a tree as I size Kai up again.

'Ready, Princess?'

'I've been waiting for you, Prince.'

He runs his eyes over me, watching as I step closer.

I attack, but I hold myself back, waiting patiently for the right moment to come along. Swinging my sword towards Kai's right shoulder, I'm met by a blade. I jump back, dodge right and attack right. He matches my every move. I need to throw him off.

I keep to a similar routine for a moment, as I work out what would take him by surprise. He knows my every move and how I think.

I leap back and watch him before launching forward to attack. Kai is ready, waiting for me and at the last moment, as he moves to match my attack, I retreat. He hesitates and I attack, disarming him. A smirk appears on my face as I best him.

He steps back, eyes tracking his sword as it flies to the ground and slowly raises his hands.

'I win.'

He lowers his hands and moves to pick up his sword. 'Good.'

'I know,' I say, grinning.

I look across at Hunter, he's watching us warily. He meets my gaze and holds it.

I can almost see the words he wants to spit. *Trained killer. Monster.*

Kai walks up to my side and I pass him my sword. He gives me a questioning look but doesn't ask as I stride up to Hunter.

He bites his lip as I stop in front of him, the only sign of his fear.

'What is your issue with me?' I finally demand.

He doesn't back down from my gaze.

'I don't like you. I don't like him.' He nods his head at Kai. 'And I don't like your kind.'

'Oh my, I am heartbroken,' Kai mutters from behind me.

'Then why are you here?' I'm tempted to roll my eyes at Kai's comment.

'I am here because I know what my mother has done is wrong, and I am here to save my people, so they're not slaughtered by you.' He takes a step closer, and I recognise the slight challenge in his tone, the quickening of my pulse in anticipation.

'Because your mother certainly hasn't slaughtered hundreds of people either,' I snap back, taking a step closer.

Kai steps up by my side.

'She did it in the best interest of her people, of the citizens of Roseguard and the other cities across Asada.' Hunter lets a nasty grin slip onto his lips. 'You can't say that what you're doing is right, you're about to march onto a city of innocent people.'

Kai finally speaks up. 'Careful, Hunter.'

He turns to Kai, hatred sizzling in his gaze.

I realise Hunter is stupidly brave. Maybe he really does love his people, the innocents in Roseguard. And he's proven it by approaching his enemy to stop a war.

I take a deep breath, calming my own anger.

'Hunter,' I say, and his gaze turns back to me. 'Listen to me carefully.'

He only raises an eyebrow.

'Neither side is innocent, both you and I have blood on our hands.' He moves to open his mouth, but I push forward. 'You may not be the one releasing the arrow, but you gave the command to fire. Now there might be a way I can stop this war without our people suffering at all.'

'Why should I trust you?' he snaps.

'You wouldn't be here if you didn't trust me and my word,' I say back.

Hunter hesitates. I turn to Kai.

'I've got an idea, but Rayven's not going to like it.'

'Danica...' Kai grins, and I return it.

# CHAPTER THIRTY-TWO

## DANICA

Throwing a saddle onto my horse, the black leather almost the same colour as the Natari's silky hide, I focus only on staying quiet.

The moon is out and bright, shining down over the army. It's the early hours of the morning and although many warriors are asleep, there are still some awake, keeping an eye on the camp, going about jobs. None of them take any notice of Kai and I hiding in the shadows. We saddle up our horses quickly and quietly.

Only the crackle of the campfires and the quiet conversations of other warriors can be heard as I vault onto Oak. Sitting up straight in the saddle, I gently nudge him with my spurs. Kai follows as we make our way out of camp and the forest that hides our army, avoiding the few sentries that watch over the camp.

We have a lot of ground to cover, so I push my stallion into a slow canter. Kai's horse keeps pace behind me.

We had spent hours that afternoon hidden in his tent discussing the potential of this plan and had decided that the best way to determine if it could work would be to go and see for ourselves.

We don't talk as we canter across fields and through trees, the moonlight marking a clear path as we follow deer trails north, making a loop around Roseguard. I breathe in the night air, taking in the freshness of it and letting it wash over all my still-healing wounds. The night air is a sweet kiss of escape. An escape from my life, from the good and bad memories. That sweet kiss is the moment where I can be no-one else except who I am now, a young woman on her horse in the moonlight. The only sounds are the slight breeze and the steady beat of the horses' canter as we make our way north.

The trees begin to get fewer and fewer as the landscape evens out into the grasslands that surrounds Roseguard. In the distance, the walls of Roseguard stand, the towers visible and fire lights flickering. There are thousands of people within those walls, sleeping, partying, trading and gambling, and only the minority know how much danger they are in.

I slow my horse to a walk.

'I don't think I want to kill Melissa,' I break the silence, keeping my gaze on the walls. 'But I've also made a promise that she will die.'

'Why?' he asks softly.

'I don't want to be the person Hunter thinks I am, I don't want to kill his mother despite the horrors she put me through.'

'You care for Hunter's opinion more than you should.'

'Aye, but I don't want to give him another reason to label me a monster.'

'Okay, so we'll let someone else make the killing blow, either the king or queen.' Kai looks over at me. 'You told Hunter that *you* wouldn't kill Melissa. You never said anything about anyone else killing her.'

'I guess…' I trail off, thinking.

We walk for a while, enjoying one another's companionship.

'When I first met you, you would have handled the argument with the Cole boy in a completely different way than you did today. That would have ended up physical.'

'Well, I guess I'm starting to figure out who I am. And also, how to negotiate and strategize like Rayven.'

'Indeed. And Vixy?'

'Her death will forever be a dark shadow, but I think it closed the door on who I was before, who I was on the front line.' I hesitate before going on. 'I'll admit I may have been a bit irrational and focused on survival before.'

Kai laughs and pushes his horse into a trot again.

We keep clear of Roseguard's walls, staying along the perimeter of the tree line as we make our way to Thorn Gap.

As the ground begins to change from smooth grasslands to rocky cliffs, we halt the horses and tie them to nearby trees before setting out on foot, jogging to the closest edge, the western point of the great chasm.

It takes us longer to make it there than I hoped, especially as we have to crawl around rocks and cliffs before we're able to gaze down into the ravine that has been in the world since it was created.

'Hunter wasn't lying when he said Melissa had an army,' Kai says quietly, just loud enough to hear over the roar of the waterfall, the water rushing to the bottom of the canyon.

My breath catches and the rock is rough, sharp, beneath my grip at the edge of the cliff as I gaze down. I can make out the individual fires for each camp and it's like looking into a sea of stars. I allow myself a few moments to take in the sight below me, to comprehend how large this army is and how small I feel hidden among the cliffs. I feel as if I'm looking down into a whole new world.

Taking a deep breath, I can smell the wet earth, the smoke from the campfires and the scent that brings memories from the front line with it, human sweat, leather, stew… it smells like the trenches.

I shake my head, focusing myself. I notice a river flowing through the middle of the gap, the stars above and the firelights reflecting in it. At the western end is a waterfall, which pours into a small river flowing through the centre, before vanishing underground. Although we can't see the eastern end from here, I do not doubt the maps or Rayven's word.

'Do you think it could work?' Kai asks quietly.

'I think so,' I say as I gaze down at the Red Army below us.

As the moon makes it path across the starry sky, giving way to that soft twilight before dawn, we lie gazing down at the Red Army, watching, calculating.

I sit up a bit when I notice all the Red Soldiers rising and moving into a formation. It's as if they're expecting … Melissa Cole. There she is. A small figure strutting through Thorn Gap. The sun hasn't even risen yet, and she's already down here. What would she be doing up so early…?

I point her out to Kai. 'There's Melissa.'

He tenses and launches into a crouch, his gaze focused on Melissa. He doesn't say anything as he pulls out his bow.

'Kai. What are you doing?' I sit back, watching him.

He doesn't say anything as he stands, pulling an arrow from his quiver.

'Kai,' I snap at him.

He doesn't acknowledge me.

I launch myself onto him, tackling him as I grab his bow, yanking him to the floor, so close to the edge and freefall.

'Let me go,' he growls, so different from his usual easy tone.

'What are you doing?' I demand as I keep my knee on his wrist.

He tries to stand up, but I push him back down with as much weight as I can. I flip a dagger out of my boot and place it on his neck.

He finally stills now that I have his attention.

'What are you doing?' I demand.

'I don't answer to you, Princess. Let me go.' His voice is serious, but he doesn't move beneath me, not with my knees pushing down on his arms, my dagger at his throat and all my weight on his chest.

I hesitate. 'Talk to me, Kai.'

He doesn't say anything, only stares at me, his pale ice eyes piercing into me.

'You were going to try to kill Melissa, weren't you?'

He doesn't respond, but his eyes flicker and I recall his reaction when he first saw Melissa.

'I'm the reckless one, and I wouldn't even attempt that! Only Dimitri would be able to pull off that shot.' I snap at him. 'I know you want that bitch dead, so do I, so does everyone in our army.

'You can't win this one! I understand you want her dead; I understand you want revenge for Luca.' He flinches, and I know I've hit the mark, figured out his one desire and the one dark shadow that haunts him. 'I understand, Kai,' I say again.

His body relaxes, and I remove my knees from his wrists. I keep my dagger at his throat and my weight on his chest.

'Talk to me, Kai,' I say again.

A shiver goes up my spine as his hands grip the backs of my legs, and I feel like I'm the one in danger.

'You're right.' He hesitates. 'I spent ten years learning how to control myself, so the moment I came in contact with Cole, I could kill her. Yet both times I've lost all self-control.'

'If I take my dagger away, will you be reasonable and smart, or will you try to leap off this cliff to get to Melissa?' I ask, unsure how to respond to the truth he'd let me hear.

Kai gives me a lazy grin and squeezes my leg. 'I'll be reasonable and smart.'

'Good,' I say as I remove the dagger, relieved that he's put that casual and teasing mask back on.

I hesitate as I realise that I am on top of him, and I swallow as I gaze down, at how close I am to him.

His eyes flicker and he grins. 'Congrats on winning this round, Princess.'

I roll my eyes and climb up. 'We should go.'

'You're no fun,' he says, following me up. That easily, he's back in control of himself.

'I never have been,' I say, glad that the darkness will cover the faint pinkness in my cheeks.

The ride back to our camp is quick and quiet, neither of us talking.

# CHAPTER THIRTY-THREE

## DANICA

I lie in my bed, listening to the quiet rustle of the camp going about its business. This morning, I learned more about Kai than I had since we first met. I learned that he isn't nearly as relaxed and easy going as he seems, it's all just a mask to hide his true feelings … to hide what he thinks is his weakness.

Dimitri bursts into my tent and I instantly launch out of my bed, already reaching for my dagger on instinct.

'What's wrong?'

My blood goes cold at the fury on his face, and when Rayven prowls into my tent, I know with a single glimpse of her face that I am in trouble.

Dimitri stops centimetres away from me.

'Where were you early this morning?' Dimitri growls and I freeze.

I have only ever seen him this angry once before, when I snuck off past my bedtime to play with Falcon when we were at the Moonstone Palace.

I stand up a bit straighter.

Rayven comes up next to Dimitri, radiating anger. 'Our spies reported that two horses made it out of camp and somehow slipped back in again just after dawn.'

'Where were you and who did you go with?' Dimitri snaps.

I keep my shoulders back, chin high as I stare down my parents.

'If you plan on leaving the camp, then you will inform your father or myself,' Rayven snarls and I understand why they're so angry, they lost me once before. That's why I decided not to tell them in the first place. We've only just found our way back together, and by travelling to the enemy's city, with only Kai, I put myself in a lot of danger.

'Who said I left camp last night? Anyone could have taken those horses,' I finally say.

'Falcon saw you leave your tent and later return to it,' Rayven states. 'It wasn't too hard to figure out that you went on a little adventure after we heard about the horses.'

I clench my jaw. Falcon!

Stubbornness sets in. 'I am not going to apologise for leaving the camp. And I will not tell you who I was with last night either.'

Dimitri turns and marches out of the tent, calling out over his shoulder. 'We'll see what Kai has to say about this.'

I follow and wait just outside my tent. I don't let any expression show on my face as Rayven watches my every breath.

Minutes pass and I keep my head high.

'Why are you so angry?' I finally demand, despite already knowing the answer.

I turn to meet Rayven's glare, unsure if she'll confess the real answer to my question.

'Because your father and I can't lose you again.'

'Dimitri let me go when it was just Hunter and I.'

'He knew what you were doing, and he also knew Falcon was on his trail and would find you,' Rayven snaps at me. 'You're to be the next queen of our people, you cannot behave in this manner, Danica.'

I fold my arms and wait for Dimitri to return.

He does moments later with Kai in tow.

I notice Hunter watching from the other side of the campfire, along with Falcon and Autumn.

Kai raises an eyebrow at me, and I shake my head slightly. *They don't know what we did last night.*

'Well, Kai, was my daughter with you last night?' Dimitri demands, and I watch as Kai stiffens slightly at the demand. Dimitri isn't his father or his king.

'I can't seem to shake Danica, she follows me around everywhere,' Kai keeps an easy grin plastered on his face, despite his tense body.

Dimitri glares at him and then sets his glare on me.

'Father,' I say, trying to keep my anger under control. Angry that he went to Kai and involved him in this argument. 'Kai and I went for a ride to discuss possible plans to prevent a war.' I try to change the topic. I don't lie but I don't tell the whole truth either.

Rayven tilts her head slightly, assessing me.

'And why didn't you tell us you were going?' Dimitri asks and I swallow, lost for words.

'I asked Danica not to tell anyone because I knew word would get back to my father, and I didn't want him to ask me about it.' Kai saves me and I shoot him a grateful look. 'I'm sorry. I was being selfish and didn't think it through.'

Dimitri sizes Kai up and I know he is trying to decide where his opinion of Kai lies.

'Anyway,' I interrupt. 'Kai and I did come up with a possible course of action that could prevent a slaughter.'

Rayven tilts her head again, and I know she is going over every word I've said and what my next words might be, like a game of chess. I notice the small crowd of foot soldiers watching, judging. And with more confidence than I have, I say, 'I have a plan. A plan to avoid as much slaughter as possible on both our side and our enemies.'

'Kill the Red bastards!' a satyr in the crowd shouts.

I watch the satyr for a moment. He has probably been to war before, considering their extended life spans, and would have been very aware of what has happened in the last ten years. 'I do not want unnecessary blood to spill.'

Rayven and Dimitri step back to watch me handle the situation. Kai's eyes are also on me.

I can feel the crowd considering my words, my worth. They had all just heard how I went behind the queen's back.

Someone spits, 'If you were really *our* princess, you would kill the Reds for what they've done to us! What they've done to you!'

I tilt my head at the challenge, trying to figure out my next words carefully, as Rayven would.

'Prove that you're our princess!'

'You want me to prove my loyalty?' I ask quietly.

'Prove it!'

'You're a Red! You fought for them!'

I stride to the centre of the crowd, surrounded by a crowd of Asadians that falls under the protection of the Treaty my kind made to stop innocents dying.

'You want me to prove my loyalty!' I shout, turning around and meeting the eyes of those gathered in the crowd. So many different species, most of them older than me. There are a few Ritenvold warriors watching in silence.

I peel my shirt up, revealing the nasty scar across my stomach, my muscles tense. 'That's what the Red bitch hidden in those walls did to me when I was just ten years old, to stop me from killing the Red Soldiers that broke into my home.'

Now I have the crowd's attention. 'I fought for the Reds because I had no other option! I was a ten-year-old girl surrounded by enemies. I was a ten-year-old who was tortured when I didn't kill my allies,' I shout at the crowd, even as the memories I had kept down so well resurface. Red Soldiers putting swords into me when I refused to walk forward, knowing I would heal by the time I made it to the line. Red Soldiers giving me a physical beating when I said a word wrong. Huddled in a corner of one of the trenches struggling to keep from sinking into despair, telling myself over and over *what happens, happens,* and deciding in that dark corner to keep my head low, do as I'm told while I gather my strength, my knowledge of what was happening around me and to keep feeding the fire that burns within me.

'Melissa Cole will never stop trying to overpower us. I learned that in those trenches. I gave Queen Rayven ten years to unite our people, not just in Asada, but the people of Ritenvold as well, and create the army we have today! If I had my way, I would slaughter every person with a rose on their armour!'

I meet Hunter's gaze and see the concern and worry in his eyes. 'But I won't because I am better than my enemy. *We* are better than our enemy, and I have a plan to spare those who are innocent. You want me to kill the Red bastards … how does that make us any better than them? You kill a snake by cutting its head off, not the tail. Roseguard is a snake, and Melissa Cole is the head.'

I look out at the crowd. 'So, have I proven my loyalty? I was a slave for ten years! I won't be a slave to my enemy ever again, and I won't let my people be enslaved and suffer as I did either!'

Silence settles over the crowd. I take a deep breath, worried I have said the wrong thing.

'Danica!' Someone shouts.

'Danica! Danica! Danica!' My name becomes a beat, a war cry as I grin at the crowd.

# HUNTER

Hours later, Rayven and Dimitri seem to have forgiven Kai and Danica for their little adventure as they discuss how to beat the Red Army, the fae among them. The fae who have betrayed them.

Danica approached me after her little motivational speech and asked if I would like to participate in the meeting.

Danica … I have her so fooled.

I have stayed quiet the past few days, watching her.

The night Vixy died, I felt sick with fear, worrying how Danica would retaliate. Any humanity Danica had left would have died with Vixy. Mother and I had a screaming match about Vixen's death. The next day, we had reconvened in the war rooms and discussed our next plan of action. It was when I had seen smoke drifting up above the trees that an idea had formed. When you're playing against creatures twice as deadly, you need to play twice as dirty.

I had been dreading the plan, but it was also perfectly brilliant, and I kept telling myself that as I had said my goodbye to Mother and began the trek through the forest.

And so, I found the army of Nightwalkers … the Night Army to Mother's Rose Army. Well, the scouts had found me.

When I saw Danica, I felt like my last meal was going to make a second appearance as dread and fear almost consumed me.

Yet Kai, who had been such a shock and revelation when he revealed himself, held her back, and she listened to him. Danica who never listens to anyone, who allows no-one to hold her leash, had let this male stop her from killing me. Danica had revealed the only one who has power over her. That leash Kai has on her, that unknown control he has ... I want it. I want to be able to control someone as destructive and powerful as Danica.

She has changed. From the time I escaped, to when I found the army, she has changed from a cold, stubborn and vicious creature to one who seems to have control. The reason for her control over herself is Kai.

I don't know which is scarier: the creature that would go to the ends of the world to save the red-haired fox or the deadly controlled princess, with the equally deadly and controlled prince by her side.

Kai... he is an unexpected turn of events. One that explains why Luca's death hadn't caused the internal war as planned. They still had a prince for their throne and a leader that was of Narakuya and human blood. So, they went to war against the person who killed one of their princes, they went to war against Mother and Roseguard.

Yet I still can't understand why Danica seems to listen to no-one except Kai.

The other change I notice is that Danica and Falcon aren't on speaking terms anymore. Falcon is still blindingly loyal to her, but she won't give him the time of day. Before I escaped, it was obvious that Falcon was fond of her, but she was oblivious, and it's evident that he still has feelings for her judging by the jealousy in his eyes whenever he looks at Kai. I have noticed over the past couple of days that Falcon is growing closer to Autumn. Not just the comfort and company he offers her in the camp, but something more, and I don't think his intentions are genuine.

Falcon is the only one who actually acknowledges me, and I know that if I stray too far from the protection of Danica, I will be killed by one of the beasts that watches my every move. Autumn won't look me in the eye, won't talk to me and leaves the tent whenever I enter it.

Danica sits across the table from me, Kai by her side. Their pale blue eyes scan the maps covering the table.

The war meetings here are so different to those in the Red Towers, where they are based around strategies and statistics. Here, it's about strengths, weaknesses and the trust the Nightwalkers have with each other and their soldiers.

I listen as Danica carefully discusses the battle to come. As King Darius and Queen Rayven discuss their warriors' strengths, purposely leaving out anything vital. Every time I open my mouth to provide information about Roseguard to my enemies, these monsters look at me with distrust. They think that I am selling out my home, and Danica won't lay her plan out until I am gone. But I do notice Danica's interest in Thorn Gap, and she goes over every possible entry and exit. She does the same with the Red Towers and the war rooms. She eventually discusses the city, all its streets and hidden alleyways all the way to its walls. It's like she is able to create a map of the city and all its levels in her mind.

I give her truths and lies, all the better to set my ambush with. Mother and I both know we're running out of options.

# Chapter Thirty-Four

## Danica

I take a deep breath as I gaze into the mirror, braiding my hair. My ice eyes reflect back at me, tendrils of dark brown hair fall loose from the braid. I secure it to the back of my head and tie the rest into a ponytail.

I stand up and my pull my loose white shirt off, glancing at the scar across my abdomen before pulling on a tight black singlet, then leather armour, light and flexible the way we Narakuya like it.

I pull my boots on, tuck my pants into them and do up the laces, double tying them.

Soon, I'll come for Melissa Cole. Soon, she'll pay for what she has done.

A breeze shifts through the tent, and I breathe it in, taking in the scent of the forest, leather and smoke. The tent flaps open, I turn to see Hunter making his way into my tent.

I instantly straighten. 'What do you want?'

'No pleasantries?' Hunter doesn't laugh as he looks around my tent, eyes pausing on the sword lying across my bed.

'I have things to do.' I turn back to the mirror as I start bandaging my fists, between each finger and over each knuckle. 'What do you want to say?'

'I need you to promise you won't kill my mother.'

I glare at Hunter in the mirror. 'I thought I already did that when you came strutting into my camp.'

'Please just swear it.'

I sigh. 'Fine. I swear I won't kill Melissa Cole.'

Hunter blinks. No doubt he was expecting more push back on the matter.

'Happy?' I finish bandaging my right fist, leaving enough flexibility and movement.

'No.' Hunter looks me up and down once before walking out of the tent.

I bandage my left fist before standing up and strapping on my sword, daggers, bow and a quiver of oak wood arrows. The tent flaps open again, and I turn, ready to snap at Hunter.

It's not Hunter this time; it's Falcon.

'I assume you were expecting Hunter to come back?' Falcon asks.

He's dressed in his leather armour, a cape hanging from his shoulders.

I don't say anything; just go about strapping my weapons on.

'I've come to beg for forgiveness.' He steps in front of me.

'You, Ryker and Caden swore to protect Vixy, but you helped Autumn instead.' I hesitate. 'That is not Autumn's fault and I'm grateful that she's alive, but I can no longer trust you. Crynn was the only one to make an effort and he's dead.'

'Autumn was closer. I assumed someone else would save Vixen.' Falcon's face darkens. 'And yet you don't hate Kai for not trying to save Vixy.'

'Because Kai never swore the oath that you did! He didn't break my trust because he didn't promise me anything!'

Falcon glares at me. 'When this war is over, I'm going home.'

I just stare at him.

'And you'll be coming back to the Palace.'

'Your point?'

'Kai will be going back to Ritenvold.'

I ignore his comment, and I just look at him. 'I know what you want, Falcon.'

I push past him and out of the tent.

Outside, the camp is busy with the army preparing for battle. The clink of metal as armour is strapped on, swords put to the blacksmith's hammer a final time, horses stamping and snorting in anticipation due to the energy and atmosphere surrounding the camp, campfires crackling and hissing as they're extinguished. Warriors test weapons on one another; the few who are unable to fight are busy preparing those about to go to battle. The air is humming with adrenaline.

I stride towards the meeting tent as the sun sets over the forest.

Inside, the Narakuya commanders are gathered with Rayven, Dimitri, Darius and Kai.

Kai shoots me a glance, and I give him a quick nod to let him know that I am ready, before turning back to listen to Rayven. I don't say anything, listening as Rayven finalises where our warriors will be placed, where the archers will be and where the cavalry will charge.

I watch my mother. She's in fighting gear like mine but has two swords strapped across her back. And she has black paint on her face. It's tradition that when we go to war, warriors paint their faces in a mixture of Moonstone dust and oak wood, to bestow us good luck and safe passage into the next life, should we die. Above Rayven's brow is a black circle for the moon that we are born, live and die under. Leaves branch out from Rayven's pale eyes representing the oak forest we call our home.

I look over at Kai. He too has the moon painted on his brow, but instead of leaves, his jaw is covered in jagged black paint. It takes me a few moments before I realise that it's a mountain range.

My eyes travel over all the commanders. All the Asada warriors have the moon and leaves; the Ritenvold warriors have the moon and mountain range.

I turn back to watch Rayven finish her speech.

'This war has dragged on for ten years. And for ten years, the enemy held our heir hostage.' Rayven pauses, letting the words sink in. 'There have been many battles with Melissa Cole but it's time we finish this war once and for all.' Rayven looks out over the crowd before continuing.

'Now, not all are guilty in that city. The moment Melissa Cole surrenders, we cease fighting the humans. The moment the fae surrender, we cease fighting them. However, the fae are guilty of treason and we will punish them accordingly.'

We all nod our heads in agreement.

Rayven finally takes a dagger out and pricks the palm of her hand. 'We live under the moonlight and fight in darkness, we are the ones that hold the line between good and evil, the line that the Three Sisters Celestial, Selenia and Zodia created. When we fight today, we fight knowing we hold that thin line and those we fight have fallen through the holes in that line, those we fight have lowered themselves to evil.'

'Aye!' a Ritenvold commander next to Kai calls out, giving Kai a friendly nudge in the ribs. Kai nudges him back and grins.

'Let's go fight!' Rayven shouts.

The commanders thump their shields with their armoured hands.

I watch them leave. Rayven nods her head at me once before following them out. A queen leading her people.

'Where's your war paint, Princess?' Kai asks as he comes to stand beside me.

I shake my head.

'Danica, you're one of us and you're fighting for your people.' He steps in front of me, and I look up at him.

'I ... I don't think I should wear it.'

'Why not?'

'Because when I come for Melissa, I want her to know it's me coming for her.' I look him in the eye and give him a feral grin. 'I want her to know that she made a big mistake making me her soldier.'

'You're out for revenge.' He grins.

'Of course I am. Just like you, and Rayven, Dimitri and Darius,'

'Ready, Princess?' he runs his eyes down and up my body.

'I was ready a long time ago.'

Outside, warriors are leaving the camp, marching to battle. I watch as the cavalry leads the way with Rayven at the head. King Darius is at Rayven's side in metal armour like the rest of the human soldiers from Ritenvold. Behind Rayven and Darius are the two commanders of each army. I spy Dimitri on a horse leading the archers, just where the famous sharpshooter should be. Falcon, Ryker and Caden are on foot, marching as they follow their commanders.

Kai offers me the reins for a stallion, and I pause, the stallion isn't Oak.

'Couldn't find your usual horse,' he rolls his eyes.

I easily vault into the saddle.

'Danica!'

I look up to see Autumn running towards me. 'Kill that monster!'

I nod my head. 'I promise you that Melissa Cole will be dead by the end of today.'

'For Vixen.'

'For Vixy.' I nod my head and look at Kai in his leather armour, reassuring myself that he is still at my side. He just grins at me and aims his horse towards the forest.

I follow Kai and keep my breathing relaxed as we push our horses into a canter and aim for Roseguard. We pass the army in the distance, and we keep going, keep pushing the horses.

The horses hold a steady canter all the way to the grasslands in front of Roseguard, halting at the tree line as we gaze at the city. The sun has already set, our army is on its way.

I guide my horse to follow along the tree line, pushing him back into a quick canter. Kai's horse keeps up and we weave between the trees as we aim north.

We pass by Roseguard, travelling on the western side of the city, our horses sweating hard but never faltering, never hesitating as they fly over the ground, faster than a common bred war horse, faster than any of the horses that Roseguard will have. I lean down and stroke my stallion's thick black neck, my hands damp from the sweat dripping down.

Soon the ground changes from woodlands to rocky outcrops.

I slow my horse.

Kai prepares to vault off.

'We can get closer on the horses,' I gaze out at the land, darkness beginning to descend.

He only nods his head and pushes on.

We weave our way between the rocks until we're forced to go on foot. We quickly untack our horses, hiding our saddles and bridles before giving the horses a pat and making our way on. I look back once to see the horses grazing, ears listening to the wind.

'The moon has risen,' Kai says from in front of me.

'The warriors would have arrived then, with the moon,' I say, watching his shoulders as he makes his way around the cliffs of Thorn Gap.

I take a steadying breath before clinging to the cliff and following him to the waterfall at the western end of the giant canyon.

'I'm amazed that Rayven let you do this.' Kai grunts as he heaves himself from one ledge to another.

'It didn't take much convincing.' I pause as I step carefully around a loose edge, focusing on keeping my footing. 'Rayven's too much like me.'

'You are your mother's daughter,' he mutters.

We continue on in silence until we reach a larger ledge next to the waterfall. I gaze down at the canyon floor, right below us is the pool where the waterfall lands. 'Do you think the army's gone?'

'If not, we're in for some excitement. But I imagine that they will be at the walls, Melissa would have had them march the moment she sighted our army.'

He turns around to face me, his back to the sky behind him.

I quickly ask, nerves starting to build, 'Ever done anything like this?'

He shrugs, 'Once or twice with a friend.'

I check that my sword is secure one final time before looking up at him.

'Ready for some freefall, Princess?' He asks. He leans back and falls over the edge.

I grin at the moon before launching into a sprint and leaping into thin air.

# CHAPTER THIRTY-FIVE

## HUNTER

Breathing hard from the desperate dash back to Roseguard, I push the doors of the war room open.

It hadn't been hard to lose the guard with the chaos already happening around camp, especially with how little of a threat he believed me to be. Oak was the only stallion that hadn't pinned its ears back at me, and I thought it was ironic that I was escaping on Danica's stallion.

I had been terrified that I'd get caught, but the army had been so busy getting prepared that they hadn't notice me slip away.

Except for Falcon.

He had seen me just before I had made it out of camp. He'd watched me for a moment before turning back to the clearing, letting me escape.

Relief washes through me as I spy Mother at the head of the table, her eyes meet mine.

'Well?'

'The heirs are coming through Thorn Gap.' I breath, still trying to catch my breath. 'The army will be here shortly.'

Mother walks around the table and places her hands on my shoulders. 'Good. You have done well Captain.'

She turns to look back at the gathered generals, her short hair swaying. I take her in, she's wearing a clean red suit.

'You all know what's about to happen and have your instructions.' Mother takes me by the upper arm, not harshly, and I let her guide me to the head of the table. 'I, Melissa Cole, Commander of Roseguard, name my son Hunter Cole to be my successor.'

I bite my lip, I had known this was coming but it still sounds like music to my ears. I meet each of the generals' eyes. They all dip their heads in respect.

But Mother continues. 'Should our ambush for the heirs fail, Rayven will not stop until she has my head. I have accepted this fate, and will willingly sacrifice myself during this battle, for if we lose this battle, it does not determine the outcome of this war. If I die today, the plan, as already discussed will be to bow our heads whilst we wait for reinforcements. We've already played the long game for ten years, another few won't matter if it means that we are able to secure a future free of the Nightwalkers for humankind.'

'As the successor for Roseguard,' I begin, 'I promise you that I will not stop fighting for our freedom. I have learnt many things about the Nightwalkers, especially the princess. She is unfit for the throne, and their kind will suffer greatly if the throne is made available for her. She and Queen Rayven are the last descendants of Celestial's bloodline. I intend to wipe out these bloodlines before I die.'

A round of applause fills the room, and I smile.

'Now, we prepare for this battle, and I will take my position.' Mother dips her head. 'It has been an honour working alongside all of you and defending this city. Now I would like to spend a small amount of time with my son before taking my position.'

Mother dips her head to the crowd and silence follows us as we make our exit. Two horses wait outside for us and we make our way home in silence. The streets are quiet, empty, the smell of sweat, spices, cooking food missing. Everyone is hiding, preparing for the battle ahead.

There is adrenaline in the evening air, anticipation for what is about to happen.

Upon reaching our home, we dismount the horses and make our way inside.

'Get changed quickly, freshen up, and I'll lock all the doors while you do so.' Mother says. 'Meet me in the basement once you're finished.'

'I won't be too long.'

I make my way up the stairs, breathing in the smell of home, refusing to consider if this will be the last time I do so.

*****

Quietly, I make my way into the basement. I have a sword strapped to my belt and I carry the lucky charm Danica had given to Vixy. Pushing open the basement door, Mother is seated, her uniform looking immaculate and out of place in the dark, cool room. I close the door behind me before taking a seat beside mother on the old couch.

'You're going to make a great commander.' Mother says quietly.

'Thank you.' I say and begin unthreading the leather strap on the charm and rethreading it with a chain.

'What's that?' Mother asks, raising an eyebrow at the metal in my hand.

'I don't know, but Danica gave it to Vixy to protect her.' I give it to Mother, letting her inspect it.

I frown when her eyes widen as she takes it in, and she glances at me once before turning it around in her hand.

'You know what it is?' I ask slowly.

'Where did Danica find this?'

'In a well in Eagles Canyon, the nymph told her about it I think.'

Mother passes it back to me, wrapping my hand around it. 'Many have hunted for this.'

'What is it?'

Mother swallows once. 'One of the fragments of Selenia's crown.'

I open my palm and inspect the bit of metal. The small fragment is covered in twisted metal, like tree vines. Nothing special.

'Wasn't Selenia one of the Three Sisters the Nightwalkers believe in.'

'Yes.'

'Why haven't you tried to find all fragments?' I look up at Mother, at the scars on her cheek.

'I do not know where they disappeared to. It's a fool's quest, as Maristela is a dangerous place, unpredictable.'

'Right…' I trail off, considering everything Mother had just told me.

'But you can always use that fragment as a bargaining chip one day, both Rayven and Darius would pay handsomely for that bit of metal.'

'I will keep this on me like my life depends on it.'

Mother nods. 'Good.' She pulls an envelope out of her pocket and passes it to me. 'Inside are instructions on how to get in contact with your aunt.'

'I thought you said she is estranged?'

Mother frowns. 'She is, but I would rather you reach out to her than your father should you need some family to support you.'

'Okay, thank you.' I tuck the envelope into my pocket. 'I will destroy Danica one day.'

I meet Mothers gaze, and she gives me a sad smile. 'I hope you finish what I started, Hunter.'

# Chapter Thirty-Six

## Danica

The water is freezing, it soaks my clothes and fills my boots. I scramble, searching for a grip on anything as the current pushes me under. Someone grabs my shoulder, and I gasp as my head breaks the surface, drawing in as much air as I can.

'You good, Princess?'

Kai keeps an arm around my waist as we swim towards the shore. My feet touch rock and I straighten up, already checking how many of my weapons have stayed with me. Fortunately, I had taken the time to secure my arrows in the quiver strapped to my back. The only missing weapon is a dagger from my hip.

I look up at Kai and laugh.

He frowns. 'What?'

I laugh again before answering. 'It looks like you've just come from a mud fight.' The war paint is smeared all over his face.

He goes to rub at the paint, and I catch his hand.

'Here.' I reach up and wipe it away, my fingers turning black.

His ice eyes don't leave mine as I take my hands away. 'All better.'

He catches my hand. 'Thank you, Danica.'

I smile and turn towards the caves. Tents are set up, campfires hiss, but there's no-one down here except us. Picking my way through the abandoned army camp, I aim for the wall with the door, according to Hunter's description of the gap.

'Rayven once killed a basilisk down here,' I say quietly. 'Apparently it was when she was younger, and her parents sent her to Roseguard to meet with their leaders and spend some time among the humans, learning their culture. She found out about the basilisk and went and dealt with it.'

'I never knew my mother,' Kai says, equally as quietly. 'But apparently she was full of life and loved her people very much.'

'Ada was your people's queen for a reason.' I look across at him and smile.

He returns my smile, and we make our way towards the furthest wall.

When we reach the wall, I notice white bone farther along. I hesitate, then stride towards it, curious to see the skeleton of the beast my mother killed. Kai doesn't say anything but follows behind me.

Small doors with metal bars are attached to the cave walls. Beside the hinges, bones have been cemented into the walls, creating an uncomfortable feeling as I look at the doors.

I take a step back.

'Those are cells.' Kai runs a hand over the metal bars.

I look at him. 'And they believe us to be beasts, they believe us to be the monsters in the night.'

'Autumn informed your mother that she and Vixy were held in a cell with metal bars.' Kai says to me. 'They kept two young girls locked in these cells.'

I close my eyes for a moment, focusing on keeping a leash on my anger. 'Hunter was a part of this. He could have helped but he didn't. He knew Vix.'

Kai takes my hand. 'I'm so sorry, Princess.'

I open my eyes and turn to the door. 'Come on, we've got a job to do.'

The door is made of wood and gives easily when Kai jams his shoulder into it. I lead the way up the stairs, stairs that seem to go forever, longer than the stairs to the Underground. No doubt Tyke will be hiding there tonight.

The air is cool, moist and smells of rot. I crinkle my nose at the smell of damp soil and stale air. The only noise echoing along the stairs are our footsteps.

Eventually, a door in the distance becomes visible. I sigh in relief when I see it. Thousands of soldiers would have marched up these stairs recently, and yet it looks as if no-one has been here in centuries. I take a moment to wonder how long the stairs have actually been here, especially if Rayven took the same route into the gap as Kai and I did.

We make it to the door at the top and Kai draws his sword, ready for soldiers on the opposite side. I shake my head and crack my knuckles. He grins and takes a step back, bowing at the hips to let me go first.

I step up to the door and quietly ease it open, slowly so I don't draw attention as I peek outside. Hunter had been right. Two guards.

I signal two behind my back for Kai before slipping out and up to the closest guard. I wrap my arms around his neck at the same moment the other guard spies me, Kai already behind him.

Using all my strength, I squeeze; the guard squirms, one hand gripping my arm, pulling at it. I watch as the other hand goes for a dagger at his belt. He throws his arm back with the dagger at the same moment I drag him to the ground, his dagger misses, and I kick it out of the way.

The guard's body goes loose, and I look up at Kai. His guard is dead, and there's a scratch on Kai's cheek, blood dripping down.

I nod at him and together we drag the guards in their red armour towards the stairs, pushing them inside and closing the doors.

We've come out into a small room, and I realise we're standing in one of the barracks that surrounds the Red Towers. Fortunately, there is a hallway that leads to the Red Towers, meaning we're not going to be exposed out in the open.

In the distance, screaming and war cries fill the air, and even this far from the grasslands, the smell of blood and fire is strong. This is my kind of chaos, the right kind of chaos to allow Kai and I to sneak in.

I take a moment to consider how the battlefield would look. Warriors in black with swords fighting humans and fae. No doubt the fae will be trying their best to use their small magics to slow the Narakuya down.

The fire might cause a bit of an inconvenience, but not much as we have a natural defence to anything controlled by magic.

I take a long look around me. The war rooms sit between all four towers, the hallway leads us there with stone archways on each side.

'Something isn't right,' I say quietly as I gaze at the paved floor in front of us.

The road is too empty, too quiet.

I draw my sword.

'Should we split up?' I ask, keeping my gaze on the road in front of me.

'Never,' Kai answers. 'We stick to the plan.'

I nod my head, and together we walk up to the double wooden doors of the war rooms. We stand on either side and gently push the doors in. They are unlocked and move with no resistance. I tilt my head in question at him, and he holds up one finger before poking his head inside.

'Clear,' he mutters over his shoulder before stepping through the doors.

I follow, keeping my footsteps light and glancing over my shoulder one final time. Stepping into the large war room, the hair on the back of my neck goes up and I hesitate before taking another step. I look around, it is completely empty, the walls bare and Kai standing in the centre. He turns to look back at me, the only light is from the moon seeping under the door.

At the far corner of the room is another door. He glances at me before approaching the door and opening it. The moment the door clicks open, a smash echoes through the room, sending me diving towards the closest wall. Kai is beside me as I glance around me, trying to work out where the noise came from, and my eyes fall onto the front doors. They're shut.

I look up at him.

He launches himself at the doors, trying the handle and pushing it open with brute strength. Nothing.

With my sword in front of me, I go through the other door and look into a hallway. At the end of the hallway, there are stairs leading up towards the next room above us.

Glancing over my shoulder, I say to him, 'They were expecting us.'

He raises an eyebrow, his ice eyes on me. 'Princess. Of course they were.'

'No, not like this they weren't.' I make my way along the hallway, cautiously peering up the stairs before going up them. 'Melissa has guessed Rayven would send someone this way.'

He doesn't say anything.

We make our way up the stairs, passing a number of doors, each locked with no sound coming through, without finding anyone. Finally, we reach a door that isn't locked.

I push the door, and it gives way easily. Beyond it is a flat stone surface, no fencing from the edge. I realise we're on the roof.

An arrow slams into the wood next to my ear and I dive back inside.

'Ambush?' He asks.

I nod.

'Now what?' He keeps a hand on the door, holding it closed. 'We're stuck on an island with archers aimed at the door.'

I close my eyes and lean against the wall, taking a deep breath. 'When something doesn't go as planned, you improvise.' I look at him, a grin forming as I come up with a plan. 'Now it's time to have some fun.'

Kai raises an eyebrow, and I pull my quiver of bow and arrows from my shoulders, passing them to him.

'Cover me,' I say and shift into my true form, my *killing calm*.

My limbs extend, fingers become long claws, teeth become fangs, and every muscle strengthens. My senses magnify and my nerves and thoughts of revenge disappear as I take a deep breath and try to recall what I am supposed to be doing. As I breathe in, I get the scent of humans fifteen yards away.

'Twenty,' I say, voice cold and controlled. Twenty soldiers who are about to die.

I fling the door open and run. Sprinting the ten yards to the drop off, the gap between the wall and where I am now would be a struggle to make across if I were in my human-like form.

Arrows fly at me, and I dodge each one easily. I watch as a black arrow flies towards the wall, striking true and a human falls from the wall.

As I reach the edge of the roof, I push off, up and out, flying through the air. Wind whips my hair back and I don't hesitate as I throw my arms out, grabbing onto the edge of the wall and hurling myself over. Humans rush at me and I slaughter each and every one of them, blood drips from my hands as I punch through throats, chests. Most of the humans don't have a chance to draw their swords as I send them to their next life. I listen to the sounds of footsteps, the sounds of the war playing out in the distance.

There is movement behind me and I spin, my hand aiming for their throat.

Even through the almost unemotional haze, I recognise him.

Kai.

I yank my hand back as I meet the ice eyes.

'Danica.'

His voice is soothing, gentle and more powerful than a human's.

I stare at him.

'Danica. Shift back.'

He watches me, not moving.

'You've killed all the soldiers.' He pauses as he steps forward. 'We are done here.'

I take a deep breath allowing my body to relax; the adrenaline fades as I shift out of my *killing calm*. As my body returns to its human-like form, it's like diving into water and trying to listen, smell, talk, move beneath water. Everything becomes blurry—sight and sound. My movements become sluggish. I had forgotten what it was like to be that powerful, have that much strength.

'You did it, Princess,' Kai says.

I look down at my hands, at the blood coating them and then at the dead soldiers. There is blood everywhere and I take a deep breath. I just slaughtered almost twenty men.

I reach down to the closest soldier, gently closing his light brown eyes, and pushing back his dark blond hair. Stepping back, I look at all the bodies. 'You were born from the Shadows and so you shall return. Let the moon guide your path and be a beacon in the dark. May you win your fight and rest during the immortal night.'

Kai doesn't say anything for a moment before offering me my bow and the few arrows that are left. 'They underestimated us, a pretty pathetic attempt at an ambush.'

'Melissa Cole wasn't in her war rooms,' I say quietly as I strap my weapons down. 'I think I know where she might be.'

'And where is that?' He steps closer.

'If your city was about to be overrun, where would you go if you stood no chance of escaping?'

'Somewhere I know and could hide from the battle cries.'

'Like your home?'

Kai's grin turns feral.

'Follow me, Prince,' I say, and lead the way to Melissa Cole's home.

# Chapter Thirty-Seven

## Danica

Looking down from the wall at the city is like looking down on a map. Everything is laid out in neat rows—houses, shops, stables, inns—a city built to thrive. But outside the far wall, the moon gives me perfect vision. I can see an army of red speckled amongst black, small fires scattered across the plain. Cries and screams come from the battlefield where the armies fight, but in the streets … silence. They are entirely empty.

'It's a ghost town,' Kai says from beside me and I nod my head.

'You still got that rope?'

'Of course I do, Princess.'

'I know which house is the Cole's, Hunter once told me he lives on Highhill with the best view of Thorn Gap.' He passes me the rope and I tie it to a post on the outer side of the wall. All along the wall, about twenty yards apart, are posts with banners, the Roseguard emblem big and bright.

'However, we'll need to go through the streets to get there.'

'Sounds like a plan.'

I grip the rope and lower myself down the wall, watching below for any unexpected visitors.

Finally, my feet touch the ground, and I straighten myself as I look up at Kai. 'Your turn.'

He nods and begins climbing down the wall.

He's halfway down when a crack fills the air. He freezes, hanging in mid-air. I look up at the post; a massive split runs up the centre of it.

'Go Kai,' I shout at him.

I clench and unclench my hands as I watch him slide down the wall.

Another crack sounds, and I launch into action, ready to prevent him from injury. He lands smoothly on his feet, and I watch the post come down, straight towards his head. I dive, ramming him out of the way moments before the post hits the ground. Chunks of wood go flying, and I grunt as something hits me just below my neck.

I don't move.

Kai looks over at me. 'Almost even.'

I grimace at the thudding ache on my back.

'Let me have a look,' he says and sits up.

I don't move as his fingers pull my armour back and then my singlet.

His fingers gently brush over my back, slightly to the right of my armour on my shoulder. I can feel something warm and wet.

'You'll be fine, Princess,' he says, his fingers hesitating on my back. I groan, instantly fisting my hands as he pulls something from my back.

'I know, Prince.' I grit out. 'Just a scratch.'

His fingers disappear and I sit up. Over my shoulder he passes me what had been lodged into my back, a small chunk of wood.

I stand up and brush myself off, the pain in my muscles fades as I turn my focus to the street, hoping no-one heard the commotion, but it remains empty. I bite my lip, where is everyone?

Unsheathing my sword, I turn to a northern street. Kai pulls two light swords from across his back, ready to fight. Together, we sneak down the paved roads, keeping to the walls. I test a few of the doors along the way, all locked and the windows boarded up.

'Roseguard wasn't like this the first time I walked through here,' I say quietly to Kai. 'It was thriving, full of people, smells, sounds …' I trail off as the memory plays through my mind.

*'Careful Danica, you might decide you like the social life.'*

*'Don't get your hopes up, Captain.'*

I swallow at the memory, remembering how it had felt to be amongst it, to not be looked up to, to not be a leader, but a simple girl having a night out, those brief few steps between the door and the table.

'You alright, Princess?' Kai asks, and I realised I've stopped moving.

I nod my head and follow him. 'When I was first here, I had Hunter with me and there were a few moments when I discovered what it was like to be someone without responsibility.'

Kai stops and turns to me. 'You get to be whoever you wish to be, but you and I both know that you'll always be more than one of those people without responsibilities.'

'Everyone has responsibilities. Our responsibilities just happen to be the ones our ancestors have always had.'

He gives me a grin. 'Come on.'

Our footsteps are silent along the streets, and I am careful not to make any loud noises that might attract attention, even though the city seems deserted. The houses are all made of red brick, house after house, one after the other. It's so different to the memories I have of the Moonstone Palace, where waterfalls tumble from cliffs and little rooms are carved into the mountains. Where oak trees reach for the sun and the water in the river is clear and forever flowing. The night sky filled with constellations above the palace.

In the distance, I can still hear metal clanging, war cries and screams. Armies fighting for power.

Kai's ice eyes are forward, on the street ahead and his dark hair is damp. Dirt clings to him. He catches my gaze and holds it as we make our way towards our enemy's home.

# Chapter Thirty-Eight

## Danica

Like ghosts, we make it onto the balcony of Hunter's bedroom with no noise. The doors are reinforced, however with a bit of force the lock gives way, and they swing open. The scent of rose and copper is overwhelming, the scent of Hunter. His room is neat and tidy, a double bed in the centre, red rugs and desert wolf hides covering it, and on each side is a small table. I step up to a shelf on the wall, looking over the small items Hunter has collected over the years. A badge of honour with the Roseguard crest on it, a small ruby, an old painting of the tropical city of Carramera, and a sketchbook.

I pick the book up; Kai looks over my shoulder as I turn the pages. It's full of drawings, incredible drawings. I hadn't realised that Hunter was talented in art.

The first drawing is a rose in bloom and the second is of a rose dying.

The next few pages are of landscapes—a forest, the desert, mountains, the ocean and lakes. There are a few pages of the different cities of Asada. I turn the next page and stop, immediately recognising the image. The drawing is a head split in half. The right side is some form of monster, some of the lines scribbled and blurred to look like absolute chaos with a massive canine tooth coming down from the mouth dripping with blood, lips pulled back in a war cry, the pupil is dilated in the white eye, crazed with bloodlust, a horn, almost like a deer antler comes from the temple of the creature, blood dripping down the length of the horn. The left side is my face.

Hunter has drawn me as if I'm screaming a battle cry. Blood covers my face, my eye wild, hair loose.

I don't say anything as I close the book, replacing it on the shelf before turning to Kai.

'At least Hunter got one thing right about me.'

Before Kai can reply, I push past him and aim for the door. Outside the door is a hallway and I think back to the night I first visited Roseguard. To the night when I was a starving creature looking for any sort of power and revenge. But now, as I prowl along the hallway, I am no starving creature, I keep my chin high. I am princess to the deadliest creatures to prowl Raguia.

The house is quiet, but I can sense people in it. I lead Kai through the house, our footsteps silent as we quietly determine where Melissa will be hiding. We go down a flight of stairs and pass through the kitchen.

I hear whispers from behind a stone door.

Familiar voices.

Kai nods at me before I turn to it, drawing my sword.

I stand next to the stone wall as I push the door open. The whispers fall silent.

Kai nods at me one more time and I stride into the room.

I meet Hunter's eyes, my body freezing.

He stands there, not moving with a sword pointed at me. His other hand is held up to his chest, gripping something I can't see clearly. Melissa Cole sits on a ruby red couch behind Hunter, the scars on her cheek are clear.

Kai steps up to my side, eyes focused entirely on Melissa, and I throw out an arm to stop him getting any closer.

'Why, Hunter?' I say quietly, ignoring Melissa.

Hunter keeps the sword pointed at me. I had underestimated him yet again.

'Because why would I believe a monster? You agreed to not kill my mother, yet here you are.' I notice sweat dripping down the side of his face.

I had agreed to Hunter's condition too easily for him to believe me, so he had gone straight to his mother… or he was manipulating me the entire time and was playing at being a spy. He revealed to Melissa everything he told us, about how he would have guessed where we would enter the city, why we'd been so interested in access into Thorn Gap. He'd set up an ambush, and it would have worked had we been human.

Slowly, so Hunter doesn't get a scare, I put my sword away. 'You know nothing about me Hunter Cole. You call me a monster, yet here you are,' I say. 'You jump between ships whenever one takes a turn you don't like.'

Melissa finally speaks up. 'You're one to talk.'

I look Melissa up and down slowly.

'Melissa Cole,' Kai begins, his voice dark. 'You murdered my twin to create an internal conflict. You murdered an eleven-year-old boy and then kidnapped a ten-year-old girl and forced her to slaughter her own allies.'

Hunter flinches but Melissa turns to look out of the window. 'I do not regret what I have done.'

I turn to look at Hunter. 'Put your sword down, Hunter Cole. You will not win this fight.'

Hunter glances between Kai and me, then towards Melissa.

He launches at us, and Kai disarms him in mere moments, sending him flying towards the stone floor. He scrambles back, towards the couch before swallowing once and slowly climbing to his feet.

Melissa nods at Hunter. 'You will be the leader of our people Hunter, but now you must stay alive.'

He looks towards me. 'Danica, you have sworn not to kill my mother.'

'I have and I won't harm Melissa Cole,' I say clearly.

Hunter breathes a sigh of relief and steps aside.

I make my move, pulling out my dagger and pressing it to Hunter's throat. I feel his body tense and still.

'What are you doing?' Hunter yelps.

Melissa has gone still, watching.

'Like your mother said, you will be a leader of your people. So, I need to make sure you stay alive,' I say into Hunter's ear. 'I have sworn not to kill Melissa Cole, and I have also sworn that Melissa Cole will die tonight.'

Hunter's jaw clenches. 'Please, Danica.'

'It's not me you need to plead with,' I say and nod at Kai. 'Kai has more reason than I to want Melissa dead. She killed his family.'

'Thank you, Danica.' Kai glances at me. 'However, this war is between Melissa and your mother. Rayven should make the killing blow.'

I nod my head.

Kai takes his sword and places it at Melissa's throat.

'Stand,' he orders, and Melissa slowly rises, not saying anything.

This still feels too easy, despite the ambush. It's almost as if Melissa had accepted that she would be found.

'Where are all your city's inhabitants?' I ask for my own curiosity.

Melissa watches me for a moment. 'They left last night through Thorn Gap. The fae helped to hide them and get them as far north as possible.'

Kai walks around Melissa so his sword is pointed at the back of her neck. 'Now you are going to make your army surrender, then I'll take you to Rayven.'

Melissa nods and begins walking, Kai on her heels. I push Hunter in front of me, the dagger to his throat.

Melissa keeps walking and doesn't look back at Kai. 'If I may have one request, promise me my people will be safe.'

Kai glances back over his shoulder at me. 'Your kingdom Danica, it's not for me to say.'

I take a moment to consider. 'The humans can keep Roseguard, and Roseguard will be the only city that welcomes humans. If any humans are found outside of the city's farms, they will be criminals in our eyes.'

Melissa is silent, then, 'We'll have an emissary who will be allowed to travel without consequences, and we want to keep trade routes open to and from other cities.'

'We choose your emissary. And you're allowed to keep trading with other cities, however the other cities will have to travel. Roseguard traders stay in Roseguard,' I say, then add. 'We will also have a permanent garrison of warriors residing in the city to ensure you keep to your word.'

'Thank you,' Melissa says quietly.

# CHAPTER THIRTY-NINE

## DANICA

We follow Melissa out of the house and towards the Red Towers. The battle cries and screams are louder now. The fighting must have moved closer to the wall. I can imagine how many humans would have died for Melissa's pointless quest for power.

Melissa reaches into her pocket and produces a key. She so slowly, as if on purpose, approaches the door to the war rooms, unlocks it, and pushes it open. Kai is careful to use Melissa as a shield in case it's a trap. I keep nudging Hunter forward as we follow Melissa and Kai.

As we make our way up the stairs, Hunter asks, 'How did you get through the ambush?'

'I did not appreciate having arrows fired at me.' Kai answers for me. 'You forget that we are not human.'

Hunter doesn't respond, and although I can't see his face, I know he'll be glancing between Kai and his mother.

The only sound is our footsteps as we make our way up the stairs, the click-clack of Melissa's heels. When we reach the second highest floor, Melissa produces a key to unlock this door as well. The room is empty, other than a few desks pushed up against the walls. There is a large red and yellow patterned rug covering the wooden floor. In a corner is a stone bench, with a lever on it. Melissa pulls this once, breathes a sigh of relief and aims for the roof floor.

The moonlight greets us, and I notice the towers now have red smoke coming from them, the wind taking the smoke slightly to the east.

'That's your surrender?' Kai asks.

Hunter nods. 'The lever below, it's connected to the towers and releases the smoke. Our armies will stand down at the sight of the Rose smoke.'

'How will the humans see it at night?' I ask.

'The Narakuya will see it. My people will then realise.' Melissa says quietly.

We stand there for a few minutes, listening to the noise from the battlefield as it begins to fade.

Unease at how easy this has been fills me, and I inspect Melissa from over Hunter's shoulder. She's too calm.

'Why did you surrender with such little fight?' I ask her.

She meets my gaze. 'Because your kind is too powerful, and I know that if I go without a fight, my son will survive to see another day. I know that despite losing this battle, there will be many in the future that we will win.'

Its silent for a moment, then Kai laughs and I look at him.

'She's actually delusional.' he laughs.

I frown but say to him quietly, 'We did it.'

# CHAPTER FORTY

## DANICA

The scent of metal and coppery blood taints the air, and I take a deep breath in as I stare out at the battlefield, bodies piled up against the stone wall of Roseguard.

The majority of the dead are Red Soldiers, and I realise that all the red uniforms are on the dead fae. Melissa kept all her people hidden in the walls of Roseguard and let the fae fight her war. The fae are strong, but we're stronger.

Kai and I pick our way through the battlefield to where a group of warriors in black are disarming fae soldiers. We hang back for a couple of moments, letting the Narakuya finish their job. Melissa and Hunter, still with blades at their throats, watch the commotion. I notice Ryker holding a horse and I instantly turn my eyes away from him, remembering the vow he made and broke along with Caden and Falcon.

Kai speaks up. 'Where can we find Queen Rayven and King Darius?'

An older woman looks up at us, her gaze flicking between the Coles and us. A small grin appears on her lips, her dark hair is starting to grey, wrinkles cover her tan face and blood drips from her sword.

'The Queen had the camp moved closer, just in the southern tree line. I believe she went back to her meeting tent the moment Roseguard surrendered.' The woman rolls her shoulders once. 'Normally, she'd still be out here helping with the recovery; however, I believe she is dealing with King Jules Vesper.'

The fae king.

Kai looks around the small group of warriors. 'Can four of you help escort our prisoners?'

Four step forward, and I recognise one of them as Sage, one of the warriors I first met after we'd kidnapped Tyke.

Kai turns to look at Ryker, at the horse he's holding. 'Can we use your horse?'

Ryker nods his head, glancing at me. 'Of course, Prince.'

I stand back as two of the warriors take my place behind Hunter, the other two behind Melissa. Ryker hands the reins over to Kai, who easily vaults into the saddle, and holds out an arm for me. His muscles are sleek, and I don't fail to notice how powerful he feels as I grip his forearm and swing up behind him on the horse. The horse moves off steadily, easing into a slow walk as it manoeuvres around the dead bodies, not snorting or shying at the smell of blood. A trained war horse, with warriors on its back. The other warriors follow behind, Melissa and Hunter between them.

I keep my arms wrapped around Kai, my head on his shoulder as I peer over.

We soon make it to the tree line; tents already being set up. Kai aims the horse for the centre of the camp, where a bonfire has been lit. I brace myself as he pulls the horse to a halt; a young boy runs out to take the reins, pale blue eyes watching with admiration as Kai easily dismounts and offers me a hand. I give him a grin before handing him my sword instead as I get down myself.

'Untack and water the horse before putting him on the horse line,' Kai says to the boy, adding a grin.

The boy nods his head excitedly. 'Yes, my prince!'

We wait until Melissa and Hunter arrive with the warriors until we make our way to the meeting tent.

I can hear voices coming from the tent as we approach. Pushing the flaps open, I take in the sight before me. Rayven, blood splattered and sweaty, her crown still nestled on her head and fire in her eyes; Dimitri with few arrows in his quiver, some Roseguard arrows, dirt sticking to his face and bruised knuckles and jaw; the centaur leader whose name I still haven't learned, with surface cuts across his legs and body, and a fae chained to a chair, his blonde hair matted with blood, gashes across him.

Rayven turns to look at me, breathing out a sigh of relief.

Dimitri takes one step forward and also breathes with relief.

'Melissa and Hunter Cole are outside,' Kai says clearly to everyone gathered. His gaze then turns to Rayven. 'We thought we'd let you do the honours.'

She nods. 'Let's end this now.'

Rayven strides outside and everyone who was gathered in the tent, follow. She stops in front of Melissa, the warriors stepping back, out of the way.

I watch as Melissa swallows, and the warriors keep a tight grip on Hunter.

'Kneel,' Rayven commands, and Melissa drops to her knees, looking up at her executioner.

'It's been a while since I last saw you, Cole.' Rayven tilts her head slightly; the habit always appears when she's focusing on something. 'Any final words?'

Melissa doesn't look frightened. As if she's already accepted her death.

'This battle might be lost, but I sacrifice my life to the war.' She turns to look at Hunter. 'Remember what I told you, my child.'

I glance at Hunter, seeing him quietly sobbing while nodding his head.

Melissa turns to look at Rayven again. 'I will never forgive you.'

Rayven leans forward, her fingers tracing the scars on Melissa's cheek. 'I would never expect you to.' She stands up straight. 'I, Rayven, ancestor of the sister Celestial, Queen of the Moonstone Palace of Asada, sentence you, Melissa Cole, to death for breaking the Treaty of Asada.'

Dimitri hands Rayven a sword, one I hadn't noticed him pick up. Rayven raises her arms. With one smooth swing, she beheads Melissa Cole.

Melissa's body falls forward, her head rolling over the grass and coming to a stop a few feet from her body.

I take a deep breath.

Melissa Cole is dead.

It's like a weight has been lifted off my shoulders. After years of imagining her death, I am happy that my mother was the one to kill her. For if I killed her, she and Hunter would win. It would prove to them and myself that I am driven by revenge, a monster.

Rayven passes the sword to Dimitri and turns to Kai and I. 'Thank you for bringing her.'

'Where's my father?' Kai says suddenly.

I frown, glancing around the room and realising that Darius had never been here.

Dimitri answers. 'Last I saw, he was on the western wing of the armies. I assume he is tending to his people.'

Kai nods his head, his gaze going to the fae. 'What's going to happen with the fae of Asada?'

This time it's the centaur that answers. 'We have decided that we shall imprison the fae in the city of Carramera.'

'The same punishment I gave Hunter Cole and his people,' I say, a small grin pushing at my lips. 'Except to Roseguard.'

'Good job, little warrior,' Rayven says.

'She's not little anymore.' Dimitri grins.

'No, I'm not.'

A commotion outside catches our attention, shouting and crying.

Rayven turns to the centaur. 'Watch the fae!'

The centaur immediately pulls a sword out and goes to the tent.

I jog behind Rayven as we make our way to the commotion. A group of warriors are surrounding something.

Rayven stops, but Kai pushes forward, and after a moment I follow. The noise of the crowd becomes a hushed murmur, the closer we get to the middle.

Kai hesitates as he gets to the centre, and I peer over his shoulder, my blood going cold. A sheet covers a body on the ground.

My gaze goes to Kai as he slowly takes a step forward and crouches down beside the body. He gently pulls the sheet back, revealing King Darius.

My stomach goes queasy as Kai leans forward, touching his brow to his father's brow. 'No.'

I swallow, not daring to take a step closer.

'Not you, too,' he suddenly sobs, his voice cracking. 'I can't lose you, too.'

The entire camp has gone silent.

'We won; you can't go.' He shakes Darius's shoulders.

Kai lifts his head, and I kneel across from him, on the other side of the dead king. He looks up at me, his eyes blank. This is not a side of Kai that I ever wanted to see.

I bite my lower lip as I look down at Darius.

Kai's fingers gently close his father's eyes, closing them forever before he pulls the sheet back over his head and slowly wraps Darius up.

I speak to the gathered crowd. 'Build a pyre.'

The crowd moves.

I stay with Kai as a pyre is built beside us. He doesn't say anything, just sits staring at the body in the sheet and I watch him, his gaze unfocused as he sits in silence. His normally straight shoulders and relaxed posture hunched forward.

Among the crowd gathered stand Rayven, Dimitri and many warriors dressed in black.

The sunlight appears on the horizon as the pyre is finished.

Kai glances once at the pyre before standing and picking his father up, one arm around Darius' shoulders and one under his knees. I follow him as he walks to the pyre and gently places his father on it. A warrior hands him a torch.

Kai says the final goodbye to his father. 'Tonight, we have gathered to witness the final fight for my father. King Darius Vold was a father, a leader and an inspiration to the people of Ritenvold. He has been loyal to his allies and ruthless to his enemies. Darius died a warrior's death, fighting for freedom and peace, Darius died serving his crown and kingdom.' Kai's voice quietens as he says to his father on the pyre, 'I hope you find Ada and Luca again.'

Those gathered around the pyre say the final words. 'You were born from the Shadows and so you shall return. Let the moon guide your path and be a beacon in the dark. May you win your fight and rest during the immortal night.'

Silence settles over the camp as Kai steps forward and touches the burning torch to the pyre, which bursts into flames as the sun rises over Asada.

# CHAPTER FORTY-ONE

## DANICA

I stand beside Kai until the pyre and Darius are nothing more than ashes in the wind. I stand beside him not saying anything, just offering company as he had once done for me. The sun is high in the sky, and warmth has filled me after a night of fighting for my people, my home and myself.

Rayven and Dimitri have long since returned to their duties. Rayven dealing with the traitorous fae, Dimitri a step behind her. Dimitri had always been the rock and Rayven the wildfire. I have taken after my mother.

Narakuya, humans, centaurs, satyrs, minotaurs, the Ritenvold fae, werewolves—all the different species that roam Ritenvold—remain gathered as they mourn their fallen king.

Footsteps approach from behind, but I don't acknowledge them.

'A life for a life,' Hunter's voice says.

I spin around the moment Kai does, and the look on his face … I would be running if I were Hunter.

Behind him are four warriors, both guarding and watching him. All are centaurs.

Kai doesn't move, he just stares at Hunter blankly for a moment before opening his mouth. 'Careful how you speak to a king, boy.'

And despite the situation, I grin at his comment.

Hunter's face pales as he runs his eyes over Kai. He still wears his armour; blood and sweat are stuck to him. Hunter wears a loose red shirt with black pants.

'My mother. She deserves to rest.' Hunter doesn't look either of us in the eye.

To save Kai from having to answer, I step forward. 'We'll build a pyre.'

'There will be many more pyres built today.' Kai glances across at me before stalking off in the direction of his tent.

I watch as he walks off, notice the slouched shoulders. He certainly doesn't look like a king, but a man who's just lost his father, and I vow to find Kai as soon as I've dealt with Hunter.

Hunter watches me, hatred in his eyes. I stare back, finally able to look at him without revenge in mind.

'I will never forgive you for this,' he hisses. 'I lost my mother today because of you.'

I take a deep breath. 'I lost Vixy because of your mother. I lost ten years of my life because of your mother.'

'You're not innocent either.'

'Neither are you.' I take a step towards him. 'I will see you later.'

I push past him and aim for my tent, walking among the black tents, among the small campfires where warriors recover from the fighting. When I arrive at my tent, I let my eyes wander across to Kai's, silence emanating from it, before pushing the flaps of my tent open.

Slowly I undress, removing each piece of leather armour and one by one dropping them into a pile on the floor. The water in the bath is warm, the fire beneath it still hot, and I let myself slide into the water, scrubbing at my skin with the scented soap, hissing as water touches the wound on my shoulder.

Clenching my teeth, I scrub my newest wound, my other hand grips the lip of the tub as pain shoots through my back. I squeeze my eyes shut and dunk my head under water, letting it wash over me.

When I surface, I keep my eyes shut and reach for the flannel on the tray. I rub the soft material over my face, my hair and finally the rest of my body. The water is a faint red colour, and I grimace, reaching for my towel and standing up.

Wrapping the towel around myself, I step over the edge of the tub and stand in the middle of the tent, blocking out the sounds from outside as I stare numbly at one of the walls.

It's all over.

Melissa is dead, I'm free and now I can go home.

I can finally go home to the oak forests, to Moonstone Palace.

'Danica?' A voice says from outside the tent, a small female voice.

I grip the towel tightly around me and step back, out of view of the doorway.

'Come in.'

The flaps are pushed back, and Autumn appears. Her bright orange hair is in a high ponytail and the bottom of her dress is muddy.

Her light brown eyes scan the tent.

'Sorry, I didn't realise you were getting changed.'

'It's fine,' I say as I pull the changing screen in front of me, adjusting it so it hides me from the rest of the tent. Behind me are a set of drawers with clothes. 'What did you come to ask?'

'I saw Queen Rayven kill Melissa.' Autumn remains quiet for a moment. 'Thank you. You're a hero.'

'Rayven made the killing blow,' I say quietly as I stare down at the contents of the drawer.

'Still, thank you.' I listen as Autumn sits at the small table and chairs. 'I also heard about the new law you made for Roseguard.'

I reach down for a black long-sleeved shirt with silver thread. The shirt has a big V cut over my chest and gently dips at the back.

'And what is your opinion of that, Autumn Kyler?'

'Where do I go? I was never a part of this war. I was a victim of my own people, and now I can't even go home to Salt City in fear of being sent to Roseguard for the crime of my people.'

I swallow hard and close my eyes. 'When Kai goes back to Ritenvold, I'll get you a Ritenvold horse to carry you in Kai's personal guard.'

Autumn is silent and I open my eyes, grabbing the nearest pair of pants, they are black and close-fitted.

'I don't want to go to Ritenvold. I want to stay with you, I want to stay with Queen Rayven and with Falcon.' Autumn sighs.

Pulling on the soft leather pants, I push the screen back and reach for my boots.

'I have to be fair and treat all humans equally, otherwise it will cause an uprising. They will ask why some are getting special treatment.' I look up at Autumn, worry lacing her face. 'But I will try to find a loophole for you.'

'Thank you.'

'Stay with Falcon, however. Stay close to him.' I finish lacing my boots up and sit on the bed.

'You and Falcon don't get along?' Autumn watches me warily.

I don't tell her that he broke my trust and loyalty by rescuing her, instead of Vixy.

'Falcon is a good man, but not someone I necessarily want in my guard. Falcon and I have had a few disagreements,' I say carefully.

Autumn nods. Falcon must have said something similar to her.

I stand up and go to the entrance of my tent. I can feel her eyes tracking me.

'Danica!' I've never heard Autumn use that tone before and I spin around.

'Yes?'

'The wound on your back.' She stands up.

'What about it?'

'You need to get stitches in that.'

'It has stopped bleeding.'

'Danica,' Autumn says, and I stop moving. 'I've trained as a healer. You need to get stitches in that.'

I turn to look at Autumn again. 'Our bodies are different to human's. Our blood clots immediately, our skin and bones heal quicker, and bruises fade within hours of receiving them.'

'Have you even seen the wound?' Autumn raises an eyebrow.

'No, but Kai did when I got it, and he said it was fine.'

'Yes, fine to finish the fight and go find help. You've helped me, now let me help you.' Autumn takes a step forward.

I rub my face and stride to the full-length mirror, turning around and looking over my shoulder.

The wound is ugly, skin peeled back on either side and flesh raw and red on the inside.

'I've had worse.'

'I know.'

I frown at Autumn and turn to look at her.

'You're covered in scars.'

'Which ones have you seen?'

'Only the ones on your arms and shoulders.' Autumn grimaces and I laugh.

'Those are nothing. More often than not, I forget they're there. I like to keep my scars as a reminder that I won.'

'Danica.' I tilt my head at the way Autumn says my name, as if she's unsure how to continue on. 'I know you want to look strong, tough and capable – and you are. But it's a special sort of strength to ask for help.'

'I know,' I say and push through the tent flaps, adding over my shoulder, 'I need to find Kai.'

Outside, I take a deep breath and survey the tents around me. Kai's, Rayven and Dimitri's, Darius'. The royalty from two of the three kingdoms. I doubt there will ever be tents set up for the Kingdom of Maristela. There had only ever been Selenia to wear the crown of the ocean. No-one in Rayven's lifetime, even in her mother's lifetime, had come close to finding the missing fragments of the crown.

I aim for Kai's tent.

'Danica!' Rayven's voice calls, and I turn to find her standing in front of her tent.

I glance at Kai's tent once more before turning to her.

She holds the flaps of the tent up and I nod my head in appreciation as I walk in. Dimitri is seated at the table, and I take a seat across from him. There is no blood splattered on him, but the bruising on his knuckles and jaw is still a deep purple colour.

Rayven has taken the seat at the head of the table, a glass of wine in front of her, and she swirls it in the glass as if she has no intention of drinking it.

'With Kai now King of Ritenvold, it is your duty to keep the alliance strong with the Volds,' she begins. I roll my eyes like a petulant teenager.

'I know.' I let out a breath. 'I know I've been gone the last ten years, but I'm still the princess of Asada. I know what my duty is.'

She tilts her head in consideration. 'Don't forget that, Danica.'

'She knows, Rayven.' Dimitri sighs and stands up.

'The girl, Autumn Kyler, has requested to return to the Moonstone Palace with us,' I say, before Rayven starts talking again.

She raises an eyebrow. 'You know we can't favour any humans.'

'I know, but Autumn has suffered at the hands of the Red Soldiers.'

Rayven rubs her face.

'She's training as a healer,' I add.

Dimitri turns to me. 'I'll take her in as an apprentice sharpshooter and healer. Teach her what I learned when I was training.'

Rayven looks up at him. 'That could work.'

I straighten in my seat at Dimitri's words; he has rarely spoken of his training, where he learned his deadly aim.

'Please tell me, father, where did you train?' I push, seeing if he'll finally tell me after all these years.

He looks away and Rayven doesn't speak for a moment. 'I think Danica has the right to know, especially now that Melissa is dead.'

He nods his head once and takes a deep breath. 'You've heard the story of how Melissa Cole sent me to assassinate Rayven.' I nod my head. 'Melissa was a difficult person to say no to, especially because you never knew how much power she had. She was her father's favourite daughter, so when Melissa asked for Rayven's death by my hand, Weldon Dame was quick to summon me to his quarters. Melissa and I knew one another well, as after my father, your grandfather, died, Weldon trained me.'

I feel my mouth gaping open. 'Melissa's father trained you?'

'Aye.'

'How did you know each other then?'

'It's a long story… but my father, Lark, was one of your people. My mother, Sierra, was human. Weldon spent years trying to capture Sierra's attention, but she had fallen in love with Lark. He would come through Roseguard once a month, and they would meet up and spend all their spare time with one another. Weldon soon realised that my mother would never return the feelings he had for her and later married a woman named Mabel. Sierra died when I was fifteen, Lark was out of the city, and I sat on my mother's deathbed holding her hand while she took her final breaths, along with Weldon, who had never stopped caring for her. She made Weldon swear to look after me until Lark returned. When Lark did return and learned of his lover's death, his grief became too much, and he attempted to kill the basilisk with no weapons – a suicide mission and he knew it.

'Weldon continued to look after me, train me along with his two daughters, Melissa and Mary. Weldon was a skilled warrior, and he taught me everything he knew. He never, however, approved of the Narakuya and their power because of Lark. That opinion is evident in Melissa, especially after her conflict with Rayven.' Dimitri turns to look at me. 'The conflict between Rayven and Melissa … that's a story for another time.'

I sit there for a couple of moments, my head in my hands as Dimitri's words sink in. It all makes a bit more sense now, Melissa Cole's hatred. Dimitri had lived and trained with Melissa, left her city on a mission for her, only to fall in love with the enemy he was supposed to kill.

I look up at my father. 'Why tell me this now?'

'Because the past is a tangled mess of grief, betrayal and hatred.' Dimitri turns to look at Rayven. 'I certainly didn't think our past would carry on to my child, but I was wrong. And now that Melissa is dead, your own hatred soothed, you should know why it has soothed ours.'

'So why did you offer to train Autumn?'

'Because already Autumn doesn't like humankind, and I will teach her differently than Weldon Dame taught me.'

# Chapter Forty-Two

## Danica

At sunset that evening, Rayven and Kai carry Melissa's body towards the pyre.

I haven't had a chance to talk to Kai again. After speaking with Dimitri and Rayven, I'd gone to find food and then caught up on some much-needed sleep.

Almost an hour ago, the horns blew to signal the end of the war and that Melissa's body was about to return to ash.

Kai moves forward, his shoulders pushed back as he holds the side of the make-shift coffin. I watch as he keeps his blank eyes forward, his chin up. He's dressed in a white shirt and dark pants with tall black boots. On the other side of the coffin, Rayven wears the Moonstone crown with the waning crescent moon in the middle.

Although Kai hasn't been crowned yet and isn't wearing his Moonstone crown, I can already imagine him in his, with the waxing crescent moon.

The crowd has fallen silent, and I relax slightly as Dimitri puts his hand on my shoulder.

Rayven and Kai approach the pyre and lower the coffin to the ground. Kai reaches in and picks up the wide plank of wood that Melissa's body rests on, a black sheet covers her body, and her head has been placed just above her neck, her face cleaned. Her eyes are closed and the four scars on her left cheek seem to glow in the fading light.

I watch as Rayven leans in and whispers something in Melissa's ear, then brushes the back of her hand along the scars on Melissa's cheek. Rayven steps back and picks up the wood from the opposite end, at Melissa's head. Together, they place Melissa's body and head onto the pyre, rearranging her arms so they are crossed over her chest.

I look across the crowd at Hunter. He's surrounded by our warriors and wears his red jacket, the Roseguard crest over his heart. His hair has been combed back and he's staring at his mother's body, his hands clenched tightly.

My gaze goes back to Rayven as she starts speaking.

'Today, a war has ended. A war that has lasted ten years.' Rayven lets the words sink in as she turns to look out at the crowd. 'Many have suffered, but we have peace again through our kingdom. The Treaty of Asada is once again the law.'

Rayven looks over at Kai, who speaks like a king. 'It should not be me saying these words, but my twin, who would have taken the crown.

Yet here I am, here we all are. Today I have avenged Prince Luca Vold and all those who have suffered.'

Kai takes a torch from one of the warriors and holds it out in front of Melissa's body. 'You were born from ashes and so you shall return, enemy of the Moonstone Crown.'

I listen as Kai says the vows to the enemy. 'Our people are born from the shadows, our enemies from the ashes, as our people will continue on in the afterlife, but enemies will turn to ash and scatter in the wind.'

Silence follows as Kai places the torch over Melissa and her body begins to burn. All who have gathered remain until Melissa is no more than ash. No-one talks, no-one whispers or makes a sound. The only noise comes from the crackle and hiss of the flames.

I look over at Hunter and meet his gaze. His face doesn't change, but he turns on his heel and walks away from the crowd, in the direction of Roseguard. As he walks away, my stomach turns at the stiffness in his back, the anger, the hatred in his walk.

I look back at the pyre, smoke high in the sky.

Despite ten years of being Melissa's slave, she was also a teacher of sorts. Not a teacher who cared how I fared, but one who gave me my dark way of fighting, my resilience and patience. She taught me that despite ten years of turning me into a monster, it will be I who decides whether I'm that monster or not. Not Melissa, not Hunter, not Kai or Falcon or Rayven. Only me.

There is a commotion in the crowd, and I turn to look as the fae commander is brought forward. He looks as if he has accepted his fate, as a centaur leads him forward on an iron chain. Rayven follows behind, a sword in her hand and I know what is about to happen.

Another execution.

The fae is pushed to his knees in front of the pyre, and Rayven stands beside him, looking down at his bowed head.

'You are guilty of acting against the Treaty. You have allied with the enemy,' Rayven says clearly to the fae man. 'Do you deny this?'

The fae does not look up. 'I do not.'

'I, Rayven Arlet, ancestor of the sister Celestial, heir to the Moonstone Palace of Asada, sentence you, Jules Vesper to death.' She pauses for a moment. 'Any last words?'

The fae doesn't say anything, and Rayven raises her sword.

The entire crowd is silent as Rayven drives the sword down, decapitating the fae king. I watch as his head roles to a stop before the pyre, the burning embers already catching onto it, ready to consume it.

# Chapter Forty-Three

## Danica

Hours later, when the fae king of Carramera is nothing but ashes in the breeze, I make my way over to Kai's tent. Inside, he is sitting on his bed fiddling with a dagger. He's still wearing the clothes from this morning, smelling of smoke.

'Hey,' I say quietly as I make my way in.

'Hey,' Kai replies, looking up.

I sit down at the small table.

'How are you?' I ask softly.

He rubs his face. 'Recovering. I'll be fine.'

'You will be.' I lean forward in the chair. 'The camps are packing up, and I spoke to Rayven on my way here. We're leaving for the Shadow tomorrow morning.'

He looks up at me. 'You need to go home.'

'And you need to go to the Moonstone Castle to be crowned.'

He nods his head.

'I guess I've come to say goodbye for now.'

He stands up and walks over to the table, taking a seat across from me, taking my hand in his.

'Indeed.' He looks up at me. 'Time for the princess to go home after ten years.'

One corner of my lip pokes up at the thought of going home.

'I can only remember it as if those years were a hazy dream.' I glance down at our hands, my memories surfacing. 'I remember the oak forests and the Moonstone Palace gleaming on the side of the mountain, the moonlight shining through the pillars. And I've had dreams of running barefoot through those forests, laughing and playing at being a warrior.'

Kai smiles at me. 'You have been away for too long. You have proven beyond anyone's expectations that you deserve to live among the Moonstone.'

'And what about you? You left a prince, and you're going back a king.'

He looks down at our hands. 'It's something I'll need to figure out for myself.'

We stay silent for a while as the wind whistles through the camp preparing to go home.

And with no-one listening but Kai, I speak the one truth that's been haunting me since Rayven told me we'll be leaving.

'When I was on the front line, I wasn't scared because I didn't know any better, and I had anger to keep me going.' He looks up at me and I squeeze his hand. 'When I escaped, I wasn't scared because I had Vix to look after, I knew what I had to do. When I decided it was time to fight again, I wasn't scared because I had my plans for revenge, and when Vixy died and when we jumped off the cliff into that river, I wasn't scared because I had you.' I blink away tears for a moment. 'I'm scared now.'

He squeezes my hand, but remains silent, waiting for me to finish.

'I'm going home, but I'm not sure I know *how* to go home, when this is the life I know. I don't know how to be a princess, and you won't be there to help me. You have saved me time and again, and I don't know how to go home without you.'

With his free hand, he caresses my cheek. 'Danica. You are the strongest person I know, and when you don't know how to do something, you create your own way to do it.'

I swallow.

'We will see each other again, and when we do, we'll have time to be together,' he says quietly.

I embrace his heavy gaze and his company. Company that I know I won't have again for a while. I lean into his warmth, and we stand like that for a while, then he leads me to the bed, and we stay in one another's embrace for the rest of the night. All night he holds me, and I don't let go as I breath in that familiar scent of summer rains and oak. I let myself relax, knowing that I am safe in his embrace.

*****

The next morning, when I'm in my riding leathers mounted atop Oak with Rayven on my right side, I look over at Kai and nod my head, saying my final goodbye.

He returns the nod, reins in hand for his own horse before he begins the journey east and I west.

# Chapter Forty-Four

## Danica

After a couple of weeks of riding with the Narakuya army, we finally cross the Yulara Mountain Range separating Asada from its Shadow. Over the weeks, the armies of the other species have dispatched, travelling towards their own homes, their own cities now that the kingdom is free again, until it is just us Narakuya.

Rayven has left a handful of her most trusted commanders and warriors to deal with the remaining fae and humans. It has been a quiet couple of weeks, and I've spent most of that time either riding next to Autumn or with Rayven. Dimitri had to go to Ritenvold to witness Kai's crowning as a representative of Asada and will be returning home soon after.

Days ago, the pine trees became fewer and more oak trees appeared. Sunlight gleams through the leaves as we ride through the oak forests.

'Danica.'

I look over at Rayven.

'Are you ready to arrive home?' Rayven tilts her head slightly in anticipation as she looks over at me from her horse.

'As ready as I'll ever be.' I grin and look forward.

Rayven pushes her horse into a trot, and I follow behind.

After a few minutes we ride out of the oak forests and enter a glade. Gleaming down on me is a palace made of Moonstone, the rock dug from deep beneath where that star fell from the sky millenniums ago, its pale silver gleam almost the same as the crown. I pull my horse to a halt as I gaze up at the stone palace, my heart racing.

Among the pillars, through the windows, I can see movement.

My gaze travels from the top of the palace to the bottom, where a stone road leads to the gates, on the other side of which people are gathered, watching Rayven and me.

I smile and push my horse into a canter, aiming for those gates.

Cheering starts from the crowd.

'The princess has returned!'

'Danica!'

'Princess Danica is home!'

As my horse carries me through the gate, a weight lifts from my shoulders, a weight that has been pressing down on them since that night ten years ago when Melissa took me from my home.

Despite the tensions disappearing, I can feel a flutter in my stomach, something like doubt beings to creep into the back of mind. It's small, but it's there.

A warrior I am, but a princess with people to lead? That, I have no idea how to be.

# Acknowledgements

Firstly, thank you to you, the reader, for having enough faith in me to pick up this novel. I really hope you enjoyed meeting Danica, Kai and Hunter and I hope you enjoyed the adventure. You're support means the world to me and I am so incredibly grateful.

The idea for "Where Monsters Hide" was crafted on the back of a horse. I would like to think that those horses that I could take for a trail ride and completely zone out of reality and into fairyland helped come up with Danica's story. Those awesome horses are Marley, Flicka, Olly, Goldplay and Dollar.

I would like to thank my dad for stopping at the Bindoon Bake House on the way up to Moora and dad asked what was on my mind, and I replied with something along the lines of 'I want to write a book'. Dad, you were so supportive, and we spent the hour and half discussing the seeds of the story.

I would like to thank my mum for reading my first ever manuscript, it was shocking, and I hope it never sees the light of day, but you said it was great, and you edited the whole manuscript for me with so much support.

Thank you, Jo Chalmers, for being the first person to professionally edit Danica's story, I am forever grateful. To Chelsea & Alaina for your many edits, you guys are amazing! I am thrilled that you not only wanted to help edit but edit multiple times. You guys are absolute legends. Thank you to the Bookstagram community and all the authors who are so willing to offer advice and help me out.

A huge thank you to my little sister, Anna, for putting up with my nagging and piecing together the vision I had, creating something even better. You are the most talented artist, and I am beyond proud to display your artwork on the cover.

Next, I would like to thank my incredible and amazing fiancé, Steve, you support me so much and I am a very lucky girl. Thank you for challenging me and helping me on this wild journey. Words can't express how much I love you.

# About the Author

Emily Agnew is an author based in rural Western Australia. Born in 2001 and growing up on a farm in the Wheatbelt region; one's imagination must be vivid to keep themselves entertained. As a horsey girl, Emily found her passion of reading through horse books and having read every book in the library that mentioned horses, Emily picked up a fantasy novel for the first time, and the rest is history.

During senior school, Emily decided to test her abilities and see if she could write a novel. She discovered that not only could she write a novel, but she absolutely loved it and decided that becoming an author would be her career goal. And so, after thinking, plotting and structuring an entire storyline, "Where Monsters Hide" was born.

Now living in a coastal town with her fiancé and dog, Arlo, she worked tirelessly on drafting, editing, formatting and designing this story between working fulltime and all other life commitments.

If you enjoyed this novel and want to hear updates on book two in "The Moonchildren Trilogy" or wish to support Emily, please review and share the novel with your friends and family. Additionally, you can find Emily on Instagram @emilyagnewbooks .

www.ingramcontent.com/pod-product-compliance
Lightning Source LLC
Chambersburg PA
CBHW031735180726
48283CB00005B/1521